ANNIE MURRAY
The Narrowboat Girl

PAN BOOKS

For my daughter, Katie

First published 2001 by Macmillan
and in paperback 2001 by Pan Books

This edition published 2005 by Pan Books
an imprint of Pan Macmillan Ltd
Pan Macmillan, 20 New Wharf Road, London N1 9RR
Basingstoke and Oxford
Associated companies throughout the world
www.panmacmillan.com

ISBN 0 330 39628 5

A CIP catalogue record for this book is available from
the British Library.

Typeset by Set Systems Ltd, Saffron Walden, Essex
Printed and bound in Great Britain by
Mackays of Chatham plc, Chatham, Kent

All Pan Macmillan titles are available from www.panmacmillan.com
or from Bookpost by telephoning 01624 677237

Acknowledgements

Thanks are due in large measure to David Hearmon, owner of *Raven* for so generously sharing his time and expertise, and for his e-mail friendship; to my sister and brother-in-law Julia and Timothy Woodall for their hospitality and help, to Stoke Bruerne Canal Museum and to the staff of Banbury Museum.

I also owe a debt to canal enthusiasts Ray Shill, Wendy Freer and the Birmingham Canal Navigations Society for their publications. Above all, thank you to Sheila Stewart for her wonderful book about life on the cut – *Ramlin Rose*.

PART ONE

One

Ladywood, Birmingham, 1926

'Oi, Maryann – pack that in or your shoes'll be all scuffs. You'll 'ave our mom after yer!'

Sally Nelson sat primly on the step of the Garrett Arms, skirt pulled well down over her knees, thick blonde hair fastened back with a rag ribbon, and her baby brother clasped tight on her lap. There was a frown on her round, pretty face as her younger sister skipped impatiently up and down, aiming kicks at the grime-encrusted wall.

Maryann turned, sticking her tongue out as she sprang back and forth, an ice cream in one hand and ample signs of it in evidence round her top lip. She stopped for a moment and stared down the length of her skinny, scab-kneed legs to her feet, pushed into an old pair of cast-off shoes, their buckles dulled with wear.

'They're all scuffs any'ow, so what yer on about?' She licked urgently at the ice cream before beginning again on her hopping and twirling, her bobbed, black hair flying wildly round her face. 'Oh – where's our dad got to? 'E should be 'ere by now!'

Sally's big-sister bossiness couldn't rile her today. Maryann was as full of fizz as a bottle of Nanny Firkin's dandelion and burdock and just as close to exploding with excitement. It was 17 September, her twelfth birthday, the sun was still shining even though

3

the summer was over and they were back to school, and today was the day their dad had promised they'd go and fetch the kitten home from Nanny Firkin's. Even though she'd have to share it with Sal and Tony and babby Billy, really it was going to be *hers*.

After school that day she'd come dashing home well ahead of Sal, her excitement even overcoming her wariness of her mother. 'Mom! Mom! You there?' She tore up the entry, to find Flo Nelson in the yard still toiling away on the mangle outside the brewhouse. It was Monday, washday. Billy, with just a vest on, was stamping to and fro in a scummy puddle of washwater with his little peter out on show, the lot. Wet clothes strung on lines along the yard, flapped against Maryann's face.

'Course I'm 'ere. Where else would I be, sunning meself in the South of France?' Flo Nelson snapped, wiping her wet hands in an irritable gesture over her blonde hair to keep it out of her face. She was a broad-hipped, rather stately woman, once as beautiful as Sal would one day be, but sagging now. Her manner was petulant and long-suffering. 'And keep yer grubby 'ands off of there. I ain't been slaving away all day for you to come and bugger it all up. 'Ere—' She reached down the front of her blouse for a twist of cloth from which she took a sixpence.

Maryann's eyes widened with glee. Mom was never going to give 'er a whole tanner! Blimey, she knew it was her birthday, but Mom never handed out even a farthing without being *asked*! Flo Nelson bent and hoiked her youngest son to his feet.

'You and Sal go and find yerselves an ice cream – and get some drawers on 'im and take 'im with yer – 'e's running me ragged.'

A beam spread across Maryann's freckly face.

'Ice cream, oh *ta*, Mom. Come on, Billy – eh Mom, what about Tony?'

Her five-year-old brother would be whining round her if he saw her with an ice.

''E's round with Alec.' Flo jerked her head towards the wall adjoining the next-door yard. 'What 'e won't know won't hurt 'im. Make sure yer finish 'em before yer get back 'ere!' Her face surrendered to a rare moment of softness at the sight of her scallywag of a daughter. 'Go on with yer, birthday girl. This time twelve year ago I weren't enjoying meself any too much I can tell yer.'

Sal was just coming along the road.

''Ere Sal! Our Mom's being nice today – I've got a tanner!'

The girls found an Eldorado ice-cream cycle on the corner of Garrett Street and went back and settled by the door of the pub. Dad wouldn't be back yet, however much Maryann willed him to be. They'd long finished the ice creams, wiped Billy's face and were trying to stop him crawling in to play on the beery, sawdust strewn floor of the Garrett Arms when the men started coming out of the factories.

'Awright, Sal?' some of them said, coming into the Garrett for a pint or two after work. 'Waiting for yer dad, are yer? 'E'll be 'ere in a tick, Walpole's is out.'

Maryann noticed that when some of the men spoke to Sal, their voices altered, as if they were telling her a joke that Maryann didn't understand. And one or two of them would give her a wink. Sal favoured her mother's fair looks: the pale skin, gold hair, the white, rounded body. Quite the young lady she was and they treated her almost as if she was a grown-up woman.

5

They didn't do that to Maryann, a skinny whippet of a kid, with her black hair hacked off straight round her jaw and her face all freckles. She didn't care: she was a tearaway, a tomboy, besotted with animals and hungry for adventures.

She carried on skipping about. Walpole's were out! Walpole's, a firm making aluminium ware, was where her dad worked, the only man she cared about. After all these years he had a proper job and was earning a good wage and everything was getting better and better. Next year Sal would turn fourteen and there'd be two wages coming in. Then Mom'd never have to take in washing again.

Sally turned from bending over Billy to find Maryann shinning up the lamp-post on the corner by the pub.

'Oh get down before yer kill yerself,' she snapped. ''Ere, look – it's our dad. Yer that busy fooling about you've missed 'im coming.'

Maryann slithered down the pole and tore along the road, all sharp knees and skirt flying.

'Dad!'

Harry Nelson, a tall man with a lean, tired look, watched his daughter's wild progress along the street, followed more sedately by her older sister and baby brother. Harry stopped, throwing his coat over his shoulder, a grin spreading across his face. He held his arms out as Maryann catapulted herself at him.

''Eh – you're getting too big for that!' He laughed, fending her off.

'Dad, Dad – can we get the kitten now?'

'Well—' He eyed her, teasing. 'I had in mind a couple of pints with the lads first.'

'Oh *Dad*!'

He laughed. Harry Nelson had big, tombstone teeth

6

and needed only to part his lips to look as if he was smiling. 'There'll be no peace till we do, will there?'

'She's been keeping on and on,' Sal said, trying to sound superior, although in truth she was almost as thrilled about the kitten as Maryann.

Maryann dragged him by the hand. 'Come *on* then!'

Nanny Firkin lived in a back house on a yard off Ledsam Street, along from the Borax factory. It was a short way across Ladywood, the other side of the railway shunting yard and the cut in which lay the sluggish, scum-ridden water of the Birmingham Mainline Canal to Wolverhampton. The house where Maryann and the rest of the Nelsons lived was also a back house, with two tiny bedrooms on the first floor and an attic, but Nanny Firkin's house at the far end of the yard was more by way of a cottage: two up, two down, with a little patch of garden at the front, and Maryann loved going there. Nanny Firkin, a widow of some years, loved animals too and told Maryann she was a 'chip off the old block'.

When they reached Ledsam Street, Maryann ran on ahead, heart pounding with excitement, up the entry to Nan's and across the greyish-blue bricks of the yard. The door was open, as it nearly always was, and one of Nanny Firkin's cats, an exceptionally hairy ginger tabby, was curled, asleep on the front step. Maryann peered into the dark kitchen, which smelled of coal and onions and the sour odour of the parrot's cage.

'Nan? It's me, Maryann! Dad's brought us up for the kitten.'

'I didn't think it'd be long before you made an appearance.'

7

Nanny Firkin limped over to the door, a twinkle in her eye. She was a tiny lady, thin as a wisp, who lived on next to nothing and was always dressed stiffly in black, but with a little wizened face from which looked two eyes, watery and blue, and brimming with warmth and vivacity. She was full of affection for her granddaughters and son-in-law. It was her own daughter Flo she found it less easy to rub along with, forever mithering and carrying on, although Nanny Firkin had done everything in her power to help Flo while Harry was away fighting – and the pair of them once he came back from France. Flo was a houseproud chit but lazy and self-pitying with it. Always hankering for a spick and span house but thinking it ought to get done by magic instead of knuckling down and doing the work herself. Flo Nelson called her own mother's house a 'bloody flea-ridden menagerie – yer go there alone and you come back with company.'

But Maryann had hardly ever caught a flea at her nan's. She'd be more likely to pick up company of that sort at her friend Nancy's house in another yard across Garrett Street, if the truth be told.

Nanny Firkin's kitchen was a cosy place. Her grandmother had been chopping an onion at the table and the kettle was hissing on the hob over the black range. Beside it was squeezed the old chair with its horsehair stuffing bulging out through holes in each of the arms. In one corner, balanced on a crate, was the cage where Walt her parrot lived, named after her late husband.

'Talks to me a darn sight more than Walter the flesh and blood man ever did,' Nanny Firkin often said.

''Ello, Walt!' Maryann called to him.

''Ello,' Walt said. ''Ello.' And added a metallic

8

sounding shriek for good measure, closely resembling the noise that came from one of the factories behind the yard.

When Harry Nelson appeared at the door with Sal and little Billy, Maryann was already bent over the black cat who was lying under the big chair with her litter. Out of the mass of warm, hairy bodies, Maryann saw a tiny face, tiger-striped grey and black, with shiny brown eyes gazing up at her.

'Oh look, Nan! Look at this one – the little tabby!'

She took the creature on her lap and it settled there, seeming quite content.

'Ain't they grown, Nan!' Sal exclaimed. 'No, Billy – yer must be gentle with 'em.' She restrained Billy's strong, pinching fingers.

'Oh Nan, can I 'ave this one!' Maryann looked into the animal's eyes and knew he wanted to be hers. 'Look at the way 'e's looking at me.' The kitten twisted playfully on to its back and pawed at her fingers.

'Don't I get a say then?' Sal stood over her, but she was smiling in spite of herself at the kitten's antics.

'It *is* madam's birthday,' Nanny Firkin said, brewing tea for Harry. She was always mothering him, trying to feed him up. 'Anyroad, I reckon 'er's picked the best of the bunch.'

While her dad gratefully drank his tea and ate Nanny Firkin's sticky ginger cake, and Sal and Billy played with the other kittens, Maryann sat with her new pal in her lap, laughing as his fur tickled her bare knees. She could scarcely believe it: a living creature, so tiny and perfect and beautiful, and he was all hers ... She stopped, looking carefully at him and turned to her grandmother who was sitting, as she always did, perched at the very edge of her chair as if in her long

9

life she had never learned to take her rest and be comfortable.

'Is this one a boy or a girl, Nan?'

'Oh that's a lad, that one. Tigerface I call 'im.'

'Tigerface—' Maryann cocked her head at him. 'I think I'll just call 'im Tiger.' She nuzzled her cheek against him, brimful with delight. 'Thanks, Nan. 'E's the best ever.'

Maryann lay cuddled up close to Sal that night on the bed they shared in the attic. There was a strong whiff of damp, but they barely noticed, being used to it. They had an army blanket and a couple of old coats, and apart from that they had to keep each other warm. The nights were still quite mild now but it was perishing cold in the winter. Now she was older, Sal refused to have a 'bucket of wee' by the bed and, however cold the night, if she needed to go, she took the key and went off down the yard to the freezing toilets. Maryann wasn't so fussed and would go down and relieve herself in the bucket in Tony and Billy's room if needs be. Sal was getting far too particular, she thought.

'Move over,' Sal moaned. 'I'm half hanging off the edge of the bed over 'ere.'

'Sorry.' Maryann shuffled along the lumpy mattress. There was a pause. A mouse scuttled across the floor. 'Tiger's so lovely, ain't 'e?'

'Oh Gawd, not again. Yes, Maryann, 'e's lovely. 'E's the most perfect cat in the whole blinking world. Now will yer shurrup?'

There was silence for a moment, then Maryann poked her in the ribs and Sal rolled over, giggling. 'Oi, pack that in!' But she was only pretending to be cross.

The two of them snuggled up together. Despite being so different they were close. They'd had to be, the way their mom was.

There'd been great excitement when they carried Tiger home. Nancy Black and three of her brothers had invaded to look him over until Flo Nelson unceremoniously shooed them out again. Maryann had spent the whole evening holding him and playing with him and even Flo admitted he was 'awright, I s'pose'. Now he was asleep, exhausted, on a strip of rag by the range.

Maryann lay looking up at the dim rectangle of sky through the uncurtained attic window. The nights were drawing in now. 'I don't want to leave Tiger when I go to school,' she whispered. 'I wish 'e could come too.'

'Don't talk so daft,' Sal murmured. They lay together talking fondly about the kitten's antics until the downstairs door opened and they heard their father's tread on the stairs. Flo Nelson was always harassed and irritable in the evenings and hustled them straight from playing in the yard up to bed out of her way. She had Billy to settle down and didn't want any added trouble from them. But their dad always came up to say goodnight. Maryann squirmed with delight. It felt so cosy in bed, with Dad coming up to give them a kiss.

He had been a stranger to them when he came home from the war in 1919. Sal had been eight then, and Maryann five and it had taken them some time to get used to one another. Flo, exhausted after years of coping with two young daughters alone, of scrimping and queuing and struggling, had expected a man to come home who she could lean on, who would take over. Instead, for those first years, she had an unpredictable, helpless wreck on her hands. Often she exclaimed angrily that the men who came home may

11

have survived, but they were 'no bloody good to anyone, the state they were in'. The girls didn't understand what it was all about. They didn't understand the war, or the suffering of the soldiers, or that the man who had come home was one who had changed and couldn't fit in, wouldn't, for a long time, be able to hold down a job. But they did know they were loved. Harry Nelson was a man who felt incomplete away from his family. He adored his children, and that separation, added to the horror and degradation of the war, had increased his trauma further.

'How's the birthday girl?' he said, stooping his long body and sitting down on the bed.

Maryann giggled.

'That little Tiger of yours is asleep. Worn out.' Maryann felt him rub her back with his warm hand and he gave Sal a pat. 'Night night.' He leaned down and kissed them both. Maryann felt his lips press her cheek, the prickle of stubble on his top lip.

'Eh – 'ow about you sing to me, eh – our special song? Just the first bit. How'ds it go?'

The song was one Sal had sung at school while the war was on, a prayer for the soldiers and sailors. She had told her father about it when he came home and they had sung it many times. Now they both piped up:

> God bless our soldiers
> Guard them each day
> Make them victorious
> All the way.
> In the great conflict
> May they endure,
> And God bless our soldiers
> And make victory sure.

In the early months after he came home, he would ask for the song, and when they sang it he would sit on their bed, his shoulders beginning to shake until he was weeping uncontrollably. It had frightened them at first, but he was such a kind, gentle man that they used to sit beside him and put their arms around him. Flo had become resigned to his suffering and fractionally more understanding. They had had the two boys, who filled Harry with joy. It had taken years, but now, with the passing of time and the help of his family, in particular his children, Harry Nelson knew that the emotional wounds of the war were slowly healing.

Now he no longer wept when they sang to him. He sat quietly listening, then stood up as they finished.

'Nice voices, you wenches. Sleep tight.'

Maryann listened to him going slowly down the stairs to see the boys, the familiar creaks of each tread. She closed her eyes. She felt safe and warm and loved. Later, looking back at those cosy nights, she would wonder how she could have taken them for granted, when they were all too soon snatched away.

Two

It happened two months later, quickly, horribly, all in an afternoon.

Maryann was with her friend Nance. Nancy Black had been Maryann's best pal ever since they'd started school together. Maryann loved going to the Blacks' because there was always something going on. Even when Nance's dad came home tanked up he never took any notice of her – he and Mrs Black had a right lot of shouting matches, but he'd never done her any harm. As often as not when he arrived, Maryann and Nance'd shoot across the road to Maryann's house to keep out of the way until the trouble died down.

The Black family consisted almost entirely of boys: Nancy was sandwiched between three older and four younger brothers. Her dad, Joe Black, known as Blackie in the district, scratched what might have been a reasonable living as a cooper, going round the yards mending the maiding tubs, if he hadn't parked his barrow and drunk his earnings away most afternoons. Nancy's mom, Cathleen Black, had a head of salt and pepper curls, one crossed eye and a moany voice. Maryann's mom said Cathleen Black was a Catholic and 'not up to much' and having one eye crossed like that 'served her right'. Nancy said her mom was born like that so Maryann never understood how it could serve her right. Did God do things like that? Didn't he like Catholics? And was that why she had to take in washing and cart other people's bundles off down the pawn shop on a Monday morning to make ends meet?

'Well, it's no good relying on that drunken bastard,' Cathleen said, placidly, of her husband. 'Or we'd all've starved to death by now.' But then, with a distant look in her eyes, she'd add, ''E was never like that before the war.'

Cathleen Black seemed to overlook the fact that Nancy was a girl most of the time and except for school, Nance wore her brothers' cast-off shorts and shoes, and her hair, black and curly as her mom's, was cropped short. Nance strutted about with her elbows stuck out and you didn't cross her. She was tough. Flo Nelson said it was a shame, her never looking like a proper girl, but she was damned if she was passing down her girls' clothes to people like that.

It was chilly that November afternoon, threatening rain, the air damp and rank with factory smells from all around and the stink of the yard privies. Both Maryann and Nancy had been ordered to keep an eye on their baby brothers, and Billy Nelson and Horace Black were at one end of the long, narrow yard, playing with a collection of marbles.

'Don't you go putting 'em in yer mouth, Horace,' Nancy shouted to him. 'They ain't rocks for sucking.'

Billy's fair head and Horace's dark one were close together and they kept picking up the marbles, throwing them at the wall, watching them bounce off and roaring with laughter.

'They're awright,' Nancy said, long-sufferingly. 'Let's leave 'em be.'

She strode over in her patched, baggy shorts to

where two of her older brothers, Jim, thirteen and Percy, ten, were trying to cobble together their own cart out of a wooden meat-crate they'd bought for tuppence – the proceeds of selling empty jam jars – and some old pram wheels.

'Get lost!' Perce scowled at her as he did something important with a piece of wire. 'You'll only muck it up.'

'Let's play hopscotch,' Maryann suggested. 'I gotta bit of chalk.'

For all her boyish ways, Nancy loved having another girl to play with. Blowing on their cold hands, they ran up the yard and started marking out a hopscotch grid. Nance started the game, throwing a pebble along the ground and jump-hopping back and forth. Mrs Black came out of the house with a scarf over her head and a cigarette jammed in one corner of her mouth and started hanging out a line of washing. She took the fag out and turned to them. 'Yer'd better not muck this lot up or I'll belt the pair of yer.'

The girls ignored her. One or other of their moms said this to them several times a week every week and had done ever since they could remember. It had the same effect as 'Don't get dirty', which also went straight in one ear and out the other.

'Is yer dad in yet?' Maryann whispered to Nancy as she took her turn on the hopscotch.

Nancy pulled her mouth down and shook her head. Not many minutes later though, they heard his voice in the entry, mumbling furiously to himself as he staggered along. He was a red-eyed, barrel-chested man, with such skinny legs to support his rotund girth that they looked as if they'd been pinched off someone else's body. He came lurching into the yard, cap in hand and swearing fit to blister paint.

'Oh, 'ere we go,' Cathleen Black said, vanishing inside her house to clear away the breakables.

Blackie stormed into the middle of the yard and bawled, 'Someone's nicked me fuckin' barrer!'

Nancy and Maryann looked at each other. Nancy's big brown eyes rolled expressively skywards.

Jim and Percy straightened up at the end of the yard. Other neighbours round the yard barely turned to look, this was such a usual occurrence. Blackie's favourite watering hole was the Beehive Inn in the next street. He'd bring his barrow, loaded with iron strips for mending the maiding tubs in which everyone did their washing, and leave it out at the front of the pub. By the time he came out it had almost invariably gone – moved for a lark by local lads who then watched Blackie's alcohol-befuddled indignation at its disappearance. Week after week he never seemed to remember that if he left the barrow outside the pub, the same thing would happen. That, Flo Nelson said, was because he was 'so bloody thick yer could stand a spoon up in 'im'.

'You sure, Dad?' Jim said, cautiously.

Blackie attempted to stride masterfully towards them, but ended up struggling to keep his balance.

''Course I'm bleedin' shewer! What d'yer take me . . .'

'It'll turn up, Dad,' Percy said. 'It always does, don't it?'

He and Jim weren't going to volunteer to go and get it and face the jeering ridicule of the lads in the next street.

'Someone's nicked my . . .' Blackie was just beginning all over again, when Sal came rushing up the entry, her face white as a china doll's.

'Maryann – oh Maryann!' she cried, then burst into hysterical sobbing. At the sight of her sister's emotion, a sick, cold feeling came over Maryann. For a moment they all stood numbly, waiting.

'Our dad's been in an accident,' Sal blurted out at last. 'A terrible accident.'

Cathleen Black left her sozzled husband to his own devices, picked up grime-streaked little Horace and marshalled all the children across the road to the Nelsons' house. Maryann immediately caught hold of Tiger and hugged him to her. Her chest felt tight, as if it was going to tear open. Nancy watched her with wide, concerned eyes.

'Our mom's up the h-hospital.' Sal sat down, still crying, at the table. 'This copper come and said our dad'd been hit by a c-car and 'e couldn't come home and Mom had to go with him. M-Mom told me to come over and get Maryann and stay 'ere with Tony and Billy till 'er gets 'ome.'

'Did the copper say 'ow yer dad is?' Cathleen stood over her. She couldn't stand Flo Nelson, always looking down her nose as if from a great height, but she was fond of the Nelson children, and she couldn't just leave the kids in a state like this.

Sal shook her head. Maryann started crying then. They'd taken her dad away and she'd never been inside a hospital and didn't know what it was like, only they looked big, frightening places, and he was hurt and she just wanted him home and everything to be back to normal. Her tears started Tony and Billy off crying too, and Horace looked at them all and began bawling as well.

The evening passed like a terrible, blurred dream. They tried to eat the mash and mushy cabbage Mrs Black cooked for them, but Maryann felt as if her throat had closed up and she could hardly swallow. The older ones went out into the yard after tea, but all Maryann wanted to do was play with Tiger and hold him tight.

Nancy tried to get her involved in a game, but Maryann just shook her head. Her dad, was all she could think of. She ached for him to come home, to pick up Tiger in his big hands and say, 'How's our little moggy then?' But the evening dragged on and still he didn't come, and neither did their mother. Everything felt strange and horrible.

It was after eleven when Flo Nelson finally walked in. Cathleen had got Tony and Billy to bed. Tony had cried and screamed and Maryann went up and sat with him, stroking his head until his eyes closed, his distraught little face relaxing finally into sleep. Sal and Maryann had been adamant that they would not go up until their mom came back. They sat silently at the table, Nancy with them, draped wearily over its surface, too tired to do anything and too worried to sleep. The younger Black boys had dozed off on the floor and Horace was fast asleep on his mother's lap with his thumb in his mouth. His nose was bunged up and his breathing was the loudest sound in the room.

Despite the fact that Cathleen Black barely ever set foot in her house normally, Flo Nelson showed no surprise at them all being there. As she came in through

19

the door, Maryann knew immediately that everything was different. Her mother's eyes wore the glazed, exhausted look they had had in the days after she had given birth to Billy, only then she had been cheerful, had carried him proudly about. Now her pained, defeated body looked as if she had been punched so hard she would never stand straight again. She closed the door and turned, seeming unable to raise her head and look at them all.

'How is 'e?' Cathleen said, softly. She struggled to her feet, still holding her sleeping son.

Flo Nelson shook her head. She couldn't speak. After a moment she put her hands over her face.

''E's not...?' Cathleen was deeply shocked. She hadn't thought it would be the very worst. Not this. 'Flo, 'e's not...?'

Flo nodded, hands still over her face. Slowly she pulled them away, staring at the table, not looking directly at anyone. 'Ten o'clock. 'E never came round – never knew what happened. 'E was in Icknield Port Road – it was a motor car knocked 'im down – his head...' She put a hand to her own head. At last she looked directly at her neighbour, eyes wide with shock and bewilderment.

'He was on the Somme, Cathleen. He came all through the Somme.'

Maryann and Sal lay clinging to one another in the cold darkness.

'We'll never see 'im again,' Sal sobbed.

The word 'never' stabbed through Maryann like a sharp sword. Never. Ever. No – it couldn't be true. Wasn't real. Tomorrow he would come back, she'd

20

wait for him outside the pub, take Tiger for him to stroke with his long, rough fingers. Sundays they'd go down the cut or go over to Edgbaston reservoir with a fishing line and a jam jar. She'd hear him slowly, wearily climb the stairs to say goodnight, the same rhythm of his tread night after night ... Never. Never again. She pressed her face against Sal and felt sobs jerk out from the very depths of her body. Everything felt frightening, and cold and utterly lonely.

Three

During the time between Harry's death and the funeral, his children stayed away from school. Flo couldn't cope with any of it and the girls had to take over their brothers completely. Sal minded Billy, while Maryann looked after Tony, helping him get dressed, trying to keep him occupied and out of Flo's way. For two days their mom scarcely moved from her bed, lying there with her pale hair matted round her head, face swollen with crying, and it was Nanny Firkin who came to take charge. She was not one for kisses or cuddles but she kept them fed and her busy presence in her rustling black dress was a great source of comfort. As she had all through the war, Flo leaned on her mother for help. Nanny Firkin came and cooked for them and stayed with the children while Flo hauled herself out of bed to go to the undertaker's on Monument Road, to make arrangements.

'Where's my dad?' Tony kept asking. He was five, and he didn't understand death. His dark-eyed little face was so solemn, so hurt, that Maryann could hardly stand looking at him.

''E's not coming 'ome again, Tony,' she said, gently at first.

'Why? Where's our dad gone?'

''E's – 'e's had an accident, Tony, and 'e ain't coming back.' She sat him on her lap, cuddling him, stroking his soft, squashy legs.

Night-time was the hardest, when he didn't come back from work. They couldn't hear his voice through the floorboards from downstairs, his loud yawn as he came up to see them. The house felt so quiet and empty. Their mom's sobbing was the only thing they heard, sometimes with Nanny Firkin's voice trying to comfort her.

'What 'm I going to do?' she kept saying over and over again. Every time she said it Maryann froze inside. Her mom was afraid they'd all starve! 'Four children and no 'usband! 'Ow're we going to get by? It were bad enough in the war, but then you 'ad to put your own troubles aside when they were over there fighting. But now there's four instead of two, and there'll be no end to it all . . .'

'You'll 'ave yer widow's pension,' Nanny Firkin said.

'But that's next to nowt! 'Ow'm I going to keep 'em fed and clothed?' She was tearful again. 'Life's cruel – so cruel. After all these years, these bloody 'ard, struggling years, Harry gets 'imself a decent job and then this 'as to go and 'appen!' She sank into a chair by the table and broke down. 'We'll not 'ave a stick of furniture – I'll 'ave to sell it all. Oh, I can't go through all that again – I want a bit of rest and comfort in my life, not scratching and scraping for every farthing till the end of my days!'

Nanny Firkin pursed her lips. It grieved her more than she could ever express that Harry had been killed. She'd loved the man like a son and her own heart was leaden with it and even more at the sight of her grandchildren's faces, especially little Maryann, so like him in looks and his favourite. The child was heartbroken, clinging to that kitten. They should have had a better life, Harry and Flo. Married at eighteen, then Sally had come along. Harry had an apprenticeship then and they looked set for a fair passage. He was going to work his way up to being a skilled worker, then emigrate with his family. There'd been big advertisements before the war, asking for people to go to Australia. That was Harry's dream, to start a fine new life away from the stink of Birmingham factories and the shabby, vermin-ridden houses of old Ladywood.

'I've got the energy of two men,' he used to say. 'You'll see, Mother Firkin. This family's going up in the world, up and out of 'ere and right the other side of the world. Flo and me'll live like kings – and we'll see to it you do as well. You can come and join us when we're all set up.'

And then the war came, and instead they faced the shadow of a man whom the fighting had spat out and sent home to them: used, then discarded, abandoned to eke out a future on ruined health and confidence, on shattered nerves. Whatever rays had broken through from that bright, possible future had faded and gone out and now all was darkness for Flo.

But Nanny Firkin had never been one to get carried away by dreams. You could dream, oh yes, dreams were what kept you going, kept you living one day after another. But stepping right into them and thinking life would pull itself round just to suit you – that was something else. Moonshine, that was. She watched her daughter's grief, day after day, and she saw things very clearly as they were.

'Well, Flo,' she said in her cracked little voice. 'You know I'll give yer all the help I can. It's no hardship to me spending time with my grandchildren – when I'm

24

allowed,' she added rather tartly. Flo looked up at her, her tear-stained face desperate. 'But as for you, you're gunna have to get yerself a job, one that pays enough to keep this family together. I can't do that for yer, Flo, I'm past all that. If I 'ad anything to give yer, yer could 'ave the teeth out of my head, but I ain't even got them now. You'd best get yerself into a factory on the best wages yer can find.'

In Loving Memory of
Harold Nelson
Who entered into rest 16th Nov 1926
Aged 33 years
Interred at Lodge Hill Cemetery

Funeral furnished by N. Griffin & Son,
Monument Road

Harry's funeral was held at St Mark's Church, next to St Mark's School, where Maryann and the others attended. Maryann sat next to Tony in the immense gloom of the church while grand words from the Book of Common Prayer whirled round her head. Her dad's coffin was draped with a Union Jack, the reward of respect given to a serviceman of the war.

At the cemetery they stood round in watery sun-shine and a cold wind. Flo was distraught. She seemed to have no comfort to give to her family. She stood across the grave from them, being consoled by her younger brother Danny and his wife Margie. It was Nanny Firkin who stayed close to the children, arms stretched out, trying to spread her tiny frame behind them like a fan. Tony clung to Maryann. As they lowered the coffin into the grave, Tony turned and buried his face against her.

The undertaker, Norman Griffin, was a tall, respectable-looking, middle-aged gentleman, his broad shoulders encased in a smart black coat with a white wool muffler at the neck, black gloves and shoes gleaming with polish and elbow grease. She could see, from under his bowler hat, that his hair was a faded ginger, and his complexion also had the faded freckliness of the redheaded. His manner was tactful and deferential. When they had driven back to the house from Lodge Hill and Mr Griffin had dispatched the carriages, he lingered in the street with them for so long that eventually Flo felt obliged to say, 'Can we offer yer a cup of tea or summat for your trouble, Mr Griffin?'

'Well, I must say,' Mr Griffin said, rubbing his hands together, giving a practised, moderate, undertaker's smile, 'it's a right cold day – I won't stop for long, of course, but I'd be very grateful, I truly would.'

Flustered moments followed of building the fire and Nanny Firkin fetching water for the kettle while Mr Griffin sat by the hearth, looking round the room and lighting up a cigarette. Maryann watched him. He had sat himself, without a by your leave, in the chair that had been Harry's when he came home from work. Maryann gritted her teeth. She didn't like the smell of Mr Griffin's cigarette smoke (her dad had never taken to smoking), and even more she didn't like him parking his backside in her dad's chair, however much of a gentleman he was. Besides which, it was the most comfortable seat, so Nanny Firkin was left perched on a hard chair by the table.

Flo laid out their handful of best cups and saucers and poured the tea after the eternity it seemed to take to get ready, while none of them had anything to say. She spooned condensed milk into the cups, her fingers trembling.

'I'm afraid it's a bit on the weak side,' she apologized miserably, as if the tea was representative of their desolate state. 'Get Mr Griffin some sugar, Maryann,' she ordered, adding in a hissed whisper, 'and don't bring it in the packet.'

Maryann tipped the large grains of sugar on to a saucer, found a spoon and dutifully offered it to Norman Griffin, coughing as his blue smoke wafted up into her nostrils.

'Ah—' Mr Griffin turned to her and she felt herself turn red under his close examination. 'Thank you ... er, my dear.' Close up to him, as well as the smoke, Maryann could smell sweat and some other funny chemical smell. Without meaning to she wrinkled her nose. Now he had taken his hat off she could see his hair was thinning on top and was smoothed back with soap or Brylcreem. He sat very straight, with an almost military bearing. As well as his smell, Maryann disliked his affected way of talking as if he was really posh, and the way he had ousted Tiger from by the fire with a rough shove of his shiny shoes, their soles muddy from the cemetery.

But they had to be polite and thankful to Mr Griffin. He had handled Harry's funeral at a discount: the hearse pulled by gleaming black horses, the wreath, the cards announcing the death. In the circumstances, Flo Nelson had genuine cause for gratitude.

'We couldn't 've managed it – not proper like – without yer being so kind,' she was saying, from a wooden chair opposite him, a tremor in her hands as she held her cup and saucer.

The children sat round, dumb with misery; Maryann squeezed on to a stool next to Tony, each of them with one leg on, one off. Sal was sitting holding Billy, asleep in the dim gaslight. Cathleen Black had looked after him for the day and he'd worn himself out playing with Horace. Mr Griffin seemed to take for ever to drink his cup of tea. Maryann could see the strain in her mother's face, her need to be left alone, not to have to be polite, to weep.

'Of course, I understand your feelings at this inauspicious time,' Mr Griffin was saying, clinking his half empty cup down on the saucer. His fingers were pale and stubby, the backs of his hands freckly and still red from the cold. 'My own dear wife passed away not two year ago.'

'Oh,' Flo Nelson said, with an effort. 'I'm sorry to 'ear that, Mr Griffin. I didn't know.'

''Course I've only the one son – worked for me in the business for a bit, till 'e decided to go his own way. I tried to persuade him to stay – 'e made a beautiful coffin when 'e put his mind to it...' As he spoke he looked round the room again. Sizing it up, Maryann thought.

'You've got yer 'ouse looking nice, Mrs Nelson. Daresay you'd move to a bigger place given the chance though, eh? Very cramped these yard 'ouses – with all the family you've got.'

''Er's always managed,' Nanny Firkin put in, sharply.

'We ain't got much chance of moving now,' Flo said. 'To tell yer the honest truth, Mr Griffin, I don't know 'ow we're going to manage with my Harry gone...'

Unable to hold back her emotion any longer, she burst into tears and Sal began sobbing as well. Maryann felt her own emotions swell inside her as if she might explode, but she wasn't going to cry with *him* here! She folded her arms tight across her bony ribcage, pressing herself in.

Mr Griffin leaned forwards, breathing loudly through his nose. 'Oh dear, oh dear, now, now. I am sorry for your trouble, my dear. I do know what a terrible time this is for you . . . You know, I feel very sorry for you, a woman left to fend for 'erself with family. Now if you need any help – if there's anything I can do for you . . .'

Maryann squeezed her eyes tightly shut. *Go away, you horrible smelly old man!* her mind screamed. *Get out of our dad's chair, and out of our house!*

At last he stood up, seeming to take up half the room, and put his hat and coat on. Suddenly he turned and enacted a little bow towards Sal and Maryann.

'Goodbye then, girls. You'll help look after yer mother, now won't yer?' They sat, mute, not even meeting his eyes.

'Thank you again, Mr Griffin,' Flo said meekly. 'I don't know what to say, yer've been that good to us.' She saw him to the door.

'Goodbye, m'dear.' Mr Griffin lingered for a moment. 'Now don't you go forgetting what I've said, will you?'

Flo stood on the step, staring thoughtfully after him as he disappeared into the smoky gloom.

Four

December 1927

'And where d'yer think you're going?'

Flo's question was flung furiously across the room, through the paper streamers which hung in sagging loops from yesterday's Christmas festivities, at Maryann, who was by the door, forcing her arms into the sleeves of her coat.

'Out.'

Flo advanced on her, hands still black from shovelling coal.

'Oh no you ain't, yer little madam. You get back 'ere and find a civil tongue for Norm – for Mr Griffin for once in yer life. 'E'll be 'ere any minute and yer can sit there and be polite. There's summat 'e wants to say to you all.'

But Maryann was already out and across the yard, still pulling the coat round her, the door rattling shut in Flo's face. It opened again.

'You get back 'ere, yer uppity little cow!'

Maryann disappeared at a run, down the entry to the street. She felt the cold come down on her like a weight, the raw air biting into her cheeks on this day of deep, silent midwinter. The cobbles were icy and the slates glazed with it: the sun hadn't broken through all day. She pushed her hands deep into her pockets, thrusting her chin down. She had on a pair of Sal's old stockings, held up with garters. Everything she had handed down

30

from Sal was on the big side. She could feel the stockings wrinkling down her legs.

Flo's angry words seemed to propel Maryann along the road. 'I'm not staying in there – not to see *'im*,' she said out loud, her breath swirling away from her, thick and white.

She turned down towards Nanny Firkin's. In her left pocket she found a halfpenny, and gripped her hand round it, squeezing hard. She and her mom had never been what you'd call close, but nowadays all she ever seemed to be was on the wrong side of her. All year it had been like this, getting worse and worse. Since her dad had died and since Mr Griffin kept on coming round week after week bringing presents: joints of meat, cakes, thrusting bags of sweets under their noses, sitting himself by their fire on Sunday afternoons. He had even begun to take off his shoes and park them up against the fender as his socks steamed in the heat.

Maryann knew exactly what Mr Griffin wanted to say that afternoon. She was sick at the thought, because it had been coming all year. He was going to sit there in the chair, her *dad's* chair, with them waiting on him hand and foot. There'd be her mom's, 'Oh yes, Mr Griffin, no, Mr Griffin,' which had gradually turned into, 'Oh yes, *Norman*, no, Norman,' as Flo recognized a chance if ever she saw one. Mr Griffin was going to sit holding a cup of tea in those pudgy, freckled hands and tell them he was going to marry their mom. And he would say it in that wheedling, smarmy voice which made Maryann want to be sick all over his shiny shoes.

She knew this as clearly as anything, because as his visits had become more frequent, Norman Griffin had come making hints and promises.

'You're a good woman, Mrs Nelson, showing such

kindness to a poor old widower like me. You shouldn't 'ave to spend the rest of your days slaving away on yer own . . .' 'Nice little family you've got 'ere, Mrs Nelson – you need someone to take care of yer . . .' And gradually, 'You want to get yourself wed again, Flo – the factory's no place for a fine woman like you . . .'

Late in the summer, when a reasonable period of mourning was seen to have passed, and Flo had wept and worried and worked so hard in the brassware factory she had turned scrawny, she started going out for the odd walk with Mr Griffin on a Sunday afternoon, returning with flushed cheeks and a hard, determined look in her eyes.

When he came to the house Maryann tried to avoid even looking at him. She hated him being there and refused to speak to him unless forced to. Sal was more biddable. She missed her father but brushed out her long, pale hair on a Sunday, made tea and was polite. Maryann pulled hideous faces behind his back and dropped dust and dead ants in his tea, reduced to being childish by her powerlessness over the situation. She missed her dad with a terrible ache in her that never seemed to get any less.

She kicked at a rotten piece of wood on the pavement and it skittered into the gutter. She bent over and spat on it. 'Norman! Bloody sodding *Norman*!' She stamped and spat until tears ran down her cheeks.

Walking on, wiping her eyes, she crossed over the railway and went along to the spot where there was a hole in the fence and she could get down to the cut, scrambling down through scrubby bushes and alongside the wall of a warehouse on to the path. Down here it felt even more cold and utterly still. Fog hung thickly over the canal so that she could see only a few yards ahead: the factories, chimneys and warehouses were all shrouded in the saturated air. The place felt completely deserted. It was Christmas of course, and she saw the water of the canal was frozen over. Near where she was standing a stick poked up, frozen in at an angle, black against the grey ice. She walked along the path in the eerie whiteness, in towards the middle of Birmingham, over a little humpbacked bridge and past the Borax Works towards the wharves at Gas Street. Ahead of her she could just see the ghostly shapes of the wharf buildings and in front of them two rows of joeys, the boats which mainly did journeys of a day there and back. They were tethered shoulder to shoulder along the Worcester Bar. As she moved closer, she became aware of a sound coming to her intermittently through the fog. She wasn't alone down here then. Someone was coughing, a laboured sound which went on and on.

Then she saw him, on the path in front of her, close to a boat which was tied by the bank. He was bent over, coughing from drenched-sounding lungs and struggling for breath. At first she assumed he was an old man, but as she approached, intimidated, yet somehow fascinated as well, she saw this was not so. He was quite unaware that she was there because he had to submit completely to the process of coughing and this made him seem somehow vulnerable. Maryann was also drawn by the look of him. He had a thick head of curls and a beard, all deep auburn, which appeared to glow in the greyness of the fog like a sanctuary lamp in a church, and he was clad in thick, brown corduroy trousers and heavy boots, and a thick jumper with a worn, black worsted jacket over the top and a muffler at the neck. As he stooped, hands pressing on his thighs, one hand also held a black cap.

She saw that the boat by which he was standing was a horse-drawn family boat, and she noticed too that the man's hands, clasped so tightly on his thighs, were black with coal dust. Near him, on the ground, was a galvanized bucket.

At last the fit passed and he stayed in the same position for a moment, seeming exhausted by it, let out a low groan and shook his head quickly from side to side as if to shake the fit off. Then, still bent over, he raised his head and looked up along the path. Maryann felt her heart beat with panic, and she stayed quite still. For a moment the two of them looked at each other in silence. The man had a round face, though his cheekbones jutted a little, adding a chiselled look to it. His eyes, from the distance at which Maryann stood, looked dark and his gaze was strong and unflinching. He stared at her without hostility. Just looked, taking her in. Then slowly, he straightened up and replaced the cap on his head.

''Ow long've you been stood there?' His voice was soft and quite gentle.

Maryann swallowed. She had been ready to run if he was angry or strange, but didn't feel the need now. The man didn't talk like Birmingham people, she noticed.

'Only a minute.'

'What're you doing out? It's Christmas, ent it?'

Maryann shifted her weight from one foot to the other. She felt conscious of her stockings, wrinkled round her ankles. 'Well, you're 'ere.'

'Well – yes, that's true.' She thought she heard him give a wheezy chuckle.

'Why?'

He indicated the boat. 'I live 'ere. We ent s'posed to be 'ere – brought a load of coal from Cannock to the

34

Borax Works – before Christmas that was. And got blooming iced in, dint we? They ent 'ad the icebreaker out to free us up. I've been smashing it up at the edge 'ere to give 'er a wash out.' He indicated the bucket. 'Got to get the coal washed out, see, before we can put a new load in.'

Maryann nodded and moved closer. The long hold of the boat was black with coal dust and the rope fenders were grubby with it too, but apart from that she looked in good trim. She was painted red and yellow, with castles painted in the panels of the cabin doors, roses round the edge, and on the side of the cabin was painted her name, *Esther Jane*. Maryann looked at her with great curiosity, at the painted water can on the roof, the brass trimmings on her chimney, from which drifted dense yellow smoke. She looked round.

'Where's yer horse?'

'Old Bessie? Stabled up. Having a rest.'

'Can I see inside?'

The man smiled. She saw he had big, square teeth. The smile creased up his face and gave him a comical, cheeky look. 'You'll get dirty.'

Maryann shrugged. 'Don't matter.'

'Come on then – just for a minute but mind where you put your 'ands.'

She thought he seemed pleased. He climbed aboard ahead of her and when she stumbled climbing down into the boat, he gripped her arm. He felt very big and burly and strong.

'Go easy!' Another low chuckle came from him. For some reason he seemed to find her rather amusing. 'You don't want to hurt yourself. Look – that's the tiller – what we steer the boat with. Now, come on in.'

He opened the cabin doors and Maryann found herself stepping down into a miniature house. The man, who was too tall to stand upright in the cabin, sat down on a bench along the side, and gestured for her to sit beside him.

'There you go – this is our 'ome in 'ere.'

She gazed round, astonished. It was like being in a magic story where everything had shrunk. In front of her was a little black-leaded range, which made the cabin so stifling hot that Maryann unbuttoned her coat and took it off. There was a brown and white teapot and a big brass kettle, well polished, on the hob, which gave off a lovely warm glow. To her right was what looked like a cupboard, which jutted out into the cabin, and further back, a little area where there was another bench, divided off by red and white check curtains, tied back at each side. On the near side of the cupboard and on shelves on the wall by the stove were pretty china plates, some with lattice edges with velvet ribbons threaded through and tied in a bow. The man watched her taking it all in with some amusement.

'We pull this down 'ere—' He opened a small cupboard in front of him and the flap folded outwards. 'That's our table. That cupboard you can see' – he pointed towards the back – 'folds down for a bed.'

'But it's so . . . *small*!'

'It's small all right.'

'Don't you 'ave a house to live in an' all?'

'Nope. I was brung up on 'ere – lived 'ere all me life. Only time I been on the bank was in the war.'

She gaped at him. 'I've never seen in one of these before.'

'I can see that!'

'Who lives on 'ere with you then?'

'My dad, my little sister, Ada – she'd be a bit younger 'un you I'd think – and Jep, that's our dog. They've gone off to get us some food and see about who's going to get the ice broke up. We can't stick around long, you see – 'ave to get moving. We was s'posed to be at Napton by Christmas but we got stuck 'ere. We ent starving yet though. 'Ere—' He reached to a little shelf at the side of the cabin. 'Want a bit of this?'

'Ooh yes!'

She took the two thick squares of Cadbury's chocolate, nibbled and sucked slowly, making them last. The man bit some off too, smiling at her enjoyment. He had such a kind face, she thought, somehow old and boyish at once.

'How old're you?' Maryann said.

'Me? Old as the hills.'

She frowned. ''Ow old's that?'

'I'm going on twenty-nine. What about you, since we're asking?'

'Thirteen. What's yer name?'

'Joel Bartholomew. And what's yours?' He was making a game of it. Maryann found the corners of her mouth turning up.

'Maryann Nelson. I'll *always* be Maryann Nelson.'

'Will you? Why?'

''Cause no one's going to make me be called anything else.'

'Well – that's settled then.' Joel watched her carefully, rubbing his huge hands on the legs of his trousers. Then he stirred himself. 'Best get on – the others'll be back soon and they won't take to me idling.'

They stepped back out on to the bank. It felt very cold outside after the snug little cabin. Joel showed no sign of being cold, but he saw her shivering.

37

'D'you live far, Maryann?'

'Garrett Street.'

This meant nothing to him. 'Shouldn't yer be at home?'

Maryann shrugged, miserable again at the thought of home. 'I wish I could come with yer.'

Joel smiled. 'Not this time o'year you don't.'

They stood by the bank and she felt shy again, as if she'd stayed too long. She put her coat back on.

'Better go then.'

Joel suddenly held out his hand in a teasing way and she took it. His was big and very rough.

'Nice to meet you, Maryann Nelson.'

'Can I come and see yer again?'

''Course you can – if you can ever find us. T'ent easy that, on the cut!'

She turned and left him, pulling her too-big coat in closer round her, face and hands aching with cold. Reaching the bridge she turned back and saw Joel watching her. She waved, and for a moment he raised an arm.

She went to Nanny Firkin's house next, although she didn't say a word to her grandmother about Mr Griffin and why she wasn't at home and her nan didn't ask. She could see the girl's unhappiness in every line of her. She'd had words with her daughter and would have more, but she wasn't going to inflict more on her granddaughter.

'Yer just making up to 'im for a meal ticket!' she'd accused Flo, and Flo whirled round, livid.

'Yes – I am! 'E's said 'e'll move us into a bigger 'ouse and I'll not need to stand in that stinking factory turning out kettles all day long. I'll be able to live without being worried to death about where every meal's coming from. Harry's gone – 'e ain't coming back and a meal ticket's what I need, without any sodding lectures on the subject. I don't want to end up like you, living on nothing and surrounded by mangy flaming cats for company!'

Maryann stayed with Nanny Firkin, warming herself again by the fire and drinking a cup of tea. She sat stroking the cats and talking to Walt the parrot, in the musty familiarity of her grandmother's house and she waited long enough so that Mr Griffin would have gone through his usual rigmarole of wiping his mouth, putting on his jacket and shoes and standing, holding his hat in front of his stomach and thanking her mother, with a little bow, for the afternoon tea which, he always said, brightened his lonely life. She thought about Joel and the boat and hugged this to herself as a lovely, warming secret.

When she got home she pushed the door open cautiously, making absolutely sure she was not going to see Norman Griffin's head, with the pasty, balding patch at the back, still in place in the chair.

Sal was putting away cups and saucers on the shelf. She turned and raised her eyes to the ceiling, implying that Flo was upstairs, then shrugged, with an expression of sorrowful resignation. Tony ran to Maryann.

'Where've yer bin, Maryann? Our mom's ever so cross with yer and she's going to get wed to Mr Griffin. Don't say anyfing and make a row, will yer?'

They heard their mother's tread on the stairs. She had almost reached the bottom and stopped, staring across towards the door. Maryann waited for her temper to erupt, but she just stood there and they all gazed back at her. Maryann looked at Sal, then back to her mother.

''Ow can yer, Mom?' Maryann said quietly. ''Ow can yer do it?'

'I'll tell yer how I can do it.' Flo came down the last of the stairs and across to fix her younger daughter with the steely, determined expression that had become hers since her husband's death. 'By thinking about what life'll be like if I don't. Norman Griffin's got a business. 'E's got enough money to keep us, we're going to a new 'ouse and 'e's got a job lined up for Sal.'

'Do I 'ave to work with 'im, Mom?' Sal asked timidly. 'I like where I'm working now.' Sal's first job after school was with a local bakery.

'*Yes.* You do. We'll be all right now. We shan't 'ave to worry. I know 'e's not yer dad, but from now on 'e'll be the head of this family and you'll treat him with respect and a bit of gratitude. D'you 'ear?'

Five

1928

'There's someone at the door, Maryann!' Flo Nelson shouted.

Maryann went to the front door and found Nancy grinning in at her. 'So this is yer new 'ouse then!'

Maryann's solemn expression broke into a smile as well. 'Come on – I'll show yer.' Nancy went to St Peter's, the Catholic school, so the girls didn't see one another in the daytime.

Flo and Mr Griffin were married in the new year, and soon after he announced that there was a house waiting for them two roads away in Anderson Street and they were to move in immediately. He had it all planned. It was a little bit nearer his premises, where Sal had started work straight after Christmas, and was a two up, two down, with a tiny yard out at the back behind the kitchen and definitely a step up from a back-to-back.

You stepped straight in off the street into the front room. By the hearth was a peg rug, which Flo and Sal had botched together, and Harry Nelson's chair. Apart from that, the only piece of furniture which came from the Nelsons' old house was a small cupboard. The other two chairs and a low table were provided by Mr Griffin. He had a little china cabinet, a table and chairs and another comfortable chair (although he still preferred Harry's) and a heavy brass oil lamp which he liked to keep well polished and light in the evenings. It had been his father's, and his 'beloved mother' who lived in Handsworth, had passed it on to him.

Nance's eyes were wide, looking round.

'Ooh, it's nice, Maryann—' After the cramped squalor of her family's back house this seemed almost palatial.

Flo was in the kitchen cooking and there was a smell of ham knuckles boiling.

'Oh – 'ello, Nancy,' Flo said, rather snootily. Cathleen Black may have helped her out in her time of need, but that didn't make them equals in Flo's eyes. They had only moved two streets away, but it felt far enough to represent a new start. Flo was managing to pull herself up in the world and she was going to do it, no matter what the cost. There always was a price: that was just how it was. She hadn't anything in the way of feelings for Norman Griffin, except for gratitude that he'd come along and been prepared to take on her and her family. That was no small thing. But he was gentlemanly in his ways, and he'd shown her the gateway out of absolute poverty: she never, ever wanted to be faced with that again. She'd have to live with his mauling her about in bed of a night – she shuddered slightly at the thought of Norman's white, flaccid body, his thick lips and tongue. But that wasn't too high a price to pay, she thought: he wasn't one of these oversexed men, thank heaven. And he showed great consideration – never went all the way, so to speak. They'd agreed that there weren't to be any more children. Her own four were enough of a handful.

'Go on and show Nancy upstairs,' she said, irritated by the girls watching her.

'You ain't been round our 'ouse for ages,' Nancy complained as the two of them clattered up the stairs.

'I know. We've been busy. Moving and that.'

Upstairs were two rooms, one shared by the new Mr and Mrs Griffin, with Billy on a little bed on the floor, and the girls and Tony in the other. Maryann wrinkled her nose as they went in. She could smell urine from where Tony had wet the bed again that morning. He was forever asking if he could get in with her and Sal, but they said they weren't having him wetting them too. Tiger was curled up asleep in the middle of the bigger bed that Maryann shared with Sal. She and Nance sat down on it and Maryann reached for Tiger and stroked him. He arched his back, purring.

'D'yer wanna come and play out then?' Nancy said. She wasn't one for sitting still for long.

Maryann kissed the stripy top of her cat's head, between the ears. He was such a comfort, amid all the changes.

'Maybe – in a bit,' she said. She felt edgy, almost tearful, sitting there with Nance. Nance was her best pal, but there was a distance between them suddenly that Maryann didn't know how to overcome. Her emotions were all tangled up and confused and she couldn't find the words to tell Nance how she was feeling. She cuddled Tiger tightly. The day they moved their few possessions out of Garrett Street, Norman Griffin had stood in the living room and prodded Tiger with the toe of his boot.

'We don't need to take *that* with us, do we?' he said.

Flo looked at him, not understanding for a moment. 'You mean the cat?' Even she could hardly believe what he was suggesting.

'We don't want a cat in the new house, do we? Dirty animal, under yer feet all the time. I nearly tripped down the stairs over the thing the other day. Be a good time to get shot of it.'

Maryann stood behind him, so tensed with shock at what he'd said that for those moments she couldn't react. She saw her mother look across at her. Flo ran her hands over her pale hair, as if preparing herself, and stepped closer to her new husband.

'Norman – I really don't think we can leave the cat behind. The children ... I mean, it's Maryann's. It'd break 'er heart.'

Norman turned and saw Maryann's piercing expression. For a moment he hesitated, then decided to smile. 'Oh, awright then. If we must, we'll take the thing. It'll most likely follow us over there anyhow.'

So Tiger had come. At least her mom had stood up for her over him. That was something.

''Ow's Sal getting on?' Nancy asked. 'What's she doing at Griffin's? Eh—' She dug Maryann in the ribs. 'She ain't building coffins?'

'No!' Maryann elbowed her back. 'Don't be daft. I dunno. She's in the office. Bits and bobs. Messages, taking down details for cards and that. She ain't really said a lot.' Sal never seemed to say a lot about anything nowadays.

'Sounds awright,' Nancy said. 'Soft job that.' With a giggle she added, 'If yer go for that sort of thing.'

Maryann managed a laugh, feeling Nance dragging her up out of her gloomy mood.

'Yer dad home yet?' she asked Nancy.

Nancy rolled her eyes. 'Sleeping it off. But we could go over the yard, take Billy – Tony as well, if you like?'

'Awright then.' Maryann stood up without much enthusiasm.

'We're going over Nance's!' Maryann called out, downstairs.

'Take Billy with yer then!' Flo predictably shouted back.

It was cold, but bright outside. The girls set off with Billy between them holding their hands, and Tony dragging his feet behind so they kept having to turn round and call, 'Come on, Tony – get a move on, will yer!'

Maryann took a deep breath of the freezing, acrid air and managed to grin at Nance. This is better, she thought. Away from that house, *his* house, she felt lighter, free again.

'I'm glad yer came over,' she said to Nance.

Norman Griffin had habits of almost clockwork precision. On certain nights of the week he locked up his premises, went down to his favourite pub, the Duke of Wellington, for a pint, then came home. Every evening he expected them all to polish their shoes and line them up against the fender ready for the next day. He inspected them every night, turning each one over, frowning if there was obvious wear in the sole. On Sundays they all had to go to church with him, and afterwards he spent the rest of the morning in Handsworth with his mother. But for once tonight he was late, and Flo was especially exasperated as it meant Sal was late too, and she had the dinner all ready.

Maryann was pleased. The later he came back the better so far as she was concerned. The place felt much more like home, their real family, when he wasn't there. It was quite cosy with the gas mantle popping away and the warmth from the range. Flo was dishing up stew and potatoes when they heard the door open out of the dark winter evening.

''Bout time,' Flo muttered, relieved. Norman didn't take too kindly to them starting without him.

'Summat smells good!' they heard him say. Sal, her face paler than ever in the gaslight, slid into the room and sat down quietly at the table.

Norman came through, smoking the butt end of a cigarette. Maryann didn't like it when he stood over them. He was so big it felt intimidating. She saw Tony shrink down in his seat.

'What's happened, Norman?' Flo asked, serving his food. 'You seem pleased with yerself.'

'Oh no, no – nothing much. Just glad to be 'ome with you, my dear,' he said, sitting himself at the table. As he did so, Tiger stirred from where he had been sitting under the table and brushed against his legs.

'Get that thing out while we're 'aving our tea!' Norman said, scraping back his chair. He stood up and kicked Tiger out through the door. The cat let out a screech of pain and Norman slammed the door. Maryann burst into tears.

'Never mind.' Flo, startled by this sudden outburst, tried to appease her. She watched Norman anxiously. He was breathing heavily. 'Shoosh now,' Flo snapped at her. 'T'ain't summat to blart about.'

But Maryann couldn't stop. The tears just kept on coming out of her eyes, though she tried as hard as she could not to make any noise. Norman kept eating, steadily. Tony and Billy were wide-eyed, but they ate up obediently. Sal kept her eyes on her plate. Eventually Maryann let out a loud sniff and Norman leapt to his feet.

'Go on – get out of 'ere! I'll not 'ave yer snivelling and blarting at my table. If you can't eat quietly you'll not eat at all.'

Maryann, keeping her head down, left the room and ran upstairs. She lay curled up, crying, the clogging taste of the stew still in her mouth. When she was calmer she lay looking up into the darkness. She thought about her father, about the dreams Nanny Firkin had told her about. That he'd said he was going to take them to Australia.

That's what I'm going to do, Maryann thought. The resolve burned through her. I'm going to get out of here, as soon as I can. She didn't know where to: her young life had given her experience of nothing further away than these few Ladywood Streets and an occasional rare trip to the Bull Ring. But there was more out there, there had to be, beyond these smoke-blackened houses and stinking streets.

Comforted by this, she was already almost asleep when Sal came in to put Tony to bed and get ready herself. She brought a candle with her, and Maryann watched as she bent over and roughly undressed her younger brother. Her expression was tight, wooden.

'Sal?' Maryann wondered if she was cross because it was usually her job, not Sal's, to look after Tony.

'What?' She didn't look round.

'D'yer want me to do our Tony?'

'I've done 'im now. And don't you go wetting the bed again!' She pushed his shoulder. 'D'you 'ear me?'

When Tony was settled she turned away and undressed. Maryann frowned, looking at Sal's curving shape in the candlelight. She was clearly in a mood over something, turning her back like that, when normally she just pulled off her clothes casually and flung on her nightdress. Tonight her movements were abrupt. She put her nightdress over her head and her arms through the sleeves. Suddenly she sat down on the edge of the bed and put her hands over her face.

''Ow's it with the job, Sal?' Maryann asked.

There was no reply.

Maryann sat up and moved nearer, laying a hand on her sister's shoulder. 'What's up?'

'Nothing!' Sal flung her off and stood up. She threw her clothes savagely into the corner of the room, then climbed into bed. She turned her back on Maryann, blew out the candle and wouldn't say another word.

The next day, when she came home from playing with the Black children, Maryann ran up to the bedroom looking for Tiger. He was always her first thought when she came home, and very often she found him curled up in the dip of hers and Sal's bed. But he wasn't there. She peeped into her mom's and Norman's room. No sign there, either, nor was he in any of the warm spots downstairs, by the range or the chimney breast.

''E must be out,' Maryann said, disappointed.

Not long after, Flo got in, tired and irritable from an extra afternoon of chores. Nanny Firkin was feeling poorly and Flo had felt obliged to go and help.

'You seen Tiger?' Maryann asked her.

Flo stoked the range. 'Course I bloody ain't – I ain't been 'ere all afternoon, 'ave I?'

'Is Nanna better?' Tony asked.

'Not as yer'd notice,' Flo said. ''Er's in bed and that ain't usual. But she said to leave 'er, she'd be awright.

I've rubbed 'er chest with goose grease and left 'er 'er tea.'

When their own meal was over, Norman stood up behind Sal, hands on his waist, looking round at them all with a satisfied expression on his face.

'We'll all 'ave a game of cards, eh?'

He did this, every so often. Decided they were all going to sit together, 'be a family' and play whatever he was in the mood for.

'After I've got our Billy to bed then,' Flo said, sounding pleased. 'That's nice of Norman, ain't it?'

'I don't want to play cards,' Maryann murmured. 'I want to go and look for Tiger.'

'Look for Tiger!' Norman snorted with laughter. 'Yer don't want to bother with that! Cats can look after themselves, that they can.'

'I'm tired,' Sal said quietly. 'I think I'll just go to bed, 'stead of playing.'

Norman laid his hand on the back of her chair. 'Oh, I don't think a game of cards'll hurt before yer turn in, Sal.' His voice was soft, but Maryann heard a firm edge to it which always meant Norman wasn't going to be crossed. 'Young girl your age shouldn't be tired this early. Come on – help yer mother clear up then we can get to it the sooner.'

They had no choice but to do as they were told, as was the case with all his 'treats'. His taking them to church every Sunday, visits to the pictures, walking down the street all together, usually to see something that was too old for Tony and Billy, who would sleep or fret through it all. Maryann did like the pictures, but she loathed sitting anywhere near Norman.

Before going in for the dreaded card game she opened the back door into the little yard.

'Tiger! Come on, puss – where've yer got to?'

Nothing. No sign of him. She was filled with unease. He'd never done this before. What if he'd got under a train – or a car like her dad. Or what if he'd fallen in the cut?

Sal stuck her head through the door from the front. 'Come on – 'urry up. Let's get it over.'

'Coming,' Maryann said reluctantly.

Norman had pulled out the little table and was sitting shuffling his dog-eared packs of cards.

'Come on, our Maryann,' he said in a jolly voice as she slipped into the room.

Maryann sat down next to Tony.

'We'll 'ave a game of rummy,' Norman said, licking his thumb and dealing the cards. He paused to light a cigarette.

'You play with me,' Maryann whispered to Tony. Flo sat yawning. She wasn't the least keen on card games, but if Norman said they were going to do something there was no arguing.

'I'm not used to being a family man,' he'd said to her. 'I'm out of practice, Flo. But I'm doing my best . . .'

He jollied them along through a couple of games, laughing loudly at the least thing except at one moment when Tony picked a card to play and he frowned and said, 'Stupid boy . . .' and Tony turned his dark eyes on Maryann, looking worried about what he'd done. He lived in constant nervousness of Norman and his exacting ways. His lisping voice and tense face only seemed to aggravate Norman further.

'S'awright,' she told him, loud enough to be heard. 'You ain't stupid, Tony.' She put her arm round his shoulders, avoiding looking at Norman. Apart from that, and Norman's efforts at thawing them out, they barely said a word, all waiting for the moment when they could go.

Finally, Norman sat back at the end of a game and said, 'Well – that's enough for one night, I'd say.'

Maryann jumped up. 'Come on, Tony!' she said, and they ran upstairs, anything to get away from him.

By the time they went to bed, Tiger had still not come back, although Maryann had been to the door several times to check if he was waiting out there.

'What if 'e comes back in the night and wants to come in, Mom?' she said. 'Can we leave the back door open for 'im?'

'You mad?' Flo said. 'It's perishing cold. 'E's a cat, Maryann – 'e knows 'ow to fend for hisself without you coddling 'im!'

But Maryann lay in bed that night, miserable without Tiger's warm shape at her feet.

Six

Sally Nelson sat behind the desk in the austere office of 'N. Griffin's, Undertaker's'. In front of her lay two open ledgers and a small pile of newly printed death cards, almost identical to the ones they had had for her father. On another pad on the desk were Norman's various tottings up of the prices of coffin, hearse and cards. It was Tuesday evening.

Sal's demeanour was anything but relaxed. She sat chewing hard on the end of her thumb. Every so often she got up and tip-toed over towards the staircase leading down to the double cellar which ran under the building, and stood, head cocked, listening. After waiting at the top of the staircase for a long time on one occasion, she crept halfway down and stopped. She could hear Norman Griffin's voice, talking to Fred, the lad who worked down there building coffins. The last boy had left not long back and Norman was training Fred up. On Tuesdays he sent Fred home early.

'Shall I put all these away now?' Sal heard Fred say.

Then Norman's voice. 'No – leave that to me. I keep that cupboard locked, with the chemicals and that about. You can get off now.' She heard the clink of a key. Fred was about to leave. Her heart beat even faster. She opened her mouth to speak but her throat had dried out and she had to swallow before she could get any words out.

'Mr Griffin?' she called downstairs. She knew it was futile, but she had to try it. She felt she was going to explode inside. 'I'll be off 'ome now – our Mom'll be needing some help.'

Norman Griffin's face appeared round the cellar door, pale and moonlike in the gloom as he looked up at her.

'No, Sal – yer not to go yet. There's a few things want finishing.' He spoke in the low, respectful tone Sal and Maryann called his 'Undertaker' voice.

'But—' She tried to protest.

He closed the cellar door behind him, and then came another of his voices. 'No, Sal.' Now the voice was soft, wheedling. 'Yer to stay a bit longer. Don't want yer going home yet – or you know what'll happen, don't yer?'

Sal returned to her chair upstairs, trembling from head to foot. She was in such as a state she felt as if her throat had closed up, that she couldn't swallow. Oh God! She could run out and down the road now. But she daren't. Couldn't. Sooner or later she'd have to go home. And when she got home he'd be there. And she couldn't tell anyone and she'd have to come back to work with him and then he'd . . . he'd . . . She dug her nails into the palms of her hands.

They were coming up the stairs, Fred clumping along in his boots. He was none too with it, Fred wasn't. Gangly, greasy brown hair, big feet, yes, Mr Griffin, no, Mr Griffin, everything Norman wanted.

'G'night then—' He nodded at Sal, and Norman Griffin stood at the door as he went out.

Norman pulled his watch up from his weskit and squinted at it.

'Ah yes – time to close up.' He locked the door,

pulled the blind down over the door and windows and turned to look at her.

'Don't do that again, will you?' He spoke casually, but she could hear the threat underneath.

'What?' She could only manage a whisper. The tension in her was like a crushing sensation in her chest.

'Don't talk back to me in front of my employees like that,' he said, as if he had a whole empire of workers, not just herself and Fred.

'I'm sorry.' She kept her gaze on the desk in front of her, hands clasped tightly together in her lap. Her heart was beating so hard it hurt.

Then the wheedling voice was back. 'Come on then, Sal. You know what *will* please me, don't yer?'

She didn't answer, just kept her head lowered, and she heard him moving towards her. Sal squeezed her eyes tight shut. When he reached down and took hold of her hands she cried out, startled.

'Oh, don't get in such a state,' he said impatiently. His voice became clipped and cold. 'You know what yer 'ave to do – and then it's over and yer can go home. Simple. It ain't asking much.'

Much, she thought, as he pulled her towards the stairs. Ever since that first time, the start of it, when he had come up behind her and pressed his hands over her breasts, hurting her, it had been much. Far too much.

The cellar was a double one, extending under the premises behind. At the back end, through a white door, was the chapel of rest. The walls in there were plastered and distempered and it was kept very neat and clean. It contained a long trestle table and a small side table on which were a Bible, a candle and an arrangement of dusty silk flowers. There was access to it from the street behind, and any visiting bereaved were escorted in through there and all hammering silenced while they were there. Tonight, on the long table in the Chapel of Rest, a Mr Alfred Johnson lay in his coffin. His family hadn't wanted him at home taking up the room. The front end, under the shop, was much more workmanlike: unplastered brick walls, cobwebs trailing under the grating through which only shreds of light filtered from the street so that it had to be lit by gas lamps all day long. At one end, abutting the wall of the Chapel of Rest, was Mr Griffin's cupboard, but most of the space was taken up by a workbench and a long table. On the workbench tonight sat the almost completed coffin which Fred was due to finish the next day.

Mr Griffin was breathing rather fast. He reached up and made some adjustment to the light so that it burned less brightly. 'Now then, Sal, my dear.'

'No,' she begged, starting to cry. 'No – please. Not today. I'll do it tomorrow, but not today – I feel a bit bad today and I can't . . .'

'Sal—' He was speaking in his soft, fluid voice. 'You're just not used to it, my dear. You're young – you have to learn to enjoy it.'

She was shaking her head, wretchedly, unable to stop the tears from pouring down her cheeks.

His mouth was right close to her, his hot breath wafting the words into her ear. 'And if you don't, you know what'll happen, don't you?' He pointed to the far end of the cellar. 'There's my cupboard.' He patted his pocket. 'And here is the key. And you know what's in my cupboard, don't you?'

Sal nodded, gasping.

'Right then.' There was nothing wheedling about his speech now. It was icy, clipped. It made Sal wither inside. He pulled at the buckle of his belt with one hand, reaching out with his other to grasp her by her long hair, yanking her close to him.

His other hand was under her skirt, tugging, tearing.

'Let's get on with it.'

When Maryann got home from school that day she ran straight in shouting, 'Mom – Mom! Is Tiger back? Has 'e come home?'

Flo Nelson shook her head. She hadn't given a thought to the flaming cat. 'No – I ain't seen 'im all day.' She saw the hope drain out of Maryann's face. Maryann had been so sure he'd gone wandering and would be back by now. Her lips quivered and her eyes filled with tears.

'Tell yer what.' Flo saw an opportunity for a few more minutes peace. 'Yer could go and ask up and down the road if anyone's seen 'im – the neighbours and that. Someone might of done. 'E might be asleep by the fire in someone's 'ouse just along the street, yer never know. Or maybe 'e's sloped back off to Garrett Street. And take our Tony with yer, eh?'

A little cheered by being able to do something, Maryann called Tony. They went to Garrett Street and called at the Blacks' house. Blackie came to the door and the usual stink of urine and soiled baby's napkins assailed their nostrils as it opened. He stood blearily in the doorway, not seeming to know who they were. His shirt was unbuttoned halfway down and she could see black, springy hairs on his chest.

''Allo, Mr Black,' Maryann said. 'It's me – Maryann Nelson.'

'Oh ar,' Blackie said. For a second Maryann felt

sorry for him. He looked such a wreck. But she had more urgent things on her mind.

''Ave yer seen my cat? 'E's a little tabby with a face like a tiger . . .'

'Cat? No – I ain't seen no cat . . .' He stood looking at them, as if thinking what to say next.

'Maryann, is that you?' Nance came running downstairs. 'What's up?'

'It's Tiger – 'e's gone missing.' Maryann felt a lump come up in her throat again. ''E never came in last night and I dunno where 'e is. Our Mom said to come looking over 'ere.'

'I'll 'elp yer,' Nance said. She'd changed out of her school clothes and put on a grubby pair of boy's trousers.

Maryann was pleased to have some more company for the search besides Tony who kept saying 'Where d'yer fink 'e's gone, Maryann?' until she wanted to scream at him. They asked round some of the backyards in Garrett Street, Maryann saying hello to some of their old neighbours who asked a bit sniffily how they were getting on. Flo hadn't been back to visit a single one of them. Then they went back to Anderson Street. As the afternoon wore on, Maryann grew more and more dispirited. No one had seen Tiger.

'Ow can 'e just've disappeared into thin air?' she said to Nance. 'Someone must've seen him.'

'Yer never know with cats, do yer?' Nance said. She grinned, showing her wonky teeth, trying to cheer Maryann up. 'Knowing 'im 'e'll be back large as life. P'raps 'e's gone and got 'imself a lady friend!'

Maryann tried to smile. 'I 'ope so. It's lonely at home without 'im. Come on, Tony – we'd best go back. D'yer wanna come round ours for a bit?'

'Will yer dad be there?'

'*E ain't my dad.*'

'No, I know. Sorry, Maryann. I daint mean anything by it.'

They went back to the house where Flo put out a plate of broken biscuits for them. 'Ooh!' Nance cried, her face lighting up. This was sheer luxury by her standards. She tucked in as hard as she could and sat at the table chatting away happily to Maryann and Tony. Then Tony went to the back door, trying to open it, clutching himself urgently at the front with his other hand.

'D'yer need a wee?' Maryann opened the door as Tony nodded emphatically and ran out to the privy in the yard and pulled the door squeaking shut.

A few moments passed, the back door swinging open into the darkening afternoon, then they heard Tony shouting, 'Maryann, Maryann! Come 'ere – 's a nasty fing!'

He was standing at the end of the yard, his eyes wide, fascinated, beckoning urgently.

'What's up, Tony?'

Maryann and Nance both went out and looked along to see what he was staring at. Between the privy and the low wall at the back was a gap of almost a yard, which had a load of rubbish chucked into it by the last occupants. It was smelly down there, the corner of the yard best avoided. But Tony's gaze was fixed on the pile of refuse. What had caught his eye was a little patch of white, the white of a small, furry throat.

It was Nance who went down the gap and very carefully picked up the cat's cold, rigid body. She kept her head down as she came back, and only when she was standing right in front of her did she look at Maryann.

'Tiger?' Maryann whispered. 'No – not Tiger!' She just stood and looked, dumb with horror. Then she shouted, 'What's happened to 'im? Oh, Tiger!'

Beside herself, sobbing, she took him from Nance, who also had tears in her eyes, and hugged him to her.

'Oh, Tiger – my poor little Tiger!'

She held him away from her, looking for signs of blood, of injury. There was nothing to see, but as she did so, his head flopped back all at the wrong angle.

'Oh my God – look! His head's all – oh look, Nance!'

Tony was crying as well then and Flo Nelson came out of the back door to see what the matter was with them all. As she did so, Nance said, 'Someone's broke 'is neck. They must've throttled 'im and broke 'is neck.'

Maryann started running then, still hugging the cat's body to her, through the house and out of the front door .

'Maryann – where're yer going? Wait for me!' By the time Nance reached the front step Maryann was off down the road, disappearing into the dusk.

Her eyes were blurry with tears so that she could barely see, but she knew the way well enough. Every so often she slowed and looked down at the precious friend she was carrying in her arms. For a second each time there was a flicker of hope. It was all a mistake. Tiger wasn't dead. He'd look into her face and purr at her and close his eyes as she stroked the side of his head, then he'd wriggle around because he wanted to be let down to play. But Tiger didn't raise his head. His fur was bunched into damp points from lying out in the wet. In the half-light, just for a second it seemed his eyes opened and she gasped. But of course it was a trick of the light and her own wishes. His eyes were two tight, pained lines and his face didn't look like him any more. All the cheeky, fiery life that was in him had gone. Maryann could hardly stand to look at him, with his poor, floppy neck. She ran along the street sobbing her heart out.

'Oh, Tiger, my little Tiger!' She didn't care who saw her. And mixed with her grief she could hear Nance's words in her head, 'someone's broke 'is neck ... throttled 'im and broke 'is neck' and the terrible knowledge, as she ran along, that she knew who that someone was. Someone who kicked Tiger out of the way with his shiny boot every time the cat crossed his path, the someone who liked to have clean hands and clean nails, who had sat making them play cards with him when all the time he knew where Tiger was because *he* must have put him there. She thought she might burst with her rage and hatred of Norman Griffin.

She ran down Ledsam Street and tore across the yard to her Nan's cottage, pushing in urgently through the door.

'Nan, oh Nanny – look what that bastard's done to Tiger!'

But Nanny Firkin was not in the kitchen and the place was as cold as ice, no fire in the range. Maryann had been in such a state she hadn't noticed the unusual darkness of the windows. There was a rank smell of cat urine and as Maryann burst in the three cats all rushed at her, tails up, miaowing for food, their fur appearing to be standing on end in the gloom. Walt the parrot shifted silently on his perch. There was a dish on the table containing the dried-up remains of porridge.

'Nan?' Maryann wiped her eyes with the back of one hand, the eerie feel of the place breaking through her grief over Tiger. The other cats were rubbing against her legs. 'Nanny, where are yer?' It was unheard of for her Nan not to be in her kitchen. Then she remembered Nanny Firkin was ill, that she'd had a cough and her chest was bad. Hadn't her mother been in that day? The cats were acting as if they hadn't eaten for a week.

Maryann went to the stairs. 'Nanny? It's Maryann.'

But there was no reply. She laid Tiger on the floor and climbed up, somehow feeling she needed to tip-toe. Maybe Nanny Firkin was asleep.

The old lady was lying in her bed. Maryann saw the little bump where her little feet were sticking up under the cover. The room smelt stale. When Maryann went over to her she saw in the dimming light from the window that her grandmother's hair was down out of the pins and straggly round her face and her cheeks looked hollowed out. She was on her back with her eyes and mouth half open and she looked like a wizened doll. There was no movement from her, not a flicker.

'Nan?' Maryann whispered. She knew there would be no reply, that whatever it was that really made Nanny Firkin her Nan, was gone, but she couldn't take it in. Nanny Firkin was always there like the sky, she was supposed to live for ever. This wasn't really her any more, this body lying here. Maryann suddenly felt a prickle of terror pass through her, her whole body shuddered and she backed away, and ran back down the stairs. She left Tiger and ran all the way home again.

'Mom! Mom!'

Seven

The lamplighters were round lighting up as they all ran back to Ledsam Street, Flo still in her apron, with Maryann, Tony and Billy. Flo told the boys to stay out and play in 'Nanny's yard' and snapped at Tony when he tried to come into the house. A Mrs Price, one of Nanny Firkin's neighbours, on hearing what had happened, asked if the boys would like to come into her house. She said she was sorry she hadn't been in to see old Mrs Firkin, hadn't had any idea how ill she was.

At that, Flo poured out her own guilt.

'I never realized myself,' she said to the woman. 'She weren't so bad yesterday – just a bit of a cough like. I'd've come earlier, only with it being washday and that I've 'ardly 'ad a moment to spare.' Maryann watched her mom as she spoke. She was full of grim, pounding emotion. Was it true what her mom was saying? How could Nanny Firkin have not seemed ill if she was poorly enough to die?

She followed Flo back into the dark house. Flo lit a candle, her fingers trembling so much that she had difficulties handling the match, then, carrying the flickering light in front of them, they went up to Nanny Firkin's bedroom.

'Oh—' Flo's hand went up close to her mouth as she looked down at her mother. 'Oh my word – fancy 'er going like that. 'Er heart must've given out. I'd never've

62

thought . . .' She looked across into Maryann's reproachful eyes. 'I ain't stopped all day! I can't be everywhere at once, yer know. I never knew she were this bad – anything like. She just 'ad a bit of a chest on 'er. I was only 'ere yesterday afternoon. You can't say I neglected her – my own mother!'

'I ain't said a word,' Maryann said stonily. 'Did yer feed the cats yesterday, when yer come over?'

She saw her mother's brows pucker in the candle-light. 'No – I never thought. I mean, she were in bed, but I thought she'd been up and about . . .'

Clearly Nanny Firkin had been putting a brave face on things when Flo was there.

'Anyroad – I've got more to worry about than sodding cats. Maryann – go and get the range lit and ask Mrs Price who's nearest to lay 'er out . . . And Norman'll 'ave to come . . .'

Maryann found another candle downstairs. There was a small amount of coal and slack in the coal bucket and she stoked the range, as she had seen her mom and dad do on so many occasions, standing over it to check it was burning. Then she went across to Mrs Price's house. She felt numb and strange, suddenly, as if she were moving through a dream.

'Oh, it's Eve Leadbetter you need,' Mrs Price told her. She gave Maryann the address, directing her to another house further along Ledsam Street.

Mrs Leadbetter was a strong, jolly-looking woman.

'A death in the family, is it? Well, 'er won't be going nowhere – give me an 'alf-hour and I'll be over. Ask yer mom to 'ave some water ready.' She looked down into Maryann's solemn little face. 'Yer nan is it, bab? I'm sorry for yer, that I am. Tell yer mom I'll be over.'

As Maryann walked back across the old, familiar

63

yard, she saw the shape of the house she'd known as her nan's all her life. Maryann stopped, the biting cold and smokiness of the air hurting inside her nose. The moon was rising, half full, casting a white sheen on the slates. There was still a candle burning in the upstairs window, and another where she had left it on the table downstairs. It looked as if Nanny Firkin was in, going about her normal evening's jobs. But she wasn't in. Nanny wasn't there, despite the frail old body lying stiffly in the bed upstairs. She would never be there any more to go to for comfort, to tell her about school, about Tiger and his antics as he was growing up ... With a terrible jolt she remembered the earlier events of the day. Tiger was lying there in Nanny's house, at the bottom of the stairs! And soon Mrs Leadbetter would come, and Norman would come – she would be sent to fetch him. No – she couldn't stand any more.

The front door was ajar as she went quietly into the house. There was no sign of the cats, but the fusty, urine-soaked atmosphere in there persisted. Maryann picked up Tiger's body, cradling him in her arms once more.

'Mom,' she called up to Flo. 'There's a Mrs Leadbet-ter coming. She said she'd be about 'alf an hour.'

'Oh thank God yer back,' Flo called down the stairs. Maryann heard her coming closer and she shrank back. 'Now listen to me, wench – there's a few jobs I need yer to do.'

'What's them, Mom?' Maryann was creeping back through the downstairs room. As her mom descended the stairs, her feet loud on the boards, Maryann pushed the door open and slipped out. She was away and across the yard in seconds.

*

She was running as if her life depended on it, as if by doing so she could escape the terrible events of that day. She still had the feeling of being in a dream.

It's not true, she thought. None of it. Please let it not be true.

Clutching Tiger against her chest was making it hard to breathe and she stopped for a moment when she'd turned out of Ledsam Street and stood panting under a lamp. For the first time she tried to think where she might go. If she went home Norman would be there. Before, she'd have run to Sal to pour out everything that had happened, but Sal was so odd and shut off from her nowadays. And she could go to Nance's. They'd be kind to her, but she couldn't face being there tonight. The house was always so smelly and chaotic and you never knew what state Blackie might be in.

Running on, she climbed through the gap in the fence and down into the cut, near to the bridge where the road passed over the canal. Down on the path, she was suddenly forced to stop. It was so dark! It felt as if a blanket had been thrown over her head and she couldn't see where to take her next step on the muddy path. From under the bridge she could hear, magnified, the drip of water and behind her, in the distance, the clink of a horse's harness. Thank God, someone was coming along – she wasn't alone down here!

She waited a few moments as it came closer, seeing the dim light from the oil lamp on the boat growing stronger, and the shadowy movement of the horse along the bank. She pressed back to let it pass, not wanting to attract attention to herself, then followed on behind. The boat was a joey, a long open cargo boat with a tiny cabin at the back, and a man was standing up at the back, steering it in towards the bank. The carrying area was filled with a dark, gleaming cargo of coal on its way to fuel a factory boiler-house in Birmingham. The horse was walking slowly, wearily, but at a steady pace. As the prow of the boat slid alongside the bank, another man, who Maryann hadn't even noticed, jumped across on to the bank in front of her and reached for the horse's harness.

'Awright!' he called out. 'Come on,' he said to the animal. 'Let's just get 'ome now.'

Maryann was extremely glad of their presence. She knew that sooner or later something would have come along on this busy stretch of water, but the idea of walking along the path, edged by dark warehouses and wharves was very frightening. She soon realized, as the joey continued its journey in front of her, that another boat was following not far behind. She waited for it to pass and saw it was a horse-drawn family boat, also laden down with coal. She couldn't read what it said on the cabin in the darkness, but it looked the same sort of boat as the *Esther Jane* and she followed behind, holding Tiger, comforted by the leathery creak of the horse's harness. They passed under bridges and between such a density of high buildings that even in the daytime the canal at that point was forever in shadow, and the only thing visible was the tiny light from the oil lamps on the boats. The joey had vanished ahead, and she followed the boat to the basin where the cargo was to be unloaded. There were other boats underway with the task, the sounds of shovels digging into the coal or scraping at the boards of an emptier vessel to gather up the last pieces into the waiting barrows to be trundled into the boiler storehouses. Maryann could hear voices and the hard breathing of men exerting themselves, men who had already worked

66

for sixteen or so hours that day. The horse stopped and they found a place to tie up. There were gas lamps here, and she saw the breath unfurling from the animal's nostrils. The lights of the basin jittered brokenly in the black water.

Maryann stood on the edge of this activity, looking along the row of boats, her eyes searching in the dim light. Could it be – please God could it be that the *Esther Jane* was here, and Joel? She crept along peering into the gloom. Many of the boats were joeys, with a few family boats among them. Looking down into one she saw it was nearly empty and the man shovelling up into the barrow on the bank was having to lift each shovelful almost five feet in the air to get it into the barrow. Every time he lifted one he gave a loud grunt at the effort required. Small pieces of coal rattled back into the boat. Noticing her watching, he straightened up, expelling air loudly from his mouth and pressing a hand to the small of his back. He rested on the shovel, wiping the back of his arm over his forehead.

'What're yer after?'

'I want to see a man called Joel Bartholomew,' Maryann said. She was still holding tight on to Tiger and felt small and silly. She wondered if the man could see what it was she was carrying.

'What 'd 'er say?' The figure who had just approached behind the barrow, waiting to empty it, spoke up and to her shock, Maryann realized it was a woman.

''Er's after some bloke, Joel what was it?'

'Bartholomew.'

The two of them were silent for a moment.

'I dunno 'im,' the man said. ''E work on the day boats, does 'e?'

'No – 'e's on a boat like that one—' She pointed. 'Called the *Esther Jane*.'

'Oh well—' The man bent over to start work again. 'Sounds like one of the Number Ones. 'E could be anywhere, bab, if 'e's a long distance ... Needle in a bleeding 'aystack.'

The woman stood braced by the barrow as the man started shovelling again.

'Tell yer what,' she shouted over the racket. 'We'll keep a look out for 'im, like. The *Esther Jane* did yer say?' She called over to another man who was passing. 'D'yer know the *Esther Jane*? One of the Number Ones I should think.'

The man shrugged, seeming almost too exhausted to speak. 'No. Can't say I do.'

'We'll ask around for yer,' the woman yelled across. 'And who shall we say was asking for 'im?'

'Maryann Nelson,' she said, without hope. She wasn't going to find him tonight and that was what mattered.

'Awright then. Cheer up. Word gets about fast.'

Maryann thanked her and turned back along the towpath. There were more joey boats, pulled by plodding horses and mules towards the city's canal loops and basins from the Black Country coalfields, so it was not completely dark, the edges of things picked out by the glow from their lamps. The disappointment that Joel had not been there was an ache in her that cut through her numbness. She hardly knew the man, but he was kindness and warmth; she knew instinctively that he was someone who could help her bear all the feelings that were welling up in her. Of course Joel wasn't just going to be there, like he had been the time before when she came down here by chance! How could she have been so stupid, as if she could just will him to appear? The horror of that afternoon came flooding back to her. First Tiger, then Nanny Firkin. And Sal had gone all funny and wouldn't speak to her any more ... If only there was someone she could run to ...

'Oh Tiger!' She held him to her and brushed her cheek against his fur but it was wet and nasty and pent-up sobs began to shake her. She felt her way to the side of the path and laid Tiger in the undergrowth, covering his body as well as she could with grass and cold leaves, then she wiped her hands down the front of her coat.

'Goodbye, Tiger,' she sobbed. 'I loved yer, that I did.'

She walked back, still crying, beside the black water, towards home. Where else could she go? The cold sliced through her now, and under the bottomless winter sky she felt more alone and lost than ever in her life before.

Eight

May 1928

'Where're yer going? Oi come on – wait for me!' Nance trotted imploringly along beside Maryann.

'Down the cut.'

'Can I come with yer?'

'No.'

'Well, *sod* yer.' Nance stopped, hands clasped to her waist as Maryann strode off between the rows of terraced houses without even a glance back in her direction. Bloody charmed, I'm sure, Nance thought. What a pal she'd turned out to be. There was no getting near Maryann these days. Nance turned back towards home. She'd come out specially to see her friend after school. Now she'd be stuck playing with all her brothers again, if they'd have her.

'Still – better than that mardy little cow any'ow.' But she was hurt. She missed Maryann and the days when they'd been able to tell each other anything. Best pals they'd been, ever since they were knee high. But nowadays Maryann was just closed in on herself and they saw rather more of Sal at the house, hanging about, making eyes at Charlie. She'd never much taken to Sal though. She was older than Nance and she'd never been such a laugh as Maryann.

Nance stopped for a moment, almost changing her mind and following Maryann down to the cut. She'd had a few things to tell her about Charlie and Sal and what they were getting up to. But her pride got the better of her again. She'd keep it to herself. She wasn't going where she wasn't wanted. Maryann could stew if that was the mood she was in.

Kicking an old Woodbine packet irritably into the gutter, Nancy slouched back towards Garrett Street.

Maryann climbed through the fence and down through the scrubby trees at the edge of the cut. The leaves were bright green, crumpled and newborn-looking and even with all the various pongs in the air from the factories – metallic, chemical, getting in your throat – down here just in this scrubby little patch you saw some green and got a whiff of spring, which lifted her spirits. She spent all the time she could down here now, drawn to the back-to-front magic of the canal, the way it felt like another world when you were down there, closed in from the rest of the city, somewhere where, for her, the normal troubles of life no longer existed. You saw everything from the other way round down here: the rear ends of buildings, the low level of the path making you look up at things, the watery veins of the canals flowing round and through and under the heart of Birmingham like its secret circulation. It smelled of the murky, bitter water and of the trees, it smelled of a root to the country and of freedom.

'Did you know, children,' Maryann's teacher once told them, 'that Birmingham has more canals running through it than Venice? By length that is, I assume.' She had smiled. 'That's quite something, isn't it, when you consider that Venice is built only on canals instead of roads.'

'What's Venice, miss?' one of them asked.

'Well, I was hoping you'd ask . . .' She had grainy pictures of black and white poles edging canals in front of grey and black houses, gondolas tilting across expanses of dark water towards churches.

'Venice,' she said. '*Venezia*.'

'Bet our canals are a darn sight muckier,' one of the boys said and the others laughed.

'Well, perhaps. But they're very dirty in Venice too, when you consider that *everything* gets tipped into them.'

Everyone sniggered and made revolted noises. Venice didn't really sound like a real place. Real life was contained in these streets of Ladywood, collecting pails of horse muck and jam jars to sell for pennies. Maryann found herself smiling as she reached the path. Only two years ago that had been. Happy days. At school, and her dad and Nanny and Tiger all still alive. The smile fell from her lips and her face took on the scowl it wore habitually now. People had commented for a while: teachers, Cathleen Black – 'well, *she* don't look any too 'appy nowadays' – even her own mom. Now they'd just got used to it.

'I don't know what's come over you two girls,' Flo complained to them. 'There's Sal with a face like a wet Sunday and now you're even worse. And your behaviour to Norman, Maryann – I didn't know where to put myself.'

She'd come back from the canal that night, leaving Tiger's body with the cold companionship of the undergrowth and canal rats. They were all back by the time she got in. She had no idea how long she'd wandered in the cold but it must have been longer than she realized. She expected Flo to scream at her – the usual 'where've *you* been?' – but they barely seemed to notice when she walked in. They seemed only just to have got in themselves: Flo cooking, Norman Griffin sitting by the fire, feet up on the fender, his presence seeming to fill the room. Maryann slipped past and upstairs, where Sal was settling Tony and Billy. Tony was crying and without a word to each other the two sisters sat and tried to comfort him.

'It's awright, Tony,' Maryann told him, starting to cry again herself. 'Nanna's going to heaven to see God and Jesus and all the angels – and our dad an' all.'

'Bu-b-b- . . . I wanna . . . I wanna see 'er!' He was so bewildered, upset and tired.

'I'll see to 'im,' Maryann whispered, and Sal nodded and got up, sniffing. Maryann could see from her expression that she'd been crying too. The children had all been very fond of their Nanny Firkin. She'd always been good to them. Maryann expected Sal to go downstairs, but instead she went across and lay on their bed, the springs creaking as she sank down on it and put her hands over her face.

'And 'e took all Nanna's cats away, and Walt, and I dunno where 'e took 'em!'

'What're you saying?' Maryann turned to Sal.

Sal raised her stricken face. 'Norman took them outside and . . .' She made a wringing movement with her hands. Maryann went cold.

'Not Walt? Not *all* of them?'

Sal nodded, glancing anxiously at Tony.

Choking back her feelings, Maryann managed to sing a lullaby through her tears, stroking Tony's head until his breathing changed and she could tell he was drifting off to sleep. Sal lay on the bed, buried her head in her arms and shook with sobs. The smells of cooking floated upstairs: liver, potatoes, cabbage. The boys had

73

had slops and if it had just been the family there they'd have had the same, but Norman Griffin had to have his meat and two veg whatever the time of night. Maryann got up and went over to Sal, tapping her gently on the shoulder. It was like after their dad died when they'd cried together up here and Maryann expected her to sit up so they could put their arms round each other. But instead Sal seemed to shrink from her.

'Get off me!' Her voice came out muffled but the venom in it was unmistakable. 'Just don't bloody well touch me.'

'Please yerself,' Maryann said, feeling more tears well in her eyes. Why was Sal being like this? And today, of all days, when they'd lost their nan? The two of them had always been different and they'd always fallen out a lot, but in the end they had been close. But these last few months Sal seemed to have changed so much Maryann couldn't get near her, and tonight those changes felt unbearable. She was going to move away, but she looked back at Sal. She was curled on her side now, her hands over her face as if she couldn't bear to see anything. Now she was looking carefully at her sister she noticed the boniness of her fingers – Sal, bony! She'd always been the plump one. Maryann felt a sudden physical shock go through her. She knew her sister had been strange, moody lately. You couldn't miss the fact. But people said that was wenches for you when they began to get a bit older: she was just going through it, growing up. But now Maryann saw it was more than that.

In a soft, hesitant voice, she said, 'You don't look well. What's up with yer?'

Sal sat up with an abrupt movement and Maryann flinched, thinking for a second Sal was going to slap her. Her blonde hair was wild round her face and she spoke through clenched teeth. 'Why should there be anything up with me – eh? Just bloody well leave me be, stupid!'

Maryann stood up and backed away, leaving Sal glaring at her in the candlelight.

'I dunno what's 'appened to yer' – a sob caught in Maryann's throat – 'but you ain't like my sister any more. Yer 'orrible, I 'ate yer . . .'

'Oh who cares.' Sal lay down, indifferent. 'Just sod off, will yer?'

Maryann got halfway down the stairs and then sank on to one of the steps in the dark, hugging her knees, utterly miserable. She sat rocking for a moment, everything flashing through her mind, all the horrible things that had happened. Norman had done away not just with Tiger but all Nanny Firkin's animals! The swelling, explosive feeling built and built inside her until she could hardly breathe, she was so full of hatred and grief. At last she got up, not giving herself more time to think, and ran down to the front room where Norman Griffin was reading the *Mail*. She snatched the paper out of his hands, screwed it up and threw it into the grate before he had even taken in what was happening. The fire leapt into a great yellow blaze.

''Ere! What the . . .?'

Maryann saw his slitty eyes widen with astonishment and he sat forward as if to get up.

'You killed Tiger, didn't yer?' she shrieked at him. 'Who d'you think you are, killing my little cat and my nan's pets and throwing them out like bits of rubbish! I *hate* yer, you 'orrible man, coming 'ere thinking yer can take over from our dad. Well, yer can't because 'e

75

was a good man and you're just a ... a fat, murdering pig, that's what you are and I 'ope someone cuts yer bloody throat for yer!'

There were a few seconds of stunned quiet while the clock ticked and the fire crackled, then Flo's voice, 'Maryann!' at the door, her expression more appalled than Maryann could ever remember seeing it before. But she was past caring now, she was in a storm of crying, kneeling on the hearth rug, beside herself with grief and exhaustion.

'How could you've let him, Mom? 'E's a nasty, cruel man. 'E put his hands round Tiger's throat and squeezed the life out of 'im and that's the man you're married to, Mom ... What'd Tiger ever done to 'im, poor little thing?'

The slapping Flo Griffin administered at that point almost floored Maryann, an almighty swipe across the side of the head.

'What d'you think you're on about, yer little bitch! Shut your mouth before I knock the living daylights out of yer!'

'Flo ... Flo ...' Norman Griffin's voice was calm, measured. 'That's enough now – calm down.'

The heat from the fire was intense on Maryann's back and her cheek was raw and burning. She looked out from behind her hands, keeping her gaze lowered, to see them both standing over her. Her eyes were at the level of their thighs. She knew without looking that her mother's face was contorted with rage. Next to her, Maryann looked down at Norman's stockinged feet planted wide apart. His shoes, well shined, were tilted up against the fender beside her. Slowly, she raised her eyes towards him. He seemed immense, looming over her, his face a great doughy ball on the end of his neck. She looked for the fury in his face, the eyes narrowed with loathing. But instead she saw something more puzzling. Norman Griffin looked relaxed, not smiling but as if a smile was waiting under the surface of his face. He seemed in some way triumphant. Maryann stared uncertainly at him, waiting, but then Flo started up.

'I'm so sorry, Norman, for Maryann carrying on like this. The girl's a disgrace, but what with losing my mother today and all . . .'

'Feed the girl and get her to bed,' Norman said. The expression on his face didn't alter and he spoke evenly, betraying no emotion. 'Today's not an ordinary day, is it? We don't want her going hungry.'

'Oh Norman.' Flo sounded quite awestruck. 'D'yer hear that, Maryann, after all the terrible things yer've said? Norman did the only thing that could be done with all yer nan's animals – we couldn't bring them 'ere, the filthy things. Now you get on yer feet and say yer sorry or you'll feel my hand across yer again, wench. Yer've got far better from Mr Griffin than yer deserve, that you have.'

Maryann stood up, her eyes fixed on the coloured splashes in the rug. She was astonished herself, but she couldn't say sorry. The word bulged like an egg stuck in her throat but it wouldn't come out. Sorry! She wasn't bloody well sorry. She wished she'd said far more. She wanted to get a red-hot poker and burn and burn him till he screamed.

'Maryann – say yer sorry!' Flo was almost shouting at her.

Maryann shook her head.

'Let it go,' Norman Griffin said quietly. 'We'll let it go. For now.'

Maryann lay in bed next to Sal. Sal hadn't come down, despite Flo calling her repeatedly. By the time they ate it was eleven o'clock and Maryann almost collapsed into bed and, exhausted and overwrought, fell asleep.

But she was wakened in the dead of night by Sal, moving restlessly at first, whimpering, then thrashing about more and more violently. Her arm came over and whacked Maryann across the chest.

'Eh – Sal!' Maryann pushed herself up on one elbow. 'Sal? You dreaming?'

Sal sat up suddenly and started gagging. Maryann's heart was going like a drum.

'Sal, Sal!' She tried to put her arm round Sal's shoulders, shaking her to wake her. Sal's whole body was heaving as if she was choking on something, her breath coming in sharp, desperate gasps.

'Sal, for God's sake stop it – say summat to me. What's the matter with yer?'

She gabbled on and on at her sister until Sal suddenly took a huge gasp as if something had come unblocked and her breath calmed a fraction. Maryann held her tight.

'Maryann?'

'Oh Sal. You frightened the living daylights out of me! I thought you was choking.'

For a moment Sal seemed to snuggle into her sister's skinny arms as if glad of the comfort. 'Help me, Maryann,' she said sleepily.

''Ow can I help yer?'

'Help me – I've got to get out.'

'Sal—' She wondered if her sister was asleep or awake. It was so dark she couldn't see if her eyes were open. She stroked Sal's shoulder and kissed her. 'I wish yer'd talk to me. Tell me what's up. Yer never talk to me these days, Sal. I want us to get on.'

There was silence then Sal said, 'Don't ever let 'er make you work for Mr Griffin.'

'I won't.' Whatever was she going on about? 'I wouldn't any'ow. Don't think 'e'd want me.'

Sal gripped her arm. 'Just don't. Promise me.'

'I promise.'

Nine

All that spring Maryann stayed away from home as much as she could and haunted the canal bank. The paths were not readily accessible – they were kept well walled and fenced off to stop thieving from the wharves – but she had her place where she could squeeze through. It was her secret escape route through which she could climb into this other world, different and hopeful. She was keeping out of everyone's way and it suited Flo Griffin to keep the cheeky little bint well out of her hair, except that she'd have liked her out of the way with her brothers in tow as well and Maryann had other ideas. Sometimes she took Tony with her, out down to play in the street or to the rezzer, but she never took him to the cut. That was her place. She tried to sneak out as quickly as she could every day, before Flo could tell her to mind her brothers, sometimes even slipping out the back, over the wall and away.

No one had got round to cutting her hair in months, and it hung in black trails each side of her thin face. When school was over she untied the strip of rag which held it back all day, put on her cotton frock in faded checks of dark and lighter blue and old rubber-soled pumps with no socks and she was off, the air on her bare arms, the sun pricking out freckles on her nose.

Ever since the morning a few weeks ago when Sal had sat up to find an ooze of blood between her legs, and Maryann learned that Sal had 'got her first monthly and become a woman' Maryann had decided she didn't want to be a woman very much herself. If it meant putting rags in your knickers and sitting about looking weighed down, groaning that your stomach hurt, they could keep it. And to have to marry horrible men like Mr Griffin so she could live in a half decent house and have meat every day of the week. She wanted to stay as she was for ever, light as wisp, to slip through the fence and run and run along the canal bank until there were fewer factories and more trees and she could lie looking up into leaves arched over her like a great green cathedral.

But she did have a companion to take on her wanderings. That week, after Mr Griffin murdered Tiger, Sal came home from work and, when they were alone, slipped something into Maryann's hand.

''Ere – saw this in the pawn shop. S'for you.'

To her delight, Maryann saw a little china cat, painted quite crudely in grey and black. It was lying down looking up with an alert expression. It didn't have a white throat, but in every other way it could have been Tiger.

'Oh Sal – ta!'

'S'awright,' Sal said.

It didn't make up for Tiger of course, and Sal soon sunk back into herself, but it meant such a lot that she'd thought to buy it. That Sal had reached out to her. Maryann loved the china cat. She called it 'Little Tiger' and carried it everywhere with her in the pocket of her frock.

At the weekends she went down to the cut and walked miles, closing her mind tight against her family, her life at home. She'd been down on the path out through Selly Oak, round the back of Bournville, her mouth watering with the smell of chocolate from the Cadbury factory as trains rumbled past close by, purple lupins amid the grass. Up Winson Green way, on a cold day, water outlets from factories making steam hiss up out of the icy canal, the routes winding and looping round the back of firms and out again, the path darkening under dripping bridges. And when she looked up and took notice she began to realize that Sal was sloping out every weekend too. Nance told her Sal was turning up round their place and she and Charlie were going off together. The park, they said. Never spelled out where. When Nance said it, Maryann shrugged.

'Good for them.'

'I don't know what's got into yer,' Nance said, offended. Before, they'd have gossiped and giggled about this development. Sal and Charlie – ooh, what was going on there!

'There ain't nothing wrong with me,' Maryann said. Nance got on her nerves nowadays. She seemed young and daft, wanting to play games all the time. Maryann just wanted to be away from it all, on her own.

But all the time, even though the canal had become a place of refuge in itself, she was on the lookout for that man, with his big smile and glowing red beard. Joel, who occupied her mind like a great burnished rock. The canals were busy with traffic day in, day out, mostly the joeys, day tripping, doing local deliveries round the factories, but among them were the family boats, the kings of the cut. Maryann narrowed her eyes when she saw one coming, looking for the right colours, the *Esther Jane*'s reds, yellows and greens, the scrolls, roses and castles painted on her doors. One day she thought she saw her, moving slowly along, a mile or so further out from where she had first met Joel. She ran towards the boat, full of excitement. But when she got closer she saw that it was wrong, everything was in a different place from what she remembered. The horse turned out to be a mule, not Bessie, and the boat was called the *Mariella*. A woman stood at the back holding a baby. Walking beside the mule, there was also a boy, about the same age as herself.

'D'yer know a boat called the *Esther Jane*?' Maryann asked him.

The boy hitched up the sleeves of a huge shirt.

'I dunno. *Mom!*' he bawled across towards the boat. At the same full volume he repeated Maryann's question, still plodding along as the mule towed the boat.

A man appeared. '*Esther Jane*? That'll be Darius Bartholomew's,' he called across.

'And Joel Bartholomew?' Maryann shouted.

'Ar – that's 'is son. You looking out for 'um?'

The boy's father gave the same promise as the coal-shovelling man had, those months ago, that he would pass word round. And why didn't she leave a message with the toll clerks?

So she had, a little note saying:

Dear Mr Bartholomew,
    When you pass this way again I'd like to see you, please keep an eye out for me. I'm on the path most afternoons.
        Yours,
        Maryann Nelson.

And one day she was suddenly there, a hazy afternoon when the cut seemed clogged with factory smoke and no breeze to blow it away. She'd walked out almost as far as Smethwick Junction. The horse was skewbald, a solid little mare, and behind her Maryann saw the red, yellow and green of the boat and once more her pulse speeded as she ran closer. Before she could read the name she saw a man in a black hat standing holding the tiller, a huge white beard curling across his chest and, standing behind the small fore-cabin, staring out, a dark-haired girl of about ten years old. On the roof a brown mongrel dog was standing by the water carriers, wagging a long tail. Maryann's excitement drained away. No sign of Joel. It was the wrong boat again.

But as it drew alongside she saw the writing on the side of the cabin. *Esther Jane*. It was her! But where was Joel? Was the old man steering the boat his father?

She was too shy at first to call out to him. He looked rather grand standing there, face shaded by his hat, his back straight, beard billowing in the slight breeze, looking straight ahead of him along the canal. Maryann followed behind the horse towing the *Esther Jane*, and she kept glancing across to see if there was any sign of Joel. After a while, she saw the old man had noticed her and he raised his hand and saluted her. He reminded Maryann of a king in a fairy story, or what she'd been told God was supposed to look like. She waved back, uncertainly. She heard him say something into the cabin of the boat and in a moment she saw Joel's head appear out of the cabin. He waved as well and Maryann felt her cheeks turn pink with pleasure.

'Maryann Nelson!' he called across to her, and she giggled. She heard old Mr Bartholomew call to the girl at the bow of the *Esther Jane*. His voice was deep and growly and Maryann liked the sound of it. The girl began pulling on the tow rope, guiding the boat into the side. The old man moved the rudder and the *Esther Jane* glided up beside her. The girl leapt across the gap once she was able, and caught hold of the horse's bridle.

'Keep her moving, Ada,' Mr Bartholomew ordered. Maryann stood waiting nervously as the boat slid slowly along the bank. Now he was close to her, she could see that Darius Bartholomew had piercing grey eyes under the bushy white brows, and a forehead criss-crossed with lines like a railway junction. When he spoke he had several missing teeth. But best of all, she saw Joel smiling and reaching out his hand to her.

'Come on then, Maryann Nelson, hop in quick.'

She took Joel's hand with no hesitation and her own felt tiny, gripped in his palm, which was caloused and rough as a brick wall. She jumped across into the *Esther Jane* as it glided along, on to the tiny platform from where the boat was steered, and they pushed off again, Darius holding the long tiller while the girl stayed on the path guiding the horse.

''Ere,' Darius said to Joel. 'Tek over.' He stooped and disappeared into the cabin.

'Ent no locks to stop us along 'ere, see,' Joel said.

Maryann nodded. She was rather pleased with their little feat of getting her on board. And she liked the way he treated her as if it was quite natural that she should be there. The dog, who Joel said was called Jep, jumped down beside them, tail wagging frantically.

''Ello!' Maryann cried, patting him.

She stood with Jep beside Joel, looking round. The city began to close in on them more and more, factory walls blocking out the sky and from behind which she could hear clanging and shouting and the roar of machines. The boat moved smoothly along, her paint-work vivid against the blackened walls and leaden

85

water. In places there was a pall of smoke across the cut. She had never felt so excited. There were plenty of other boats coming the other way; some empty, others filled with different cargoes: metal products from the foundries, boxes or barrels of provisions, heaps of refuse. As they passed other boats, Joel touched his cap and called 'How do!' and usually got a reply. Maryann was standing inches away from his elbow. His sleeves were rolled and she could see the red down of hair on his brawny left arm. She could hear his breathing, rather fast, his lungs seeming to make a rustling sound at each breath.

'So – you've been on the lookout for us?' he said eventually. She had been comfortable with his silence and was quite startled when he spoke.

'I wanted to see you again.'

'Bloke in the toll office said. Just tell 'im next time – 'e'll pass it on. Letters ain't no good to us.'

'Oh.' Maryann looked up at him. ''E don't like to be left letters to look after then?'

''E don't mind, but we don't read, us. Never 'ad much schooling. D'you want a go at this?' Joel indicated the tiller. Maryann nodded and Joel showed her where to put her hand, then laid his over the top of hers. 'It's busy down 'ere. Once we get round there we turn in and we can get unloaded.'

He guided her, tweaking the rudder, feeling his way.

'Is that your sister?' she asked, nodding over to the girl leading the horse, who kept looking round at her, curiously.

Joel nodded. 'That's our Ada.' Maryann was wondering how old the girl was, when Joel said, 'Ten years of age she is now. She could pretty well run the boat 'erself if she had to.'

86

She heard the pride in his voice. How she'd love that! To know how to look after a boat, steer it all herself, live in one of these cabins, away from the streets, from everything about home! Although Ada was younger than her she found herself looking at her with awe. She'd grown up on a boat and knew everything! She was a skinny girl, with dark brown hair and a pinched face, but in Maryann's eyes she looked very capable and grown up walking along at the side of the horse.

After a time of winding through the network of the city's canals they turned into one of the shadowy loops of water branching off it, where they brought the *Esther Jane* to a halt for unloading behind one of the factories. Joel told her they were carrying firebricks from 'up Staffor'shire'.

'Yer can get off of 'er for a bit now,' Joel said. Darius had emerged and was standing out on the side. Ada was strapping a painted can of feed under the horse's nose.

'I don't want to get off,' Maryann said and she heard Joel give his chuckle, like a wheeze in his chest.

'Awright – well, yer can stay on if yer want. But it'll take a good while.'

A little round man with glasses came bustling over, smiling.

'Yer early, ain't yer, pal – what're yer feeding that pony o' yours?'

It was more than two hours before all the firebricks were unloaded. After a time, as Joel, Darius and two other men shifted the cargo, hand over hand, working as a team, Maryann jumped out and went to see Ada and the horse. She was standing watching Bessie finish off her fodder, patting her brown and white neck. Jep was near by, sniffing round.

'She's called Bessie, ain't she?' Maryann asked.

Ada nodded.

'She yours?'

'Oh ar – she's our 'orse. She's a good'un, Bessie is.'

'Never seen an 'orse eat out of a bucket before.'

'That ent a bucket – that's a nostern!' Ada laughed. Maryann liked her cheeky face. 'I got to fill up wi' water. You coming?'

'Awright.'

They each took one of the colourful metal water cans, both covered in painted flowers, and went to a tap round the side of the factory. The ground was a crunched up morass of broken brick, dust and mud.

'So you're Maryann Nelson,' Ada said, holding her can under the tap. 'You met our Joel.'

Maryann nodded.

'You writ a letter.'

'I wanted to see Joel again.' She looked over at him. Joel had stopped, was coughing.

'Why?'

''E was nice to me. And I like the boat.'

'She's called the *Esther Jane* . . .'

'I know,' Maryann said, rather impatiently. It was her turn to fill her can. She heard the water rising in it and supported it with both arms.

'That was our mom's name.'

'Where is she then?'

'She passed on when I was born. Our dad called 'er the *Esther Jane*. Joel says before that she were called *Elizabeth Ann*.'

They carried the water back to the boat. Once more, Maryann was able to go inside the cosy little cabin and she watched as Ada stoked up the range, stood a big pot on the heat and made cups of tea, handing them out to the men. She gave one to Maryann, with lots of sugar in, and the two of them sat out, balanced on the edge, each side of the stern. Ada told her that she and Joel had an older brother called Darius who worked what she called 'fly' on a Fellows, Morton and Clayton boat. This was the city's biggest carrying company, Ada explained seriously, and Maryann nodded: she had seen boats with their name on many times. Working fly meant having a shift of five or six men working day and night to cover the long distances.

''E goes down London,' Ada said. 'Works the Gran' Union.'

Ada asked a little bit about her family, but Maryann could tell as she talked that Ada didn't really understand what her life was like, just as Maryann didn't hers. Ada had never lived in a house that stayed still in one place, the same every day. She was a boat girl, born and bred. Maryann could feel the difference between them. The weather-beaten look of Ada's face, the confident way she dealt with the boat, the horse. Her strength, thin and small as she was, the way she thought and spoke differently.

When the butty was finally empty, Joel came over to them. He looked exhausted.

'Got the stew on, Ada?' he asked. 'And you'd better get yerself home, hadn't yer, little Maryann?'

'But I don't want to go 'ome!' Maryann protested. 'I don't ever want to go home!'

Ten

The light was fading now and the two Bartholomew men's faces were hollowed out with shadows as they stood looking at her. Jep was between them, looking up at their faces questioningly. Maryann presented them suddenly with a strange puzzle, an obstacle to be overcome. Darius, as if at a loss, moved stiffly away and the dog followed him.

'Well, you can't just stay 'ere, can you?' Joel suggested gently.

'Why not?' Her voice was fierce. 'I don't want to go 'ome. I'd rather stay with you.' She looked imploringly at Joel, who was standing with his arms folded. '*Please* – just for a bit.'

'Look – come up 'ere—' He reached his hand out and pulled her up on to the bank, going down on one knee in front of her. 'What's all this, Maryann? You've got a mom and a dad . . .'

'I ain't got a dad!'

'What about your mom?' Ada said. 'You can't just stay out, can yer?'

'She most likely won't even notice,' Maryann said mutinously. She gripped her hand round the little china cat in her pocket, felt her lip begin to tremble. More than anything she'd wanted ever, more even, she thought, than wanting Tiger, she longed not to have to go home that evening. Home meant Sal's terrible silences and Mr Griffin being horribly oily and nice to her. There was something wrong with that after the way she'd shouted and raved at him and she felt as if she was living on borrowed time, that he was cooking up some punishment for her, made all the worse because she didn't know what it was. And there'd be Tony with his big eyes, imploring someone, anyone, to take some notice of him.

'I'll run back in the morning,' she pleaded. 'I'll go to school. And I could sleep anywhere – outside if I 'ave to!' But saying this, she hugged herself, running her hands down her bare arms. It was chilly now the sun had gone down and all she had on was her cotton frock. She put her head on one side, looking with the full force of appeal into Joel's face. He was watching her with a mixture of amusement and concern.

'Sleep outside . . .' He shook his head and she heard him laugh, his chest making a rustling noise. 'Look, Maryann – this ent right. We'll be loading up at dawn and then we're off out of Birnigum again . . . You can come on the boat again – leave a message with the toll clerks. Let me walk you back to your house tonight and see you safe, eh?'

She looked down at her shoes and wanted to cry because it felt as if Joel was babying her, as if she was younger than Ada. She swallowed hard and looked him in the eyes, annoyed at the fact her own were swimming with tears.

'Please, Joel,' she whispered. 'Just once. I won't get in your way.'

'Go on, Joel – let 'er,' Ada said. She seemed excited by the idea. 'She can bunk up on the bench. I'll go on the floor.'

Joel sighed and pushed himself upright so he was

standing over her, hands on his waist and she stood looking up at him like one might at a mountain. She could see his beard silhouetted round his face. She knew he was exhausted, that they'd had a long, hard day's work and why would he relish the thought of having to walk her back home through unfamiliar streets, houses pressing in, to be greeted by her angry family?

Eventually he said, 'Best 'ave summat to eat, then.'

Maryann turned to Ada and saw her grin, her teeth gleaming, and she smiled back, hugging herself even tighter with excitement.

Joel lifted the lid off the stew pot and stirred the contents. Maryann went with Ada to stable Bessie for the night. On the way back Ada explained cheerfully that they had a bowl in the cabin and if she wanted to wee she'd have to go off and find somewhere. Maryann blushed.

'I'd best go now,' she said.

Ada handed her the bowl and Maryann slipped off in the dark and squatted down near the edge of the canal. She decided she liked weeing in the open even if it was a bit nerve-racking – anyone might come along. She saw that the moon had come out.

When she climbed down into the cabin of the *Esther Jane* over the coal box which was used as a step, she found a big smile spreading over her face. She was enchanted every time she stepped inside. However did they manage to live in a space this small? The house she'd grown up in in Garrett Street had been cramped enough, but here the whole living space was nine feet by seven.

'You sit 'ere—' Ada indicated the side bench, next to Joel. Maryann sat shyly beside him, smelling the delicious frying potatoes he was cooking. Jep came up and sniffed at her and she stroked his head until Joel said, 'G'won – out with you,' and he squeezed out past Ada on the step of the cabin.

Darius Bartholomew who was already sitting on the bench at the far end, dressing a wound on one of his fingers with a strip of rag, had given her a grunt of acknowledgement. She was shy of Darius, but sensed that he was gentle, even if he was not sure about her being there. Now he had taken off his hat Maryann saw he had a fine head of grizzled hair. An oil lamp fixed to the cupboard beside the range cast a cosy light round the small space, though she could see Darius was squinting to see properly. She looked round at the grainy ceiling, the pretty paintings of roses and castles on the cupboards, the strips of crochet work edging some of the shelves. It was warm in the cabin from the heat of the stove and the steam gushing out from the kettle. Maryann enjoyed every moment of it.

'You hungry?' Joel said.

Maryann nodded. Joel suddenly grinned at her. 'Nearly ready now. Table down.'

Joel swivelled the lamp round on its bracket so they could see better. Her eyes felt stretched very wide, taking everything in. Joel chuckled again at her amazement and she saw Darius smile as well, his bushy moustache making the smile appear even broader. They were enjoying seeing their own life through her eyes, this quaint little wench from off the bank, who saw things that they had always known and taken for granted as new and surprising.

They ate what tasted to Maryann like the best meal she had ever had. Mutton stew with big chunks of carrot, fried potatoes, bread, from pretty plates and a cup of sweet tea. No one said much and that suited her. Jep was peeping in through the door, nostrils working. She could feel the weariness of the men, although Joel said it had been not too hard a day for them. He was squeezed in on the bench next to her, her skinny legs dwarfed by his solid thighs. She could hear his jaws working as he chewed on huge bites of bread, and in the confined space, the wheezing sound of his lungs. During the meal he started coughing and had to go outside. She heard the coughing go on and on and he came back wiping his eyes.

'Where's she going to sleep, then?' Darius asked. Maryann saw that though he was the older man, the father, it was Joel who was in charge of the *Esther Jane*.

''Er can 'ave the bench,' Ada said again. 'I'll go down under for tonight.'

Joel nodded, patting the bench they were sitting on with his hand. 'This is your bed then, Maryann. How d'yer like that?'

'Ooh yes,' she said. 'Ta, Ada.'

Ada laughed. She seemed to find a lot of things Maryann said funny.

She watched, after they had cleared away the meal and folded back the table, as Darius pulled out the door of the bed cupboard and inside was a thin mattress and a couple of blankets. She thought for a moment he was going straight to bed, but it seemed the men were off to the pub.

'Back a bit later,' Joel said. 'You'll be all right with Ada 'ere.'

Ada grinned, shuffled herself down under the bed with another blanket, rested her head on her coat arm and, to Maryann's surprise, fell asleep straight away. Jep was allowed to come and curl up next to her.

'You can have this,' Joel said, handing her what felt like an army blanket. He indicated that Maryann should lie on the bench. Maryann settled herself down. The bench was hard, but she didn't care. The cabin felt so snug and warm. Joel took off his jacket and folded it roughly. 'Put this under yer head.'

The jacket was worn and the material scratchy, and it smelled of Joel.

'Ta,' she whispered.

Maryann dozed for a while in the light from the lamp, and was woken by the two men coming back in. Darius manoeuvred his way across the cabin and was very soon just as fast asleep as Ada.

'You awright, little 'un?' Joel asked. She caught a whiff of beer on his breath.

'Yes – ta,' she whispered.

'Oh – you won't wake them two – not once they've gone off.' But he still spoke in a soft voice. She watched as his huge shadow moved round the walls of the cabin.

'Joel?'

'What's that then?' He came and sat beside her, his feet up on the step.

''Ve yer always lived on 'ere?'

''Cept for the two year – nigh on – I were in France.'

'Our dad was in France. 'E was a soldier. Were you a soldier an' all?'

Joel nodded. There was silence before he spoke. His talk came in brief bursts, as though he had to get himself ready for it.

'Was 'e killed in the war?'

'No, by a motor car.'

Joel watched her face. 'You got to go back in the morning, little 'un. You shouldn't be 'ere, should you?'

'I know. I will. I just wanted . . . I just like it 'ere.'

For a second she felt his huge hand laid on her head. 'Sleep, that's a girl.'

''Night, Joel.'

He put the lamp out and the cabin was in complete darkness while she heard him move carefully across and settle himself on the bed beside his father.

She did not sleep well that night. The bench was very uncomfortable and she kept feeling she was going to fall off it. It was quite stuffy, and she could smell Jep's doggy smell and it was all strange being there, with no Sal beside her and no Tony across the room. She lay listening to the silence, thinking of the water under them, wondering if she was sleeping above any fish or frogs. After a time she realized it had started to rain, the drops drumming steadily on the roof, which made the cabin feel even more of a cosy refuge when the sky was only a thin shell away. Lulled by its rhythm she dozed, but later was woken by Darius Bartholomew snoring. Some time after that Joel was moving about, coughing, and once he got up and left the cabin. She listened to him straining for breath outside. The sound made her feel sorry for him; a big man's cough so loud, such a wrenching, painful noise.

When she heard him come back in, she said, 'Don't your cough ever get any better?'

He felt his way across, hands moving over her feet, and sat down on the edge of the bench. She heard him say 'Lie down!' to Jep.

'So you're still on the go, are you? Was it me woke you?'

'No.'

'Have yer heard of gas?'

''Course.'

'The sort they used in the war?'

96

'Did you get gassed?'

'Could've been a lot worse. But my chest's always bad. Worse in the winter.'

'Don't you 'ave a missis?' Maryann asked.

She heard another small seizure of laughter from Joel. 'No.'

'Don't yer want one?'

'Me?' There was a pause. 'Well – yes, course. But it ent happened yet. You don't meet up with people for long, working the cut. Here today, gone tomorrow. Don't s'pose I'm very easy to live with, neither.'

'I wouldn't mind living with yer,' Maryann said.

She heard Joel's laugh again. She liked the way he laughed when she said things, as if he found her surprising and funny.

'Don't know what yer mom'd say about that. She won't be very pleased with you in the morning, will she?'

'No. I s'pose not. But can I come and see yer again?'

'I told you you could. We work up and down this route. We can send word when the *Esther Jane*'s coming through.'

'Oh, *will* yer?'

Joel stood up. Once more she felt him pat her, this time her shoulder. 'You don't give up, do yer? Go on – off to sleep.'

They were up at dawn, the sky grey and rain still falling, the men with many hours of work ahead of them. Maryann said her goodbyes and thanked them.

'Look out for us!' Ada called to her.

'Oh – I'll be back!' She was shivering in her thin frock in the wet, but so happy she didn't care.

She watched as the *Esther Jane* began to slide along the wharf, off to collect her next load to be moved north, Jep standing on the cabin roof, Bessie plodding along, the white blotches of her coat standing out in the overcast morning. Joel waved at her.

'Go on now – I want to see you on your way!' he called, then coughed.

'Come back soon!' she shouted, watching until they were out of sight before she tore back round on to the towpath towards home. She had to get changed into her school clothes!

It was fully light when she got home, the lamps were out, people were setting off for work. When she opened the front door she could hear the sound of her mom shovelling coal. The cellar had flooded so they were keeping it out the back under a tarpaulin. She stood in the front for a breathless moment, hearing footsteps on the stairs, which came down into the corner of the front room. The stairs door opened and Sal appeared, face white as a sheet.

'Maryann! Oh my God, Maryann. Where were yer? I thought summat 'ad happened to yer! Our mom's going to 'ave yer for this!' To Maryann's astonishment, Sal flung her arms round her, sounding tearful.

Flo came and stood in the doorway, hair still plaited from bed.

'Well—' she began menacingly. 'Where in God's name 've you been?'

Maryann shrugged. She wasn't telling *them*. 'Out.'

'Out!' Flo was about to get herself worked up but then the effort seemed too great. She badly wanted a cup of tea and there was obviously no harm done. 'Well – you're back now, ain't yer? We'll 'ave to see what yer father 'as to say.'

Eleven

That evening Maryann was settled in the kitchen after tea, about to start on her bit of homework. She was still wondering with astonishment why no one had said anything. They'd all sat through the meal together and there'd been not a word. Had she got away with it? Then she heard Norman Griffin's voice from the front.

'Maryann – come through 'ere.'

Her heart started racing then, stomach tightening in dread but she kept her expression blank as she went through to the front room, clutching one of her books to her chest. Sal had stood up and was hovering behind Flo's chair. Maryann didn't look at her stepfather. She fixed her gaze on the grate: the poker with its brass handle was lying across the fender. The room stank of his cigarettes.

'I've not heard anything in the way of an explanation about you disappearing off for the night, Maryann, worrying yer mother half to death.'

Maryann hung her head.

'So where were yer?'

She said nothing. Nothing on God's earth was going to make her tell him, even if he took a stick to her. She'd slept on the *Esther Jane*! That was something they couldn't take away from her and she'd never forget it.

'Are yer going to tell me, or what?'

'What.'

Norman propelled his rotund bulk up out of the chair. 'Why, yer impudent little bugger!'

'Maryann!' Flo sat forward on the edge of her chair, eyeing her husband. 'I'll not 'ave yer speaking to Norman like that. Now come on – spit it out. Was you at Nance's, or what?'

'I ain't telling yer.' She looked up into Norman's face. Her legs had gone weak and trembly. Sal had a desperate expression in her eyes, her hand over her mouth.

Norman seemed at a loss for words. 'Go up to bed,' he said, his voice tightly controlled. 'But you needn't think I've finished with yer.'

'Don't do that, Maryann,' Sal said when they were upstairs, undressing in their candlelit room. 'Just tell 'im where yer went for God's sake, we was all worried. Where were yer?'

'I'm not telling you neither!' Maryann flung her cardigan on the chair. Her voice was a fierce hiss. 'And I bloody ain't telling 'im, Mr Smelly Pig!'

'Keep yer voice down – you'll wake Tony. You're a silly little cow, Maryann. You're just making trouble for everyone.'

'Not for everyone – just me. You ain't in no trouble, are yer?'

'That's what you think – you don't know what 'e's like, none of yer – you ain't got no idea . . .' Sal's voice started to crack. She put her hands over her face. 'Oh God, Maryann . . .'

'What the 'ell's the matter now?' Maryann managed a rough transition from being furious to sounding sympathetic. At least Sal was talking to her for once and not just telling her to shove off. She was really crying her heart out as well, shaking with it. 'Come on, Sal – I'm on your side, you know I am.'

'I can't...' Sal was shaking all over, could hardly speak, teeth chattering. 'You don't know what 'e might do!'

'Don't talk daft – what's 'e going to do? 'E can't do nothing!'

But the emotion she could feel coming from Sal was so strong that she hugged her tightly with one arm, taking her hand with the other, trying to steady her. 'God, Sal, you're freezing! What's happened – you can tell me. I won't breathe a word, you know I won't. Cross my heart.'

'It's ... it's ... I can't ... It's too dirty ... I'm dirty ...'

'Sal!'

But they both froze then, eyes meeting each other's, as they heard the door open at the bottom of the stairs.

'Don't you worry, Flo love, I'll deal with it my way. You stay 'ere – it'll all be sorted out in a few minutes.'

Moving as one body the girls blew the candle out and flung themselves into the bed, half undressed as they were, the springs on the bed giving them away as they pulled the covers up over them, lying down and squeezing their eyes tight shut. Maryann could feel her heart thumping as if it might burst.

The heavy steps came closer. He was in the room, standing looking down at them. They could hear his breathing. Maryann felt Sal grip her arm, squeezing until her nails dug in.

'I know you're not asleep. I don't need a candle to know that.'

There was a long silence, so long that Maryann had an odd floating sensation as if she was dreaming, that

101

he was not really there, but she couldn't open her eyes because it felt as if Norman Griffin could see everything, each flick of an eyelid, as if the room, for him, was full of light. It wasn't completely dark outside and you could just see the outlines of things in the room. She felt Sal give a gasping little breath. What was he waiting for? Why didn't he say anything? Then at last he moved closer along Maryann's side of the bed.

'So – secrets, eh?' Speaking more softly this time, almost singsong.

Another pause.

'Maryann?'

She said nothing, stopped breathing, remembering to do so again with a gasp.

Norman cleared his throat. 'We all have our little secrets, don't we, Sal? See, Maryann, Sal and I've come to a sort of agreement, haven't we, Sal? And I don't see why you shouldn't be part of that now as well. Sal's getting older and there are certain things older girls ain't no good for.'

Maryann felt him sitting himself down on her side of the bed and she squirmed further across towards Sal. What was he talking about? She didn't understand at all. It was no use carrying on pretending to be asleep. She forced her eyes open and, though fully aware that he was there, she jumped when she saw him leaning close, looking at her. Her heart was racing frantically. With an abrupt movement he pulled back the cover and laid his hand on her chest, fumbling round her tiny breasts. His hand felt hot and heavy, pinching and hurting her, and Maryann whimpered.

'Don't touch my sister!' Sal sat up, trying to find a thread of courage, then her own voice trailed pathetically. 'Please Mr Griffin. Not 'er as well. 'Er's only a child. It ain't right.'

'Oh – jealous now, are we!' He laughed. Maryann had the same feeling she had the night she found Nanny Firkin dead, that this couldn't really be happening. It was a horrible dream.

'D'yer want it an' all, Sal?' He reached across and Maryann heard Sal cry out.

'Stop it – I'll call our mom, yer dirty man.'

'Call yer mom!' he mimicked her. 'D'yer think she'd believe a word you say, little Sally Griffin. She ain't gunna believe any of this in a month of Sundays. And you ain't so brave, are yer, not normally.' The voice was hard now, cold as steel, talking on and on, and they had no choice but to hear it.

'Just remember, Sal, what I'll do if I 'ave any trouble from you. Do I 'ave to remind you again, eh? You ain't no good to me now, and I need someone who is. And this one' – Maryann felt him prod her – 'she's still clean and she's got a bit of spirit to 'er an' all. You can leave school in a couple of months, can't you, Maryann? And then we'll see about a job for yer.' He ran his hand down the length of her body, hovering at the top of her thighs. 'Secrets, Maryann. Yer a good wench if yer can keep a secret. Because if you say a word . . .'

He left the threat hanging over them, unfinished, as he got up and went off downstairs.

Sal turned away, crying, curling herself up as tight as she could.

'Sal – oh Sal, don't! Talk to me!' Maryann felt horrible, having him touching her, but she didn't understand what it was all about, she just knew it was all wrong. 'Why was 'e doing that? Sal, tell me what 'e's been doing!'

'I can't.'

'Why not?'

'I just can't tell yer – couldn't say the words. Just, Maryann—' She rolled over, peering down intensely into Maryann's face. ''E's bad and dirty and I don't want 'im going anywhere near you. 'E does things 'e shouldn't.'

'What d'you mean?' Maryann asked in a small voice.

'Things you shouldn't even 'ave to know about. Look, Maryann – you're better at standing up to 'im than me – do anything yer can, even if you get into trouble. But don't let 'im make yer work in that place. Get yerself another job after you've finished school.'

'I will,' Maryann said. 'But why don't you leave an' all? You don't 'ave to stay there, do yer? Just walk out – 'e couldn't do nothing about it.'

'I can't,' was all Sal would say.

Maryann couldn't understand her. It was as if their stepfather had cast a spell over her and she couldn't resist anything he did, wouldn't stand up to him. She just couldn't get Sal to tell her more. She lay awake, full of disturbed feelings at the thought of Norman Griffin's hand moving over her. At the end of this school term she would reach the end of her education, of being a child. She was nearly fourteen. What had he meant when he said Sal wasn't clean any more? Was that to do with the bleeding? None of it made any sense. All she knew was that nothing at home felt safe any more. She thought with sudden longing of Nance. Nance had always been a good pal and she'd treated her badly. If only she could patch things up with her. She needed Nance now more than she'd ever needed her.

Twelve

''Ello there, stranger!'

Cathleen Black appeared when Maryann knocked on the half-open door.

'Well – we ain't seen you in a while, even though Sal seems to think she lives 'ere nowadays! Awright are yer, Maryann?'

'Oh yes, ta,' Maryann said, distracted from everything else by the sight of Cathleen Black's enormously swollen belly. It would have been impossible not to notice that she was expecting another child, she was so big she looked as if it might decide to pop out any moment.

'Look who's 'ere, Nance.' Cathleen waddled over to the range and picked up her cup of tea.

Nancy was doling out spud at the table to the four youngest, and a grubby lot they were, all grime and snot but cheerful. Perce was eleven now, William and George, nine and six, and Horace who was two and a half and kept sliding off his chair and running about. Nance tutted and banged the pan down.

''E won't keep still, Mom!' She picked Horace up and slammed him down on the chair again. 'Just park yerself and for God's sake stay there!'

'Ain't yer going to say 'ello to Maryann?' Cathleen said.

Nance's eyes were unmistakably hostile under her curly black fringe.

'So yer've turned up all of a sudden then. Don't I stink after all?'

Maryann blushed. Nance was in the right. She had been vile to her for ages. 'I know I've been a bit mean to you, like, Nance. Only I wanted to see you.'

'Go on with yer, Nance.' Cathleen put her cup down. 'Get yerself a plateful and yer can go and eat it on the step and cant with Maryann – I'll see to this shower in 'ere.'

'S'awright, Mom,' Nance said stiffly. 'I'll 'elp yer first.'

'Don't talk daft.' Cathleen waved a hand at her. 'You've been carrying on about 'ow yer ain't seen Maryann, so get off with yer. You'll 'ave plenty of 'elping to do when this babby comes, so yer might as well enjoy yerself while yer've got the chance.'

Nance doled the unappetizing food out on to a plate. Maryann watched with a pang of guilt. Her family had much better food than the Blacks – meat every day! 'What won't fatten will fill,' were words often on Cathleen Black's lips, and most of the Blacks' meals were in this vein. Then they both sat squeezed in side by side on the step. The yard was full of metal smells from the foundry at the back.

'Sorry I ain't been over,' Maryann said. 'Only things at 'ome 've been a bit ... well, you know ...'

'Is it yer old man?' Nance asked through a mouthful of tater.

Maryann hesitated, then nodded.

''E killed that cat, daint 'e?'

'Who else?' She wanted to pour everything out to Nance. Coming back here again felt nice. Mrs Black chatted to her children, asked them the odd question about school, was always on about one or the other of

106

them's First Communion. She took an interest, unlike her mom. Being here was a taste of the old times and it made her long for everything to be as it was before, back on the old footing, without all the horrible things going on at home. But she didn't have words for all of it. How could she say what had happened last night, Norman Griffin pawing at her through her nightshirt? She couldn't tell Nance or anyone that, but she did want to joke and laugh like they used to, before her dad died and everything went bad.

'It's my birthday next week,' Nance said. 'I can walk out of that school and never go back – get myself a job of work. You can an' all soon, eh?'

Maryann shrugged. 'S'pose so. Where're you gunna go?'

Nance grinned. 'Kunzle's'd be nice. Eat cakes all day! I'll go round the firms, see who'll 'ave me. Eh—' She nudged Maryann. 'If you're looking too, why don't we go round together?'

'I've got a bit of time to go yet.' Maryann felt cheered. Nance was so warm-hearted and she already felt forgiven.

'Oh ah, that's a thought. Anyroad, I'll let yer know what it's like, wherever I end up.'

They chattered on a while while Nance scraped up the last of her food, and they had a bit of a giggle.

''Ere—' Nance grinned and budged up a bit closer. 'I saw your Sal and our Charlie at it kissing the other night. They was in the brew'us and they never knew I was 'aving a look in!'

'They never!' Maryann didn't know whether to feel glad or not. Sal had turned fifteen. She was growing up. But she'd never said a word about it. There were too many things about Sal she didn't know nowadays.

'She was all over 'im,' Nance went on with relish. 'She ain't backward, your Sal, and that's a fact!'

The two of them were tittering over it, but while Maryann was intrigued – Charlie Black was a handsome devil, there was no denying – she felt hurt and left out.

'She never breathes a word to me about it,' she complained to Nance.

'Well, what d'yer expect! – O-oh,' Nance said as they heard loud muttering and blaspheming approaching along the entry.

Blackie appeared in the yard, walking with a gorilla-like gait, arms swinging, cap on askew, his jacket hanging open.

'Dad,' Nance said. 'Over 'ere.' She and Maryann got up out of the way and Blackie looked and looked.

'The door!' He pointed a wavering finger. 'Shome-one moved . . . the fuckin' door.'

'Oh come on in, yer silly sod,' Cathleen shouted from inside.

Blackie stumbled in through the door and they heard a grunt as he fell into his chair, followed by a loud, grating belch.

'Well,' Nance said with a wry look. 'That's 'im finished for the day.'

Friday night was bath night. Maryann got home feeling much more light-hearted after her visit to Nancy's and found Flo filling up the tin bath which usually hung on a rusty hook on the wall of the privy outside.

'Glad you're back at last,' she said resentfully. 'Yer can come and bath the boys for me.'

Maryann agreed gladly. She enjoyed soaping the

boys in the warm water, the feel of Billy's soft little body. He was nearly five now, still small, with shoulder blades like little angels' wings.

While she was pouring in a last kettle of water, Norman arrived home, bustling through the front door. Maryann felt herself tense as if there were pins pricking her skin. He was not a man who could move quietly. He was always a noisy, disturbing presence about the place. She hated the way he came and looked in when they were bathing, especially after last night. Sal refused ever to have a bath in the house now: she went down to the public bathhouse.

He came and stood at the kitchen door, hat in hand. 'Oh-ho, bath night, eh?'

Well, it's not as if we only do it every hundred years, Maryann thought. She didn't look up at him or answer, but she could feel him staring at her.

'Your tea's nearly done, Norman,' Flo said. 'Yer might as well come and sit down.'

'I'll just wash my hands.' He came and leaned over the bath opposite Maryann, took the bar of soap and rubbed his stubby white hands, using the nails of one hand to dig out the grime from under the nails of the other. She watched, repulsed. For a moment he looked into her face and she could feel his breath on her cheek. Maryann got up abruptly and moved away to call Tony and Billy.

She bathed the two of them while Norman sat at the table eating his mutton stew, Flo sitting opposite him. He ate up quickly, then sat back and lit a cigarette, watching them lazily, his eyes narrowed a little.

'I can do myself,' Tony said, so Maryann concentrated on Billy, splashing about to make as much noise as she could and drown out the sounds Norman made when he was eating. Billy laughed, pouring water energetically over his fair hair.

'Go easy,' Flo snapped. 'You'll soak the whole floor else. Where's Sal got to, Norman?'

'She said she 'ad to go to the shop for yer.'

'For me? I never asked 'er.'

Maryann rubbed Billy dry on a strip of cloth and he put his clothes on again.

'You go in next,' Flo said. 'Use the water 'fore it gets cold.'

Maryann felt her body go stiff. Not with him sitting there, she thought. 'When tea's finished,' she said.

'Oh, that's awright – you can carry on,' Norman said.

Maryann looked at her mom mutinously. 'I'll wait till you've finished.' And she walked off upstairs, knowing Flo was too idle to follow. When she was certain Norman was ensconced in the front room with his paper, she crept down, closing the kitchen door. Flo was in there, tutting about how long Sal was going to be. Maryann could hear the boys playing out with some other lads at the back.

She slipped her brown skirt off and her cream blouse, wishing she had the room to herself, without even her mom there. She felt suddenly curious about her body and would have liked to be alone to have a good look. Lately she had sensed it changing, little swellings on her chest when it used to be quite flat. But there never seemed to be a place where you could be on your own without a brother or sister or *someone* gawping at you.

She dipped one foot in the water.

'Can I 'ave one more kettle, Mom?'

Flo sighed. 'Oh, go on then. As it's boiled.'

She topped up the bath with hot water and it felt lovely as she sank down into it, even though it was scummy from Tony and Billy going in it before. She couldn't quite lie down full stretch any more, she had to keep her legs a bit bent up and in the winter you could feel the cold nibbling round whichever bit of you was sticking out of the water. But today it was warm and she relaxed, then sat up and began soaping herself. She was just rubbing suds over her shoulders and arms when the door opened and Norman came in. Maryann instinctively crossed her arms over her chest and tucked her head down.

Get out! she felt her whole being scream. *Just get out of here and don't look at me.*

He had his hands pushed down in his trouser pockets. Maryann turned away, trying to block him out.

'That looks nice in there,' he said. ''Ere – let me put some of that soap on your back for you.'

'No!' she almost shouted. 'I can do it myself.'

'Oh, don't talk so silly, Maryann,' Flo said irritably. 'Norman won't bite yer – 'e's just trying to give yer a hand. You can't reach yer back, can you?'

He was kneeling down, rolling up his sleeves and grinning at her. She cringed away from him.

'There you go—' Round and round he rubbed the soap in his hands until they were frothy with it. Her back was rigid. She wanted to jump out of the bath and run away from him, but she couldn't move.

Flo went to the back door. 'Billy? Billy! Get in 'ere now. It's time you was getting to bed.'

He was kneeling on her left, she could smell him. Death, he smelled of. He began to soap her back, his right hand circling round and round, caressingly.

111

'There,' he said. 'Nowt wrong with that, is there?' The soap slid from his left hand into the bath with a plop. 'Oops. Now where's that gone then?'

He was pretending to look for the soap, but she saw his eyes were on her breasts, his hand still circling on her back.

'That's the trouble with soap . . .' His breathing was louder. 'Slippery blooming stuff . . .'

'Billy!' Flo was shouting, furiously.

Maryann couldn't believe at first what she was feeling: a hard poking between her legs which for a second she couldn't connect with anything but then knew it was Norman's finger or thumb, jabbing, forcing up into her.

'Youch!' she cried, pulling away with a splash. 'What the 'ell 're yer doing?'

'Ah – 'ere it is!' A quick sweep of the bath and he brought up his hand, triumphantly holding the soap. They looked into each other's eyes and his were as icy as pebbles. Maryann turned cold all over.

'Sorry – did I catch yer by mistake?'

Flo, oblivious to all this, was bringing Billy crossly in through the back door. 'Look at the state of yer – you'll need to go back in the bleedin' bath!'

'Language, love!' Norman stood up. 'There we go – another one all fresh as a daisy.'

'Out you get then, Maryann,' Flo said. 'Billy's dipping back in.'

Maryann sat quite still. She couldn't look at Norman, at any of them. Shame seemed to burn up from her chest to the top of her head. Was this what Sal meant, this, and more, things Maryann could not even imagine? After a moment, Norman went out again, closing the door.

'It's nice the way 'e tries to be a dad to yer,' Flo commented.

Two days later, when she went up to their room, Maryann found Sal sitting on the bed. Her left arm was held out, underside upwards in front of her. In her other fist was a kitchen knife with which she was stabbing at her outstretched arm, making jerky little digs into her flesh, some not breaking the skin, others harder. There was a thin trail of blood running down over her fingers.

For a second, Maryann couldn't believe the sight in front of her.

'Sal! What 're yer doing!' She seized the knife, stopped its jabbing motions which seemed to be happening almost independently of Sal's will. She opened her sister's fingers and prised the knife away from her. Sal looked round mildly as if woken from a dream.

'Blimey, Sal – what've yer done to yerself? Look, I'll go and get summat to wipe yer.'

She bound her sister's arm with a rag then sat beside her, half afraid to touch her. Sal looked so beautiful sitting there, pale and still, the evening light catching her hair.

'Is it *him*, Sal? What's 'e done to yer, eh?'

Sal just shook her head, seeming unable to speak.

'Is 'e . . . is 'e . . .' Maryann could barely say it, like when she had wanted to talk to Nance and no words would come, not for something like that, that couldn't really be going on, not in real life. She sensed that whatever had happened to Sal was much worse than anything he had done to her, but she didn't know about anything, couldn't imagine what it could be. 'Is Norman *dirty* with yer?'

To her enormous vexation Sal suddenly started laughing, head back, until the tears ran down her cheeks.

'Well, *what*?' Maryann said furiously. She was trying to help and this was what she got. 'What's so bloody funny then, eh?'

'Dirty! Oh, Maryann!' Still laughing away.

'Well, I meant like the other night – touching yer and stuff.' She couldn't go on.

Sal turned to her, solemn again. 'Don't let 'im near yer, Maryann, that's all.'

Thirteen

anding, the little fire sput...
to be a horse ... lide ...
To you it was m...
While something s...
ent, calling at an inn ... t...
the loosebox was firm ...
Maryann limbed the stairs...
Maud Stamp. ''Wendy...

Cathleen Black had her new baby. Nance had been allowed to help out with the birth and there was great celebration when it turned out to be a girl.

'I tell yer, Maryann,' Nance said after, 'I never want to go through that in my life. Our mom says it's like passing a pig's bladder. She was on the go till right the last minute an' all. I kept telling 'er, "Mom, just go and 'ave yerself a lie down," but she says, "No, Nance – I've got to see the lads 'ave 'ad their tea. Any'ow, the longer I'm on my feet, the quicker the babby'll come."'

Maryann had her first peek at baby Lizzie when she was only one day old, with her mop of black hair, scrumpled up face, closed eyes and tight little fists. She was allowed to go up into Cathleen and Blackie's room where Cathleen lay in a motley mess of bedding consisting of what looked like rags and coats. The room was bare except for the metal bedstead and a chamber pot, and though the window was open there was a sickening miasma of sweat and blood. Cathleen looked hollow-cheeked but she raised a smile when Maryann said, 'Oh, ain't she lovely!'

'Makes a change from all them lads, don't she?' Cathleen said. ''Bout time we 'ad a wench to finish off with, 'cos I'm buggered if I want to go through all that again.'

Billy was also captivated by Lizzie, by her sheer

smallness. He stood for ages stroking her waxy hands, trying to get her to straighten her fingers.

'Why don't our mom 'ave any babbies?' he asked.

'Well, you was a babby not so long ago,' Cathleen said, adding as an aside, 'She's got more bloody sense, that's why.'

Outside, when the boys had gone off, Maryann asked Nance, 'What's yer dad been like over 'er?'

'Oh, 'e's soft as anything with 'er. 'E's always wanted another girl. Said she were 'is life's work or summat – and that were before 'e'd been down the pub!'

'Nance—'

'What?'

'How do – I mean, how does the babby get in there – d'yer know?'

'All I know is it's got summat to do with a man's – yer know – thing. 'Is willy.'

'Oh.' Maryann's brow puckered. 'Has it? You sure?'

''Course,' Nance said, all worldly-wise, though she wasn't really sure at all.

Maryann had never seen a man naked, except for her brothers. When she was younger she'd wondered whether their little willies grew with them when they got bigger, or did they stay the same size?

But she knew the answer to that now, for certain. On Sunday afternoon, Sal had gone out, and Flo was with her brother Danny and her sister-in-law Margie who had come on with her babby and she'd promised to help if she could. Norman was in the front room. Maryann was just about to call the boys to go up to the Blacks'.

'Maryann—' She heard his voice calling softly through to the kitchen where she was clearing up.

'What?' She stuck her head round the door.

'Come 'ere a minute, pet.' His voice was wheedling. It didn't quite sound like him.

She went and stood beside the chair. He was lolling back, feet up on a stool, and his face was flushed even though there was no fire in the grate.

'Fancy going to the pictures?'

'What, now? All of us?' She had had other plans, but she did love the pictures. There were the talkies now, too, people really speaking instead of just the piano banging away while you tried to read the words off the screen.

'I'll give yer a shilling and you and that Nance can go with the lads. Treat yerselves.'

'Oh – ta,' Maryann said awkwardly. Was this him 'trying to act like a dad' again? Anyway, if he was in a good mood she might as well make the most of it.

'C'm'ere first.' He beckoned her closer. 'Part of the treat for yer. There's a couple of tanners in 'ere – you come and get 'em.'

He held his pocket open, shifting in his seat.

'Go on, Maryann, I won't bite!' He was grinning, showing his yellow teeth, sweat on his forehead.

She slid her hand into the open pocket, expecting her fingers to find the two sixpences tucked in the soft material. But as soon as her hand was in there Norman slapped his own hand over it and pulled hers over, pressing it down on to his hard willy, waiting down there. She yanked away, managing to pull free and run to the door.

'Tony! Billy! Come on, quick – I'm going now.'

He was laughing. 'Don't you want your shilling then, eh?'

He wouldn't leave her alone these days. Watching

her all the time, so the feel of his eyes on her made her feel dirty. Once or twice, when he got the chance, he'd rub against her, or feel her round her chest. She could never relax when he was about and she stayed out all the time she could. Outside, at school or with Nance it was all right. She could shrug it off because these disgusting things weren't happening away from the house. It wasn't real out there, and she could forget. She dreaded being at home. Sometimes Maryann thought about trying to tell her mom. But any little thing she criticized about Norman and Flo was down on her like a ton of bricks. She'd never believe Maryann. She was always on his side. He seem to infect everything. Even when he wasn't in there were reminders of his presence: the oily dent in the chair where his head went, the paper thrown on the floor where he left it, the smell of his fags hanging about the place. Always there. Always.

It was well into June and the weather was warm now. Thin shafts of evening sunlight had found their way in through the back windows, dust motes swirling in them. Maryann smiled, remembering how Tiger used to jump up and biff at them when he was a kitten.

Sal had come in with Norman from work, had eaten her tea and the last Maryann had heard from her was the slam of the front door as she took off out again. Huh, Maryann thought, covering Tony up in bed. But she couldn't really blame Sal. She really seemed to be sweet on Charlie Black and if Maryann could have thought of a place to go she'd have gone out as well. She was beginning to get the hang of when the *Esther Jane* might be likely to be in town from the run to

Stoke. She left messages at the toll offices and ran down to ask. But she didn't hang around the cut any more, waiting. She'd seen Joel, Darius and Ada once since her night on the boat, but they'd been held up along the cut and were pressed for time, so Maryann just walked along a bit of the way with Ada and Bessie and Jep, and left them to get on. They all seemed pleased to see her though, and Joel waved.

'See yer next time!' she yelled as they headed into the gloomiest part of the cut.

She'd sung Billy a lullaby and was coming downstairs again when she heard a knock at the front door, then Flo's voice, 'Danny – what're you doing 'ere? Oh my God, what's up?' Danny's wife Margie had also given birth to a little girl, Cissie, who was now four days old.

Maryann heard her uncle panting. He must have run all the way over.

'It's the babby, Flo, 'er's bad and Margie's in a right state over 'er. Can yer come over and 'elp us, right quick? 'Er breathing's terrible.'

'Well, I don't know as there's much I can do,' Flo was saying. 'You'd be better fetching the doctor out.'

'We 'ave, but she wants you there – please, Flo—' Maryann came down into the front room and saw her Uncle Danny looking as if he was going to burst into tears. 'We'd feel better if you was there. You know what to do with babbies – we don't know 'ow to go on!'

'You go, Flo,' Norman said. 'Yer brother needs yer – there'll be summat you can do, with all your know-'ow, I'm sure.'

'Awright,' Flo agreed reluctantly.

Maryann watched her mother disappearing out

through the front door, and it was only then it dawned on her. If Flo went out she'd be all alone in the house with Norman, except for the boys sleeping upstairs. She tore out behind her mom as if she was on springs.

'I'm coming with yer! I might be able to 'elp.'

'Oh, don't be daft, Maryann!' Flo was all flustered. 'Go on in with yer. Danny and Margie've got enough on their plate without you getting under all our feet.'

'Please, Mom, let me come!'

'Maryann, go back inside.' Danny spoke roughly in his anxiety. 'Do as yer mom says. We need 'er for now.'

Maryann knew she couldn't argue. She stood on the step watching them disappear along Anderson Street. The sun was sinking now. Martins' huckster's shop was still open of course, along the way. She felt like going and standing in there, amid all the mixed smells of rubber and soap and sweets until her mom got back, but she had no money and whatever could she say to Mrs Martin?

'Come in and shut that door, Maryann,' Norman Griffin ordered her.

Her heart was thudding. The idea of being left alone with Norman Griffin now alarmed her so much that the hairs on the back of her neck were standing up and her hands shook as she closed the door. But how could she refuse?

There he was, sat in his chair as normal, she told herself, clasping her hands together so that he should not see the tremor in them. What was there to worry about? He was just sitting, looking across at her. And she knew better than ever to put her hand in his pocket again.

'So, then,' he said.

'I think—' Maryann swallowed. She was straining to keep her voice casual. 'I'll go up to bed now.'

'Oh, it's too early for that, ain't it? Why don't yer come over 'ere and sit with me for a bit?'

'No, I, er . . .' In her awkwardness she rubbed one shoe against the back of her other leg like a much younger child. 'No, thanks.'

Mr Griffin leaned forward with a grunt and eased himself up out of the chair. Blood started to pound in her ears. But Norman went over and drew the curtains, even though it was still light outside, so that the room turned dim and green. He lit the gas mantle and the pop-pop sound started up. Then he stood with his hands straight down by his sides, looking at her. Maryann ran her tongue over her lips and looked down at the floor. Slowly, knowing in her heart that he was not going to let her go, that there was something he wanted badly from her, she began to edge across the room towards the door to the stairs.

'No, don't go!' His voice had a hard edge. 'I said stay 'ere with me.'

He walked over to her.

'I like you better than your sister, I must say.' He picked at a lock of her dark hair and stroked it. She drew her head back. 'D'you know why, Maryann?'

Still not looking at him, she shook her head.

'You ain't like her. You've got more fire about yer and I like that in a woman.'

Woman? Maryann thought. *But I'm a girl, not a woman. I'm still at school.*

'Sal were good to me for a bit. Helped me out and did what I told 'er. See, we men are different from you women.' He spoke in a very reasonable voice. 'We need – satisfying – now and then. That's what comes natural

121

to us, see, that's all. And you girls have a way of getting me ... excited.' He was taking his jacket off. She heard him throw it on to the chair.

His hands came down on her shoulders and she cried out.

'No need for that. I'll show yer what to do. This is what wenches're made for. I'm just teaching yer, that's all. Now – you just do as I say and we'll 'ave a nice time.'

His arms came round her and she felt herself lifted off the ground and carried to the peg rug by the hearth. When he pushed her down she banged her head on the floor and gave a moan of pain, which seemed to arouse him. She heard his hard, ragged breathing.

'What're you doing?' Her voice had gone squeaky. 'You shouldn't be doing this.'

'Who says so?' His voice had lost its wheedling tone and was as cold as the frozen east wind. 'Who's gunna stop me now? You, yer little bitch, eh?'

His hands forced up her skirt and she felt him tearing her underclothes down.

'No!' She lashed out, trying to kick him. 'Stop it ... stop it! Get off me.'

'Shut yer mouth.'

Everything went darker as he leaned over her, blocking out the light and his weight came down on her so she was struggling then only to be able to breathe, gasping. Her legs were being forced apart and that hard prodding started like in the bath until she was sobbing it hurt so much, with him pushing and jabbing, burning his way up inside her, panting in her face, filthy words dropping from his lips.

When he climbed off her she was like a rag doll, dizzy, her back sore and smarting. She went very cold, starting to shiver until her teeth chattered, wet stuff oozing out down her legs as she stood up.

Mr Griffin went out to the kitchen and she heard the splash of water. He came back, buttoning his fly.

'Now. That's it then. Sal could keep a secret and I know you can. Anyhow – your mother wouldn't believe a word if you started on about this – you know that, don't you? You can go to bed now.' He turned away. 'I've finished with yer.'

She could barely remember getting to bed, struggling to wash first, shaking so much she could scarcely attend to herself. All the water in the sea could not wash Norman Griffin off her. She lay alone in the bed, hugging herself tightly with her arms, sobbing and shaking. She felt frightened and sick and bereaved, as if there was something enormous that she had lost, and she wept for all the losses she could think of: her lovely dad, her nan, her little cat. All those she had loved and would never again be able to hold in her arms.

Fourteen

She slept for a time in fits and starts, crying at first, dozing, dreaming dark, broken dreams, and still feeling, even in sleep, the ache between her legs. Then she jolted awake as she heard Norman Griffin coming up to bed. The light of his candle and his shadow moved past the crack in the door, and for those moments she stopped breathing. Was he coming to her room...? Not with Tony here, surely? She gripped the cover close to her throat.

But she heard him go to his and her mother's room across the tiny landing. She knew from the solitariness of his sounds that Flo was not here, had not come home. There must be something dreadfully wrong with baby Cissie that she'd had to stay out at Uncle Danny's house so long. But even more worrying was that Sal was not lying beside her, and that had never happened before. Where in heaven could she have got to? She lay there, hearing him moving, fear and anxiety growing in her until she could hardly breathe.

She wasn't going to be able to sleep. She got out of bed, tiptoed over to pull the door open and listen. She could hear Norman's loud, stertorous breathing from the front bedroom. Pig, she thought. She pulled on layers of clothes and crept downstairs to the front. The fire was dead in the grate so, as quietly as she could manage, she scraped the ash out, leaving it in a metal pail by the back door, then built up a new fire. She'd always liked putting a fire in the grate, even though it was dirty work. It made the room cosy, and she was a little comforted by the sight of her twists of newspaper as they jumped, flaming into life at the touch of her spill. The flames filled the room with warm, twitching light. She sat on the rug with her knees close to her chest, pulling her baggy cardigan down over them, and watched the fire, sometimes leaning down to blow on it, or adding a few more bits of coal to keep it going properly. Behind her the room was very dark, but the fire in front of her felt like her warm protector.

She tried to shut out any thoughts of Norman Griffin, even though this was the very spot where he'd forced her down on the floor. If she hadn't been so sore still it wouldn't seem real now. But she wouldn't let her mind dwell on it.

Where are you, Sal? she wondered again and again. With each half-hour she grew more worried. The fire was glowing a deeper orange now. After some time there was a tiny rattle of the mechanism from the clock on the mantle before it struck its gentle bong-bong-bong, then it went quiet again and there was only the sound of the fire.

She woke to the sound of Norman Griffin's feet on the stairs and found herself lying cold and cramped by the grey ash of a dead fire. Her heart pumped violently at the sound of him approaching and she sat up. The clock said half past seven. When Norman appeared he was already dressed.

'Where is everybody?'

'Mom must still be at Uncle Danny's.' Maryann sat hugging her legs again, shivering.

'Sal still abed?'

Slowly Maryann shook her head, though with a sense of unreality. Perhaps Sal *was* in bed after all? Maybe she'd been there all the time, or slipped in after Maryann had fallen asleep?

'Well, where is she?'

He turned impatiently and went back upstairs, looked in girls' room, then was back down. 'Where's 'er gone?'

'She never come in,' Maryann said, looking down at her knees, the loose-knit mesh of her blue cardi stretched over them. She knew then for certain that something had happened.

'No bloody breakfast on the go neither, I s'pose.' There was a coarseness to Norman this morning, usually hidden under his oily smoothness when Flo was about. 'Get the kettle going, wench – at least yer can make a cuppa tea.'

Maryann did as she was ordered, then went up to wake Tony and Billy. She sorted out breakfast for Norman and the boys, blanking out all other thoughts.

'Tony, you'll 'ave to go to school with Alec,' she told him. 'I'll have to stop here till our mom gets home.'

'Oh Maryann!' Tony complained.

'Do as your sister tells yer!' Norman said, with such savagery that Tony cowered.

'You'll be awright,' Maryann said to him. 'Only I've got to stay – who's going to mind Billy, else?'

Tony nodded, dumbly.

'Tell that Sal to get 'erself down the shop when 'er turns up,' Norman said, putting his hat on by the front door. 'I'll 'ave a few things to say to 'er, that I shall.'

'Come on, Billy – we've gotta go out.' Maryann impatiently shoved her little brother's shoes on. 'Push yer feet in, will you!'

'Where we going, our Maryann?'

'You'll see when we get there.' She dragged him out and along Anderson Street, then softened. 'You can come and play with Horace.'

'Oh!' Billy moaned. 'Horace is a babby, I don't wanna play with 'im!'

'Well, 'ard luck 'cos yer gonna 'ave to.'

Pulling Billy along so he had to run, Maryann went as fast as she could to Garrett Street. They were about to run down the entry but found it blocked by Blackie Black and his barrow coming the other way, loaded with his tools and metal hoops. He wasn't looking any too good but he managed a wan smile.

'Awright, Mr Black?' Maryann said.

'Awright,' he murmured amiably. Maryann turned to watch him, saw how his walk had become a shambling, dragging gait. But he didn't seem to have noticed anything was amiss, anyroad.

Everyone was out except Cathleen and Horace and the baby Lizzie. The room was in a right state, spilt tea and crumbs all over the table, and on the floor, dirty clothes, a pile of nappies, the lot.

Cathleen was at the table, Lizzie tucked in on her lap, feeding. She pulled her blouse together a little, but not before Maryann had seen the white, mottled skin of her breast. 'What're yer doing 'ere, Maryann? No school?'

'Mom's at Uncle Danny's – the babby's took bad,' Maryann said. She felt tears come into her eyes. All the fear and worry of the night welled up. 'And our Sal's disappeared. She daint come home last night so I come to see if she was 'ere last night, sleeping over?'

Cathleen gave a laugh which dislodged the baby from her breast. 'Sleeping over – 'ere? Where d'yer think 'er'd sleep – in the coal scuttle? Sorry, Lizzie – 'ere yer go.' She pushed her nipple back between the baby's gums.

'But she was with Charlie last night, wasn't she?' Maryann was frustrated by Cathleen's lack of concern.

'They went off together in the evening. I never saw 'em – Charlie must've come in late last night. I were that tired what with this one up and down, I got me 'ead down when I could, and Blackie were too kalied to notice, or 'e'd've been giving out to 'im.'

'So Charlie was here this morning?' Maryann struggled to be patient.

'Well, I s'pose 'e was – I never saw 'im though, come to think of it. 'E must've come down and gone off to work, like.'

Clearly Cathleen had no real idea whether either of them had ever come back the night before.

'They'll turn up,' Cathleen said serenely. 'I s'pect they're both at work by now. Don't get mithered.'

Loath as she was to go anywhere near Norman Griffin, Maryann called in at Griffin's Undertakers. There was no sign of Sal.

'I'll tan 'er bloody hide when I find 'er,' Norman ranted. 'We've got a lot on today.'

*

Maryann spent the rest of the morning worrying and trying to occupy Billy. She could see why he drove her mom mad with his non-stop chattering.

At last, just as Maryann was thinking she ought to get something for his dinner, she heard the front door open and she rushed through from the back, leaving Billy in the yard. Flo came in, exhaustion showing in every line of her. When she turned from closing the door, Maryann saw that her eyes were red and her face was different, somehow, tighter.

'How's little Cissie, Mom?' she whispered.

Flo shook her head, taking off her hat. 'She daint make it, Maryann. The doctor came, but she breathed 'er last this morning, poor little mite. I stayed for a bit to be with Margie.'

'Oh Mom!' Maryann was so tired and worried that she was not far from tears as it was, and the thought of babby Cissie dying brought them on fast. Poor little thing, what had she ever done to anyone!

Flo sat down, filling up herself. 'Oh, it's a terrible thing to see a babby die, Maryann. Thank God I never had any more of yer to worry about.' Unguardedly she added, 'I've been lucky marrying a man who's not that way inclined, that I have!'

'Mom—' Maryann wiped her eyes, though the tears just wouldn't seem to stop coming. 'It's – I know yer've got enough to worry about, but – it's Sal . . .'

'What?' Flo's tone was sharp. 'What about 'er?'

'She never came 'ome last night, she ain't at work and Mrs Black don't know where she is neither.'

'Mrs Black? Why the hell should she know where our Sal is?'

'Because—' Maryann stopped. Sal didn't want

129

anyone to know, that was obvious, or she'd have told them herself.

'Because what? Come on, get on with it.'

'Well, Sal's been knocking about with Charlie Black – and Mrs Black ain't quite sure 'e came home last night neither.'

Flo stared at her as if none of the sense of this was getting through to her brain. 'You mean they might've took off together?'

'I dunno,' Maryann said miserably.

Flo sank down on the chair behind her. 'They can't've done. What would Sal want to do that for? She's comfortable enough 'ere. Got no worries. Anyone checked where Charlie works?'

Maryann shook her head.

'Go on. See if 'e's there.'

It was quite a walk to the place where Charlie had his current employment, a dark workshop in a side street where they turned out copper rods and wire. Charlie Black? No, he hadn't been in. And if he missed another day there were plenty of others who could do his job.

By the time Maryann got home Flo was asleep and she slept for the rest of the afternoon. The evening wore on and there was no sign of Sal. Norman came home in a bad humour because he had been without his general dogsbody all day. After tea, Flo ordered Maryann upstairs, took her into their room at the back and closed the door.

'Now look – what's going on?'

'I told yer – Sal's gone. Charlie Black weren't at work today. I think Sal's sweet on 'im. They must've gone off together. And she . . .'

'She what?' Flo hissed.

'She – I'm ever so worried about 'er. She ain't right in 'erself and ... and ...'

'Ain't right – what're you on about?'

''E touches us. Mr Griffin. Where 'e oughtn't – and 'e – 'e's a dirty man, Mom ...'

Flo had been soft and emotional over babby Cissie: they'd almost felt close in those few moments. Surely her mom would take her word on this? Maryann started sobbing all over again.

'What *are* you saying to me, yer foul-mouthed little bitch?' Flo sprang at her and slapped her face so hard that Maryann cried out at the pain. 'How dare you say such a filthy thing! I've a good mind to put carbolic on your tongue for that. Where d'you get such disgusting ideas from?'

'From 'im!' Maryann sobbed. 'Where else would I know 'em from?'

She received a matching slap, this time on the other cheek. Flo swelled with self-righteous fury. 'How *dare* you? Norman's a good, clean-living man. Almost a gentleman, that 'e is, and I ain't having that talk in my house from my own daughter!'

Holding her burning cheek, Maryann went up close to her mother, speaking right into her face.

'You don't see what's in front of your nose, Mom, do yer? You think more of that disgusting man than you ever do of yer children 'cause 'e buys you dresses and keeps you comfortable. But 'e ain't what you think. 'E's evil, but it don't suit yer to see it, does it?'

Flo stood before her, speechless, and Maryann fell sobbing, distraught, on to her bed.

Fifteen

Days passed, and still Sal didn't come home. Charlie Black didn't make an appearance either, and it was obvious they really had done a bunk together. Maryann couldn't stop thinking about them: where had they gone, and was Sal all right? Sometimes she was angry with Sal for leaving her alone. Mostly though, she was just worried.

Norman was all concern.

'I just don't know what can've come over the girl, Flo,' he said, shaking his head. 'I'm only sorry she's causing yer all this worry. That's young 'uns for you – selfish, never give a thought for anyone else. Don't you get upset, my dear – the pair of 'em'll be back with their tails between their legs sooner or later.'

'You 'adn't 'ad words with 'er had you, Norman?' Flo asked cautiously. 'Not done anything to upset 'er?'

'Oh no!' He laughed. 'Not our Sal. That Maryann's the minx I'm most likely to 'ave words with, as yer know. But not Sal – a good girl that one. I've been very pleased with 'er.'

Flo was appeased by the fatherly tone in which he spoke. He was right – Maryann *was* a minx, running off here, there and everywhere, making up terrible stories, like about Norman killing that kitten – and now, all that filthy language she'd come out with. She needed watching, taking in hand, that she did.

Flo went reluctantly to Cathleen Black, picking her way grandly across the yard and smoothing her hair as if she was too superior ever to have set foot in such a place before. Cathleen, who was holding the baby, looked very worried.

'Sal's been coming 'ere ever such a lot of course,' she said, laying Lizzie down on a blanket on the chair. She felt her own poor drabness beside Flo's relative glamour. The woman was wearing lipstick and powder. 'Look – won't yer 'ave a seat and a cuppa with me now yer 'ere?'

'No ta,' Flo said, wrinkling her nose at the frowstiness of the house. 'I'll not be stopping long.' Heaven only knew what you might sit on if you accepted a chair in this house, and as for drinking from one of their cracked, grimy cups, oh dear no! She wanted to be angry with Cathleen, to lay blame on her and her son, but she felt at a great disadvantage as a mother who had known nothing of her daughter's whereabouts for what had apparently been quite a long time. It made her look very bad.

'So,' she probed, 'Sal and Charlie've been knocking about for quite a time?'

'Ooh yes – din't yer know, Flo?'

'Well, of course I *knew*.' She could hardly let Cathleen Black realize she'd had no idea Sal could prefer spending her evenings in this slovenly household. 'What I daint know was she was hanging round with some idle good-for-nothing who'd make off with 'er to Christ only knows where!'

Cathleen rounded on her. 'Don't you come 'ere carrying on about my son like that! Your Sal wouldn't've gone off with 'im if she weren't a little trollop – you obviously ain't seen the way 'er's been

133

carrying on lately or yer wouldn't be as surprised as you are. You want to pay a bit of attention instead of preening yerself, Flo Griffin, with yer frocks and yer warpaint. Looking down yer nose at my family – we may be rough and ready but we rub along. You want to look at what's going on under yer nose, 'cause one thing's for certain – your Sal never wanted to go back 'ome when she were 'ere, and that's a fact.'

'Don't you talk to me like that, yer filthy slut!' Flo yelled back. 'Yer the lowest of the low you are – look at this place! I'm surprised that babby of yours 'as survived in this filth. You ain't any place to carry on at me with yer drunken husband and yer bloody idle sons. I just 'ope our Sal comes to her senses before long and gets 'erself back 'ere because what sort of life's she gunna 'ave with one of your lot, eh?'

Flo stormed out of the Blacks' house and across the yard, all too aware that her old neighbours had probably heard all that loud and clear.

Life for Maryann at home had become one of constant fear and dread. Every time she stepped into the house she began to feel sick. The very walls were tainted with Norman Griffin. Once she heard him come home she could never relax for a moment. His eyes seemed to be on her so much of the time, watching, waiting. Her mom showed no sign of having believed what she'd told her. There was no one she could trust or rely on. She missed Sal dreadfully. School was the one thing that got her out of the house: it was somewhere to go.

One morning, though, as they were all having break-

134

fast, Norman said to Flo, 'Our Maryann's almost finished with school now. When can she leave?'

'She's got to see out till the end of term,' Flo said. 'She ain't fourteen till September.'

'Well—' Norman sat back at the table. Maryann watched him link his hands over his belly. 'No need to see out the last stretch, is there? Dragging it out, that's all, when 'er's fit and ready for work. Let's 'ave 'er take over where Sal left off – I'm short-handed and I could do with it. Start 'er straight away.'

Even Flo was not oblivious to the pleading look of horror on Maryann's face, and Cathleen Black's remarks hadn't entirely passed her by.

'But, Norman – if Maryann leaves early she won't get her bit of paper from the school and that – for getting work.'

'Well, she won't need it if she's coming to work with me, will she? I'd see 'er awright, Flo, you know that. I say start 'er today – soon as possible.'

'No, Mom.' Maryann's tone was desperate. 'I 'ave to stay – Miss Bentley said. I *do* 'ave to!'

'It's only another couple of weeks, Norman,' Flo reasoned. 'Then she'll be ready for yer.'

Norman pushed his chair back and leaned over to kiss the top of Flo's head. Maryann looked away.

'Awright then, my sweet. Whatever you say. You can twist me round yer little finger, can't you?'

Maryann looked back in time to see Flo glancing at her. She experienced a rare moment of gratitude towards her mother.

'I do think it's for the best, Norman. I'm thinking of Maryann's future.'

*

135

After school every day she haunted the cut. She left message after message at the toll houses and was becoming a familiar figure to the workers there.

'Look,' one of them said to her that week. 'I think they'll be through in the next couple of days if they're on the normal run. I'll make sure they get yer message.'

The next couple of days! Maryann could think of nothing else. But suppose she missed them? What if they came through when she was at school? She *had* to see them, to see Joel above all, hear his lovely country accent. The very thought of him was comforting. She didn't know what she could say to him, she couldn't tell him what was happening to her, that she would not, could not work for Norman Griffin, not for anything ever. But she did know he was the one person with whom she felt safe and happy. And she liked Ada, with her raucous voice and cheeky face as well. She longed to see the *Esther Jane* come gliding along the cut with Bessie plodding alongside.

The next day she was so keyed up with nerves she could hardly stand it. She set off to school with Tony and his pal Alec. She waved them off at the boys' entrance.

'See yer later, Tony!' But he hardly took any notice, he was so thick with Alec. Maryann smiled with relief. She was glad Tony had such a good pal. She didn't feel able to give him any attention herself.

She looked round, making sure none of her own classmates was in sight, and darted off again down the road, looping round the back and along to where she knew she could get down to the cut. In each of her pockets was tucked a piece of bread she had sneaked from the kitchen. That'd keep her going. This could be the day they came and she couldn't miss it – just couldn't!

They came in the late afternoon, when the sun was sinking behind strips of candyfloss cloud. She saw them as they drew into view near Soho Loop. Peering into the smoky gloom she wasn't sure at first. There was the horse, all her white splotches standing out, no one walking with her on the bank. Maryann ran forward to meet her. A train clattered over the iron bridge across the loop, but Bessie barely even twitched her ears. It *was* her, and there was Joel, she could see now, standing majestically at the tiller. The boat was clothed up, tarpaulins tied over to cover the cargo, so she couldn't see what was in there. They must've come through rain.

'Joel! Joel!' Maryann bounced up and down, waving, saw him turn his head, then the slow arc of his wave back to her. Could she see his smile, or did she imagine that? After a moment she saw Darius's head appear out of the cabin and he waved as well.

'Shall I walk along with Bessie?' Maryann shouted.

Joel nodded. 'We'll need yer!'

'Where's Ada?'

His voice floated over to her. 'Gone.'

Gone? It was too far to talk properly. She'd have to ask when they stopped. Where could Ada have 'gone'? And where was Jep? She patted Bessie's neck, feeling the dried sweat on it.

'Have you had a hard day, Bessie? Poor old girl – you'll soon be there and have yer nostern.'

She felt proud, knowing a word of the canal dialect. It was different, the way they spoke. Birmingham was

Birnigum. She'd heard Darius call Rugby 'Ruckby', and Ada had run together the names 'Fellows, Morton and Clayton' as if she had no idea where each began and ended. Reading and writing was a mystery to her. She had no pictures of words in her head to know the edges of them.

The city closed in on them and every so often there was a horse bridge where Bessie had to be led over. It grew darker and darker, the blackened walls and filthy overhead enclosure of roads, railways, mills and foundries. The canal had been so built over that in parts it was so dark the gas lamps burned day and night. The water was horrible here, choked with scum and oil and refuse. No wonder Joel said Birmingham was always the grimmest part of their journey. Once she saw a man's sleeping body slumped by the wall at the side, which she mistook at first for a pile of rags. She shuddered. The place felt gloomy and hostile and she was glad Joel was not far away.

Eventually he shouted to her that they were to turn into the private wharf to unload. As the *Esther Jane* pulled in, Joel stepped across on to the bank, ruffled Maryann's hair in greeting and handed her the nostern containing Bessie's feed just as if she was Ada. Maryann grinned and tried not to show she was struggling as she fastened it on.

She knew the next couple of hours would be spent unloading. She left Bessie for a moment and went timidly up to Joel.

'Shall I make you and Mr Bartholomew a cuppa tea?'

'That'd be grand.' Joel's brow wrinkled. 'Think you can manage it?'

Maryann grinned. 'Just 'cos I'm off the bank don't mean I don't know 'ow to do nothing.'

'Go on with you then.'

He walked off, smiling. He seemed well and cheerful.

She was dying to ask where Ada was, and Jep, but she knew they were preoccupied. In the meantime she stoked the little range in the cabin, filled the kettle from the water can, which was always in place on the cabin roof, and put it on the heat. When it was ready she took the tea out to them, Joel winking at her in thanks. She made herself busy then, looking for a spot where the water didn't look too mired up to pull bucketfuls out to do some cleaning. However did Joel and Mr Bartholomew manage to keep things clean without Ada?

She found they weren't managing all that perfectly and the cabin was well in need of a scrub. To the grunts and shouts of the men unloading the firebricks outside, she wiped down the shelves and surfaces in the cabin, moving things off carefully and replacing them. She eyed the crochet pieces along the shelves, the precious work of the real Esther Jane. It was grimy grey in colour.

'I'd give *you* a wash given the chance,' Maryann said, stroking a hand over it. 'But there ain't no time for that now.'

She swept and scrubbed and kept the range going and eventually all the unloading was done and she stood up on the steering platform, watching as Joel and his father finished off with the factory men and finally turned back to the boat.

Joel climbed aboard, followed by Darius, who gave her a nod.

'I'm going for water, Joel,' he said, and went off with the can.

Joel and Maryann went into the cabin and he sat on the bench, looking at her with amusement in his eyes.

'So, little Maryann Nelson. Can't keep away from the cut then?'

She beamed. 'No, I can't. D'yer like what I've done?'

Joel looked vaguely round the cabin.

'I've been cleaning for yer.'

'Ta. She could do with it.'

'Where's Ada gone?'

'Oh, working another boat, the *Lucy* – another of the Number Ones. Their little 'uns're all grown now and they needed some 'elp.'

'But to send 'er off without you!'

'It's done on the cut. Times are hard, Maryann – more boats than cargoes these days and we're all chasing the work. You don't keep moving, you don't eat. Ada's a good little crew – she'll earn 'er keep on there. They let her take Jep with her.'

'But don't you need her?'

'We could do with 'er, but needs must. Good job you came today to find us. We're starting a new route tomorrow. Going south, Oxford way, back to where us came from. Any'ow—' He rubbed his hand wearily over his face. 'I'd best start on cooking.' He pulled a paper bag with some bacon in it off the shelf and put a pan on the stove.

'How's our Maryann then?'

The question was asked lightly but it brought tears flooding to her eyes. Oh Joel, she wanted to cry out, help me! Please help me!

'I'm awright.'

Joel turned to look at her. 'Don't sound too happy to me.'

Maryann didn't say anything. She shrugged and sat

140

watching Joel as he went back to work. He cut thick chunks of bread. She wanted to touch him, feel close to someone. Most of all she wanted to curl up in his arms for comfort, like a child.

'Joel—' she burst out at last. She wanted to speak to him before Darius got back because she was more shy of talking in front of him.

'What's that?'

'Please let me come with yer! I could help – do all the things Ada ain't 'ere to do, like cleaning and stabling Bessie and ... and everything. And I wouldn't get in yer way and I don't eat much, honest I don't!'

'No, I shouldn't think yer do, the look of yer.' Joel sat back and gently put his arm round her. She leaned against him, feeling the great warmth he gave off. 'Maryann – what's wrong with being at 'ome with yer own folk, eh?'

'I just – nothing. Only I know they won't miss me, not at all. There's nowt happening now – it's the summer holiday and it'd be awright, I promise.'

She knew Joel would have no idea when school terms began and ended. 'I ain't fourteen until the autumn and then I'll 'ave to start work, but I could come with yer till then – my mom'll be glad to get me out of the way!'

She felt Joel looking at her, his face close to hers.

'Well – I dunno,' he said eventually, sitting back. 'It's one thing having an extra from another boat, but one off the bank is different.'

'I'll learn. I'll do anything!' Maryann begged excitedly. She touched Joel's hand. '*Please*. I don't know how else to tell yer 'ow much I want to come with yer!'

'Oh, yer not doing too badly,' Joel said wryly. 'But

I don't want it causing no trouble, them turning up saying we've taken yer off or anything.'

'No – I'll go 'ome and tell them. I'll get some things. Oh Joel!' She was jigging up and down with longing to hear the word 'yes' come out from Joel's lips.

'Well—' he said again, ruminatively. Then looked round at her. 'Go 'ome and see. If it's awright, meet us back here with your things tomorrow – not too much mind. We'll be gone before daybreak so make it early.'

'Oh!' Maryann's face was alight. 'Oh Joel, you're the best!'

Sixteen

She was back at the wharf by five in the morning in a light mizzling rain, her coat pulled round her and a bundle of belongings in her arms.

On her bed she had left a note:

Dear Mom,
    I am going away for a bit. Don't worry I'll be safe, no need to look for me.
    Maryann.

She had crept downstairs, weak-kneed with anxiety, and once she reached the street she tore along until she'd turned a corner, convinced she was going to hear a shout or running feet behind her and equally anxious in case the *Esther Jane* had already left without her.

The men were up and having breakfast when she arrived, frantic and panting, and she climbed on to the steering platform helped by Joel's outstretched hand.

'Morning, nipper.' He gave his slow smile. His cap was shiny with minute droplets of rain.

Maryann grinned, overjoyed. She was here – at last!

Joel sat her down inside and handed her a cup of tea and a thick, man-size wedge of bread.

'I don't know as I can eat all that,' she said.

'I should get it down you. You'll need it.'

Darius Bartholomew had not said a word in greeting,

so Maryann turned to him. 'Morning, Mr Bartholomew.'

In reply she received a reluctant-sounding grunt from behind the magnificent white beard, but Darius didn't meet her eye. After a few moments, chewing on the last of the bread, he got up, bending over as usual in the low cabin, stuck his hat on and ducked out through the door.

The joy had faded on Maryann's face. ''E don't want me 'ere, does 'e, Joel?'

Joel finished his mouthful, ruminatively. You couldn't hurry these men into speech.

''E's glad of an extra pair of hands. It's only that, well, living on a boat's quite a close life, intimate like. It'll take a bit of getting used to, someone about who ent family. But we'll manage. Plenty of others do.'

'I'll do whatever you want,' Maryann said desperately. 'I'll do yer washing, cooking – anything, only let me come. Don't send me back 'ome!'

Joel ruffled her hair again. 'I know yer will. We'll manage for a round trip. Don't you fret.'

When Darius came back, Joel went out and spoke to him, the two of them standing over by the stack of firebricks, and when they came back in, Darius nodded at Maryann.

'Mornin'.'

'Morning, Mr Bartholomew. I shan't be any trouble, I promise.'

Darius nodded. 'Let's get on then.'

Warmed by her breakfast and by Darius at least acknowledging her, Maryann went with Joel to fetch Bessie from the stable and watched with great attention as he harnessed her up.

They moved round to a new wharf to load up. Maryann stood watching with Bessie munching beside her as a crane lowered the cargo of iron pipes, load by load, down into the *Esther Jane* with much clanking and banging in the morning air. As she waited there it stopped raining and grew lighter though the rising sun was obscured by cloud and the smoke and smuts in the air. Joel went off to pay the toll and Darius went to fill up with water once more. Maryann offered to go, but he seemed not to hear her. She watched his slightly stooped back moving away from her.

At last they set off: Bessie straining hard against the harness to get the *Esther Jane* on the move, her hooves sliding and scraping, easing the boat forwards until it would begin to drift off and gather its own momentum. Joel led the horse, telling Maryann to stay on board with Darius.

She felt her eyes stretching wide to take everything in, thrilled at the boat beginning to start off slowly under her, and so caught up in the sight of the wharves and chimneys and canal cottages sliding past that she forgot to feel anxious standing beside Darius Bartholomew. She felt bubbly with excitement. They were really going, and she could leave it all behind her: home and school and Sal's disappearance and most of all, Norman Griffin. He'd be livid that she'd given him the slip – there he was commanding her to go and work for him without even giving her a say, and she wouldn't be there in two weeks after school ended, she'd make sure of that. Miss Bentley was a kind teacher and she'd persuade her somehow to give her her school leaving certificate. She'd cross that bridge when she came to it. But for now, in this one precious week, she was going to learn to work the cut and see something of outside Birmingham for the first time in her life. Up until now she'd hardly set foot outside Ladywood!

She held on to the cabin of the *Esther Jane*, a smile on her lips as she watched Joel stepping along the bank. She took in a great lungful of air. Stinking and smoky as it was, just then it felt like the breath of freedom.

The days that followed she would always remember as the closest heaven ever came to earth. It was the newness of it all, how right it felt – her being on the boat and life opening out in front of her like a picture in a storybook. For the first time in such a long while, she felt safe.

That morning, as they moved south, Maryann watched carefully, drinking in every detail as Joel and Darius manoeuvred the boat through Camp Hill Locks. Gradually the dark city began to fall away, the sun burned through the clouds. They left Birmingham with a cap of cloud over it, but outside the haze cleared and at last the sky was a rich summer blue.

'Is this the Oxford Canal then?' Maryann asked, excited.

'Oh no – we don't get on the h'Oxford till after Wigram's Turn – down at Napton. This is the Warwick and Birnigum. We're headed for a cleaner part of the cut now, you'll see,' Joel told her. They referred to 'Birnigum – that stinking 'ole' and as they progressed out into the Warwickshire countryside, Maryann could see why. She kept gazing round her, enchanted by the space, the wide, rolling country with its green pastures, black and white cows, its cornfields and snug-looking cottages, amazed at being able to see so *far*, further than she'd ever been able to see in her life before.

She could have sat and stared around quite happily all day, but she was anxious that Darius shouldn't regard her as a 'good-for-nothing' while she was aboard. Also the place felt rather lonely without Ada and Jep and she wanted to keep busy. She asked Joel what she should do.

'Well, you could give the brightwork a polish,' he said, pointing to the brass fittings on the chimney, kettle, horse brasses and handles inside the cabin. Since Ada left they hadn't had the time for 'prettifying' the place and the brasses were tarnished. Gladly Maryann set to work until they were smooth and gleaming and she could see a distorted version of her face looking back at her in them. Then she cleaned the cabin, wiping out all the smuts and dust and sweeping the floor. She was small and agile, kneeling to poke right into the corners in a way she could see was hard for big, muscular men. The cabin was so small, yet so prettily decorated inside with its scumbled paintwork, its roses and castles and scrolls, and its shelves of china, that Maryann felt as if she was playing houses. She had to remind herself that this really was their house and that Joel, and certainly Darius, had never known any other home.

In the middle of the afternoon, with Joel's help, she pulled a bucket of water out of the cut, and with a chunk of soap set to and washed the cabin's crochet work until she had it looking, not gleaming white, for it was already yellowed with age, but at least a good deal better.

'Can I hang them out to dry?' she asked Joel. She

147

always went to him instead of his father, although the two of them were both there in the stern. Bessie knew the routine and plodded along for a lot of the journey without being led.

'Oh – can't rig up a line any too easy with a load on,' Joel said, dismissively. 'We do that when the boat's empty, see.' But he caught the crestfallen look on Maryann's face. She had so wanted to do something to help!

'Awright then – I'll see what I can do. Those little bits don't need to hang down far, do they?'

Maryann felt Darius's eyes on her and wondered what he was thinking. She watched nervously as Joel climbed forward over the cabin and made his way along the planks which were laid over the cargo. He was holding a line attached to the cabin and unravelling it. He stretched it across to the low mast at the front and tied it, creating a washing line.

'There y'are!' he called to her, scrambling back across the planks.

It was obviously her turn to climb over. Joel handed her some pegs which she put in the bucket. She was glad it was a calm day without wind, and that the boat didn't have its tarpaulin sheeting on – the planks would be positioned higher, over the top of it, if they had to cover the load. The only time she felt really wobbly was when she straightened up after bending over to pick one of the cloths out of the bucket, almost losing her balance and falling off the planks. It wasn't far to fall but she was determined not to lose her dignity. Soon, not far above the cargo, the line of crochet work was fluttering like bunting. How pretty it was! Fancy being able to make things like that, Maryann thought. She saw Darius exchange a quiet smile with Joel as she came back to them. Suddenly Darius said, 'Why don't you 'ave a sit up there and look round. You've bin working enough I reckon.'

She realized he meant she should sit up on the cabin. He said he could see past her.

'Ooh,' she said, climbing up. 'It's hot up 'ere again!' The roof of the cabin was baking to the touch in the sunshine. Joel handed her the soaking mop. Periodically, in the heat, they swabbed down the roof of the cabin to stop the heat shrinking the timbers and cracking the paint. Maryann laid her coat on the damp roof and sat feeling the sun blazing down on her skin, screwing her eyes up against the bright sunlight on the water. Life on the cut was so quiet and peaceful compared with home, where there were always factory sounds, the whirring, whining, clanging of machinery, trams and buses and people shouting over all the other racket. Out here there were just the gentle noises of Bessie's hooves, mostly muffled by mud now they were out in the fields; the boat passing through the rippling water; the creak of the tiller and the men's occasional speech. Maryann began to attune herself to new sounds: birdsong from across the fields and in the trees, the occasional lowing of a cow, waterbirds quacking away from the boat and the breeze in the grass. There was nothing to look at that was grimy or ugly, just fields, trees and sky, farm cottages and church spires, and the bright paintwork of the boat winding along the ribbon of water. As they glided along, she thought the cut was the most beautiful place on earth.

Every so often another boat would appear, coming from the opposite direction, and the boats would pass one another a few inches apart in the middle of the channel, the boatmen exchanging a 'How do!' or more if they were better acquainted, as they often seemed to be. A couple greeted Darius and Joel with, 'We ent seen you for a bit!'

She was still sitting dreamily on the cabin roof that afternoon when there came another, incongruous sound advancing towards them, a ceaseless 'phut-phut' getting louder and louder, until round a bend in the cut they saw a vessel coming along with smoke streaming out from it.

'See that?' Joel shouted up to her. 'That's one of they moty boats!'

As it drew closer Maryann saw it was towing a butty, both of them clothed up with tarpaulins over the cargo so she couldn't see what it was. The noise it made seemed extraordinarily loud after all the quiet. The family aboard all waved and shouted greetings, trying to make themselves heard over the engine. Maryann turned to watch it disappear behind them and saw that Joel and Darius were doing the same. Darius was shaking his head as if in disapproval at this noisy 'moty boat'.

Joel leaned over to her. 'You don't get many of them down the h'Oxford,' he said. 'The locks're wider down 'ere to London.' On there, he explained, the boat could tow a butty through all in one go, whereas on here they had to pull them through the narrower locks one by one and it all took time. Maryann was learning that the one overwhelming command on the cut was 'keep moving!'

That night they tied up near a pub called the Cape outside Warwick, a little distance after the long flight of locks at Hatton which Joel told her were called the 'Steps to Heaven'. There were three other boats tied up there too. Once Bessie was fed and stabled, Joel, Darius and the other men caught up with the gossip in the pub. Maryann sat out on the bank and played with two little children from the other boat and their mother seemed grateful to have them occupied while she got on. Joel and Darius came back with groceries they'd bought from the pub.

Maryann bedded down on the side bench again that night, as she had before when she slept on the *Esther Jane*, and watched Joel ready himself for bed. She was lulled by the reassurance of his presence, his huge shadow moving round the cabin. Neither of the men undressed much for bed. They left their boots by the door and took off their jackets, undid their belts which they fastened at the back to keep the buckles from digging in when they bent over, and unfastened a few buttons. Both of them lay to sleep in shirts and their thick, corduroy trousers.

Before he lay down, Joel stepped over to her. 'You tired after your first day, Maryann?'

'Ummm.' She smiled sleepily up at him. His face was in shadow. 'It's been *bostin* – the best day ever.'

He patted her shoulder and she could hear the smile in his voice.

'Night – young nipper.'

The bed creaked as he lay down beside his father.

Maryann wanted to lie awake, to hear the sounds of the countryside at night, but she could scarcely manage it, she was so exhausted after all the new sights and a day in the fresh air. Everything smelled different. There was always the smell of the canal all round them. The sounds of family life from the boat moored behind them were dying out. Her mind passed over the day they'd had, what she'd seen, how she'd learned the way a boat manoeuvred through a lock. Something screeched outside. She imagined the *Esther Jane* from the outside, under the stars, resting on the black water. And then she was asleep.

Seventeen

Soon after the *Esther Jane* set off again the next morning, they passed through Warwick and later that morning, the stately, calm town of Leamington Spa. As they approached each town, buildings and roads grew up along the cut, shutting out the view, and with more people about there was a sudden sense of bustle.

When they reached the lock at Radford Semele, Joel said, ''Ere – you give me a hand this time.'

The day before he had told her to stay on the boat at most of the locks, but today he took her with him and showed her how to attach the windlass and turn it to open and close the gates. Maryann watched with intense attention, all her senses alert to learning to do everything as quickly and as well as possible.

He brought her round in front of him and she took the handle of the windlass which was warm from his grip on it. Each of the men had a favourite one or two of these implements for turning the locks, and the handle of Joel's was smoothed with use. His rough hand tightened over hers, concealing it completely and together they turned on the windlass, opening the gate to let the *Esther Jane* through now that the water was level. Maryann felt the immense strength of Joel's arm.

Just before they reached Wigram's Turn where Joel had told her they would join the Oxford Canal, Maryann was in the cabin and heard Joel and Darius suddenly start shouting and calling outside. She was astonished to hear them so voluble and excited and she poked her head out to see them both waving like mad at a boat approaching from the other direction.

The man at the other tiller was waving back.

'Who's that?' she asked.

'That's our Darius,' Joel said.

As they drew nearer, Maryann saw a large, muscular man with black hair curling out from under his cap, dark eyes and strong, chiselled features. He wore a rather solemn, austere expression. He reminded her of Ada except he didn't have her cheeky grin. She wondered if old Mr Bartholomew had looked like that as a young man. The younger Darius was one of the crew on a Fellows, Morton and Clayton boat which was lying low in the water, its hold heaped high with packing cases.

There was a lot of 'how do'ing and exchanges of greeting as the boats passed.

'You're low in the water,' Joel called out. 'You'll 'ave sparrows drinking from yer gunwhales!'

The young Darius grinned back and what had looked rather a forbidding face lit up suddenly and Maryann decided he looked nice after all. Joel called out that he should keep an eye out for Ada with Josiah Morley and there were shouts of 'see yer at Christmas time if not before!' and then they were past. That was the nearest they were going to get to a family reunion. The boats had to keep moving. Maryann wanted to ask Joel more about his family but she was shy in front of the elder Darius.

She helped Joel as they went up the flight of locks south of Napton, carefully doing everything she was told. The day became blisteringly hot as they set off down the Oxford Canal, so much so that Maryann found that at times she could barely touch anything on the outside of the cabin without scorching herself. She busied herself with the mop. The sun glared off the water, blinding to the eyes, and she felt her nose and cheeks turning red and sore. There were trees in a few places close to the canal, but mostly it ran through remote, open fields, and the need to keep the towpaths clear meant discouraging anything inclined to hang down over the cut. So there was little shade either for the boat or for Bessie.

For a time, Maryann walked beside Bessie along the path, enjoying the feel of stretching her legs, the smells of the fields and the hot horse beside her. Bessie wore little crocheted sleeves on her ears to keep the flies off and she seemed to plod more slowly in the intense heat. The route wound and twisted along, nestling against the contours of hills. Sometimes there were villages and little wharves tucked right beside the canal but much of the time there were just the fields stretching into the distance, trees outlined against the skyline, and it felt as if they might not see anyone else ever again. The only sounds were the rustling reeds and the twittering of invisible birds. Once she saw a huge bird lift from the bank ahead of her, its legs trailing, flying off with a heavy, cumbersome flapping of its wings.

Later, back on board, Joel told her it was a heron. She went into the cabin. It was stifling hot in there and a heavy bluebottle was batting against the windows. Maryann felt like lying down and going to sleep, but she knew she mustn't. The last thing she wanted was to be seen being lazy.

Joel's head appeared at the door. ''Ent you got a bonnet with you?'

She shook her head. 'I ran off in such a hurry – I forgot it.'

He hesitated for a moment, then seemed to decide something. He came into the cabin, squatted down and rummaged right at the back of the cupboard he called the 'monkey 'ole'. He brought out a large, squashed paper bag and from it he drew an old-fashioned boat-woman's bonnet with a peak at the front and layers of black frills which went right over the top of the head and ended up hanging down at the back.

Maryann stared at it. It looked old and dusty, like a dead raven.

'It were my mother's,' Joel told her gruffly. 'She 'ad it made special in black when the old Queen died. These 'ere bits' – he pulled at the long material at the back – 'them's your curtains – 'll keep the sun off yer neck.'

Was he expecting her to wear it? The hat looked so worn and old-fashioned. It was a heavy, *ugly* thing and she wished she had her little straw bonnet with her.

'I can't put that on. Not if it was your mom's.' This was a rather awesome thought.

'I'd like to see yer in it.' Joel held it out to her. 'It's ten year since it were worn. She passed on before I came home.'

'Why daint Ada wear it?'

'Oh – she had her own bonnet.'

Seeing she didn't take it, he put it on her head himself. Maryann felt strange, seeing the fond look in his eyes. The bonnet felt much too loose.

'Bit big on you, ent it? But it'll do just for a bit while it's so hot. We don't want you getting caught by the sun.'

Joel was the last person Maryann would ever want

to offend so she smiled uncertainly at him. She felt like a granny in the bonnet. She had seen a few older women wearing them along the cut.

She followed him up out of the cabin. As she straightened up she saw Darius's eyes fasten on her. He actually started at the sight of her and a look of utter outrage came over his face.

'What's 'er doing in that?' he demanded.

'I thought she could wear it for a bit,' Joel said. 'She ent brought a bonnet with 'er. And it's nice to see it wore again.'

Joel had made a terrible mistake. Maryann could see just how terrible by the look in Darius Bartholomew's eyes.

'That's my Esther's bonnet – moy best mate. Not one else ever wears that bonnet. Get it off yer, lass!'

Maryann was already tearing the hat from her head, her hands trembling at the emotion in the old man's voice. Joel took it from her.

'Sorry, Dad – only I thought yer'd like to see it on again, the way I did.'

Darius was breathing heavily. 'Put it away.'

Joel ducked back into the cabin with the bonnet. Maryann couldn't look up. Her cheeks were burning and she had a horrible feeling inside as if she'd committed a crime. She had offended Mr Bartholomew so badly when what she wanted more than anything was for him to accept her. It was unbearable that he would think her uppity enough to take his dead wife's bonnet and wear it.

'I'm ever so sorry, Mr Bartholomew,' she managed to say, her voice quavering.

'It weren't your idea I don't s'pose,' Darius said abruptly.

Though she knew this was true, his rough words scarcely made her feel any better. Joel came back out and laid a hand on her shoulder for a moment.

'My mistake, not yours,' he said.

But it was not until much later that day that the feeling of discomfort this incident had brought Maryann began to ease off and she could feel a little more comfortable with Darius Bartholomew again. After that she doubled her efforts to show him she could work hard and try to please him.

That night, after fourteen hours on the go, they tied up at Fenny Compton, where there was a small wharf and a pub. A couple of other boats were tied up there and the men went out to the pub as usual after they'd eaten. Maryann didn't mind being left behind. She rather liked the novelty of having the cabin to herself.

As it was so warm, she didn't feel like slaving away cleaning the cabin. She was hot and tired and she went out and sat on the bank in the evening air. She could smell smoke and food cooking and she breathed in deeply, a great feeling of well-being coming over her.

Glancing towards the pub, she suddenly noticed that Joel was on the bridge and there was a young woman with him. Maryann screwed up her eyes to see better. She was short and rounded looking, with a wide, healthy face and curly brown hair. She and Joel were standing quite close together, relaxed, each leaning on the bridge, and now and then their laughter floated over to her. Maryann was immediately curious. Was she someone Joel was very close to? She found herself full of mixed feelings. Joel had told her he had been courting a girl before the war changed everything. Of course he'd want to get married like other men, but she had had in her mind a future stretching ahead in which she could live on the *Esther Jane* and everything would stay the same.

After a time, the two of them left the bridge and walked round the wall of the pub, out of sight. Maryann sat on, feeling suddenly desolate. She wasn't really part of all this, however much she wanted to be.

When Joel came back in she was already lying down. 'Who was that lady you was talking to?'

He frowned for a second.

'On the bridge.'

'Oh – that's Rose.' He laughed, then coughed to clear his chest. 'Ent seen 'er in a good long while. We've been catching up.'

'She's pretty,' Maryann said. She knew she sounded sulky.

'S'pose she is. Known 'er all my life.'

'Are you going to marry her?'

To her surprise, both men started laughing.

'Marry Rose? Bit late for that – she's got a chap and three kiddies, Rose 'as!'

Maryann went off to sleep feeling much happier. However much she told herself she was stupid to think she could have Joel all to herself, the thought of him being in love with that pretty Rose had made her feel jealous and left out.

The next day was just as long, and in the evening they pulled into Thrupp where the canal was edged by little terraces of canal workers' cottages. Joel told her they were now only about three hours away from Oxford.

She helped to get the range going and cook the food.

Joel had also made her responsible for unharnessing Bessie, feeding and stabling her. On these scorching days she also had to wipe out Bessie's eyes with a rag dipped in paraffin, to keep them free from flies and parasites. Mostly, as they went about their evening chores, even Maryann was too tired to speak. Darius went off and kept himself separate, collecting water, or coal if they needed it, and at Thrupp he asked around for return loads to take back north after they had delivered the pipes in Oxford. She and Joel did their chores, often in silence, but always at ease. Sometimes he looked at her and smiled and she'd grin back.

She was more than ready for bed every night after all the physical activity and fresh air of the daytime. As they drew further south away from Birmingham, home seemed more and more unreal, like a bad dream. In the daytime she was so caught up in all the details needed to keep the *Esther Jane* on the move that she barely had time to think, and that suited her very well. She wanted to forget all of it: Sal, Norman Griffin. When she did allow herself time to think, she was filled with anxiety. Where had Sal gone? Was she with Charlie Black and were they both all right? And what about Tony and Billy, left at home? Most of all she felt badly for Tony, about her going off and leaving him. But nothing would have made her give up these days on the cut. Nothing.

By ten the next morning they were pulling into Juxon Street wharf in Oxford amid a collection of boats waiting to unload. The wharf was very busy. Maryann stabled Bessie, gave her a feed and cleaned her harness. She wound her way back to the *Esther Jane* through the stacks of cargo standing on the wharf waiting to be collected: coal and stone, barrels, packing cases, sacks. The hard work of loading and unloading was going on all round and she could have stood all morning watching, but instead she hurried back and got the stove going to make cups of tea. The *Esther Jane* was due a big clean-out while they were tied up. In the meantime she heated more water, got the tin tub and dolly from off the roof and did some washing, scrubbing at the men's thick corduroy trousers, struggling to lift them when they were saturated with water.

'They're *filthy*,' she said to Joel, pummelling them wearily with the dolly. Her shoulders were aching like mad.

'You should see 'em after a hold full of coal.' Joel grinned. '*That's* filthy!'

The afternoon passed loading the *Esther Jane*, the long iron pipes swinging high in the air above her head before being deposited with a loud clanking on the bank. Joel and Darius were preoccupied with securing a return load to take north again. The country wharves sometimes wanted loads of grain taken up for grinding in the Birmingham mills, but it was close to a new harvest now and the stores were low. They needed to find something in Oxford. Joel went off to some of the other wharves, and by late afternoon he had secured a load of timber to be taken to Birmingham. In the meantime, Maryann strung the washing along the boat and helped Darius to swill her out with water. She was ill at ease being left to work with him, but she did everything he said to the letter and by the end of the afternoon she felt that even if she did not have his approval in great measure, at least he had accepted the help she was offering and she had not let herself down.

161

Eighteen

That evening though, for the first time, she felt lonely. With the work done and the cargo to be loaded in the morning, Joel and his father went to see Joel's auntie, Darius's sister, and then for a few pints at the pubs round Jericho, the area near the wharf. Maryann, as ever, was left alone.

She cleared up the tea things, put everything away. The men brought food in daily if they could, as nothing would keep in the heat, so there was only a bit of bread and bacon on board for next morning. The place was tidy, and as she had been washing and cleaning most of the day she could think of nothing she needed to busy herself with. Now they had achieved the journey down to Oxford the urgency had gone out of things. Before, she hadn't minded being left here, had rather relished having the cabin to herself, but tonight, with nothing to do, she felt suddenly bereft. She sat by the table for a time, biting her nails, and unwelcome thoughts of home and Norman Griffin began to crowd into her mind. She knew if she started on that it would just keep on going round in her head. No – she must think about anything but him.

She got up and folded back the table so she could make up her bed on the side bench with the little flock mattress and the blanket she slept under. She lay down and concentrated on the rosy light of the lamp reflected in the brass fittings. It was such a snug place and it felt like home now. Maryann found herself smiling, snuggling down cosily and growing more sleepy. Every so often she heard the sound of the water lapping gently against the wharf. She was coming to love the sounds of the cut at night. If only she could stay here! There were a few lonely moments, but nothing like the isolation she felt at home where there was no one she could turn to. There was no threat here, not with these big, quiet men. She felt safe with Joel, safe and reassured, as if he was a strong, fairytale brother who'd come to rescue her.

The thought of home filled her with dread. She would have to go back – for Tony if no one else. But why did she have to stay at home? Why could she not just live on the cut with the Bartholomews? Joel had said it was hard enough working the *Esther Jane* three-handed, let alone two, and Darius wasn't a young man any more. But what would Joel say if she asked him? And Darius? Had she proved her worth enough during these last few days?

By the time the men came in she was dozing. She woke again as the cabin door squeaked open, letting in the night air. Darius, walking unsteadily, immediately went and let down the bed at the back, gave out a loud, beery belch, then readied himself for the night. Joel, however, seemed restless. Seeing Maryann looking sleepily up at him he came and sat on the end of the bench. She slid her legs out of the way for him. For a time he just sat there holding his cap while she watched him. His wiry beard and wavy hair were a lovely bronze colour in the pink, subdued light. She looked at his gentle face and huge, worn hands and felt she couldn't imagine a time when she had not known him.

Why was he just sitting there instead of going to bed, she wondered. But she liked it, didn't want him to move, wanting instead to ask him if she could stay with them, but Darius was there and she didn't have the courage.

He looked across at his father now and then, and when Darius was obviously asleep he turned to her and said, half whispering, 'Well – it's been a soft day for us today. I don't know about you, but I ent ready to settle yet. I fancy a walk. How about you, young nipper?'

'Ooh, yes!' She sat up, immediately cheerful. Anything Joel suggested seemed good. An adventure!

She put her shoes back on and her cardigan and they climbed back out into the starry night. The moon was almost full and the wharf buildings were sharp edged, the colour of pewter under its light.

They set out along Juxon Street. Maryann found it strange to be back on a road, with buildings hemming you in on either side, after the cut. She tried to imagine how it would feel never to have lived on the bank.

'D'yer think you'll ever live in a house?' she asked, looking up at Joel.

'Oh – you can never tell, can you? There are folks moving off the cut all the time. It ent easy, with the moty boats and lorries taking over the cargoes. We'll hang on as long as we can though. It's what we know.'

'But you wouldn't give up the *Esther Jane*, would yer?'

Joel shrugged. 'I hope not. But we had to sell the butty – we had a pair before, but we had to part with one of 'em. That's how it goes these days.'

Maryann felt sobered by this. The thought of the Bartholomews living like other people was inconceivable. They turned into another street, then another, in

164

silence, except for the sound of their feet on the road. Silence was easy with Joel. It never felt uncomfortable.

'But—' she said eventually. 'You were born on the cut, weren't you?'

'I was s'posed to be born 'ere at h'Oxford. My mother was coming to town to 'ave me and I was in too much of a hurry – arrived just south of Banbury!'

'On the *Esther Jane*?'

'She weren't called the *Esther Jane* then.'

'No, I know. Joel – will you tell me about your brothers and sisters?'

They turned on to a wider road where there were a few more people about, coming out of the pubs.

'You're a proper chatterchops, ent you?'

'I ain't!'

She liked Joel calling her a chatterchops, but in fact it was hardly justified. There'd been very little time to talk much on the way down. They were always busy, or the men were in the pub or too tired.

'When'll you see Ada again?'

'Well, if we don't run into 'er on the cut, it'll be Christmas. We all try and 'ave a rally at Christmas time, tie up at Braunston or Hawkesbury for a couple of days. See young Darius and Ada.'

'Won't she miss you?'

'She will. But a lot of young 'uns work away from their families. It's the only way to do it – someone always needs a pair o' hands.'

'What about the others?'

'Darius is the oldest. There was Daniel who fell sick and passed on as a little 'un. I never knew 'im. Then there was Esther – she drownded when she was not more than fifteen. Then Ezra – 'e died in the war, and so did Sam, then there was me, then Sarah and we lost 'er to the h'influenza and our mother lost a pair of babies in between – she was very poorly after them – and then there was Ada and through her we lost our mother.'

'Oh Joel, your poor mom!'

'Yep—' he said gruffly. 'She were a good'un, our mother.'

'Did Darius go away to the war?'

'No. Someone 'ad to stay. We younger ones went and I was the one come back. Anyhow – that's how it went. How many's in your family?'

She told Joel all about Tony and Billy, and Sal running off and her dad dying and Mom marrying Mr Griffin, but she didn't want to say much about him. She could feel Joel listening beside her.

'Is your stepfather good to you?'

'No,' she said abruptly. 'Well – I mean, we eat enough and that. But . . . I don't want to talk about 'im, Joel. Don't let's spoil it – it's lovely out 'ere.'

As she began to take an interest in the town unfolding round her, she saw that it was indeed beautiful. There were a few lamps, but mainly the buildings were lit by the moon. Maryann looked up at the spires and towers, the grand, dark fronts of the colleges all around them.

'This is h'Oxford University,' Joel told her. 'They do a lot of book learning 'ere, that's what.'

To Maryann it seemed like fairy land, like nowhere else she'd ever been before.

'I'll show you summat lovely,' Joel said. 'Come along 'ere.'

He led her down a side street, then another, and into a square. All along the sides were castellated buildings, no factories or houses at all. There was a huge, rounded building in the middle. It was covered in little stone arches and columns and stone balustrades, and its roof was domed. Its windows reflected back the moonlight.

'Oh!' She looked round in wonder. 'What is it?'

'They say it's full of books,' Joel said, with a slight air of disbelief. 'Let's go down by the river, shall we?'

Maryann could tell that, while awed, he was not comfortable between all these walls. He led her out the other side of the square and across another road hemmed in by buildings that seemed like palaces to Maryann.

'D'you wish you could read?' she asked him. 'If you wanted to learn I could 'elp yer.'

She heard Joel's wheezy laugh come to her through the darkness. 'Reckon I've got this far without. There ent much call for it on the cut.'

She walked with him, down to where the river flowed past the backs of the colleges. For a moment they stood looking back. It was a beautiful sight, the old stone lit by soft moonlight.

'S'funny how many different ways there are for folk to live, ent it?' Joel said. She felt him reach down and take her hand in his, and she nuzzled against his arm, happy. 'Bet you've never seen nothing like this before.'

Maryann shook her head. 'Joel?' Her heart began thumping fast.

'What's that?'

'I don't want to go home. I want to stay with you and your dad and work the cut.'

There was silence as Joel stared down into the water, that flowed past quite briskly, not like the still, sluggish canal water.

'I don't know about that. You've been a good'un,

learning how to work the boat, no doubt about it. And I can't says I won't miss you, specially with Ada gone. But you can't just stay on without your family giving their by-your-leave. That ent right.'

'Oh *please*, Joel. I can't go home. It's not . . . I can't say why. But it's horrible at home and they won't care if I'm there or not . . .'

'Now, now—' He turned to face her. 'That can't be true now, can it? You got family – people who need you.'

'But Ada just went off to live with someone else, daint she? Why shouldn't I do it too?' She knew she sounded desperate, almost tearful.

'That's what life is on the cut. We boat people do that. But it ent the same where you come from, is it? I ent saying we don't need you – a pair of hands is like gold to us. But you should go back and make things right with your family first. I can't feel right about you just running off and them not knowing where you are, Maryann. You can see that, can't you?'

'I know.' Her voice sounded high and young. 'But I just want to stay with you, Joel.'

'Oh – now—' He pulled her towards his big, burly body and she felt herself pressed against his scratchy weskit, her little budding breasts tender against him, his strong arms tight round her. She put her arms as far round him as she could reach, laughing. She hadn't felt so warmed or happy since she was a little girl, held in her dad's arms after he came home and she nestled against him, loving the feel and smell of him. Joel could save her, he could take her away from that life at home that she so dreaded, she knew he could. He could do anything.

'Don't you get all upset,' Joel was saying, tenderly

stroking her hair. His hand felt enormous on her head. 'We'll see what can be done.'

She looked up into his face and saw his eyes twinkling down at her affectionately in the moonlight.

Nineteen

During the small hours of the next morning, the weather broke. Maryann woke in the night to hear thunder and, soon after, the sound of rain drumming on the cabin roof. The next morning it was still raining. She went out with her coat on and the water was soon running off her hair and down her cheeks.

They moved the *Esther Jane* down to Isis Lock – Joel and Darius called it 'Louse Lock'. To load up, Joel explained, they had to move from the narrow Oxford Canal on to the wider Thames, the adjacent 'Mill Stream', to where the imported timber was brought from London on lighters, towed by tugs, which were too wide for the Oxford Cut.

'When they come up 'ere' – Joel pointed after they had come through Isis Lock – 'they got to get past the railway, see? There's a bridge there, cranks up by 'and, lets 'em through.'

'But what if there's a train coming?' she said.

Joel laughed at her foolishness. 'You don't do it when there's a train coming!'

Maryann did not see any of the lighters coming through, but on the wharf waiting for them was a stack of timber sawed into all sorts of different lengths and thicknesses.

'It's one of the awkwardest bloomin' loads we ever carry,' Joel said, taking off his wet jacket. 'We've to load each bit by hand, or it won't fit in. You can help.'

Maryann soon found out what he meant. Darius, with his lifetime's experience of settling a load into a boat just the right way, stood in the hull as Joel, another worker and Maryann passed him down each plank, piece by piece. Darius said which bit he wanted next and laid them all in, fitting them like a patchwork quilt. The wood was very rough and splintery, not planed smooth. Some of the pieces were so heavy that Maryann couldn't lift them, but she worked hard taking over whatever she could. She wore a thick, hessian apron over her dress. Sometimes she squatted, resting a plank across her knees for Darius to take it from her. The rough wood burned her hands, splinters jabbing into her like needles, and she was soaking wet. The men never seemed to stop and rest: the boat and load always came first. By mid-morning, when the load was almost on board and the rain was still falling, she was close to tears she was so wet and tired, and her hands were bleeding and swollen. But she was determined not to show Darius how close she was to getting up and running off. She gritted her teeth and passed him another plank, wishing he'd at least notice how difficult she was finding it. But after they had secured the last pieces and the *Esther Jane* was now riding low in the water, Darius patted her shoulder briefly as he passed her.

'That were a good job,' he said.

Maryann beamed back at him, elated yet with a lump in her throat. She had truly done something right and won his approval! She skipped along to help Joel harness Bessie, who was quite frisky after her extra half-day's rest. Once she was harnessed up, tolls paid, coal and water aboard, they were off.

Maryann was thrilled to be on the move again. The cut stretched out ahead of them as they slid slowly out of Oxford, the spires and towers receded into the distance and they were in the country again.

'This is the proper life,' she said.

Joel grinned at her. 'If you say so, missy.'

They only travelled as far as Thrupp that day and the sun never broke through. The second morning, they woke to rain and the wind was getting up. Their clothes from the day before were still not dry even though they'd hung them in the warm cabin while they were in bed, but it was obvious that if they put their spare set on they would soon be soaked through as well. Once Joel and Darius had gone out she pulled her damp dress over her head with a shudder. It was slightly warm from being close to the stove, but it soon cooled on her and she was shivering before she had even gone outside. For the first time she started to have misgivings about this life. If this was what it could be like in the middle of summer, what must it be like living here in the freezing winter wind and rain?

They warmed themselves with a cup of tea as they went along. But the day started out as a hard, maddening one. The wind was the real enemy on the cut, pushing even a well-loaded boat about like a plywood toy from side to side. Joel stood at the tiller working it with all his strength to keep it from being blown into the bank, and the shallows where often there were reeds, and other plants with big leaves that looked like rhubarb. Maryann annoyed him by asking, before she realized, 'Will you teach me to steer today, Joel?' and he snapped back, 'Not today – can't yer see what it's like?'

As the wind got up further, Darius took to the bank

to help keep Bessie steady. Every so often the boat was caught by a gust and blown into the side. The water was the colour of milky cocoa. Joel abruptly ordered Maryann off to help pull them off. The first time, the stern of the boat was forced right into the side. Joel yelled at her, telling her how he wanted her to pull. She hauled on the rope with all her strength, the rope yanking away and burning through her agonized hands until she couldn't help crying with the pain. They'd no sooner get straightened up again than another gust would send the *Esther Jane* off at some other angle. As well as keeping the boat on course, round Banbury there were all the lift bridges over the cut to be raised and lowered again as they passed. The morning seemed endless; cold and hard and wet. Maryann was already near to exhaustion and everyone was tense and bad-tempered. Darius kept yelling at her to pull harder, Joel was cursing on board the boat. Maryann almost wished she was at home. She had a sudden longing to see Tony and Billy – someone younger who looked up to her and loved her and didn't order her about.

But the worst was to come on the afternoon. Worse than Maryann could ever have imagined. They'd passed Banbury and reached Slat Mill Lock. As they struggled into the lower pound – Joel striving to keep the boat straight, another boat following close behind, which added to the pressure on them – he shouted to Maryann, 'D'you think you can do it?'

'Yes!' she called back proudly. ''Course.'

Darius was already out on the bank too. 'You take the 'orse,' he said.

'No, please,' she said. 'I can do it. I know how.'

With obvious reluctance he handed her his windlass, which he carried tucked in his belt, and stayed holding

Bessie. Maryann fitted the windlass on to the lock mechanism and started turning. One of the men from the boat behind pushed on the gate beam to swing it open and Maryann stood out of the way, feeling pleased with herself. Joel had spelled out many times the danger of standing in the wrong place and getting swept into the cut. None of them could swim and even if they had been able to, the men especially would have been weighed down by their heavy trousers, boots and over-coats. Maryann stood with her hands behind her back, the windlass clutched between them as the two boats moved into the lock chamber and the men closed the lower gates, trying to look as if she had lived on the cut all her life and knew just what she was doing. But she noticed that on the boat behind there was a boy with only one leg, and it was a sobering sight. People with missing limbs were not uncommon on the cut. What accident had befallen him in this dangerous life?

When the lower gates were closed and the boats were secured, waiting for the water to rise, she struggled along, leaning into the wind, to the upper gates, hearing Joel shout something to her as she went. The wind whisked his words away.

'S'awright!' she called back. 'I can do it!'

She started turning. Though she'd done it a number of times with Joel, it was hard by herself but she was determined to manage. The muscles on her arms strained and eventually it was so difficult that she was leaning her whole weight on the windlass to turn it and haul it back round at the bottom. The paddles were opening and the water started to gush in with a great roar.

And then it all went wrong. She was leaning back, bringing it round, when she lost her balance. Her hands slipped off the windlass and it snapped back the other way, flying round and round, and Maryann fell over backwards. Frantic and mortified, she scrambled to her feet just as the windlass flew off the spindle. There was a metallic clink, then a splosh. She stood there, paralysed. No – it couldn't have done! Darius's precious, favourite windlass, the one Esther Jane had given to him, his wife, his best mate, had disappeared down into the cut.

Everyone was shouting: Joel, Darius, the other men in the boat. Tears welled up in her eyes. She didn't know what to do.

Darius was suddenly beside her. 'Take care of th 'orse,' he shouted at her.

She saw him go to the shaft where the windlass should have been. He looked round on the ground, then down into the water. He went to Joel, shouting to him for his spare windlass. Maryann slunk back to Bessie with the most leaden heart she had ever had. She was sick with shame. She wanted to hide her face in the horse's hot, wet neck and give in to crying, but she knew this would put her in even more disgrace.

'Your windlass taken a look in the cut, eh?' one of the men on the wharf called out to her. 'Oh dear, oh dear!'

The teasing was not unkind, but it made her feel even worse; young and stupid and incompetent. Worst of all, it made her feel an outsider again, just as she thought she was beginning to get the hang of it. Waiting to finish getting through that lock felt the longest few minutes she could ever remember. When they were through, she went to Darius, looking down at her muddy shoes, unable to face him.

'I'm ever so sorry, Mr Bartholomew.' The tears ran

down her burning cheeks. 'I never meant to lose your windlass. I wish I could go down and get it. I feel ever so bad.'

Darius Bartholomew could not seem to speak. Maryann looked up to see him trying to gather himself. He was breathing deeply and she could see he was furious, but seemingly unable to find the words to yell at her as she knew she deserved. He looked at her for a moment, then strode past. Once they were through the lock Maryann climbed back into the boat, wishing she could just disappear.

'The windlass – I lost Mr Bartholomew's favourite windlass. I don't know what to do, Joel – he's so angry with me.'

'Well, of course 'e is!' She had never heard Joel raise his voice to her in anger before. 'I told you to wait for 'im. You have to do what you're told, not just mess about! What d'you expect him to do? He'd had that windlass more'n half his life.'

'I daint hear you. I promise I daint, Joel!' Maryann was really sobbing now. It was no good thinking she could come here and be one of them and start a new life. She was hopeless, even at the first test and now Joel was fed up with her as well. She wanted to get off the boat, get away from them and from feeling so small and ashamed.

'Oh, there's no need for all that,' Joel said crossly.

Maryann stood looking out, wiping her eyes as Joel wrestled with the tiller, struggling to keep the boat moving straight. He took some time to gain control again. After what seemed a cold, miserable age, he turned to her.

'Eh – cheer up. You weren't the first and you won't

be the last.' He patted her shoulder. 'We'll make a boatwoman of you – don't you worry.'

But to her it still seemed a huge and awful thing she had done and she didn't know how she was going to face the rest of the journey with Joel's father.

Later she apologized again to Darius Bartholomew and he said gruffly, 'These things happen. It taught you, I hope.'

Maryann felt almost forgiven by the men, but she was finding it very hard indeed to forgive herself.

For the rest of the journey she was quiet and subdued. She listened with great care to what she was asked to do and did it with all her concentration, trying as hard as she could to make amends. Darius treated her much as he had before, but he did not reach out to her with any words of reassurance and she couldn't feel forgiven, even though Joel tried to jolly her along.

The last night, when the men were asleep, she gave into her feelings and lay sobbing, trying to be as quiet as she could. After a time, though, she heard the cross bed creaking as Joel sat up, then came over to her.

'What's up, chatterchops? You ent been yourself these last days. Eh – come on now, you don't want to worry so much. There ent nothing wrong.'

He sat down beside her and took her hand in his.

'Oh Joel!' She pressed his hand against her cheek. 'I feel so bad about eveything – I can't stay 'ere 'cause I'm no good to yer, but I don't want to go 'ome. I just can't go back there!'

'Now, now—' She became aware that he was stroking her hair with his other hand and it gave her such a warm, reassuring feeling. 'Don't go saying you're no good to us. You've been a good little boatwoman.

177

Everyone loses a windlass some time – that's life on the cut.'

'But Mr Bartholomew's best mate's windlass!'

'Well, that were a pity, but what's done's done. In the past now. You want to forget about it.'

But Maryann's heart was so heavy she couldn't feel consoled yet. She couldn't stop crying.

'What is it, eh?'

'Can I stay with yer, Joel? Just come and live 'ere?' she pleaded again.

'We said all this already.' His voice was gentle but firm. 'You must go back and tell 'em where you've bin. It's no good. If they're happy about it . . .' His voice trailed off.

'What? Tell me, Joel!'

'Truth is, I can't say I won't miss you. I've got used to you, sort of thing.'

'Oh please—' Maryann sat up eagerly. 'Say I can stay!'

He took her in his arms and rocked her, and she clung to him. In wonder, she felt him kiss the top of her head.

'You go 'ome and sort things out. Then we'll see. 'Ow about that, eh?'

Birmingham grew up around them, dark and rank with factory smells and the grim stenches of slum living. Buildings blocked out the light.

'I never knew 'ow much it stank 'ere till I got out of it,' Maryann said, standing on the steering platform. Darius was on the bank with Bessie. 'It's so dirty and dismal, ain't it?'

Joel laughed. 'Don't say that about your 'ome!'

178

As they moved further into the town, the noise increased: the cut busy with laden joey boats, the boatmen in a rush and shouting and swearing at each other to get ahead, trains clattering overhead dropping smuts, the air laden with factory smoke. Maryann's spirits dropped again. She had to get out of here. The narrow streets, the meanness of everything – and worse, much worse than that, Mr Griffin ... Winter on the cut, however cold and hard, could not be worse than this.

When they pulled into the wharf under the labyrinths of factories to offload the wood, Joel said to her, 'You'd best get off now, 'adn't yer – be getting back to your own people.'

'I'll be back,' she said. 'I will, Joel – I'll leave word for yer!'

She saw his slow smile. 'Well – we'll see, won't we. We'll try and stay on the h'Oxford. I know my dad's happier going down that way.' He leaned over and rumpled her hair. 'Cheerio for now, young nipper.'

She politely said goodbye to Darius Batholomew. He said, 'G'bye, lass,' in a kindly way and his leathery face creased into a smile, even though they were in a rush to get unloaded, and that made her feel better. Waving at Joel, she left with her little bundle of clothes and set off towards Ladywood.

Twenty

'Well.' Flo's face was distorted with anger and her arms tightly folded across her chest. 'What've yer got to say for yerself then?'

Maryann had made sure she didn't arrive until after Norman Griffin had left, and when she got in only Flo was at home with Billy, who ran through from the kitchen calling, 'Maryann!'

''Allo, Billy love.' She put down her bundle and squatted down to cuddle him.

'Norman's been going mad!'

Maryann's expression darkened. She scowled at Flo over Billy's blond head. 'Ain't that typical, eh? I go away for a week and all yer can say is "Norman's been going mad!"' She mimicked her mother's tone. 'That's all you cowing well care about, ain't it?'

Flo stood glaring at her, then suddenly kneeled down so her face was level with Maryann's.

'That's always the way with you, ain't it? Never a thought for no one else. Do you know why I married Norman? Do yer?'

''Cause yer wanted his money.'

'Yes – 'cause I wanted his money! And d'yer know why I wanted 'is money? So I could feed my family and keep it together. So you could 'ave the clothes you're wearing on yer back, Maryann. So's I daint 'ave

180

to hand over Tony and Billy to Barnado's when I couldn't afford to keep them!'

'No, Mom, that's the excuse you've always had but I don't believe yer. We wouldn't've starved the way you'd like us to believe. You 'ad a job – in a couple of years Sal was out at work – then I'd've been. Other people do it – look at Mrs Winters.' Mrs Winters was a widow with five children who they'd known in the Garrett Street days.

'Huh,' Flo said contemptuously. 'Yer needn't think taking in washing was the only way *that* one was making ends meet! She had men in and out of there like rats in a nest. And look at the state of 'er – 'er looks sixty if 'er looks a day and she ain't no older than I am. I weren't living like that – I struggled and scrimped all through the war, and then with yer dad coming home in the state 'e was—' She leaned closer, spitting the words into Maryann's face. 'You was too young to know what it was like. You don't feel it all when yer a babby, all the worrying and going without – you just 'ave the bread put in your mouth and that's all you know. It's the mother feels it. I'd 'ad enough, Maryann. Norman ain't yer dad – course I know that. I loved my Harry, that I did, even when 'e come home half the man 'e'd been. But when 'e'd gone I couldn't face no more. You needn't think it's easy for me. You don't know what it's like to lie every night next to a man yer've no feeling for.'

An expression of revulsion came over Maryann's face. 'Don't I? And Sal – don't she?'

'Don't start on them lies again.' Flo turned away in disgust. 'I don't want to hear 'em.'

'No – you don't, do yer?' There was great bitterness in Maryann's voice. 'That's the one way I can rely on

181

you – not to want to hear the things that don't suit yer.'

'Norman's given us a good home and a good life – and you girls just can't see it. We could get on awright but you go running off – you're nothing but trouble. First Sal, and then you . . .'

To Maryann's vexation, her mother put her hands over her face and burst into tears.

'That's it – go on and cry then.' She walked away across the room. 'Twist everything round so everyone has to feel sorry for you. That's always your way, Mom, ain't it? You never want to hear what anyone else's got to say.'

She stamped her way upstairs, full of bitterness. The bedroom felt damp, and very cold and empty. After a moment she heard her mom following her up. Flo came and stood at the door with Billy who was watching them both, wide-eyed with alarm.

''Ve yer heard from Sal?' Maryann asked, her back to Flo.

'Not a word.' Flo wiped her eyes on her apron. 'I've been worried to death. And then you take off as well – fancy leaving a note on your bed like that. You can be a cruel, selfish little bint, can't yer? And I can smell you from 'ere. Yer stink as if yer've been living in a ditch. Where've you been?'

'I ain't telling yer.' Maryann turned, hands clasping her upper arms and her jaw thrust out. 'You can ask me till you're blue in the face. I've been somewhere where I can 'ave a better life than I ever do around 'ere with you and that dirty husband of yours. But of course you don't want to hear about that, do yer?'

Flo was breathing hard. She narrowed her eyes. 'Tell me the truth, Maryann, or I swear to God I'll take my hand to yer. You've been with Sal, ain't yer? You know where she is!' She was shouting, moving closer. 'And I bet that Cathleen Black knows an' all!'

'I am telling you the truth. I ain't seen Sal. I wish I had but I don't know where she is, on my life.' She backed away from her mother. 'But I ain't telling you where I've been. One thing is – I'm going again, soon as I can. I ain't staying round 'ere for a second longer than I 'ave to!'

'So – you're back.'

Flo was in the kitchen with the boys when he came in. For the few moments Maryann was alone with him in the front room, Norman Griffin looked older and flabbier than she remembered, such a contrast to the muscular strength of the Bartholomews. He was looking at her with undisguised lasciviousness, as if his eyes were fingering her through her clothes, and her skin prickled with revulsion.

He moved closer, speaking very softly to prevent her mother hearing, in his low, wheedling tone. 'I'm not going to ask where yer've been, so long as you're back now.' His hand reached out and stroked her left breast. 'To stay.'

Maryann's lip curled with disgust and she stepped backwards, folding her arms tightly across herself. She stared past him, at his brass lamp on the table by the wall.

'I do believe you're growing up.' He was smirking at her, undeterred. 'Quite a young lady all of a sudden.'

'Norman?'

He turned as Flo came in. She looked at them both for a moment, as if puzzled, then continued. 'Oh –

you've seen she's home?' She kept her voice light and persuasive, as if Maryann was forever just disappearing for a week at a time.

'Yes. And ready to start work.'

Maryann stared hard at Flo, willing her to speak. When things had calmed down a bit earlier in the day, Flo had said to Maryann, 'The wag man was round earlier in the week. I told 'im you was ill and lucky for you 'e didn't come in to make sure. But yer'd better get back to school next week.'

Maryann agreed readily. She could collect her leaving certificate, even if she might never need it, and it would keep her away from Norman for a week. By the time she was supposed to start work for him, it would be about the time Joel and his dad would be back from another run if they worked the Oxford Cut again. And she'd be off and away for good ... She felt calmer facing them all because she knew that. There was nothing for her here.

'So I've told Maryann she'd best get back to school next week,' Flo was saying.

Norman put on his most amenable tone. 'All right, m'dear. Whatever you think. So long as she's ready to start a week on Monday.'

It felt odd to be home. Maryann felt as if she'd been away far longer than a week. As if in those few days she had grown up and changed so much that she just didn't fit. But the changes were not just in her. She was most anxious about her brothers, how they had been while she was away. Billy seemed much as usual. Tony, though, didn't come home until it was almost time for tea and when he did he didn't seem at all pleased to see her. He slouched to the tea table and sat down without looking at any of them.

'You been out with yer pals, Tony?' she asked him.

She received barely a grunt in reply. She watched him, hurt. Tony was eight now, tall for his age and thinning out. He had a tight, closed expression on his face and was shovelling his stew down as if he wanted to get away from them all as soon as possible. Maryann looked at Flo, who shrugged.

Upstairs, when Tony was in bed, Maryann went and sat on his mattress and tried to get him to speak to her. He lay on his side facing the wall with his back to her, tucked down under the bedclothes so that she could only see dark tufts of his hair.

'Tony – turn over and look at me.'

He didn't move.

'Tony – please. I'm sorry I went away without saying goodbye and that, but . . .' She couldn't tell him where she'd been or that she was going back. A pang went through her. He felt abandoned, she knew, but it was her and Sal who were the ones at the mercy of Norman's disgusting habits. She couldn't tell Tony that, couldn't tell him why . . .

'Look, I'm back now, Tony. Can't you speak to me? Let me make it up to yer?'

But there was still no reply. She wondered if he was asleep and not just pretending, but she sensed that he wasn't. With a sigh she got up. 'All right then – let's 'ave a talk another time.'

Lying in bed, she heard Flo come up and settle herself down. She waited for Norman to come up too: the terrible, familiar sounds of him breathing heavily on the landing from climbing the stairs, his cough, all of which made her lie so tensely that she was scarcely breathing, then his murmured words to her mother as he bedded down beside her. But there was nothing. He had not come to bed. She waited for what seemed hours and she was so tired. Eventually, thinking about Joel and missing him, wondering where the *Esther Jane* was tonight, and were they missing her, she fell asleep.

It wasn't the squeak of the door which woke her. She was conscious a second before that, perhaps from his furtive tread on the stairs, or some second sense which alerted her. Before she had come to properly, his hand was over her mouth and nose and she was fighting for breath, panicking and struggling out of the bed-clothes, tearing at his arm.

'Ssssh.' He moved his hand so that it was only over her mouth and she took fierce, gasping breaths, feeling her nostrils flaring in the darkness. He was sitting on her bed, his face close to hers.

'Don't you dare make a sound, yer little bitch, or I'll do to you what I did to that cat.'

He was manoeuvring himself in the darkness, with difficulty, she could tell, hearing his loud breathing, his hand still over her mouth, though less tightly. She was paralysed with fear and horror at the thought of what he was going to do, unable to move. She heard a small whimpering sound escape from her and felt his fingers claw at her face.

'I said not a sound . . .' His voice was tight, strained. 'I've been waiting for you – I don't like waiting. I'm going to 'ave you. I've waited long enough.'

It did not take him long. When he had gone she crept downstairs and out into the yard in the thin moonlight. Dizzily she leaned over the low wall, resting her head wretchedly in her hands. After a few moments her body revolted against what had happened. She bent over and was violently sick.

Twenty-One

Maryann's teacher, Miss Bentley, didn't seem perturbed by her absence and asked if she was feeling better.

'Yes thanks.' Maryann couldn't manage a smile. She quite liked Miss Bentley, and in some ways it was nice to be back at school and see all her pals. But she felt cut off from them now. She couldn't ever tell them what went on at home. But she also felt rather superior to them all. After all, she'd been working the cut all last week, learning all that she'd learned about real life while they were still all sitting here in rows! But now she had joined them again and was back in her school frock looking round at the tiled walls with pictures hanging on them, and at all the other girls round her, there was a poignancy about those few days. Many of the children had been at school together since they were infants and by the end of this week quite a number of them would be signed off from education for ever, into the adult world of work. Some of them were talking about what jobs they were going to.

But I, Maryann thought, will be off: gone for good. She wanted to tell them, but thought they'd laugh. Children off the cut were the butt of jokes because they couldn't read or write and were regarded as dirty and ignorant. So she wasn't going to say anything. This was her secret. Only a few days now and she'd be away . . .

But on the last Thursday something happened which

she could not have foreseen. They were at home after school when someone hammered on the front door.

'Go and see who's making that racket, Maryann!' Flo shouted from upstairs.

Nancy was on the doorstep, still in her school dress. She looked astonished to see Maryann.

'Well, where've you been?' she demanded, panting. 'Your mom said you'd gone off!'

'Never mind that,' Maryann interrupted. She wasn't going to say anything, not even to Nance. 'I just went away for a bit, that's all. What's up with you, nearly banging the door down?'

'It's Charlie . . .'

'What's all this?' Flo appeared downstairs.

'Mom sent me. Our Charlie – 'e's come 'ome – just now.'

Maryann and Flo both started talking at once. 'Where's Sal then? Where's 'e been?'

Nancy was shaking her head. ''E won't say.'

'Won't say! Well, bugger that. Billy – get in 'ere! We're going out.' Flo was already heading for the door. 'I'll soon get it out of 'im!'

Hoiking Billy by the arm, she marched off down Anderson Street like the wrath of God, with Maryann and Nancy following. When they reached the old yard in Garrett Street it was full of the Black youngsters who'd obviously been sent out of the house. When Flo marched in without a by-your-leave, only Charlie was in, with Cathleen and Lizzie.

'So – where is she then?'

Charlie was in the chair by the grate, hunched forwards, arms resting on his thighs. He clearly hadn't had a haircut during the weeks he'd been away and he looked haggard and very tired. Seeing Flo, he seemed to shrink further into himself.

'I said where is she? Where's our Sal?' Flo stood by the table, grasping the back of a chair so tightly her knuckles whitened. Maryann and Nancy stayed watching by the door. Maryann couldn't take her eyes off Charlie. In just a month he seemed different. Older, and dulled. Cathleen, standing with Lizzie on one arm, looked agitated.

''E won't say,' she told Flo. 'I can't get out of 'im where they've been or what's been going on.' She advanced on her son. 'You'd better tell Flo where Sal is, Charlie my lad. You've caused nothing but trouble and worry – there's her on my back and we'll 'ave Father Maguire round again and you just sitting there – you're a disgrace, Charlie.' She was shrieking. 'You tell us where she is – now!'

''Er doesn't want yer to know,' Charlie said to the floor.

Cathleen and Flo exchanged looks of utter exasperation. Flo went to Charlie and poked at his shoulder with her finger. 'Well, why don't she? Eh? What's up with 'er? Why ain't she come with yer?'

Charlie shrugged. 'I wanted to come back 'ome and she daint, that's all.'

'Yer needn't think I ain't asked him all this before you come in,' Cathleen said. 'It's like talking to a block of wood. Will I get Father Maguire round 'ere now, eh? Will that get yer to open yer mouth?'

Flo's expression darkened further and she leaned even closer to Charlie. 'What's to hide, eh? What's ailing 'er? Have you got 'er in the family way and now she can't come back and face us? Is that it? You'd better start talking, Charlie, 'cause I ain't going away till yer do. Why d'yer just take off and leave 'er, eh?'

Charlie stood up with a fierce movement and slammed his hands flat on the table. 'Because 'er ain't right in the head, that's why.' He lifted a finger to his temple and swivelled it round. 'I don't know what's up with 'er – 'er never used to be like it. It got so's I never knew what was going to happen next with 'er, and I weren't sticking around no more to find out!'

'What d'yer mean, Sal ain't right in the head? What's 'e done to 'er?' Flo yelled at Cathleen Black. 'There weren't nothing wrong with 'er when she left.'

'You sure about that?' Cathleen said.

'What do you mean?' Flo snarled at her.

'Sal ain't been 'erself for a good long while. You only 'ad to look at the girl.'

Flo drew herself up, ablaze with defensive indignation. 'There ain't nothing wrong with my wench – or there weren't till she got in with that lout of a son of yours. What's 'e done to 'er?'

Maryann and Nancy jumped out of the way as Charlie seemed set to slam out of the house. But Flo was too quick for him. She nipped round and barred his way.

'Where d'yer think you're going, you no good little bastard? You needn't think yer can just run off. You're not leaving and neither am I. You're gunna tell me if I 'ave to beat it out of yer!'

He pushed his way to the door. 'Oh awright. Yer welcome to 'er, the silly cow.' He gave them an address in the Jewellery Quarter.

*

190

Maryann sat nervously on the tram over to Hockley, beside Flo, who had Billy on her lap. She was desperate to see Sal. Now she knew they would see her she realized just how much she'd missed her sister and was full of worry on her behalf after what Charlie said about her. *She*'d known Sal wasn't herself, and now she knew exactly why. She would have given anything to put the clock back, to feel young and innocent herself, not living in terror of what her stepfather would do next. And to have Sal back as she was – her bossy big sister, who had been full of herself and her budding young womanhood. She felt like crying at the thought of it.

'Mom – don't be too angry with 'er, will yer?' she begged.

Flo seemed thoughtful. She looked round at her. 'We might be able to talk some sense into her between the pair of us. Not that you've got much yourself. I don't know what's come over this family, that I don't. Where *did* you take off to last week?'

She kept asking this every so often. This time, though, she didn't sound angry. Her voice was soft, persuasive. 'I ain't going to keep on at yer, Maryann. I want to get this sorted out. First Sal, then you. I want to know where a girl your age goes off to if she ain't with 'er pals or 'er sister.'

Maryann almost yielded to the concerned tone in her mother's voice. What a relief it would be to be able to talk about all the confused and turbulent feelings inside her. To tell her properly about Norman without it turning into a shouting match, for her to make it stop, and about Joel and how he was like family to her, like a big, loving brother, and about working the cut.

To be able to stop having these burdensome secrets. She looked into her mother's pale eyes. She came so very close to pouring it all out. But then she remembered the last time she had tried.

'I *am* your mom,' Flo was saying. 'I was worried about yer. And Norman was. I said to him, there's summat wrong with both my daughters taking off at once. Is there summat the matter, Maryann?'

I've told you! a voice seemed to scream in Maryann's head. *I've told you and you wouldn't listen. You wouldn't believe me.*

'No, Mom.' She turned away. What was the point in trying? 'I was just . . . with some pals.'

'But who?'

'Just pals, that's all.'

'Well, next time yer decide to go gallivanting off,' she sounded indignant now, 'don't go bloody doing it without telling us. Anyway' – she shifted Billy on her lap – 'you'll be working for Norman soon, so we won't be having any of that. D'you 'ear?'

Maryann didn't reply. She stared out of the window at the streets outside.

They found Sal's lodgings in a street off Constitution Hill: a terrace with an attic. The landlady, a sharp-faced individual, looked at them suspiciously.

'I've come to see my daughter,' Flo said, pushing Billy in front of her as if he was a certificate proving her motherhood.

''Er ain't 'ere,' the woman said. ''Er's at work.'

'Well, we'll wait then,' Flo said haughtily. 'We've come a distance and I ain't stopping out on the street.'

The woman hesitated, then shrugged as if she

couldn't be bothered to argue. 'You'll 'ave to wait up in 'er room,' she said in a snooty voice. 'I'm expecting company down 'ere.'

They all climbed up to Sal's room. The first flight of stairs was covered by a threadbare runner of grubby carpet, its original colour impossible to tell. The attic stairs were bare and their feet made a racket as they went up. The room at the top was a good size, but the boards were rough and stained and the distemper on the walls was in a terrible state, flaking off and discoloured. Cobwebs hung in the corners, and the ceiling near the front end of the house was bulging with damp, right over the head of the bed. The bed was three-quarter size, and against the opposite wall stood a rickety table and chair. There was a small grate, full of dust, with no sign of a fire in it. One of Sal's dresses was hanging on a hook behind the door, her nightdress was on the pillow, and there were a few of her belongings in the room: a pair of shoes, a cup and a bar of soap on the table, a candle stuck on a grubby white saucer and, beside it, hair pins and two little pots. Maryann opened them and looked inside. One contained rouge, the other face powder.

'Well, this is a cheerless bleeding 'ole,' Flo said, peering out through the filthy, curtainless window at the houses opposite. She seemed sobered by the sight of it. 'What the 'ell does she want to stop 'ere for?'

Maryann sat on the bed in the chilly room and made Billy sit beside her. There was one threadbare blanket folded on the mattress. The idea of Sal here on her own made her want to cry. She tried to imagine Sal coming here with Charlie. They must've told the landlady they were married though, heaven knew, they looked too young.

It wasn't long before they heard voices down below, then feet on the stairs. Maryann braced herself for seeing Sal. Flo turned, standing with her back to the window, silhouetted in its meagre light, and sharply shushing Billy who'd got up and started clattering about on the bare boards.

The landlady had told her they were waiting there so Sal was prepared. She flung the door open and stood looking brazenly across at her mother. Maryann gasped. She might have walked past Sal in the street and not recognized her! She'd put her hair up like a grown-up lady's, all piled and pinned round her head, and she was all made up lipstick, the lot. There was something else queer about her face. Maryann saw that Sal had plucked out all her fair eyebrows and painted them in instead, with dark, thin lines. She looked ten years older than she really was.

Flo fixed her with a stare which took in all of Sal's altered appearance, and her mouth twisted with distaste. At last, in a bitter voice, she said, 'Well – I hope yer proud of yourself. You look like a proper tart in all that warpaint.'

Sal stayed in the doorway, as if ready to run. 'I ain't coming back if that's what yer 'ere for.'

'Look, Sal—' Flo moved towards her, realizing she'd started off on the wrong foot. 'I only wanted to see yer – see 'ow you are. After all, yer just took off, never a word or a thought for the rest of us. We've all been ever so worried about you. Look – if there's any trouble we'll get it sorted out, but you can't just stay 'ere on your own. You're only young, running off with that no-good Charlie Black . . .'

''E's a darn sight better than some I could mention,' Sal spat at her. 'Don't you come 'ere lecturing me,

194

mother. I ain't coming home whatever you say. I've got a job and I can look after myself.'

'But Charlie's left you!' Flo had been trying to be appeasing, to control her temper, but it all came spilling out again. ''E 'ad more sense than to stick around 'ere in this dump. What the 'ell's got into yer, taking off and going about looking like a trollop! You'll be in trouble soon, my girl, that you will, if you go about looking like that.'

'Charlie Black ain't the only fish in the sea,' Sal retorted smugly. 'I don't notice no shortage around 'ere. And you're a fine one to lecture me – you're no more than a slut yourself, taking up with Norman for 'is money.'

Flo whipped her hand out to slap Sal's face, but she stepped back out of the way.

'Don't, Mom!' Maryann cried. There were tears running down her face. 'Don't hurt her! 'Er'll never come 'ome if yer treat 'er like that.'

'That's awright with me!' Flo blazed back. 'You can stay 'ere and rot, you ungrateful little bitch. If you can keep yerself then all the better for the rest of us. But don't come whining round me when yer in the family way and thrown out on the streets! I've warned yer, and I wash my hands of you. Come on, Maryann, Billy – leave 'er. She don't want 'er family.'

'No—' Maryann sobbed. 'I want to stay. You go on home.'

Flo stopped by the door. 'If that's what you want.' She looked hard at Sal. 'You used to be a good girl – you were the easy one. I don't know what's got into yer, that I don't. I've done my best – whatever 'appens now, you can't blame me for it.'

They heard her clomp noisily away down the stairs with Billy, leaving the sisters alone.

'Oh Sal,' Maryann cried. 'Are you awright? I know why yer don't want to come 'ome, but . . .'

'What do you know?' Sal snapped.

'About . . . about . . . you know, *him*, what 'e done to yer.'

'Don't talk about him!' Sal came over and got her by the shoulders. 'I don't want to talk about him. I've got away from him and I'm making my own life now – and you've got to do the same, Maryann. Don't work for 'im – don't let 'im near yer. Don't let 'im get you in that cellar down there . . .' She sank down suddenly and Maryann thought for a second that she was choking, her chest heaving, but she was crying, gasping. Maryann was about to embrace her when she stood up and began banging her head against the wall, hard, sobbing and crying.

'Sal! Sal, don't!'

Maryann pulled her away, trying to take her in her arms. Sal tore away. 'Don't touch me!'

'Sal – what's the matter with yer? I know what's 'e's done, what e's like, but why're yer doing that to yourself?'

Sal stepped back and collapsed limply on to the bed. She stared ahead of her so strangely that Maryann was even more frightened. At last she whispered, 'Maryann – don't leave me. I don't know what else to do.'

Sal broke down and cried and cried, at last allowing Maryann to put her arms round her and hold her tight.

'I'm losing my mind,' she sobbed. 'Oh Maryann, I don't know what's happening to me – I keep thinking such terrible things I'm frightened to be 'ere alone. It's not so bad when I'm out at work, but when I get back 'ere . . .'

'Can't yer come home?' Maryann pleaded. 'You don't 'ave to work for Norman no more . . .'

'No!' Sal clutched at Maryann's wrist so hard her fingers were digging in. 'I'm never going back there. Never! I'm never going anywhere near 'im again – you don't know what 'e can be like, Maryann. You've got to get out too . . .'

'I will, Sal – I was going to. But I can't leave you – not like this!' She could hardly bear to look at Sal. She used to be so pretty and now, with that paint on her eyebrows, she looked cheap and horrible. 'Why did yer go and do that to yourself?' she asked.

Sal shrugged, not replying.

'Oh Sal!' She put her arms round her sister again and held her close. She wanted to say, let's go somewhere together, just you and me. Somewhere where they can't find us and we can start again. But she didn't want to live in some slum with Sal. She wanted to be out on the cut with Joel, with Bessie plodding alongside. It wrung her heart to see Sal in this state, but it also frightened her. Sal was supposed to be her big sister, but now she was different, not the same Sal. How could she live with her in this state?

'Look, Sal – I'll 'ave to get 'ome. But I'll come and see you tomorrow – and every day I can now I know where you are, awright? And Tony and Billy can come an' all. And Mom – I'll talk 'er round . . .'

Sal's eyes widened. 'Not him! Oh God, Maryann – what if she tells 'im where I am! What if 'e comes 'ere? What if 'e starts following me about?'

''E won't,' Maryann tried to assure her. 'Course 'e won't. You can tell the landlady not to let 'im in. Anyhow – he thinks he's got me now.'

Maryann stayed on until it was almost dark and then

197

she made her way home in a turmoil of emotions. This was the afternoon she had been going to leave a message for the *Esther Jane* when she came back through some time in the next few days. But how could she leave now with Sal like this? She'd felt badly enough about leaving because of Tony and Billy when she thought at least Sal was happy with Charlie. But now she was the oldest one at home: she couldn't just desert them all.

Twenty-Two

On Sunday she left a written message for Joel, hoping one of the toll workers would read it for him. 'I can't come yet because I've got to look after my sister but I'll be back again soon. Love Maryann Nelson.'

She started work for Norman on the Monday, promising herself that if it was too bad she'd go somewhere else. She didn't want to cause a family row. Flo was in a good mood, and she watched with approval as the two of them set out together.

Maryann walked beside him along Monument Road. He wore his hat and top coat although it was high summer. He had a rolling, stately walk, said good morning to people with a gentlemanly lifting of his hat and was always greeted with respect: a pillar of the community walking out with one of his stepdaughters. The shops were opening up, awnings rattling open over the pavement, cars, carts and bicycles weaving along the busy street at the heart of Ladywood. They passed all the shops with their smells: cooked meat from the butcher's, strawberries outside the greengrocer's, bread from the bakery, then the Palais de Danse on the corner. At last they reached Griffin's, with its shrouded frontage and sober gold lettering, and Norman pulled out his bunch of keys and opened up.

Inside, he pulled up the little blind that covered the

glass in the door, turned the sign round, and Griffin's was open for business.

'Right then,' Norman said, hanging up his coat. 'You sit down at the desk. You're a quick-witted young thing – you'll soon pick it up.'

Maryann did as she was told, looking at the ledgers, cards, pens and blotter. She kept eyeing the door of the shop. If only Fred, the lad who made the coffins, would come in so that she wasn't alone with Norman.

'I'll come and show you what you need to know.' Norman walked round behind the desk and her skin felt suddenly as if it had been scrubbed with sandpaper. He leaned over at one side of her and his smell of sweat and smoke seemed to envelope her. She found herself breathing through her mouth so as not to smell him.

'This is a quiet time of year compared with the winter, but then of course you're going to have people coming to their natural end any time of year,' he said whimsically. 'When someone comes in, the golden rule is you treat 'em with courtesy and respect. Our job is to be invisible. If you do it well they don't remember much about you, but set a foot wrong and you're out of business. No laughing or joking in the presence of the bereaved, *ever* . . .'

Maryann nodded, listening as Norman outlined procedures concerning dates for interments, churches, death cards, hearses and coffins. All the while she was on edge because she thought he might touch her like he did when they were alone at home, pawing at her breasts or trying to pull her against him. But he made no attempt at this. This was work. Gradually she began to relax. And after a few minutes Fred arrived, crashing in through the front and saying 'Mornin', Mr Griffin!'

in his clogged, adenoidal voice. At last, she wasn't alone!

Later, Norman went out and Maryann was left sitting expectantly in the chair which Sal had occupied all those months. Norman had told her she was responsible for keeping the shop clean but it already looked immaculate and the desk was tidy. She was soon bored. She could hear Fred sawing away at some wood in the cellar.

'Don't let 'im get yer down in that cellar...' Sal's words came to her. What had she meant? Was that where Norman had always forced his vileness on her? Or was it more than that?

Maryann tiptoed to the top of the stairs and looked down. She could scarcely see the bottom of the staircase, it was so gloomy down there and the sight of the place brought her up in goose pimples. That was where they took the dead bodies. Surely he hadn't been down there with Sal when there were dead bodies ... It was too horrible to imagine. Looking down there, she thought, *I can't stand being here*. She'd have to bring Flo's and Norman's anger down on her head and say she wouldn't work for him ...

She climbed down, jumping as the treads creaked, but Fred was making such a noise he couldn't have heard her, and she wasn't bothered about him. Maybe, she thought suddenly, if she could make friends with Fred, it wouldn't be so bad working here. She could get him to stay on until she went home each day, so she wasn't left alone with Norman ... Sal had described Fred as being 'as thick as horse shite' but Maryann was hoping she'd been exaggerating.

Peering round the door, she saw into the poorly lit

cellar. The door to the chapel of rest was closed. In the far corner she saw the cupboard, almost like a smaller room built into the cellar, with brick walls, about six foot by four, extending halfway along the far wall. The long bench on which Fred was working was at the front end under the grating.

Fred was a pale boy of eighteen, with a gaunt face and prominent lips, his eyes set far apart, and thin brown hair.

'Hello!' Maryann called out.

He looked up, bewildered, and stopped sawing so abruptly that the quiet was startling.

'I'm Maryann. Sal's sister.'

'Oh . . . ar – I saw yer. Upstairs.'

He stared at her. Maryann, with a sinking heart, began to see that Sal's assessment of Fred might have erred on the side of generosity. He stood watching her as she explored the cellar, walking over first to see what he was doing. He had sawdust all over his boots. She liked the smell of the bruised wood. She went to the cupboard and tried the door, which was locked.

'What's in 'ere?'

'That's Mr Griffin's cupboard.' He didn't leave the workbench, just turned to watch her.

'Yes. So what's inside?'

He shrugged. 'I dunno. Chemicals and suchlike for that em . . . emb . . .'

'Embalming?'

'Ar – that's it. 'E don't let anyone go in.'

''Ve you been in there?' Maryann grinned conspiratorially.

'No!' Fred looked alarmed. 'I don't want the sack – I'd never go in there! No call to.'

'It's awright, don't get all worked up. I was only asking.'

She tried the door once more. Sal knew what was in there. There was something down here that had frightened her badly. Something that had seemed to make her lose her will.

'I'll leave at half past five when Fred goes, shall I?'

Maryann was watching the clock, both out of boredom and anxiety. Norman had come back at dinner time and Maryann told him she'd had one woman in who needed to bury her mother. Maryann had felt sorry for her, had taken down her details and thought she'd handled it all right. The woman had been calm and unemotional. Norman had been in all afternoon as various people came and went, and all the time he had on his sombre, upright citizen face. But when she asked him about leaving he turned, scowling. 'You'll leave when I tell you and not before. Now get this floor swept – there's dust and bits all over it.'

Maryann obeyed, sweeping the brown linoleum of the dirt Norman seemed to imagine he could see there. She worked slowly, still glancing continually at the clock. Whatever happened she was going as soon as she could. She had to get over and see Sal. And she could sense a change in Norman as time wore on. He was at the desk, thumbing through the ledgers, not looking up at her, but all the time she could hear his breathing. As she swept beneath the chair the pace of his breaths increased a fraction. She had heard it before, when he made her put her hand in his pocket, and when he touched her. It was the barometer of his excitement.

203

Her own heart beat faster with dread and she was all nerves. Any second she expected him to reach out and grab her. She couldn't do this. Not stay and work here. Until now she had held on to herself, kept her mind aloof from it: although he'd done things to her that sickened and disgusted her, she still had her spirit. But she could not endure more of it. It wasn't going to work. She knew that much more of it and she would lose herself, like Sal, and wither away inside. As she turned, pushing the few bits of dust and fluff away with her broom, Norman's hand fastened on her thigh, pushing her skirt between her legs and she jumped, letting out a little scream and moving quickly away.

He stood up, cleared his throat and crossed the room to the stairs.

'Time Fred was off.' She saw his wide shoulders disappear through the door, heard him going downstairs.

Oh Lord, Maryann thought, *why did I come here?* Why hadn't she just stood up to them and said she wouldn't work for him? She looked wildly round the room. It was five and twenty minutes past five. She left the broom against the wall, grabbed her hat and cardigan and ran to the door, cursing the loud, tinkling bell, and fled out on to the street.

He arrived home soon after her, not taking the trouble to conceal his fury.

'What d'yer think yer doing running off before I tell yer to go? Eh?'

He became aware that Flo was watching from the kitchen door. She could see a sheen of sweat on his pale, freckly face. 'Don't you *ever* do that again,' he snarled. 'D'you hear?'

Maryann kept her gaze turned down to the floor so he should not see the defiance in her eyes.

'No, Mr Griffin. I certainly won't.'

She hurried over to Hockley that evening, but the landlady said Sal wasn't in.

'Can I wait for a bit?' Maryann asked. 'I don't s'pose she'll be much longer.'

'I shouldn't bet on it.' The woman was even less friendly than last time and sounded very disapproving. 'To tell yer the truth I'm thinking of looking for a new lodger. That feller who came with 'er weren't 'er 'usband at all, was 'e?'

Maryann didn't answer. She felt an ugly blush creep up her cheeks.

'Thought not,' the landlady said, sounding self-satisfied. She stood back, folding her arms. 'Go on up then.'

Maryann sat in Sal's dismal room, picking at the loose threads in her frock and reduced to twiddling her thumbs, until it was almost dark outside. She got up from time to time and stood on tiptoes to look out of the window, though she could not see the street properly from up here. Gradually the night came on, lamps were lit outside, and still her sister didn't come. Maryann grew more and more anxious. Where had Sal got to? Her landlady would never put up with her if she carried on like this.

Eventually she had to give up and go home, and by the time she got there Flo had already gone to bed.

Maryann realized her mistake as soon as she walked in through the front door and found herself looking into Norman's eyes as he sat waiting by the fire.

'I'm going to bed,' she said, hurrying across the room.

'Oh no – not yet.'

He sprang out of his chair and grabbed her just as she reached the door to the stairs. He clamped his hand over her mouth.

'Thought you'd avoid me today, then, did yer? I'm not 'aving that.' He ran his hands over her chest. His eyes were terrible; cold, full of hatred. 'You're turning into quite a young lady nowadays, aren't yer, eh? And I'm going to make the most of it while yer still a child. Yer no good to me once yer've got yer monthly . . .'

Maryann tried to speak, shaking her head and making a strangled noise.

'What's that?'

'I 'ave – come on. Just last week,' she babbled as he released her. She yanked herself away from him. 'You touch me again and I'll scream. I'll get my mom down 'ere and then she might believe what an evil, filthy bastard you are.' She had her hand on the door to the stairs. 'You're never touching me again.'

Norman lunged at her and Maryann opened her mouth and managed to force out a scream.

'Shut it!' He was ablaze with fury and frustrated lust. 'Shut up that racket, yer little bitch.'

He went to put his hand back over her mouth but she yanked the door open and screamed again. There came the sound of a door opening upstairs.

'Norman?' Flo Griffin's voice was full of sleep. 'What's the noise? What's going on?'

Maryann fled up the stairs, not meeting her mother's eye.

'Nothing, love – just Maryann being silly. Now she's gone and woken yer.'

'I'm not working for you no more.'

He was eating breakfast. She stood by the table, in front of all the family.

'What're you talking about?' Flo turned on her at once. 'You've only been there one day!'

'I ain't staying.' She screwed up every ounce of self-possession and courage and looked into Norman's eyes. *I'm not scared of you*, her expression said. She was, she was terrified, her hands were shaking, but she pressed them together. She wasn't going to let him see. 'I'm going to look for another job today.'

'How *dare* you talk like that!' Flo erupted. But Norman raised a hand to silence her.

'I can't say I'm not disappointed in yer, Maryann. It'll cause me a lot of trouble 'aving to get someone else. But if yer not happy – I know some people don't take to working with the dead. I don't want anyone saying I'm not a reasonable man. And if you go in one of the factories you should get a decent wage.'

'But, Norman!' Flo protested. 'You're surely not just going to let 'er get away with this, the little minx?'

'It's awright, Flo. 'Er's more hot-headed than our Sal. Let 'er go 'er own way. As long as you work out the rest of the week, Maryann, that's all I ask.'

'There,' Flo cried. 'See 'ow nice yer father's being after all the trouble you've caused!'

There was a long silence. Maryann felt Tony's eyes

on her face. She looked away across at the range where the kettle was starting to boil.

She spoke quietly. 'I'm finishing today.'

'You'll work the week out.' She couldn't look at him any more, couldn't face the cold hatred in his eyes. She knew that beneath the calm exterior, Norman Griffin was seething with rage at being thwarted.

'No,' she said. 'Today.'

She found a job at a jam factory, where she had to be in as the hooter went at ten to eight. Another went off at eight and work began. The girls all wore clogs, which were hard and blistered her feet. Fruit and sugar were brought on carts and the jam stirred in huge vats, its smell sweet and cloying. Maryann was in the labelling department, not an arduous job, but even if it had been, anything would have been better than working with Norman Griffin. She had some laughs with the other girls, biding her time. This wasn't where she was going to be for ever. As soon as Sal got herself sorted out a bit she'd be off. She spent as little time as she could at home and at night she took to ramming her bed close up against the door so it couldn't open. She wasn't going to let him get at her, never again. When she heard him come up to bed the first time, and push at her door, she lay seething with hatred of him and fierce satisfaction.

That's stopped your game, she thought.

As the summer passed and turned into autumn, she knew Norman, too, was biding his time. But she was at work all day, and she managed carefully to avoid being

alone with him at any time. Her main worry was Sal.
She couldn't keep going over every day, especially as
Sal often wasn't there. She did try and go at least once
a week. But after that time of closeness when Sal had
cried in her arms and admitted how wretched she felt,
she never let Maryann see her true state of mind again.

Twice when Maryann went in August, Sal came
home late and clearly the worse for drink.

'What the hell's kept yer?' Maryann raged at her the
first time, as Sal came staggering in after dark. She'd
been waiting ages, cursing Sal, worrying about her.
She felt as if things had reversed and she was the older
sister now, having to keep an eye on Sal all the time.
'You're in a disgusting state. You're going to have to
pull yourself together or you'll get thrown out – she's
already said she don't like the way you carry on.'

Sal lurched over to the bed. Her cheeks were grimy
with sweat and face powder, she was dishevelled, hair
all in a mess and she stank of drink.

'I'm in a disgusting state!' she repeated. She rocked
back and forth as if thinking about this, then started
laughing, a drunken, foolish laugh that made Maryann
feel like slapping her. Instead she stood over her and
shook her by the shoulders.

'Who've yer been with? Who is it's buying yer all
this booze?'

'Oh, mind your own bloody business,' Sal sneered.
Her face was grotesque in the candlelight, with its
pencilled-in eyebrows. 'I've got my own pals now, ta
very much. I've got my big strong friend Bill, looks
after me. Oh yes 'e does – 'e's a big'un now, 'e is . . .'

'You're horrible—' Maryann pushed her away.
'You're nearly as bad as Norman. Look at yourself, Sal.
What's going to become of you?' She went to the door.

'I'm not staying with you like this. There ain't no point in talking to you.'

'If you don't want Norman on you,' Sal called after her, 'just tell 'im you've come on.'

'I did,' Maryann snapped back at her. 'I ain't stupid and nor's he. He daint believe me. Don't you worry about me – not that you were. I've got my own way of dealing with him.'

A week later Sal was caught trying to smuggle a man up to her room and the landlady threw her out. She moved to another grim attic in a nearby street.

Maryann felt desperate about her. She tried to talk to Flo about Sal again, but all Flo said was, 'What can I do about 'er? 'Er's the one walked out on us. If 'er's going to the bad there ain't nothing I can do about it. I washed my hands of 'er. Sal can go to hell 'er own way, that's my way of looking at it.'

Sal was the only thing keeping Maryann at home now. And she was dangerously close to giving up on Sal herself.

Twenty-Three

Another month had passed. It was October, the nights drawing in, leaves in the gutters and foggy mornings. Maryann had been loyally visiting Sal so far as she could manage it. Sometimes Sal was in when she got there; more often she wasn't, and Maryann was fed up with waiting, anxious and hungry, in those dismal lodgings for her to come back. She kept thinking one day Sal would walk in and be the sister she had been before, bossy and hoity-toity, but kind and good for a laugh. But when she did come back, Sal was often rude and offhand.

Maryann had confided about it to Nancy only the previous weekend, she had felt so heavy-hearted. The two of them sat at the table in the Blacks' downstairs room, sipping lemon pop out of jam jars. Her mom and her dad were out and Nance was holding Lizzie on her lap and minding some of the younger ones who were running in and out. Nance hadn't got her dream job at Kunzle's and was working in a laundry, but she seemed cheerful enough about it.

'Last time I went to see 'er,' Maryann complained, 'she come in – in the end – and says to me, "What're *you* doing 'ere?" As if I was vermin or summat. She's drinking ever such a lot, Nance. And the other night I was sat there and I 'eard 'er come in. There was giggling and shushing on the stairs – I could tell there was someone else with 'er. In they come – 'er and this bloke.

Oh Nance, I swear to God 'e was the 'orriblest looking man I've ever seen, broken nose, the lot, and 'e was ever so much older than 'er.

'"Who's this then?" 'e says, swaggering about like one of them cowboys. Sal 'ad to shut 'im up talking so loud 'cause 'e weren't meant to be there. "That's just my baby sister," she says. "And 'er's just leaving, ain't yer, Maryann?" She was all nasty and superior – didn't care about me at all and that I'd been there waiting for 'er.'

'Ooh,' Nance said. She was biting at the nails of her right hand, which already looked red and work-worn. 'Fancy your Sal carrying on like that. I mean our Charlie would've married 'er, you know, when they was old enough, if things'd've been different. He was ever so sweet on 'er. And when yer think what 'er used to be like!'

'I was that upset – well, I was furious with 'er! But I could see they'd 'ad a few and I wasn't going to start a shouting match or I'd've got 'er thrown out again. But, oh Nance, it made me feel so bad seeing 'er with that great *ape* of a bloke . . .'

'So what did yer do?'

'I went 'ome and left 'em to it.'

Nance shook her head in a way that reminded Maryann of Cathleen. 'What's up with 'er then? I mean there's you and 'er – had everything the same and there's 'er going right off the rails.'

Maryann quickly looked down. She couldn't tell Nance. Blackie Black may have been a broken man and a drunk but he didn't do those things, did he? Not like Norman Griffin, who had shut them off from everyone, alone with their sense of disgust.

*

She'd delayed going back to Sal's place in Hockley, putting it off after the way Sal had treated her. Why should I keep running after her if that's how she goes on? Maryann thought, I'd be on the *Esther Jane* with Joel if it wasn't for her. She dreaded going, wondering who she might find Sal with. She knew deep down that this wasn't the real Sal, that her sister was broken and desperate inside, and it wrung her heart to see her behaving the way she was and not know what to do about it.

That day, after work, she forced herself to go. When she got off the tram her heart started pounding and her legs turned shaky with misgiving.

Don't be so daft, she told herself. Sal won't even be in yet – not this time of day.

When she reached the house, the front door was half open. The usual fusty smells greeted her. She walked straight in and tiptoed up the stairs, holding her breath. When she reached the top, Maryann stood uncertainly outside. Should she knock? Just supposing Sal was in there with some man, she'd be livid with her and the last thing she wanted was to witness such a scene. Sal had never told her anything, not directly, but Maryann knew what Sal let those men do to her. She could see it in her sister's eyes, she had seen the lust on the ape bloke's face when he looked at Sal, drunken and lecherous.

But surely it was too early for that. She leaned close to the door. Not a sound. The door opened with a squeak. She could tell immediately that the room wasn't deserted after all. It had the feel of a person in it. It smelled stale. The bedclothes, such as they were, were pulled up over the hunched shape of a body lying face to the wall.

'Sal?' Maryann cried, alarmed. 'What's up? Are you bad?' She yanked the blanket down. Sal seemed to be in a very deep sleep. Maryann nudged at her, pulled her so that she flopped over on to her back and at last Sal managed to prise her eyes open.

'Sal! 'Ve you been lying there all day like this? What's up?'

Sal winced, laying an arm over her eyes to shut out the light.

'Ooh,' she groaned. 'My *head*! What time is it?'

''Bout half past five, or later. Ain't you been to work today?'

'Nah.' There was a silence, then, 'They let me go – Monday. Said I weren't no good to 'em.'

'They didn't! How're you going to get by? You bin out to find summat else?'

Sal pulled her arm away and attempted a smile, which emerged as a sly grimace. 'There's easier ways to earn money.'

'Sal . . .' Maryann stared at her. 'Yer don't mean . . .?'

'Oh, pack in carrying on at me, will yer? My 'ead's fit to split. Go down and see if yer can get a cuppa tea out of that skinflinty old cow down there, will yer? I gotta 'ave summat to ease it.'

'Awright,' Maryann agreed reluctantly. 'But I can't see 'er handing over a cuppa tea.'

She went down the dim kitchen at the back of the house where a hairy Scots terrier, as corpulent as its mistress, was lying by the range. Without bothering to shift itself, it started up a shrill barking as soon as Maryann appeared. The lady of the house was slumped in a greasy old armchair close by, everything about her seeming to be drawn inexorably down towards the floor: her sludge-coloured hair, cheeks, chins, sagging breasts. She was drinking out of a cup and there was a jug on the table. Maryann could tell from the smell that it was ale.

'Stop that yapping, will yer!' the woman bawled at the dog. Looking round she spotted Maryann. 'What're you doing barging in 'ere, eh? Made me bloody jump.'

'Can my sister 'ave a cuppa tea?' Maryann asked as politely as she could. 'Only she ain't feeling well today.'

The woman took a mouthful from her cup, which left froth on her top lip. 'Kettle ain't on,' she said, turning away indifferently. 'And it won't be neither.'

In the end, Maryann ran down the street to find a coffee house where she bought Sal a glass of tea and paid an extra penny to retrieve when she took the glass back. Sal was still lying staring at the ceiling. The light was going and the sight of her made Maryann feel so sad she almost started crying. Her emotion made her speak sharply.

'Come on – get this down yer, sis, and pull yerself together.'

Sal hauled herself, wincing, up to a sitting position and leaned forward, cradling her head in her hands. She still had her black dress on from the night before, rucked up round her waist.

'Oh God, Maryann, I feel that bad, I do.'

'Drink up,' Maryann said, more gently. 'It's getting cold. I got it down the road – there's plenty of sugar in it.'

'Ta.' But Sal still couldn't seem to move. Her blonde hair was loose and hanging lank round her face. Maryann pulled it back over her shoulders and held the cup to Sal's lips.

''Ere—' Her voice was tender now. ''Ave a sip, Sal.'

Sal leaned towards the glass and sipped. The sisters

sat quietly together as Sal managed to get almost half the tall glass of tea down her. Maryann stroked her back.

'You can't go on with all this boozing,' she said.

But Sal stopped drinking and began to whimper. 'I'm going to be sick, Maryann!'

Maryann rushed across the room, ducked under the table for an old yellowed newspaper that was lying there and opened it in Sal's lap just in time. A gush of tea and bile pooled in the newspaper. Sal retched miserably, and when she'd finished, Maryann folded the ends of the dripping paper into a bundle and dumped it by the door. Sal panted and then her gulping from being sick turned into gulping from her tears.

'You don't want to keep on like this, do yer?' Maryann said, wrapping her arms round her. 'Oh, sis, I hate to see you like this.'

Sal cried even more, shaking her head. 'I'm scared, Maryann. I'm so scared.'

'What're you scared of? You're just feeling poorly, that's all.' But Maryann was scared too. 'You need to get some food inside you and you'll feel better. Shall I go out and see if I can get yer a couple of cobs from somewhere?'

'No!' Sal shook her head, then groaned and pressed her hands to each side of it to still the pain. 'It ain't only that, Maryann. It's . . . I think I'm expecting.'

'Expecting?'

'A babby.'

Maryann drew back, gaping at her. The thought had never crossed her mind. 'Oh no – oh Sal! Whose babby?'

Sal wouldn't look at her. 'I don't know. God 'elp me, I don't even know.'

She just couldn't tell her mom when she got home, not out with it, cold like that. It didn't seem real to her. She only had the vaguest knowledge of the connection between what men and women did together and how babies came out of it. She knew her mom'd be livid and most likely go over there and give Sal a beating.

'Well, what's ailing 'er?' Flo was demanding, standing over Maryann as she tried to force down some of a mutton chop and congealed gravy.

Maryann looked up at her. 'I've never seen 'er so bad, Mom. She ain't 'erself, and she's poorly. Will yer go and see 'er? Be a bit nice to 'er, like?'

Flo put her hands to her waist in a defensive posture. 'I don't know why Sal can't get 'erself over 'ere to see us. I mean, I've got quite enough going on, what with Billy and the house...' She saw Maryann's face. 'Awright – I'll try and get over to see 'er some time. She don't deserve it though, everyone running at 'er beck and call, that she don't!'

Maryann knew she had to go over and see Sal the next day. Poor Sal would have been there all day on her own, with only her thoughts for company and hardly the strength or will to get herself any food to eat.

She changed into her shoes and left the factory at the end of her shift, absent-mindedly calling goodbyes to her workmates as they all streamed out to the street, eager to get home. The light was fading and the air, foggy and full of smoke, stung her nostrils.

The lamps were lit by the time she got to Sal's lodgings and the pubs were already doing a brisk trade. This time she had to knock and it seemed ages before she heard the woman shuffling along the hall to open the door. The landlady peered out, suspiciously.

'Ow, it's you. I ain't 'eard nothing out of 'er today.'

Well, that ain't any surprise, Maryann thought. When you've got your nose in a jug of ale all day long. She didn't say anything, just went on up the stairs.

'Sal?' She tapped the door and went in. To her surprise the room was dark, and she felt a sudden rush of hope. Maybe Sal had been mistaken, had just had a fancy that there was a babby on the way because she was poorly. Maybe today she was feeling better and had gone out. Even Sal's old habits seemed better at the moment than the plight of being in the family way.

Cautiously Maryann stepped across the dark room.

'Blimey, it's cold in 'ere today!' she muttered. It was bad enough normally, but this was worse than ever. She stepped closer to the dormer window and heard glass crunch under her feet. From the faint light from the street she saw that one of the panes was broken. 'No wonder Sal's gone out. I wonder 'ow that 'appened? P'raps a bird hit the window.'

She decided to wait, at least for a time. If Sal was all that long she'd go out and treat herself to some faggots and peas instead of buying them for Sal. She felt more cheerful. Maybe soon she'd be off on the *Esther Jane* after all! She felt her way to the table where Sal kept a candle and a box of matches. There was only a stub of candle left. Never mind, she thought, generous in her sense of relief. She'd go out and get her some, and other things she needed. Maryann lit the candle, which was stuck on the lid of a treacle tin, and took it closer to the window again to look, but the flame began to gutter in the draft so she turned away, treading carefully over the sharp slivers of glass.

And then she jumped so hard she almost dropped the candle. The light of the flame was caught, reflected in Sal's open eyes.

'Oh my God, Sal—' She could make out Sal's shape lying along the bed. 'Why didn't you say you was in?' Maryann pressed her hand over her heart. 'Flamin' 'ell. You nearly frightened the life out of me! Sal?'

She leaned closer and smelled it, the heavy, sickening stench of blood.

'Oh Sal . . . oh Christ no, Sal. What've yer done?'

It was everywhere. Holding the candle high, Maryann saw that most of the middle part of the mattress was dyed with it and it was dripping from Sal's left arm, which hung over the edge of the bed, to a black pool on the floor. Maryann seized her arm, memories rushing back to her of Sal, that day, sitting jabbing, cutting at her arm.

Maryann heard herself whimpering, making strange, unbidden sounds. She knew now what had happened to the glass in the window, knew it all. Howling, she threw herself down on her knees beside her sister's bed, regardless of the pool of blood, kissing her poor cold face, stroking her hair again and again, beside herself.

'Oh Sal, my Sal – why did yer do it? I'd've taken care of you – I would. Oh Sal, don't die, you're my sis. We can look after each other!'

But she knew it was over, that there was no point in running to any doctor for help. Sal must have lain for hours like this. Maryann knelt with her arms round her sister, holding and rocking her, rage and sorrow possessing her like no emotions she had ever felt before. Sal was released from her agony now. Her heart was not beating. But she had not killed herself: she had been murdered slowly, brutally, over these long months, and the person who had killed her was Norman Griffin.

Twenty-Four

The day they buried Sal was wet and cold. The carriages followed the hearse to Lodge Hill Cemetery, and the horses' hooves sounded louder in the damp weather, their warm breath swirling round them in the damp. They were decked out in black feathers and smartly polished harnesses.

It was an extravagant funeral, beyond anything they could normally have afforded.

'We'll make sure she has the best,' Norman had told Flo. 'We can't bring her back – Lord knows what possessed her – but we can give her a good send-off.'

'It's more than 'er deserves really,' Flo had sobbed. 'Taking 'er own life like that – it ain't right. But it's all we can do for her now.'

They stood at the graveside as rain fell all round them, pattering on the leaves banked up at the sides of gravestones, dripping off the brims of their hats and gathering in little pools on the lid of the coffin. The priest looked thinly clad and unwell, and the only sound apart from the rain and his voice nasally intoning the burial rite was that of Flo's weeping.

As the first handfuls of earth were thrown down on to the coffin, she burst into uncontrollable sobbing.

'My little girl,' she moaned into her handkerchief. 'My baby – oh my little baby . . .' Maryann saw Norman lay his hand on her shoulder for a moment to quiet her.

221

Tony was crying silently, his hand in Maryann's, and she squeezed it and kept Billy close to her. There were no tears in her eyes. She watched Norman across the yawning slit in the ground into which Sal had been lowered, fixing him with an unwavering, icy stare. As she stood watching him across the grave she knew she would not weep here, at the funeral he had provided. Never, in front of him. Not after what he'd done.

'. . . blessed are the dead which die in the Lord,' the vicar was saying, '. . . for they rest from their labours.'

Maryann raised her eyes past Norman at the skeletal trees behind him. The wind was blowing rain sideways across the graves. In a few moments it would be over, the final prayer was being said and then they would leave the gravediggers to finish shovelling in the earth. She looked back at the coffin once more in a final farewell.

I won't let him get away with it, Sal. I'll make him pay, that I will. But you rest now, sis. You rest.

Holding the boys' hands, she followed the others back across the cemetery to where the horses were waiting. She looked at Norman's back, long and tall in his black coat, and she knew with sudden certainty what she was going to do.

She lay beside Tony that night, waiting for him and the rest of the household to settle for the night.

Flo came up first, followed by Norman, and Maryann relaxed a little, breathing more easily. He wasn't waiting up the way he did when he was going to try and come to her room. Gradually it all settled down, the padding of feet, the wrench of bedsprings, then quiet at last. The rain seemed to have stopped now but it was still windy.

She had thought she was far too pent up to sleep, but some time later she found had been dozing and woke very suddenly and sat up, her heart hammering. It came flooding back to her: Sal was dead. She had to do it, to go tonight. Now. Getting out of bed with enormous care, she lit the candle and looked anxiously across at Tony – at his thin face, his straight, dark eyebrows, so relaxed as he slept – and for a moment all her resolve withered.

How can I just go away and leave him and Billy? she thought. But then she thought of Sal, of Joel and, fortified, put the candle down on the floor and crept round the bed to gather up her few things: her shoes, bits of clothes, and the little china cat which she laid lovingly on the pile.

When it was all ready she tiptoed round to Tony's side of the bed and kneeled down by him. I mustn't touch him, she thought, or I'll wake him and mess it all up.

'I've got to go away, Tony,' she whispered. 'I'm sorry to leave yer, that I am. I know I'm not much of a sister to you, but you've still got our mom and Billy and your pals. You look after our Billy now, eh?' Tears came into her eyes at the thought of the two of them, little blond Billy and dark-eyed Tony, hand in hand as if alone in the world without her.

'Only – I've got to go tonight, 'cause if I don't, I'm gunna be in trouble, Tony. I don't *want* to leave you, Tony, honest I don't. 'Ere—' She got up again and went over to her little pile of things, took out the china cat and brought it to him, laying it on his pillow, close

223

to his sleeping face. 'You 'ave little Tiger so yer know I'll be thinking of yer.' She couldn't quite bear to go without touching him, and she reached out and stroked her hand over his head. 'T'ra, Tony.' He didn't stir.

Taking deep breaths to calm herself, she lifted the chair away from the door and blew out the candle. Every sound she made seemed deafening. The door opened almost soundlessly, but when she went to cross the small landing, one of the boards gave a loud, unexpected crack. Maryann froze, panic-stricken. The house was full of boards like that, which might suddenly betray her!

All you've got to do, she told herself, is get into that room. He sleeps nearest the door, so you can just reach across . . .

Clenching her teeth over her bottom lip, she pushed the door of her mother and stepfather's room. To her amazement it swung open without a sound. She could hear Norman's breathing, a rasping sound which helped her get her bearings as she stepped through the door. She could tell where the head of the bed was all right, with him making that racket. She stepped behind the door and, holding on to the wall, slid along the gap between it and the bed until she got to the chair. As she reached out for it her mother sighed and shifted in the bed, and she froze again, waiting. But all was well. Her hand met the scratchy tweed of Norman's jacket which was flung over the back of the chair and she felt along it, searching for that pocket he pushed his hand into when he was walking along . . . The cold weight of the keys seemed to fall into her palm as if they had been waiting for her and she clenched her fingers tight to stop them jangling together.

'Got yer,' she mouthed in the darkness.

Moments later, shoes on and holding her belongings, keys in the pocket of her coat, she slid out through the front door.

The street was deserted but it was warmer than she expected, the sky busy with puffy clouds moving across a thin crescent moon. There was still lamplight to guide her, reflected in the puddles along the pavement.

She couldn't believe she'd managed it, that he wasn't behind, following her as she walked along to Monument Road. Even though hers were the only steps she could hear on the street, she kept turning to glance behind, expecting to see him. Pulling up her collar, she shrank down into her coat.

When she reached the door of the shop a cold feeling overcame her, a creeping sense of horror. She should forget this thing she had come for, the obligation she felt towards Sal, and just go, get right away from here for good. What was it Norman had said to Sal, or shown her, that afterwards, together with those dirty things he had made her do, had meant she was never free of him? She had steeled herself to do this and she couldn't just walk away.

'Don't let 'im get yer in that cellar . . .' Sal's warning rang in her mind. She took out the keys and as she did so, she noticed in the faint light that one of them seemed to be a darker colour than the others. As she examined them, a sound came from along the street. Quickly she unlocked the door and shut herself inside. She waited, but heard nothing further.

Norman kept matches for the lamps in one of the

225

desk drawers. Groping her way over to the desk she talked to herself in her mind, trying to fight her irrational terror of darkness.

Once she'd lit the lamp she started to feel a little better. The blinds were all down so no one could see in. The office looked exactly as she remembered: a small, bare, workaday place, much as it would have looked had she been left alone there on a winter's evening. Now she just had to go downstairs, she told herself. That was all. Just have a look. Pretend Fred was down there, hammering away . . .

She lit a candle to take with her and, keys in the other hand, climbed quickly down the yawning darkness of the stairs, knowing that if she hesitated she might seize up with panic and run back out into the road. She had to unlock the cellar door – she had not known Norman kept it locked at night – and, with a huge effort of will, she went inside. She knew she must check inside the chapel of rest to see if there was anyone laid out in there. If so, she would have to rethink what she was planning to do. It took her a few minutes to find the courage. First of all she lit the gas lamps in the cellar and though the light was reassuring, she was trembling so much she could scarcely manage to insert the key in the lock and open the door of the chapel of rest. Every fibre of her was poised ready to run away should there be the slightest sound or movement.

Gritting her teeth, she swung the door open suddenly and held the candle high in the doorway. The long table was empty, with just a sheet folded on it. She let out a long, relieved breath. Thank goodness!

The place suddenly felt much more normal and unthreatening. She noticed then, though, that it was unusually messy: the floor covered in rings of wood shaving, which gave off a sweet smell, sawdust and offcuts of wood all over the place, hammer, chisels and other tools left out on the bench. Norman was so obsessed with tidiness and precision and chivvied Fred to leave the cellar looking tidy. Getting ready for Sal's funeral had evidently been a rush.

She turned then to Norman's cupboard. 'Right, mister – let's see what yer got in 'ere . . .'

Holding up the bunch of keys, she eyed the keyhole of the metal door and saw instantly the one which must fit. The keyhole had been smeared with black paint. Her heart beating painfully hard, she inserted the black key into the lock.

''Ere goes . . .'

Peering inside, holding the candle out, she could see nothing very much to start with. Her eyes grew more used to the deeper darkness in there and she saw that running along each wall were two shelves, one above the other, neatly arranged with an assortment of objects. There was a sense of order and fussiness characteristic of Norman. On one side seemed to be stored old ledgers, and a musty odour of aged paper mingled with the chemical smells. On a low shelf lay what looked like old tools – hammer, chisel, fretsaw, awl – each rather rusty, laid out straight, one by one. On the higher shelf to the left were arranged dark glass bottles and jars and beside them, an assortment of books. Stepping inside she pulled one down. It had a soft leather cover and worn gold letters on the spine. *Whiteacres' Manual for the Practice of Embalming the Human Body.* Quickly she put it back, not wanting to look inside. Her toe kicked against something and she looked down to see a can of paraffin for the stove they used in the cellar on the coldest winter days. Maryann smiled grimly. *Good.*

Turning to look at the back of the cupboard, she saw to her surprise that in the small space at the back, right in the middle, was a chair. It looked like an ordinary kitchen chair. Maryann moved closer, frowning, holding the candle higher. It took a moment for her to make out any details, but when she did the very blood seemed to freeze throughout her body. Her free hand went to her mouth.

Details jumped out at her one after another in the flickering light. The chair was straight-backed, with two struts across the back and a flat wooden seat. Fastened round the uprights of the chair back were two iron brackets which were screwed into the wall. Resting on the seat was a carefully coiled length of chain, curled round itself like a Swiss roll and glinting in the candle-light. With it was a pair of manacles – another pair was positioned on the floor by the chair legs – and a second length of chain dangled from the back in a snakelike loop to the floor. Over the back of the chair, folded very neatly, was a square of white cloth, perhaps a scarf. Maryann took in the sight, unable to move, the implications of it sinking into her mind. Had he threatened to tie it round and round Sal's mouth? Had he actually done it? Left Sal chained and gagged here – for how long? What else had he done? Was this the threat that he had held over Sal, month after month, until he had invaded her with fear, emptying her of her very self?

The restraining cords with which Maryann had held back her emotions that week burst open. She strode out of the cupboard and put the candle on the workbench. Moving with increasing frenzy, she began to gather up the mess that was strewn on the floor: the sawdust and wood shavings, the ends of wood, the sheet from the chapel of rest. Anyone who had seen her just then might have said she'd lost her mind. Going to the cupboard, she pulled out the armful of ledgers, tearing at their pages and throwing them down, their remaining pages splayed, then the books on embalming the dead. She tore into the cupboard and yanked with all her strength at the chair, trying to wrench it apart, levering it against the hold of the iron brackets, but it was strong and she couldn't release it. In the end she brought the other chair from the cellar and added it to the pyre. Going back into the cupboard, she picked up the tin of paraffin and poured it over the mess. Finally she rested the candle, with almost reverential care, on its side in the middle of it all. She stood the tin carefully by the door.

Flames immediately began to work on the dry curls of wood with a tiny crackle. Maryann stood for a moment, arms tightly folded, watching it all begin to burn.

'Burn, burn!' she hissed, her eyes gleaming. 'You evil, murdering bastard, burn!'

She seemed to do everything automatically, laughing, crying, as she did so, looking round for more things to stoke the fire. There was too much brick down here, too many hard surfaces. But she hadn't started on upstairs yet . . .

The smoke was beginning to build up, the flames reaching up towards the chair. She'd have to get out of here, but she needed to drag the trestle table out from the chapel of rest to make sure it carried on burning, or on the stone floor it might go out. She was coughing now, the cellar filling with smoke.

'Burn, go on, burn!' she urged, laying the trestles on their side amid the flames.

She heard a sound that penetrated her concentration. A bang from upstairs.

Norman. She was paralysed. It must be – he was here. Had followed her!

She stood listening, trying not to cough, but it was impossible. The smoke was getting too much. But he mustn't get her down here! If she was to encounter Norman it must be upstairs, where she stood a chance.

Halfway up the stairs, she stopped and listened, taking in deep breaths. Nothing. Was he waiting, in that spot just by the door? She could see no shadow. The smoke was winding up the stairs with her and the coughing was impossible to control. Suddenly, unable to bear it, she tore up the stairs into the office, just as there came another *bang*! The front door slammed shut. The office was empty, but the door was not properly closed, had gusted open. Maryann found she was so unsteady with shaking that she had to sit down at the desk. For a few moments she put her hands over her face and wept, distraught.

'I've got to try and forget this.' She knew even then, without time to reflect. 'Or I'll lose my mind thinking of it. Sal's gone – I'll be gone. No more girls for 'im.' She stood up, fiercely wiping her eyes. 'And this place'll be gone. I'm gunna make sure of that.'

Trying to hold her breath for as long as she could, she felt her way down the dark cellar steps once more. At the bottom she could feel the heat through the door and she picked up the paraffin can and ran up again, asping frantically for breath as she reached the top. She splashed some paraffin over everything she could manage: ledgers, the padded seats of the chairs, the blinds over the windows, the contents of the desk drawers which she unlocked and took out. On opening the bottom one she paused, looking inside. In this, the deepest drawer, Norman kept his petty cash box. She quickly searched the bunch of keys for the little one which unlocked it. There it was. She tipped all the money into her pockets.

Striking match after match, she went round the room. The blinds were already ablaze as, picking up her things, she ran out into the street and tore away along Monument Road.

Twenty-Five

Running along the cobbles which gleamed wet in the gaslight, she headed instinctively towards Garrett Street and the old yard where she'd grown up, past all those childhood places, the Garrett Arms, dark entries into the back yards, the huckster's shop on the corner near her house: all so familiar, and yet tonight everything felt changed. Because she was changed. Nothing now could ever be the same again. She had to go now, to run away. She had no choice.

In the entry she slowed, treading softly. Though it was pitch dark she could remember every lump and bump in the bricks, the big hole three-quarters of the way down on the left where you could turn your ankle and break it. In a moment she was standing under the lamp in the yard, panting, but feeling suddenly much safer.

There was no hint of dawn, the houses black against the dark sky. She had no idea what the time was. She wondered whether she should wait out the rest of the night in the brewhouse along the yard where they kept the copper for washing clothes, but there was no telling who might come in and find her there first thing in the morning and there might be chickens and all sorts in there. No, she'd have to knock up the Blacks and get them to take her in until she could find Joel.

She knocked cautiously on their door. When she'd

paused and tried a second time the door opened and a tousled head and indignant face appeared. It was Alf Black, holding a candle. He and Charlie, now seventeen and eighteen, slept downstairs.

'It's me, Maryann,' she whispered, going up close to him. 'Don't make a racket, Alf, will you? I don't want no one to know I'm 'ere.'

'What's going on?' Alf demanded.

'Ssssh – for 'eaven's sakes. Can I come in?'

'Yer do know what time it is, don't yer?'

'No.'

'The middle of the fucking night, that's what.' All the same he stood back. 'Lucky I got up for a piss or I'd never've 'eard yer – and 'e'd never've neither.' Charlie was snoring on the old lumpy sofa. Maryann looked down at him with very mixed emotions. He must have lain beside Sal like that, handsome, his dark hair curling at the nape of his neck, long dark lashes. He had loved Sal, Charlie had, or so Nance said. If he hadn't gone off and left her, maybe she'd be alive ... Alf stood at a loss for a minute. 'I'll get Nance, shall I?'

Nancy appeared a few minutes later with a candle.

'Maryann? What's going on? Flamin' 'ell, you stink like Smoky Joe. What've yer been doing?'

'Can I stop 'ere for a bit?' Maryann heard her voice turning tearful. 'I don't want them to know where I am. I've done summat terrible, Nance.'

Nance eyed her brother. 'Come up and yer can bunk down with me. You go back to bed, Alf, and keep yer trap shut about this, awright?'

Nance shared one of the two upstairs rooms with Percy, William, George and Horace. Maryann snuggled down with Nance on her single mattress on the floor.

'Come on then,' Nance whispered. 'Out with it.'

233

'Cross yer heart and hope to die yer won't tell no one?'

'Cross my heart.' Maryann felt Nance going through the motions of crossing herself in the dark.

'I set fire to Norman's offices – I 'ope I've burned the 'ole bloody lot down!'

'You *what*? What did yer do that for?'

'Because 'e ...'e ...' Maryann felt a sudden lurching inside her, as if she might be sick and she sat up, gulping. She was still shaking.

'You awright?' Nance sprang up again as well.

Maryann fought back the feeling. She felt so strange. All the time since she'd found Sal she'd felt peculiar, as if disconnected from everything around her, from her own feelings. She didn't know she was in shock. She just felt as if she was living behind a glass wall which she couldn't reach through.

'I can't tell you, Nance. I just can't. But Norman Griffin's not like what 'e seems at all, you know, kind and a gentleman. It's all lies. 'E killed our Sal, Nance – 'e did ...'

'Maryann! What're you saying? You've 'ad a terrible time with Sal ... dying and that. But that can't be right, can it? Yer stepdad daint *kill* 'er – she ...' Nance paused. 'She ended 'er own life, Maryann.'

Maryann was shaking her head. 'I 'ad to do it. I 'ad to get 'im somehow. 'E killed our Sal ...' She was gulping again. Nance's arms came round her, warm and comforting.

'Oh now, Maryann, there, there. I know yer in a state – and yer can stop 'ere with us for a bit if it'll make you feel better. Our mom won't mind ...'

'I'm going away—'

'Are yer?' She could tell Nance was humouring her

and didn't really believe her. She was stroking her arm. 'Where're yer going then?'

'I can't tell yer.'

'Awright then, Maryann. Look – you lie down 'ere with me, eh? We'll get some kip and see 'ow things look in the morning.'

'They mustn't know I'm 'ere!' Maryann was still rigid, resisting lying down. 'The coppers'll be after me.'

'Awright, awright . . .'

'I *mean* it! I need 'elp, Nance. This ain't pretend, you know. If them lot see me' – she jerked her head towards the sleeping boys – 'they'll be gabbing away to everyone.'

'No they won't – we'll just say yer've come to stay for a bit. They ain't interested. Come on – lie down.'

Maryann tried to sleep, but felt by the morning that she hadn't had a wink. The bed was cramped, there were mice scuttling round the room and she was too churned up with emotion. She got up to face the mayhem that was the Blacks' household.

Nance told the boys Maryann had just come round to 'stop for a day or two' after which they lost interest. Maryann met Blackie on the stairs, clad in a greyish singlet and trousers, who said vaguely, 'Awright? What're yer doing 'ere then?' but he didn't stop long enough to wait for an answer.

Cathleen noticed she was there sure enough. In the midst of all her sons guzzling down bits of bread, she sat feeding Lizzie who was kicking her legs enthusiastically as she suckled. Cathleen had a cold and a hacking cough and kept wiping her red nose on an old rag. When Maryann and Nance came down she squinted with her lopsided eyes, the rag halfway to her nose, then let out a huge sneeze.

'Oh – oh . . . atchoo! Jesus, Mary and Joseph – where did you spring from in the night?'

'Maryann just wanted to stop 'ere for a bit,' Nance said, making faces that indicated she'd tell more when her brothers were out of the way.

She sat Maryann down and gave her a jam jar of weak tea and a slice of dry bread, which made Maryann feel a bit better. She had scarcely eaten all week.

Cathleen stirred herself from her chair to chase her husband and children out to work and school. As soon as she moved she began coughing again, doubled up with it.

'Oh—' she groaned. 'I got through four pair of bloomers coughing last night – I'll be washing all morning . . .'

'Is it awright if I stay for a night or two?' Maryann said, hesitantly. 'I can give yer some money . . .'

'Don't be daft, course yer can,' Cathleen said, shooing the youngest ones out of the door. 'So long as your mother don't mind.'

'They mustn't know I'm 'ere.'

Cathleen turned, Lizzie under one arm. 'Ah now – I'm not so sure about that. Why's that then?'

'Please,' Maryann begged. She searched round for a reason. 'Mom and me 'ad a bit of a ding-dong. It's only for a while.'

Cathleen gave a wan smile. 'Ah well. Can't say I ever liked yer mother, she's a stuck-up bit o' stuff if ever I saw one. So she won't get nothing out of me.'

Nance grinned. 'Thanks, Mom.'

'Thanks, Mrs Black,' Maryann said. 'I'd best get off to work now.'

*

The light was fading as Maryann waited at Camp Hill Locks, later that week, her bundle of possessions in her arms. She was waiting close to the cut, as she had waited now for most of the time since she had run away. The Blacks thought she was at work. Each morning she left the house after breakfast and went to the cut. That first day she said goodbye to Nance when she turned off to go to the laundry and hurried to the toll house where she thought the *Esther Jane* was most likely to come through.

'You back again, are yer?' the man said. 'Darius Bartholomew? S'far as I know they're still working down the Oxford, tekking what comes. I'd say they'd be through 'ere soon if they'm coming. I ain't seen 'em in a while.'

She spent the days walking to keep warm. She had enough money to buy food and cups of tea to keep a bit warmer. The coins in Norman's cash box had added up to four pounds, eleven and sixpence and she felt great satisfaction in spending it on her own comfort. She was afraid of missing the *Esther Jane* but knew she could ask at the toll house. Most of the day she walked along the bank, sometimes sitting down for a while or leaning against a bridge to watch the activity on the cut, but it was too cold to rest for long. These were cold, brittle days. You could see your breath on the air all day long. Under her coat she had on a warm dress and woolly jumper and stockings, though her heels were through them like potatoes and her shoes were too small and pinched her feet. On the second day she went up into Small Heath and looked round the pawn shops for another pair, but she could find nothing but battered old shoes that were all too big. In the end she decided to spend fifteen shillings of

Norman's money on a new pair of brown boots with sturdy soles.

These'll be good for on the cut, she thought, walking along, breaking them in. She kept looking proudly down at her feet. She felt no guilt whatever at having stolen Norman's money. The boots were like the sign of a new life. But she was very, very lonely. The ache in her to see Joel was almost overwhelming. Joel, who was the only person left who felt like family, who had shown her real affection and tenderness. If only they'd come and she could climb on board with them and feel safe and warm at last!

That evening, as the sun was setting, the night growing even colder, she was standing at Camp Hill Locks, where a conglomeration of bridges crossed over the cut as the road, railway and canal all met. She was hungry, her hands and feet were frozen and she felt low and desperate. The sun was setting and the cold becoming more intense, the air sharp and smoky. A line of joey boats was queueing to get through the locks and into basins for the night, all in a hurry to get tied up, and Maryann watched as a fight broke out between two men when one tried to barge in ahead. The loud, cursing voices and snarling expressions jarred right through her, making her feel all the more lonely and desolate as if they were attacking her. It seemed to stand for all the anger and meanness in the world and she turned and walked away, her arms folded across her chest, her head down and despair in her heart.

She longed to go back to the warm, fuggy atmosphere of the Blacks' house, but it was only about six o'clock. If the Bartholomews were putting in a long hard day it could be ten o'clock before they came into

Birmingham. She walked on, past the dark backs of warehouses.

She had walked up and down for another half-hour when a family boat came out of the darkness, its dim headlight moving steadily towards her. Her heart began to race. Surely she could make out the faint glow of white patches on the horse! She tried to keep her hope at bay – she couldn't bear the disappointment if it wasn't them.

'Bessie!' she whispered, peering through the gloom. Cautiously she started to run. Surely that was Bessie, couldn't that be the light of the *Esther Jane*?

As she came close she saw someone was leading the horse, someone big, solid. The one person in the world she longed and longed to see . . .

'Joel! Joel – it's me, Maryann!'

She heard the low rumble of his laughter out of the darkness, then its lapse into coughing for a moment. Then his arm came round her and she was safe.

'How do, our young nipper! Where've you bin then?'

Twenty-Six

She was woken very early the next morning by the delicious smell of bacon frying. Someone was sitting pressed up to her feet. Opening her eyes she saw Joel, bent forward towards the range, outlined against the light from the open cabin door. He was pouring dark, steaming tea from the brown and white teapot.

'Why didn't you wake me?' She sat up. Usually the faintest sound disturbed her. The men must have got up and moved in and out doing morning chores and she hadn't heard a thing. It was the first really sound night's sleep she'd had since Sal died.

Joel turned and grinned at her. His gingery beard glowed in the white dawn light. 'You was sleeping like a baby. Seemed a pity to wake you.'

Maryann smiled back, drinking in the sight of him. Now she had seen Joel and was back on the *Esther Jane* everything felt so much better and full of promise. Even Darius had seemed quite pleased to see her last night. 'I feel as if I've come 'ome, Joel.'

He nodded. 'Reckon so. We're finding it hard two-'anded – 'arder than it's ever been. My father ain't getting any younger and we're chasing loads wherever we go. Another pair o' hands'll be a godsend. All right with your folks now, is it?'

'Oh yes.' She spoke lightly. 'S'awright with them.'

'Good. Well, that's that then.' Maryann felt his blue

eyes on her, as if really examining her for a moment, and she hugged her knees. It was a special sort of look he was giving her and she didn't know what was he was thinking, but it felt nice, him looking at her like that.

He handed her a plate on which there was a thick wodge of bread topped with crispy bacon.

''Ere you go. Get that down you.'

They loaded up that morning, their cargo sacks of bolts and screws bound for Banbury, and by midday they were well underway. Maryann worked as hard as she could, pulling on ropes with all her strength, turning lock gates with the windlass. Both men knew they didn't need to tell her to be careful. She had learned that lesson back in the summer. But she still felt nervous in front of old Darius.

'I'll try not to do anything wrong,' she told him. 'And I'll work ever so 'ard for yer.'

'That's all right, lass,' he said. 'Everyone makes a mistake now and then. I can see you're stroving 'ard as you can.'

His leathery face stretched briefly into a smile. Maryann thought he seemed tired through and through. She had seen that both his hands and Joel's were rough and cracked, the tips of their fingers split from the wet and cold, and Joel was wheezing and coughing badly.

'Your fingers look sore,' she said to him. Joel held out his enormous hands, turning them this way and that.

'Not very pretty, are they?' he said.

Maryann was proud to think she might be of help, but she knew she was about to find out about the

241

harshness of life on the cut in winter. The day was another bright, frosty one and she was very glad she'd bought the new boots. But she was ready for it all.

For that first morning she was filled with an almost insane sense of relief and excitement. She'd got away, she'd found the *Esther Jane*, she was safe, and no one would ever come and find her here! She ran along the bank, a ball of energy, taking the windlass and running at the locks until Joel said, 'Eh, steady on there. There's a long way to go yet!'

But she couldn't seem to help it. As the day wore on, though, her energy began to flag and the cold, strange feeling that had possessed her came back. They had left Birmingham behind, and she shrank into herself and quietened. For a time she climbed up and sat, huddled in her coat, on the roof of the cabin as she had in the summer, and she looked out at the beauty of winter on the cut in Warwickshire. The fields spread out around her, grass hard and sparkling with frost in the low sunshine, the reflection of which rippled along the water. Where there were hedgerows close enough she could see blood-red berries, and the grating cry of crows echoed across from the hoary trees in the distance. The sights were magical, but the further they went, the more the awful numbness seemed to possess her. She was back behind the glass screen where nothing around her felt quite real. She looked down at her hand with its bitten nails, stroking it along the *Esther Jane*'s wooden roof. Even her own hand seemed distant and unreal. She was frightened by it.

''Er's steadied down a bit,' she heard Darius say to Joel. They were at the tiller and didn't seem to expect her to hear although she was not far away. 'Like a barrowload of monkeys she was, this morning.'

Joel must've nodded or made some other sign because she didn't hear him reply. Maryann sat listening, head lowered so that her long hair fell forward. She heard Darius say, 'That child's grown up into a proper lass since we last see'd 'er. She's a proper 'and to us now, Joel, and that's a godsend.'

Maryann felt a blush rise up through her cheeks, filled with a contradictory mix of pride and self-consciousness. It was true, she had grown, suddenly, her body filling out, but it felt odd to hear them talking about her like that. Darius was pleased with her and wanted her on board! She really had found a new life where she was wanted, away from all the disgust and fear and sorrow of her life in Ladywood. Tears blurred her eyes as she looked along the cut. If only she could start to feel back to her normal self, everything would be truly fine.

They were back in the rhythm of the cut, working hard, not speaking much throughout the jouney. Maryann fell exhausted into bed the first night while the men were still in the pub. She was too tired to feel lonely. The second evening they reached Fenny Compton. It was the first of November and very cold, though not quite severe enough to freeze over the cut. By the time Bessie was stabled and Maryann had prepared the evening meal, the frost was setting in. The sun set over the fields in a glow of orange fire and the spare shapes of the trees were silhouetted against the eggshell-blue sky higher up. She saw Joel looking at her as she wiped unexpected tears from her eyes. She never seemed to know what her mood was going to be from one moment to the next.

243

They ate the stew round the tiny table without saying much, but she felt Joel's eyes turning to her often, his face anxious, and to her frustration her own eyes kept filling with tears which she had to wipe away. All that afternoon, however hard she had tried to force them away, memories of Sal kept pushing into her mind, not as she had last seen her, in despair and death, but as she had been when they were young, so lively and pretty with her long blonde hair, running and laughing in the park or leading Tony by the hand. Sal had loved having a baby brother. Maryann could hardly swallow down any of the food, however much she tried not to think of it. After a while she gave up. She went out and climbed on to the bank, trying to calm herself, looking out across the stern of the *Esther Jane* along the darkening water, her vision blurred by tears.

''Ere – you'll need this.'

Joel was holding out her coat and she put it on, glad of it.

'Come on with me, this way. We'll 'ave a bit of a walk.'

He led her away from the cut and the pub, along a footpath into the fields. There wasn't much light and she had to concentrate on walking on the frozen mud track. For a while Joel led her in silence, along the edge of the field until they came to a gateway, which opened out into another field where black and white cows were just visible in the dying light, standing huddled together not far away.

Joel leaned over the gate for a moment. Maryann looked up at him. He seemed so familiar standing there, his face, the shape of him, his big, work-roughened hands on the gate – it was as if she had known him all her life. He turned to her, one elbow still leaning on the gate.

'You ent yourself since you've come back with us, Maryann.'

'I'm ... I'm awright.' Once more the rush of tears. She wanted to stamp: stop it, stop it, I'm all right! Don't make me talk or remember. I'm where I want to be, just leave me alone!

He stepped away from the gate and put his hands on her shoulders, turning her towards him. She had grown a little, she realized. Her head now came up to his chest.

'Look, little 'un—' Despite his affectionate names for her, she sensed he was treating her differently, like someone older. There was vulnerablilty as well as kindness in his expression. 'I can see there's summat amiss. I don't know what's driven you away from your family, but I do know what a sunny face you 'ad before, Maryann, and I don't see it now. The Maryann that left us is 'ardly the same 'un that's come back.'

Maryann kept her eyes on the ground, shoulders heaving as the great swell of her grief struggled to the surface.

'Speak to me, girl,' Joel said gently. 'It can't do no harm.'

'M-my sister ...' she managed to say, eventually. 'She ki ... ki ... took 'er own life. We only buried 'er in the week.'

'Oh no – oh—' she heard Joel say. 'My poor little bird.'

He took her in his arms and she felt herself held tight against his chest as his deep, growling voice made ceaseless, comforting noises. Over and over again he stroked her hair as she wept, beginning to let out some of the reservoir of horror and pain inside her.

He held her, murmuring his comfort to her for as long as she needed it, not asking questions, just letting her weep until she began to grow quieter. She went limp, leaning against him, gulping and sighing.

'Oh Joel,' she said eventually in tired despair.

'Poor little thing.' There was great tenderness in his voice.

'I thought I'd be awright back with you, and look 'ow I'm carrying on.'

'You will be awright. In a while.' There was a pause, then he said gruffly, 'We didn't half miss you. *I* missed you.' He squeezed her shoulders. 'You ent 'alf growing up, Maryann. I can't help seeing you a bit different. I've not 'ad soft feelings for many lasses, but you – you're coming to be special to me. Silly old fool, ent I?'

Maryann felt the affection and warmth of his words go through her. She gave a tiny laugh. 'No you're not, Joel. You're just you and I want to be with yer.'

He leaned down and carefully planted kisses, first on one cheek, then the other, and she giggled as his whiskers tickled her. His face was still close to hers and he was looking into her eyes.

'You're so sweet,' he said longingly. 'Just so sweet, lass.'

His holding her, the desire in his voice, aroused a flicker of excitement in her. He brought his lips close to hers and gave her a soft peck of a kiss. When she didn't pull away, he embraced her properly, closed his eyes and kissed her more passionately, hungrily. For those first seconds as he had looked at her, kissed her, she had been deeply touched by his gentleness, his desire for her. Then she felt his tongue between her lips, his hands pressing her now more ardently, and in her hurt state, her confusion, something hard and cold slammed down in her like a shutter. What was he doing? He was supposed to be her friend, her brother! And he was starting on this dirty stuff, *invading* her like Norman Griffin had done! But this was Joel. Joel didn't do things like that . . .

'No! Stop it!' She pulled away with such vehemence that he released her immediately, confused. 'Get off me! Don't you ever touch me. I hate anyone touching me!' She was crying again, distraught, starting to run from him, but she had only gone a few paces before her ankle turned on a hummock in the frozen ground and she fell over.

Joel reached down to help her up but she slapped his hand away. 'Don't you ever touch me, yer dirty bastard. I hate yer!' She scrambled up.

'Maryann, don't – what've I done to you?' He seized her arm and made her stop. 'I'm sorry. I just thought you'd . . . You seem so grown up and I've such feelings for you, but I wouldn't hurt you for the world. Please – don't be like this. I'd never do a thing to harm you . . .'

'Take me back to the boat,' she snapped, yanking her arm away. 'Don't touch me. Just take me back.'

Joel stood, hands on hips, staring at her, completely bewildered. 'We'll get back then.' He sounded confused, irritated even.

They walked back in silence. Maryann's mind was in turmoil. How could he have done something like that? He was a grown-up man and she was just a girl! This was supposed to be her safe place, the refuge she had run to for help. But it wasn't safe. He was just like

Norman, he'd made her feel foul and loathsome, and nothing on the *Esther Jane* would ever feel right again.

She refused to speak to Joel again that night, despite him trying to make up with her. She lay down on the side bench and turned away from him. She barely slept at all, listening to the sound of the men a short distance from her, repelled by both of them, wanting now to be anywhere else but here.

The next day they docked at Banbury and work began on unloading the cargo. Darius was busy overseeing that, and Joel had gone in search of another load to take on south or back up to Birmingham. Maryann would have expected to use the time to clean up the cabin, do some washing and put a sparkle on the brasses. Instead, once the men were out of the way, she wrapped up her few things again, pocketed the last of the money she had taken from Norman and climbed ashore, looking round her to make certain both the Bartholomews were out of sight. She walked briskly through the busy wharf area and slipped away, unnoticed, into the bustling town of Banbury.

PART TWO

Twenty-Seven

1934

Maryann carried the tray along the gold carpet of the landing, at pains not to slop tea from the large cup into the saucer. Beside the cup, arranged on delicate china plates, were two boiled eggs, one in the cup, one tucked beside it in a cosy, three slices of buttered toast, a pot of Chivers marmalade and a starched linen napkin in a silver ring. When she reached the last door along the landing, she set the tray down on the floor and knocked.

'Come!'

Each day she carried his breakfast to him, after she had already been up for four hours and had had her own meal in the servants' hall. Roland Musson liked to lie late in bed and eat his breakfast late, and it had been long agreed by the rest of the family that he should because this was what was good and right for him.

'On the table as usual please, Nelson.' He was sitting, tousle-haired, on the edge of his bed, his sturdy frame wrapped in a tartan wool dressing gown although it was May and quite warm. As usual, the room was fuggy with cigarette smoke.

'How do you come to look so hot and rosy-cheeked,' he complained petulantly, arms folded tightly across his chest. 'I feel quite shivery this morning.'

Maryann smiled. 'I keep warm working – it's nonstop this time of day.'

Roland Musson didn't reply, but sat looking sunk in gloom. He had the solid Musson looks, large blue eyes and a shock of thick fair hair, but his complexion was growing ruddy from too much drink. When she first arrived at Charnwood House Maryann had found him bad-tempered, demanding and unlikeable. She asked the other housemaids why this young man, a robust twenty-seven-year-old, as he had been then, spent his life confined in the parental home, and much of the time lounged about without purpose in his room.

'It were the war,' Letty, the first housemaid, told her. 'Shot 'is nerves to bits. 'E's better now, Mrs Letcombe says.' The housekeeper could remember the five Musson children as babies. ''E were ever so bad when 'e came 'ome. Crying, nightmares and everything. Wouldn't 'ardly go out of 'is room for months on end.'

'Why doesn't 'e go and get a job?' Maryann asked, thinking this a rum way to go on.

Letty laughed. ''E don't really need to, living 'ere, does 'e? 'E's comfortable enough, and to tell you the truth—' She lowered her voice to a whisper, as the two of them were polishing the dining-room floor and anyone might be within earshot, 'I don't think *she* wants 'im out of 'er sight, what with John being gone and that.'

John, the eldest Musson, an officer in an Oxfordshire Regiment, had been killed in 1917 and Mrs Lydia Musson, an elegant, though rather vague woman with a wreath of thick, wavy hair coiled round her head, seemed to encourage her second son's invalidity. She referred to him as 'poor, dear Roland' and he remained, at once petulant and pitiable, neither challenged to leave, nor seeming to have the will or incentive to do so.

It was getting on for six years since Maryann had come to Charnwood House, four miles out of Banbury, and in that time Roland Musson did seem to get out more. He worked in the grounds in the afternoon with Sid and Wally, the two gardeners, and he had a motor-cycle on which he roared dangerously along country roads and across the fields. He had a few friends locally and they sat for hours at a time in village pubs. Mary-ann, though, couldn't help but compare his plight with that of her father, also scarred by the war, trying to adjust back to family and civilian life and having some-how to struggle on and get jobs, keep afloat, without the cushion of wealth that Roland Musson had beneath him. And Nance's father, Blackie Black, too, and Joel ... But no – she wasn't going to think of Joel. When-ever her mind strayed down any path which would lead her to think about home she blocked out such thoughts. She had found a life that was free of pain and trouble and she wanted to keep it that way. And over the years her dislike for Roland Musson had faded as she grew to understand him better, turning instead to a mixture of tenderness and pity.

Sometimes when she carried Roland's breakfast tray in he was quite jovial and chatty; other times down and sunken into himself. That morning, Maryann stirred two lumps of sugar into his tea and handed it to him, thinking today was one of his depressed days, but he suddenly looked up at her.

'How old are you, Nelson?'

'Nineteen, sir. Twenty come September.'

'You look *different*,' he said taking the cup. 'What is it about you?'

'I really don't know.' She hadn't changed her hair, her morning dress was as usual. She wasn't aware that

253

Roland ever *saw* her anyway. She was a servant, and they had to stand to one side in the corridors when a family member passed, trying to make themselves invisible.

'You look *yourself* – as if that's how you're meant to look. Chap in my unit – that's what it makes me think of.' Roland spoke musingly into his teacup. 'Went out on a night patrol – one of those bloody woods on the Somme. Can't think what it was all for now but anyhow, they were successful. We'd heard the shots – didn't know who was getting it at the time. But they came back, all of them, full of it.' Roland spoke in his odd, clipped way. 'Anyway, this fellow was one of them. When I saw him the next morning, he looked, well, *altered*. That's it. That's what you made me think of. As if he'd grown into himself overnight.' He took a long drink of the cooling tea and Maryann, puzzled, thought he'd finished and began to turn away. But he carried on.

'Day after that the chap stood up for a few seconds and bang – killed by a sniper. So what was that all about? Man grows up, becomes himself overnight, then—' He snapped his fingers. 'Like a bloody butterfly.'

A moment later he looked up at her again. 'All right. I don't expect you to have an *answer*. Off you go.'

She went back down the stairs, pausing on the landing to look out over the garden, where Wally, the elder of the two gardeners, was bent weeding the long border which edged the drive. It was at its most beautiful at this time of year, the lawn wide and green, the beds bright with flowers, trellises of climbing roses up the outbuildings and the mock orange and laburnum in blossom. The mingled scents drifted in through the open window. From close to the house, out of sight, she could hear the Mussons' two dogs barking: Freddie, a wild young fox terrier with his insistent yap, and the deeper bark of their spaniel, Lily Langtree, who was beginning to run to fat. Freddie suddenly launched himself, a black and white flash across the lawn, with Lily lumbering after him.

Different? What had Roland Musson been on about? Maryann looked down at herself. She may be different, but it certainly hadn't happened overnight. She had grown, of course, and filled out on the plentiful and stodgy servants' food at Charnwood House. When she first arrived she had had no appetite and even Mrs Letcombe cajoled her to eat.

'Come on, girl – you'll have no energy for the work if you eat like a sparrer.'

Gradually, she settled into the rhythm of the house. As she got to know the characters of the other servants and appreciated that she had a good employer and a comfortable life, she felt secure and happy. She liked the predictable routine, the steady days and years. She was under-housemaid to Letty and Alice, and once she'd got used to the place, resolved that she would try hard and work her way up through the pecking order of servants. Two years later, Letty, who was then twenty-one, had married and moved on and Maryann became second housemaid. That was a start, but the job she had her eye on was not to be a housemaid at all. The job she wanted was Ruth's. Ruth, who was in her mid-twenties when Maryann arrived, was lady's maid to Mrs Musson, and to the Misses Diana and Pamela Musson when they were at home, which Pamela still was. Ruth was a quiet, dark-haired, neat young woman, whose job seemed to be regarded in realms high above that of housemaid. As she looked dreamily out at the spring garden that morning,

Maryann was speculating excitedly about the fact that Ruth was now courting with a young baker from the nearest village. If they were to marry, surely Ruth would leave and then perhaps . . .? But would they give the post to Alice, the first housemaid? Surely not! Alice was a good, hard worker, but she was a rough diamond. Was she, Maryann, neat and respectable enough for the job? She had done her darndest to make herself so. Every morning she brushed out her long, black hair and pinned it immaculately in a bun behind her head. She kept her nails short and her uniform mended. Smoothing her hand over her apron and trying to walk with Ruth's cool serenity, she went on down the stairs. Could that have been what Master Roland meant, she thought hopefully, that she looked like someone who wasn't meant to be a housemaid? Was she really destined to be a *lady's* maid?

''Urry *up*!' Alice snapped when Maryann appeared down in the kitchen. 'You should be half done with the bedrooms by now!'

Evan, who worked under the butler, Mr Thomas, winked at her over Alice's shoulder as he passed with a tray of steaming cutlery ready for drying. Maryann ignored him. Suddenly, after a few months of banter with Evan, he was becoming too friendly. He had started creeping up on her in the pantry and putting his arm round her. 'Gerroff!' she'd say to him. 'What're yer playing at?' It made her feel horrible and prickly.

'Master Roland was talking to me,' she retorted to Alice. 'I couldn't just walk out, could I?'

'Well, you'd better get on with it double quick now's all I can say,' Alice ordered.

Maryann made a face behind Alice's back. Since she'd been first housemaid Alice had gone power mad.

She began on Pamela Musson's room. Pamela,

voluptuous, blonde and loud, was only two years older than Maryann and was the youngest of the Musson children. The room was pretty, decorated in pale blue and white, with a soft, silky bedspread, curtains the colour of bluebells and a thick blue carpet. As usual, Pamela had left her nightclothes strewn across the floor and the bedding tipped off right over the side. Her dressing table was a litter of powder puffs and perfume, there was face powder spilt on the floor, stockings dangling languidly over the edge of one drawer and coat-hangers and underslips dropped on the floor by the cupboard. Maryann sighed. When she had arrived she found it almost impossible to take in that Pamela was the same age Sal had been. She was both a child and a young woman, both so much more sophisticated and knowing than Sal, yet so much more sheltered and childlike in other ways. She and Diana had gone about in their 'flapper' outfits, or their fashionable lounging clothes in bright colours with wide flowery bandeaux round their hair and hanging jauntily down at the back. Maryann had been astonished by their energy, their colourful freedom and confidence as they danced and giggled their way through life. Diana was married now and had stopped giggling some time soon after the ceremony. Pamela, who had done secretarial training, did her 'bit of work, to show willing' and otherwise existed in a round of social visits and Young Farmers' dos and 'hops' in Banbury and kept talking about 'getting a little job in London'. Pamela was rather hoping someone would marry her quite soon too and she sometimes told Maryann about her beaux.

Maryann gathered up and folded Pamela's fine stockings. If she was a lady's maid she would deal with their pretty clothes all the time and help them do their hair instead of cleaning out grates before the sun had risen of a morning and polishing floors with beeswax and turps! She pictured herself. Maryann Nelson: lady's maid. And then her hope withered. They most likely wouldn't even think of her for the post. They'd stopped wincing now every time she opened her mouth, but she'd never forgotten Diana Musson's mirth the first time she heard Maryann speak.

'Where on earth,' she screamed, between red-lipstick lips, 'did she get that *terrible* accent?'

'Birmingham, my dear – I gather,' Mrs Musson told her, and Diana looked closely at Maryann as if she was a rather exotic wild animal.

'How perfectly extraordinary! Is the child quite well? She looks so dreadfully *thin*.'

Maryann shook out the crumpled underslips and put them out for Ruth to iron. Then she stood and looked at herself for a moment in Pamela's long mirror. A dark-eyed, serious face stared back at her. She was no longer 'dreadfully *thin*', that was one thing for certain. Slender, but curving, and rounder in the face than she had ever been.

I'm a woman now, she thought, looking herself up and down in surprise. Women were supposed to marry and have babies. Maryann had spent so much time not thinking of herself, of her body, of her past, it came as a shock to her to notice she had grown up so much.

Will I ever be able to be normal? she thought. Questions, feelings, which she had closed off in herself, were beginning to nudge their way to the surface.

She pushed the cupboard door shut, closing off her view of herself. She didn't want to look. It was too frightening.

Twenty-Eight

Charnwood House had been a haven to her, a place where she had enjoyed a long period of calm, like an animal in hibernation. Her fondest memory of arriving to work at Charnwood, after the nerve-racking interview with Mrs Letcombe (for which she prepared herself in the local baths with a good wash and change of clothes), was that first Christmas. By then she had been in the Mussons' employ just a few weeks, having arrived at Banbury in early November, and she was still thin and withdrawn, closed in on herself. Looking back on it now, she could see that she had been really beside herself, in shock at Sal's death, at her own cruel treatment by their stepfather, and by her feelings that Joel had betrayed her.

That Christmas she began to close the door on the past. By the time the celebrations began she was already getting used to the day-to-day work of Charnwood House. She liked Letty and Alice wasn't too bad, if rather petty. Letty was fair-minded and made sure everyone did their share, and life in the servants' quarters was orderly and amiable. Mrs Letcombe was a motherly person – indeed she was a widow and mother of four grown-up children. Cook was blunt and strange and there were rumours that she had been crossed in love. Her dearest pleasure was to moan and mither, but most of it was just talk, and the butler Mr Thomas was touchy and pompous, but a kind man at heart. All of them assured her she had landed on her feet, and she soon found it to be so.

The week before Christmas, Sid and Wally, overseen by Mr Thomas, dragged a huge Christmas tree in through the front door and it was set up in a gleaming brass pot in the front drawing room where there was a fire blazing for the holiday season. Maryann and some of the others were allowed to watch Mrs Musson dressing the tree, accompanied by Diana and Pamela; Hugh, the third boy, whose age fell between that of the two girls, was not yet home from boarding school. Maryann stood warming herself in the lovely room, with its comfortable chintz-covered chairs and long, sweeping curtains and watched, rapt, as the girls trimmed the tree with baubles and red and gold ribbons and a beautiful angel with gauzy wings which was pinned to the very top by Diana, on tiptoe on a chair.

'There—' She stood back afterwards and admired their work. 'How do you like that?'

She turned to Maryann, who mumbled back nervously, 'It's very nice.'

Diana burst out laughing, looked at her sister and said, 'Noice – oh isn't she a scream!'

Maryann blushed, but they laughed so much and without malice that she joined in in the end.

'Don't mind us,' Pamela said sweetly. 'It's just we've never met anyone from Birmingham before.'

Diana suddenly peered closely at her. 'You're very young, aren't you? Why have you come down here?'

Maryann's throat went dry. 'Erm – I was looking for work.'

'But however did you *get* here?' Pamela asked.

'Down the cut.'

The two girls found this hugely funny.

'Down the *what*?'

'She means the canal, I believe,' Mrs Musson said, selecting sprigs from a pile of holly and laurel leaves from the garden. 'Did you now, dear – that *is* an unconventional way to travel, I must say.'

Maryann was very relieved when they left her alone. But she couldn't stop looking at the tree, which was the biggest and most beautiful she had ever seen, and the fire beside it, stacked with apple wood which made a delicious smell as it burned.

They had had a very busy time preparing the house. Maryann drew pleasure from simply moving about in such a lovely home, with its shining wood floors smelling of beeswax, the wide staircase with its red carpet and smooth wooden banister, the long windows and beautiful curtains. So much space, such sumptuous furniture. Compared with this, the houses in Ladywood seemed so dwarfed and mean.

On Christmas Eve, the Mussons' relatives started to arrive and the house was full of cries of greeting, doors opening and shutting, luggage being carted up to the rooms and the frantic barking of the two dogs. Mrs Musson's sister came with her daughters, and Pamela and Diana ensconced themselves in their rooms in the evening with their cousins – giggling, exchanging clothes and making themselves up for dinner.

In the days before Christmas, Diana had called the three housemaids together in the hall, lined them up with an indulgent grin on her face, and said, 'Now – we always give our people a little gift for Christmas. I'd like you to think of something you'd like. Nelson – what about you?'

Maryann, standing to attention with her arms by her

sides, felt her hands begin to sweat and her heart was thumping hard. Whatever was she supposed to say?

'I ... er ... I dunno, miss,' she gasped. She looked desperately at Alice and Letty but they were both staring straight ahead of them.

'There must be some little thing you could do with, surely?' Diana Musson quizzed her.

'Well – I could do with a comb,' Maryann dared to say.

Diana gave her loud laugh. 'A comb? Oh my dear, how sweet! I think we can manage a comb, don't you worry.'

Maryann was relieved to find that Alice and Letty's requirements were barely less modest than her own. Alice asked for a roll of ribbon and Letty wanted some needles and sewing thread. Diana went away, laughing cheerfully.

On Christmas morning the family walked out along the frosty lane to the village church and came back gusting in on the cold air and still singing scraps of carols. Mr Musson had evidently been asked to read from the Old Testament. His loud, declamatory voice boomed up to her as she passed along the landing upstairs.

'The Lord has forsaken me; my God has forgotten me! Can a woman forget the infant at her breast—' There was a pause as he seemed to be struggling, with a grunt, out of his coat and there was laughter downstairs. '—or a loving mother the child of her womb?'

Maryann had slowed, listening. The words brought back the smell of St Mark's Church in Ladywood, the dark, hushed space inside. And they pierced her heart. 'A loving mother ...' A great pang of homesickness passed through her. She could picture the house in Anderson Street, Christmas Day: Tony and Billy waking to find one of Mom's old stockings on the foot of the bed with a penny and and orange, maybe a knob of sugar and a little notebook and pencil or toy inside. Her mom'd never been bad at that sort of thing. It was the thing to do and she'd always been all right at 'the thing to do'. It was anything requiring more emotional effort she couldn't seem to manage. Maryann's eyes filled at the thought of Tony and Billy. Half the family gone, no sisters to give them any love.

She wrote notes home to Tony and Nance every now and then, wanting them to know she was still thinking of them. She couldn't bear to think of Tony believing she had completely deserted him without a thought. In all this time though, she had never had letters back, as she had not disclosed her address to them. She didn't want anyone knowing where she was. But sometimes she felt so desolate, never hearing from any of them. Had Tony still got the china cat she'd given him that looked like Tiger? Did he ever think of her, she wondered. He and Billy must be quite grown up by now. Her throat ached with tears. She was just on the point of breaking down and crying when she heard footsteps coming towards her. It was Letty.

'Maryann – you all right? Mrs M wants us all down in the games room.'

When they went to the games room at the back of the house, Maryann found the servants all beginning to line up, and on the billiard table, a row of little wrapped parcels. Mrs Musson was there, and her daughters and their female cousins. Mrs Musson's greying hair was pulled back into a more elegantly styled bun than usual, and she wore a dress of rich red velvet trimmed with gold brocade, which Maryann thought the loveliest she had ever seen.

As she and Letty joined the end of the line, Mrs Musson was already calling the names of the servants one by one. Each parcel had a label in the shape of a leaf. Maryann saw Mrs Musson shaking hands with Mr Thomas and wishing him 'the good health and joy of the season'. Then Mrs Letcombe, followed by Cook. When Mrs Letcombe opened her parcel, which was rather larger than most of the others, the layers of flimsy paper revealed a batch of balls of soft, lilac-coloured wool. Mrs Letcombe did a great deal of knitting and she gasped with pleasure.

'Oh Mrs Musson, Miss Diana, *thank you*.' She laughed. 'Oh that's beautiful, that really is.'

'Now you make sure you knit something for your-self and not just all those grandchildren of yours!' Diana teased her. 'It's for *you* to have something nice.'

When Maryann's turn came, she felt her hand taken into Mrs Musson's cool, smooth palm and she glanced up at her shyly before lowering her eyes in confusion to the floor.

'A happy Christmas to you, my dear,' Mrs Musson said. 'I do hope you're settling in well with us. Mrs Letcombe says you're a credit.'

'Thank you,' Maryann mumbled, unsure where to put herself. 'It's very nice 'ere – thank you, Mrs Musson.' She glanced up again at Diana, whose red-lipped grin was bearing down on her as usual.

'Here's a gift for you, Nelson.'

'Thank you, miss.' She gave an awkward sort of curtsy as she accepted the parcel excitedly. Whatever it was, it wasn't just a little comb!

Tearing the paper off carefully, she found a brush and comb set, with a mirror included. The comb was tortoiseshell and the brush had a smooth wooden handle. She felt a big smile spreading over her face. 'Oh these're lovely, oh they are!'

Letty had been given a beautiful little embroidered sewing pouch with needles and coloured threads, a silver thimble and a tiny pair of scissors, and Alice had three rolls of satiny ribbon in green, purple and royal blue. They were all delighted.

'Back to work now,' Letty said. 'No rest for the wicked.'

The day was indeed hard work, feeding the Mussons and their visitors, clearing up and tending to all the rooms, but Maryann loved the atmosphere of the house, the comings and goings, the laughter and loud air of festivity. Christmas was her favourite time at Charnwood, even though every year since she had been there she had to fight back poignant thoughts of home.

The years gradually took on a routine. In the summer the Mussons went to the sea for several weeks, living in a cliff house they owned that looked out over the Salcombe estuary in Devon. Roland never went with them, however much Mrs Musson entreated him, saying the change and sea air would do him good. It was as if any such change to his habits had become impossible for him. But Maryann was allowed to go some years and every time plans were being made she hoped and prayed she'd be taken along. That first time, in 1929, was the first time she had ever seen the sea. They arrived, snaking slowly down the coast road on a dazzling July day, seeing the blue spread out until it faded into a blur at the horizon, and Maryann thought she had never felt so happy and excited. The month she passed there with Letty and the family was not arduously hard work and the two girls were allowed to go paddling in the sea, walk on the cliffs smelling the yellow gorse and sit on the beach licking ice creams. Maryann thought she was in heaven.

'I don't ever want to go 'ome!' she said to Letty. 'I never knew there was places like this in all the world!'

Letty laughed, wiggling her back into a comfortable position on the sand. 'Well, if you play your cards right you'll come back next year.'

And so the seasons went, and so she grew up: Christmas, spring cleaning, summer holidays, autumn coming round again; living through the events of the family: Miss Diana's wedding, Pamela's ups and downs with 'chaps', Hugh leaving school and joining Mr Musson at the bank, and Roland, who was always, disquietingly, at home. The three girls followed the lives of their employers like characters in a storybook or a play. The Mussons' events were often their events. And this suited Maryann more than she even realized. Living through their lives saved her from having to live her own.

And then Evan came and began to prise her feelings open again.

Twenty-Nine

Maryann stood in the kitchen, waiting as the toast for Roland Musson's breakfast tray browned on the griddle. The back door was open as it was a warm morning of blue sky and puffy clouds, and a breeze blew into the kitchen, dispersing the smells of egg, soap and disinfectant that lingered there. Cook was at the table laying chump chops in a row ready for lunch and murmuring about needing to 'get on and steam that pudding'.

Maryann snatched the toast from the griddle and on to a plate before it could burn and went to the pantry to fetch the butter. Out of the corner of her eye she saw Evan come into the kitchen and did her best to ignore him. She removed the eggs from the pan with a spoon and arranged them as usual on the tray. But as she was buttering the toast she sensed Evan sliding round beside her. For a second his hand rested on her buttocks.

She twisted away from him furiously, hoping Cook would notice and tick him off, but it was her turn to disappear into the pantry.

'*Don't*, Evan!'

His dark eyes looked laughingly into hers. 'You're a proper tease you are, aren't you, girl? Never mind – there'll be time for us to have some fun later on.'

Maryann looked into his round face with its habitual jaunty expression, his plump little neck squeezed into the collar of his uniform. He winked at her, as usual, and she turned her back on him again. Whatever she said to Evan, however many times she asked him to leave her alone, it seemed to make no difference.

'I dunno why you're so nasty to 'im,' Alice said to her sometimes, jealous that no one was fixing their attention on her. ''E's handsome and 'e'll get on – 'e's a good worker.' Maryann and Evan were the same age, and in the months Evan had been there he had pursued Maryann with increasing determination. She realized she represented a challenge, even if he didn't like her very much.

Maryann would shrug. How could she explain what she felt to Alice, how much the sight of Evan filled her with panic. He revolted her and she was enraged by his assumption that she didn't know her own mind, that if he kept on and on at her she'd fall willingly into his arms.

'Go on – come for a walk with me this afternoon, eh? You and I could 'ave a lot of fun. Spring fever and that, eh?' He nudged her with his elbow and gave a wink. It was her afternoon off every Wednesday and by hideous coincidence it was also Evan's.

'No,' she said abruptly. 'I don't want to walk out with yer, Evan. I don't know how else to get it through your thick head. I ain't coming with you and I never will. Now get out of my way – I've got to take up Master Roland's breakfast and you're holding me up.'

'Evan,' Cook commanded. 'Get on with your work or you won't be going anywhere this afternoon.'

Evan backed away, making gestures behind Cook's back and grinning in a way that made Maryann want to punch him. She put the teapot on the tray and set off upstairs. She felt horribly unsettled. Evan had only been in the house a matter of months, but gradually he had begun to transform it from her haven of safety and certainty to a place where she was always on her guard if he was about. She would creep softly to the door of the kitchen to check that she was not likely to be alone with him in there. She very seldom was, as Cook was almost always at her post. She checked round corners now, to see if he was coming. When he came near her the feeling of panic that rose in her set her pulse racing uncomfortably. He was so single-minded, so cunning and yet so stupid, and the combination was completely unnerving.

As she put the tray down and knocked on Roland Musson's door, the thought came to her that not once, in all the time she had been at Charnwood House, had Roland ever felt dangerous to her in this way.

'Come!'

The door swung open. He had actually got up off the bed and opened it for her. Maryann stood in the doorway, astonished.

'Thank you.' She bent for the tray but he said, 'Allow me,' and swooped down beside her, looking like a tousled-haired little boy.

'Another delicious breakfast,' he said, sniffing at the toast. 'I'm well ready for it today.'

'You won't be needing me then.'

'Oh yes, do come in. Come and do some of your tidying up or something.'

'But—' Usually she worked on his room later, once he'd gone out.

'Don't argue. I don't mind you doing your work with me in the room.' He closed the door behind them. 'In fact, you're one of the few things that breaks the monotony round here.'

He sat on the bed, pulling the small table close to

269

put the tray on, and began to eat. Uncertain for a moment, Maryann looked round the room, then began to pick up Roland Musson's clothes which were thrown on the floor all round the chair. As she was folding his shirt, trying not to watch him eating as it seemed rude, he said, 'How long have you been here now, Nelson?'

'Five years last November, sir.'

'Extraordinary. Is it really that long? God, what an appalling thought.'

'What's that?'

'Well, here're you, five years later, grown-up, opening up like a bud and a lovely one at that. Moving on, you know. And here am I, thirty-three years old, stuck here like an old fossil in a lump of rock.'

Maryann hesitated and looked across into his eyes. She felt she had to be very careful what she said. 'You had to go through the war, sir.'

'So did plenty of others. I'm not the only chap in England who's terrified of sleep, you know. Did you lose anyone in the war?'

'Yes, sir. My father. At least – no, well he didn't die in the war . . .'

Roland paused, a spoonful of egg in mid-air. 'What d'you mean?'

'He didn't die in the war. It just felt as if 'e did – in a way.'

'Yes.' He pointed the spoon at her. 'Yes, that's it exactly. You're a sharp girl, Nelson.'

After a moment he said, 'I suppose you find me a useless piece of goods. The way I've never picked up.'

'No, sir.' Not useless. What was more puzzling to her was that there was no *necessity* for him to work. It went against everything she had grown up used to.

'Don't pretend to me, Nelson, please. I have buried

myself alive here. Buried in the safety of mother love
and a full belly. But d'you know what?'

He waited for her to speak.

'What – sir?'

'I almost think that one day I shall leave here. I shall
do it. Resurrect myself. Live.'

Maryann said nothing, not knowing what to say. She
picked up his shoes and laid them straight on the gold
carpet. They were very big, moulded touchingly into
the shape of his feet.

'D'you think I could manage it? I shall go to . . . to,
let's say, Algeciras. Yes. What about that?'

'I – I don't know where that is.'

'It's somewhere Johnny always wanted to go, you
know. Don't know why now. Its name seemed to have
a magic for him. Algeciras . . .' He drifted off into
silence. Often he couldn't finish a conversation, lost the
thread of it somewhere.

'Yes,' he said eventually. 'It's all a great pity.'

That afternoon when Maryann had finished her lunch-
time duties she went up to change. Hers was a small
attic room, with a rug on the bare floorboards, but with
a high window facing over the drive and she had grown
very fond of it. She had few possessions, but over the
years had accumulated things to decorate the walls;
pictures from magazines of soft-faced, smiling ladies
with silken clothes. She loved to look at them and
imagine dressing up like that herself. And now spring
was here she had gathered a little posy of flowers from
the garden. Last time she had been out, as she sometimes did in the evening, she had come across Roland,
walking up from the lower end pushing a wheelbarrow.

Usually if she wanted flowers she asked Sid or Wally. This time though, she had not even had to ask. Roland had lowered the handles of the barrow, stepped over and picked several sprigs of orange flower which he presented to her with a shy gallantry.

'There you are. I expect you'd like those. All women like flowers, don't they?'

She'd thanked him, startled. The flowers were still sitting in the jar in her room and the scent of them came to her powerfully every time she went in. Poor Master Roland, she thought, smiling at them. His awkwardness had touched her. What would become of him?

She changed out of the grey dress and white cap and apron which made up her morning uniform and put on her one summer frock, a cotton dress in a pretty blue floral print which Pamela Musson had handed on to her, and put some money in her purse. She now earned ten shillings a week at Charnwood House, but apart from a few small necessities found little to spend her money on, and she had savings of almost thirty pounds which she kept in her room, wrapped in an old handkerchief. She had long grown out of her boots bought for working on the cut, so she kept her black work shoes on, picked up her cardigan and set off downstairs. She planned to walk into Banbury and post another note she had written to Tony. Of course, the family could have moved house by now for all she knew, but every couple of months she dropped him a few lines, and included messages for Billy. It was hard to believe that Billy must be nearly ten by now – and Tony was old enough to start work. Billy had most likely forgotten who she was, but even if that was true, she wanted her brothers to know she still thought of them and cared for them.

Carrying the letter she crept down the attic stairs, then the back stairs to the kitchen, where she found Cook dozing on an upright chair by the window, her head sagging on to her chest. Sensing someone standing close to her she woke with a start and looked, for a few seconds, quite demented.

'Oh! Maryann you didn' 'alf make me jump. Ooh my word!' she grumbled, clutching her chest. 'What're you creeping about like that for? I thought you was off out.'

'Where's Evan?' Maryann whispered.

'Oh 'e's gorn – 'alf 'n hour back I should think.'

'Oh good. That's awright.' She felt she was breathing more easily. 'I'll be off myself then.'

She walked down the drive of Charnwood House, along the scented border of flowers, between the tall elms, all pushing out fresh green leaves, and on to the side lane that, after about half a mile, joined the main road to Banbury. At the road she stopped for a moment, emerging from the shade of the trees, put her head back and closed her eyes, enjoying the feel of the sun on her face and arms. It was a warm, calm afternoon and she breathed in deeply, luxuriating in a few hours of freedom.

She walked quite briskly along the road, bordered on each side by hedges, hawthorn and blackthorn and buttercups, bindweed and blue field madder in the grass beside them. Young blackbirds and thrushes twittered from the hedges. After a few moments she stopped, moved close to the hedge and looked across to the field beyond. It was a rough pasture and a short distance away she could see the white tails of rabbits as they bucked nervously around a warren, so far oblivious to her presence. Maryann smiled, watching them. A gentle breeze ruffled the grass, but otherwise it was very quiet, not a sound except for the birds. Somewhere over there must be the cut, winding through the fields. She looked down, suddenly aware of herself, standing here alone, with time to think. It seemed very *odd* suddenly that she was here in this life so divorced from her childhood.

How did I get here? she thought. Here am I, nearly twenty – I could be here doing this for the rest of my life. She turned the envelope in her hands and looked at her brother's name. 'Master Tony Nelson'. He was supposed to be Tony Griffin, but she would never, never call him that. This was her family now: two boys who she might never see again. She didn't count her mom. A great feeling of loneliness came over her. Would she never have anyone to call her own? Would her whole life be spent here? She might become a lady's maid, but then wouldn't she just be a dried-up, middle-aged woman, living through all the events of the Mussons' life instead of having any real happiness of her own? The bleakness of this outlook brought tears to her eyes. Until now, Charnwood had offered the haven she needed. It had brought her a sense of calm. But now it suddenly didn't seem to be nearly enough.

She walked on, wiping her eyes, deep in thought, no longer noticing the beauty around her, and turned on to the main road. For the first time in a very long while, she allowed herself to think about the events that had driven her to this place. Sal's death, the fire, Joel ... Joel's betrayal of her, the disgust she had felt. She relived that journey down to Banbury on the cut, the night he had taken her out to the fields, trying to see his face in her mind. The lust in it, the disgusting, frightening emotions that drove men ... Joel's face swam into her mind, lit by the silver light of that winter night.

'I've such feelings for you . . .' He'd said that. She hadn't heard, she'd only panicked and fought him off. That face had been full of Joel's tenderness and shame and bewilderment.

I was only a child, she thought, clinging bitterly to her anger. He shouldn't've done that to me.

But now the memories came to her of the feeling of being held by him, the comfort and power of him, the sense of safety he had always given her. Had she made a mistake? Had she got it all wrong and twisted because she was young and in a terrible state? She stopped, looking up the road. Joel was long gone now, of course – she couldn't say any of this to him. But she needed to admit it to herself. There was a gateway up ahead and she decided to go and rest on it, to let herself think for a little while, however much it hurt.

On her usual visits to Banbury what Maryann normally liked to do was to spend a couple of hours strolling round the town, along the Horsefair, past the famous Banbury Cross, looking in the windows of shops, perhaps buying a few small things, sometimes more notepaper to write to Tony. She would often treat herself to a cup of tea and a Banbury cake in one of the teashops. Today she bought a stamp and posted Tony's letter, first kissing the envelope.

'Hope yer get this, Tony,' she murmered, slipping it into the posting box. Her hand was shaking as she held it out. 'I hope yer awright, you and Billy. God bless yer both.'

She began her usual wandering, peering in the window of a china shop at the beautiful Wedgwood cups and saucers, the pretty ornaments, little vases and painted animals. Further along was a dressmaker's and haberdashery store. Should she buy a length of poplin to make a skirt? But her heart wasn't in it. She wasn't very good at sewing, even with all the help and guidance Mrs Letcombe had given her, and today she couldn't seem to keep her mind on anything. She found herself wandering purposelessly among the Banbury streets, across the Market Place amid the clamour of the busy vendors and shoppers and smells of food.

Before she realized it she found warehouses growing up around her, the scents of bread and fruit fading to be replaced by more grimy smells of coal and dust, wharf buildings growing up around her and the sudden sight and smell of the cut. She had only once been back to the cut before, further along, when she wandered there by mistake a few years earlier. Since then she had kept away deliberately.

The sight of it flooded in on her. A pair of narrow-boats were gliding towards her, towed by a stringy mule, his reflection shimmering in the grey, murky water. A great rush of memories flooded into her mind. The cabin of the *Esther Jane*, the beauty of the Oxford Canal when she had seen it in glorious summertime and with the white frost of winter. And the steady, tranquil glide of the boat, with Joel at the tiller, his great strong arm guiding her. In her mind she heard his laugh, the way she had heard it that first time she met him, then later, when she ran to him in the dark by the lock. She found tears welling in her eyes again at the thought of him, at the love she had for him that she had rejected, that she had run from and turned her back on.

'Oh Joel,' she whispered. 'Wherever you are – I shouldn't have run away from you like that!'

Thirty

She went back to Charnwood House to start work that evening. When she walked into the kitchen Evan was there, leaning nonchalantly against the table talking to Alice.

"Ello, Maryann,' Alice said. 'D'you 'ave a nice afternoon?'

'Yes, ta,' Maryann said abruptly, walking past them both. 'I'll take the water upstairs,' she added.

One of her tasks in the evening was to carry up the heavy brass cans of hot water which the family used for their evening wash before dinner, draping them with a towel to keep the heat in before the water was poured into the porcelain basins. Polishing the cans was also one of her daily duties. Once they were down having their dinner, she and Janet, the third housemaid, had to scurry round tidying rooms, picking up dropped clothes, plumping cushions and, in winter, brushing round the grate and refuelling the fire. In the summer the workload was lighter.

She took Pamela Musson's water to her room and found her lolling on her bed. 'Oh my – is it that time already?' she said languorously. Next, Maryann went down and fetched Roland's water. Once the cans were full they were quite arduous to carry. She felt herself starting to sweat. She hoped Roland wouldn't be in his room as he always seemed to want to delay her these days. But when she knocked he called, 'Come!'

'Your water, sir.'

'Ah – it's the lovely Nelson again.' He'd clearly just come in from the garden and was still dressed in his working clothes. There was a glass of whiskey on the table and she could smell it in the air. 'Very civil of you, Nelson,' Roland said. 'Pour it in – usual place.' He held out his arm expansively.

Maryann obeyed, thinking, someone's been pouring something stronger down him by the look of him.

'I don't know why – I feel in a damn good mood today,' Roland said, flinging himself down on the bed.

'That'll be a bit of sunshine, sir.'

'Yes, perhaps you're right.'

She went to the door.

'Nelson?'

'Yes, sir?'

'I—' He opened his mouth, then closed it again, brow wrinkling. 'I was on the verge of saying something tremendously important just then, but I'm damned if I can think what it is. God – d'you think I'm really past it, Nelson? Is this the first sign?'

'I think it may be the whiskey,' Maryann suggested.

Roland Musson lay back and roared with laughter. ''Course it is! Course it is! Why didn't I think of that?'

She slid out of the door and downstairs. As she reached the bottom, Evan came out of the kitchen on his way to the dining room.

'Aha!' he hissed. ''Ere she is then. 'Ello, beautiful!' He came up close to her so that she had to press herself against the wall with Evan's face close to hers. She was immediately filled with panic. Every encounter like this brought back Norman Griffin, him forcing her against

278

her will. Head back against the wall, trying to get as far away from Evan as possible, she managed to look into his eyes, praying her own would not betray her fear. He was smirking at her. This was just a game to him. He breathed into her face.

'I'm still waiting for that kiss.'

It went on and on. She avoided Evan at all possible times, but it got so that everywhere she went she seemed to see his round, leering face, even if he was nowhere near. She even dreamed about him, thinking he had come into her room at night and she woke sweating with fear. All her old ghosts came out to haunt her. The horror of being pursued, trapped by a man for his own dirty purposes, rose in her until she was beginning to live on her nerves and couldn't sleep at night.

Both of them were busy most of the time. Evan was under Mr Thomas's wing and Maryann had plenty of work. But eating meals together in the servants' dining room next to the kitchen became a torment. His eyes scarcely seemed to leave her face. Every time she looked up, there he was, ogling at her until she was put right off her food. Once she found herself on the point of bursting into tears and had to hurry out to compose herself. He was always looking for opportunities to get her on her own. Usually she could dodge him, but the time that was most difficult was Wednesday afternoon: the time they both had off together.

'Alice,' Maryann asked one day. 'D'you think we could change – you 'ave Wednesday off and I'd 'ave the Thursday instead?'

Alice frowned. 'Ooh no – I don't think so.' She had

no good reason for wanting Thursday as her day off. She just wasn't one to oblige other people. 'No – I'll keep my Thursday.'

Maryann got so she was too scared to walk into Banbury in case Evan followed her. Even staying round the house she felt very uneasy. In the summer months she liked to go into the garden. To one side, near the bottom end, was a walled rose garden, bright with blooms at this time of year, sheltered to sit in and deliciously scented by the rose petals. The servants were allowed to sit there during their leisure time, provided none of the family wished to use it.

So, one Wednesday in July, a baking hot afternoon, Maryann went out of the house, looking round her as she seemed to do all the time at present. The garden was warm and peaceful. She could see no sign even of Sid or Wally, and Roland only worked when it suited him. Taking her cardigan to sit on she walked down under the trees – a mature old oak, a young monkey-puzzle tree, maples with beautiful coloured leaves – and into the rose garden. Peering through the gap in the wall she saw no one was there, and immediately she was within the walls she relaxed.

The rose garden was square and immaculately maintained, with beds all round the edge, a path running round inside them, and two large beds of roses in the middle. Between them was a long lozenge-shaped patch of grass. Though the two benches along the side received the most sun, Maryann spread her cardigan on the grass and lay down. She was tired and longed to lie in the sun, have a snooze and relax after all the hard work of the week.

It was very hot. Lying back with her eyes closed she felt immediately drowsy. Somewhere in the far distance she could hear a tapping noise, a mallet on a wooden post, which seemed to echo on the air, and closer by there were the sounds of birds and buzzing insects. The sun's rays beat down on her face and she began to fall asleep straight away.

It took her a few moments to notice that the sun had gone in and a shadow had fallen across her. She put a hand up to shield her face and open one eye, then sat up with a horrible start. Evan was standing, straddling the place where her feet had been, hands on his waist, staring down at her.

Maryann wrapped her arms tight round herself in protection.

'What're yer doing creeping up on me?' She tried to sound angry and commanding but her voice had gone squeaky.

Evan lolled down on the grass beside her, shuffling up close so that Maryann had to lean away from him.

'I saw you come down here. Don't seem to be able to find you on your own these days, Maryann.'

'What d'yer want?' As if she didn't know. She edged away from him.

'You're a funny one you, aren't you?' He sat back, leaning on his hands and looking at her. He sounded reasonable.

'Am I?'

He leaned towards her again and she felt his hot breath on her cheek. 'Look, there's not much time around 'ere, is there? Why can't you stop being so prim and proper and enjoy yourself while it's on offer?'

Maryann was all knotted up inside and her limbs had gone weak. She pulled her chin down on to her knees. 'I don't want it, Evan.'

'Come on—' He budged closer and started to play with her hair. 'You just need to get started.'

A moment later his other hand slid in behind her knees, feeling for her breast, and she felt his lips on her ear.

'Come on, girl – I've got something for you in 'ere—' He pressed his body hard against her, pinching her breast as he did so. 'Why don't we go up to your room and I'll show you? No one'll see.'

'Oh, get *off*!' Maryann launched herself to her feet, catching Evan off balance and leaving him sprawled on his side. 'Get yer dirty 'ands off of me. I don't want yer touching me.'

She saw a really ugly look come over Evan's face that chilled her. 'You're not normal, you, you know that? Not a proper girl at all.' His top lip curled in a snarl of disgust.

'Leave me alone—' She was growing distraught. 'Whatever I am, just leave me alone. I don't want yer anywhere near me. Go and make up to Alice – she'll 'ave yer like a shot. But if you come near me again I'll go to Mrs Letcombe and I'll get you sent away from 'ere.'

'She won't listen to you!'

It was Maryann's turn to stand over him. 'Oh, you're wrong there, Evan. I've been 'ere a hell of a sight longer than you have and Mrs Letcombe's been good to me. So you keep yer filthy hands to yourself from now on.'

She snatched up her cardigan, determined not to let Evan see that her legs and hands were trembling, and strode back to the house.

As the summer passed in the usual way, events in the wider world seemed very distant from Charnwood

House and its inhabitants. Mrs Lydia Musson sat every afternoon with a shawl round her shoulders and her feet up on a stool reading a newspaper, so the hunger marches from the north of England and the rise of Fascist groups constituted some of the drawing-room conversation. But they were not a highly political family. And Maryann was barely aware of the world outside Charnwood and its small domestic dramas.

Evan continued to smirk at her and make snide remarks, but he had not made any more attempts to touch her or kiss her and gradually Maryann could relax again a little. But the inner calm that she had possessed for the last years had deserted her. She felt restless and lonely. Ruth was to be married in a few weeks, but no one had said a word about who was to replace her as lady's maid. A year ago Maryann would have been on pins with anxiety about this, she had wanted the post so badly for so long. But now she began to find Charnwood confining. She loved her afternoon off and made sure every week now that she went out, into the town to the shops and for a wander along the cut to see the boats being loaded and unloaded. She liked the bustle, the smells and sounds, and the way the canal made her feel connected to things again, instead of buried alive at Charnwood. For that was how it was coming to feel.

The turmoil inside her that she had avoided for so long was returning to her like an old family chest being opened. Norman, Sal, Joel and her brothers. Round and round in her head. And her own future. Was there happiness waiting for her somewhere else? Would she be capable, after all, of love?

*

Ruth was married on a Saturday at the church in the nearest village and the staff were allowed leave to attend the service before coming back to Charnwood for a celebratory meal. Ruth, as ever, looked calm and serene; her long, dark hair was knotted beautifully and she wore a simple cream dress. Her husband, tall and blond, kept looking at her as if he couldn't believe his luck. The two of them left for Banbury in a horse and trap decorated with garlands of flowers, to begin their married life. Both the servants and those of the family who were at home came to wave them off. Maryann saw Roland shake hands rather awkwardly with Ruth. Pamela flung her arms round her tearfully and Mrs Musson slipped a little package into her hand. Maryann kissed her and wished her every happiness.

'I hope some of you'll come and see us,' Ruth said, kissing and hugging everyone. 'We're not far away, but I'll miss you.'

It had been announced that Ruth was to be replaced by a young woman called Eve. As Mrs Letcombe told them, Maryann experienced a pang of envy and disappointment, closely followed by relief and a surprising sense of freedom. If she'd been given the job, somehow in her mind it would have tied her to Charnwood, when in her heart she could feel the stirrings of change.

Thirty-One

That week, when Maryann walked into Banbury, she didn't even get as far as the shops. Slipping along the side streets, she found herself heading for the cut. More and more now, she found herself thinking about the past.

She went past the Strugglers Arms and down to the cut, walking on the towpath for a time. There were horse boats and motor boats on the go. She stood aside every now and then to let a horse go past pulling one of the boats. The smells of the water, the hot horse scent, the water splashing on the sides of the cut and the sunlight glaring on the ripples all filled her with a great sense of nostalgia and excitement. When she'd walked a way along, tied up on her side of the cut she saw a family boat called *Miss Dolly,* a rather scruffy vessel with chipped red and yellow paint. From the back on the steering platform peered three young children and Maryann heard a woman's voice shouting crossly to them from inside the cabin. Several others were playing along the bank and there was a string of threadbare clothes, stained grey with coal dust, strung on a washing line along the boat.

Maryann smiled at the children in the boat and said, ''Ello there, awright?'

''Ow do!' one of then chirruped back. The older ones were throwing stones into the cut with little plopping noises. She saw they were aiming at something floating in the middle of the channel. It was sodden and feathery: a dead pigeon turning gently in the water. She stood watching for a moment, then turned back, still smiling.

It was hard living on the cut, she remembered that very well. She knew how they rushed and competed for the loads, how the Number Ones were up against the company-owned boats, how it was work work work for long hours every day. Yet there was a freedom in it too. She stood looking north along the long, thin strand of water, following its course in her mind. On it went, out through those remote fields where you scarcely saw anyone about, only trees and birds and the sky overhead and the sun glinting in the brasses. What a life that was!

After a time she came towards the dry dock called Tooley's Yard where boats were taken in for repairs. She remembered Joel telling her about the place. Every so often the boats had to be taken there for recaulking. 'So they don't go letting no water in,' Joel had said. 'They seal up the seams and blacken 'er bottom to keep 'er watertight.'

She'd never been in the place and she thought she'd slip in and have a look. Just as she was about to go into the yard, two men came out, talking earnestly. One was a portly, middle-aged man with a red face looking out from under his trilby hat. The other, in contrast, was much taller, dark and strong-featured, with black curly hair and a large, slightly beaked nose. The tall dark man's face looked furrowed with some strong emotion, worry or anger. They passed her, talking earnestly together, and turned off away from the cut.

It was only as Maryann turned into the yard that she

realized she recognized the tall, dark man. She stopped for a moment. Where had she seen him before? If she could only think! She looked across Tooley's Yard and could just see the hull of a boat in the dry dock. Those lovely yellows and greens. And then it came to her, where she knew him from. A boat passing, Joel calling out as they slid beside each other, smiling, happy to see each other . . . the man with dark curly hair was Darius Bartholomew the younger: she was certain of it! Heart racing, she turned and ran in the direction they had gone, but they had disappeared. In any case, what could she say to Darius? He didn't know who she was, did he?

But she couldn't resist a look round the yard. It wasn't a large place – there was a brick shed and the dry dock, which would take one boat at a time, was a long, rather ramshackle building by the cut. She saw a couple of the Tooley's workers eyeing her up admiringly. She felt as if her skin was prickling. She knew she looked pretty in her blue dress, slim and shapely, black hair tucked under a little navy straw hat with a down turned brim. But she so disliked the feeling of being stared at, sized up in that way.

'Was you looking for someone?' One of the men approached her, looming over her.

'I – I just wanted to see—' She spoke timidly, but then found the courage to say, 'That man who just went out, was that Darius Bartholomew?'

The man took his cap off and rubbed sweat from his forehead with his arm. 'That 'un? Darius the younger. That's 'is boat, the *Esther Jane* down there. We'll be working on 'er next.'

'That's the *Esther Jane* – over there?' She couldn't keep the excitement out of her voice. Along from the dry dock she could just see the prow of another boat. 'Oh – can I go and see?'

The man shrugged. 'Don't see why not. Ain't no one aboard 'er though.'

He left her to walk over by herself, picking her way over the muddy ground. The boat was tied up by the bank, waiting for her turn in the dry dock, where she'd be strapped up while the water was drained out of the dock so that the men could work underneath her. It was with a feeling almost of disbelief that Maryann approached her. There she was, the *Esther Jane*! And on the roof, curled asleep, a little brown and white dog.

'Jep?' She could hardly believe it! He looked up on hearing his name and, jumping down on to the bank, came and licked her hand. 'Oh Jep – it *is* you!' He was a little grey round his sandy muzzle, but still full of life. 'Oh – is Ada back on board with you now then?' She was full of happiness and excitement. How could she have left them? How could she have stayed away so long? Still squatting, petting Jep, who was all awriggle with pleasure, she looked over the boat.

'Hello there,' she found herself saying softly. 'So 'ow're you then, old girl?'

While the boat made no reply, the state of her seemed to speak for itself. The last time Maryann had seen her she was in good repair, freshly painted and spick and span, brasses polished, her hold washed out as often as they could manage between loads. But now what she saw filled her with dismay. She looked a sad, worn-out old lady. The paint was cracking off her, it looked a long time since her brasses had had a rag anywhere near them and she was covered in grime all over. Chances were she was in the same state inside – dirty and heaving with bugs if they hadn't had time to stove her. In her dismay Maryann immediately felt like jumping aboard and setting to work but she knew she mustn't. It was clear the *Esther Jane* had fallen on hard times. Her mind was jumping with questions. What had happened? Why was Darius back running the boat? Where was his father and, above all, where was Joel?

With Jep following her she went back to look for the man who she found in the dry dock, working on another boat called the *Venus*.

'D'you know if Mr Bartholomew's coming back soon?'

The man looked at her over his shoulder. 'Oh, I should think so. That was one of Essy Barlow's men 'e went off with. Don't s'pose 'e'll stay with 'im long.'

'Samuel Barlow?' S.E. Barlow owned one of the carrying companies and she'd often seen his pairs of boats on the cut. ''E ain't selling the *Esther Jane*?'

'Seems like 'e might be,' the man said. 'E could do worse. Times're tough, everyone chasing about for not enough loads. If 'e sold out to Barlow 'e wouldn't 'ave to chase the loads 'imself, would 'e?'

Maryann was appalled. She knew how hard old Darius and Joel had always worked to stay independent, to be Number Ones like they'd always been, not tied to a boss, a company. How would Joel feel about this?

'Can I wait till Mr Bartholomew gets back? I'd like to speak to 'im.'

'Stay as long as you like.' The man winked at her. 'Don't see anyone complaining, do you? So long as you don't get under anyone's feet.'

She went over to the side of the yard. From somewhere near by she could hear the sounds of a forge: a horse being shod. She hoped Darius Bartholomew wasn't going to be too long. In a couple of hours she would need to set off for Charnwood House, but the way she felt just then she would have waited for ever and damn everything else. Having seen the *Esther Jane* it was almost as if the past six years had not existed. She was back on the cut with the boat and the people she loved and she was desperate to know what had befallen them. Suddenly it was all that seemed to matter.

Almost an hour later Darius Bartholomew came back. She saw him the second he strode, grim-faced, into the yard. He was a large, striking presence. He looked puzzled and not especially pleased to see someone standing by his boat.

'Mr Bartholomew?' she said, even before he reached her.

She found him rather forbidding, in the same way she had often found his father. Those strong, chiselled features seemed to scowl down at her.

'My name's Maryann Nelson. I—' How did she explain? 'A few years back I lived on your boat – with yer dad and Joel – and Jep here – until Ada went off. . . .'

For a moment he stared blankly at her, then his face softened a fraction. 'Did you? I remember they 'ad a lass on board for a bit.'

He seemed about to turn away, sinking back into his own thoughts again, so Maryann asked quickly, 'Only – I wanted to ask after everyone. Your father and Ada – and Joel.'

Darius Bartholomew climbed over into the *Esther Jane* and stood on the steering platform looking back at her. He shook his head. 'You won't be seeing our Ada no more. She were drownded four year ago, God rest 'er.'

'Ada?' Maryann gaped at him. 'Oh no ... No!' Not cheeky, vivacious Ada.

'They was working the Grand Union – right down to the Thames. It's all wider and faster there, with currents and that. Our Ada was knocked overboard – got swept away. Took 'em days before they found 'er.' Seeing the tears in Maryann's eyes he looked down with a sigh. 'She were a good'un.'

Maryann swallowed, wiping her eyes. 'And your father?' She could hardly bear to ask about Joel.

'I left 'im down at h'Oxford with 'is sister what lives on the bank. What with Joel and the boat in this state I said I'd bring 'er up 'ere one 'anded. He ent a young man. He's finding the life harder and harder and 'e's been poorly.'

'And Joel?' she breathed.

Darius started shaking his head in that grim fashion again and Maryann felt as if a great pressure was bearing down on her chest. Not him as well. He couldn't be drownded as well, oh please God, no!

'Bad,' Darius said. He seemed almost glad to have someone to whom he could pour out all his troubles. 'He's took real sick. He's been heading for it since the winter, what with 'is chest, but this time it went from bad to worse. I had to get him took away to the 'orspital at Birnigum even though 'e begged me not to leave 'im on the bank. But he was that burning up with fever I couldn't look after 'im and see to the boat and the loads ... And with fighting for regler loads and back loads—' He wiped one of his huge, dark hands over his face. 'It looks as if we're giving in – going to Essy Barlow. S'the only way now.'

'Oh dear.' Maryann wiped her eyes again. 'I'm ever so sorry you've had such troubles, Mr Bartholomew.

I truly am. I know how Joel and your father felt about selling up.'

'Times move on – what with the roads taking over ... Some of 'em're acting like they've never heard of the cut these days. I don't know what can be done, that I don't.' He pushed open the cabin door. 'I'm going to get the stove going and brew up. You stopping for some tea?'

'Yes please.' She was desperate to know more about Joel. She had to know how he was, where he was ...

'Come aboard – that's if you don't mind?' He eyed her pretty frock. 'It ain't spick and span like it oughta be.'

Stepping into the *Esther Jane* again after all this time was a wonderful feeling and despite her anxiety, Maryann found herself smiling as the memories poured back. She sat by the tiny table, looking round, itching to get to work and clean the place up: the plates and copper kettle and Esther's brown and white teapot. The crochet work was filthy, the whole cabin dull and dirty compared with how it had been before when either she or Ada had kept it nice. She watched Darius stoking the range and suddenly found herself aching for it to be Joel here beside her so that she could see him again. She remembered her younger self, confused and frightened, lying alone at night in this cosy cabin, this place of refuge as it had been.

'Where have they taken Joel?' she asked as the kettle was heating.

'I told you – to the 'orspital up Birnigum.'

'Yes, but which one? D'you know?'

Darius looked round at her, stooped over, scraping old leaves out of the teapot. 'I never 'ad the chance to see 'im. Our father weren't well neither and what with chasing the loads I don't know 'ow Joel is even. 'E'll not like being on the bank for long. That's if 'e even . . .' He trailed off, but she knew he was going to say 'lives'. 'Never been right really, 'e ent – not since that war.'

Every moment she sat there, she was filling more and more with an urgent determination. Joel was sick, maybe dying, and she had to see him. He'd been so good to her and she'd repaid him unkindly. Now it was her chance to do something for him. She didn't need to ask if there was anyone else in Joel's life. No one had been mentioned and Joel would only have married someone who could live on the cut, who would be his 'mate' aboard the *Esther Jane*. If there was any such woman in his life, where was she?

'Is 'e all alone there?' she asked. 'No one who can visit?'

Darius shook his head, ashamed. 'There ain't no one.'

'Can't you think which 'ospital it *might* be? Daint they say when they took him?'

Darius's brow wrinkled. 'I think it might be the one near the chocolate fact'ry.'

'The chocolate factory? Bournville. Would it be the Infirmary at Selly Oak?'

'Might be,' he said hopelessly. 'Ain't no good me knowing when I can't 'ope to get there, is there?'

'But I could go.'

Darius stopped in the middle of handing her her cup of tea. 'You?'

She reached out and took the cup and the absolute resolve in her face was plain to see. 'Yes. Me.'

Thirty-Two

'I'm sorry, Mrs Letcombe, but I really do 'ave to go – it's someone in my family.' How else could she describe Joel? 'He's very ill, maybe dying.'

'But when will you be coming back?'

'I don't know. I'm ever so sorry.'

And she was sorry. Almost heartbroken. Throughout the train journey to Birmingham the tears kept rising up in her eyes. She could go back, Mrs Letcombe said. They'd give her a week or two. But she knew that she wouldn't be returning, that everything had changed and that she could only look forward. Deep in her heart she had known that one day she would have to go back to Birmingham and face her family and now that day had arrived. And it was Joel who had brought her there. He seemed closer to her now than he had in all the years she had been away. The thought of him, and her worry about him and his weak lungs, was with her all the time. Now she knew she had to see him she was in a desperate hurry to get there. Darius had said he would try and get to Birmingham when the *Esther Jane* was ready. But she had to get there more quickly. Throughout the journey she wanted to command the train to go faster, faster!

She looked out as it chugged slowly into Birmingham. It was a hot but overcast day and a grey pall hung over the city: all the smoke from the factory chimneys and no breeze to blow it away. A blackness lay over everything and along the tracks the buildings seemed to be closing in, the workshops and warehouses, with what windows they had poky and filthy, their walls covered in soot and grime. The sight of it shocked her. What a grim, stifling place it looked! She had been away so long, had become used to the space and clean air of the country, the warm-coloured stone of the houses, and felt almost panic-stricken at the thought of being enclosed behind these dark, cramping walls again. But down there, under it all, she told herself, was the cut, slipping through and between and under. Another world, sealed off from the rest of the city, and the thought gave her hope and a way out, a sense of freedom.

When the train lurched to a standstill her pulse began to race even harder. This was really it now. She was back. People were jostling to get out of the train and she pulled her little case down from the luggage rack.

'Time to face the music,' she thought. 'But not before I've seen Joel.'

Changing platforms, she waited for a local train to Selly Oak, and it wasn't long before she was stepping out of the station. It was dinner time, a bit early to go and visit, so she went along the Bristol Road to find a place to sit and have a cup of tea and a sandwich and try to steady her nerves. She found a workmen's café and sat listening to the voices round her, remembering how much Diana Musson had laughed when she had first heard her talk at Charnwood. That place which had at first felt so strange and foreign had become a second home to her. It felt very odd to be back in this big, clanging, rackety city. Once again the thought of Charnwood brought tears to her eyes.

She had said her goodbyes the evening before. It was no hardship to part with Evan, but even the crustier characters like Sid and Wally and Cook had shown surprising affection for her. Cook had flung her arms round her and gone all dewy round the eyes. Parting with Mrs Letcombe had been very emotional even though the housekeeper herself was rather unconcerned, because she was sure Maryann would soon come running back, and kept saying, 'There there, m'dear, I don't know what you're crying about.' Even saying goodbye to Alice had brought tears to her eyes: though she'd never had very warm feelings towards her, they had spent a lot of time working together.

To her surprise, though, it had been Roland Musson who had aroused the most emotion in her. When she went up last night to prepare his room during dinner he had come in as she was turning down the bed for him.

'Oh—' he said, taken aback. 'I forgot you'd er, be ... Just popped up to er...' She saw him go to his decanter of whiskey, pour himself a generous couple of fingers and gulp them down. He turned to her, shamefaced, still holding the glass. 'Ah – that's better. Mother doesn't like to see me – you know. Says I drink too much.'

'Er—' Maryann delayed him, nervously. 'As you're 'ere, sir, I'd just like to say, I'll be leaving the 'ouse first thing in the morning. I don't know if I'll be coming back.'

Roland just stood staring at her.

Maryann blushed. 'I'm sorry, sir . . . I know it don't matter to you one way or another who makes your bed and that, but I just thought it'd be polite to say goodbye.'

296

'But, Nelson – you're not really *going*, are you? You don't mean it?'

'I 'ave to, sir.'

'This is appalling news. I mean, you can't! You're just *always* here – in fact you're the one really cheering person about the place. I rely on you, Nelson!'

She looked at the carpet, not knowing what to say.

'Well – damn it. I can't just shake your hand, not after all you've done for me over the years. Come here, girl.'

And he wrapped his arms round her in a rather clumsy but, she could tell, heartfelt embrace, and for a moment she allowed her arms to rest round him as well. She felt him kiss the top of her head.

'You're a damn fine girl, Nelson,' he said thickly. 'Damned fine.'

'Thank you, sir. And good luck to yer.'

When he'd left the room she kneeled down for a few minutes by the bed and wept silently with her hands over her face. Sitting thinking of it now, a lump rose in her throat.

Pulling her thoughts back to the present, she wiped her eyes and stood up to pay for her tea. The café proprietor stared at her curiously but she was too preoccupied to notice. Pressing her hat down she went out into the street. It was threatening to rain and she walked on quickly, carrying her case, towards the hospital.

When she enquired inside, she was told she was too early and would have to wait another half-hour. So she went out and strolled up and down Raddlebarn Road feeling more and more nervous.

What was Joel going to think of her turning up all of a sudden? Would he even remember who she was?

She felt ashamed when she thought of him, and worried. How ill was he? Was Darius exaggerating when he said he didn't know if Joel would come through? He must be seriously ill if they'd got him to move away from the cut and his beloved boat, especially at such a worrying time. Maryann's thoughts spun round and round. She turned at the bottom of the road again. It must be nearly time for them to let her in. Oh God, her heart was beating so hard! She pressed her hand over it. It felt as if all her future depended on the next half-hour. All her feelings, wounded and battered as they had been, were now reaching out to Joel with great longing. How would she find him, and what would his reaction be to seeing her again?

She approached the door of the ward with great timidity, her stomach clenching uneasily. Hospitals frightened her. They had ever since her dad had been taken away to one and never come home. The nurses in their stiff uniforms, their starchy white veils and starchy manner also intimidated her and there were those smells: bodily stenches, disinfectant.

An older nurse, with a cross face and muscly arms and legs, walked briskly up to her. 'Yes? Who is it you've come to see?'

Maryann cleared her throat. 'A Mr Joel Bartholomew . . . please.'

'Bartholomew? Chest case. Oh no – I don't think so.'

'P-Pardon?'

'No visitors. Too ill to see anyone. And you're not a relative, I assume?'

'I'm . . . no, a friend, but . . .'

'Relatives only, I'm afraid.' The woman started to turn away.

'But they can't come – any of them!' Maryann burst into tears in vexation. 'They all work on the cut and they can't leave the boat. His dad's poorly too and his brother's stuck in Banbury and there ain't anyone else and I *know* he'd want to see someone. *Please* let me – just for a few minutes. I've come all the way from Banbury myself today!'

The woman stood, considering. Maryann was afraid she'd be snooty and spiteful because she knew Joel was off the cut. But she said, reluctantly, 'Very well. A couple of minutes. But he is very ill. And don't go cluttering up the ward with *that*. Leave it with me.' She took Maryann's case and walked off with it, saying over her shoulder, 'He's just down on the right.'

She found him halfway down, a physical jolt of shock going through her when she first saw him and took in that it was him. If it had not been for his blaze of hair against the pillow she would not have recognized him. For the big, burly Joel she had known was now much thinner, his cheekbones pushing out the flesh of his face, and they had shaved off his beard. His frame, as he lay prone under the sheet, was shrunken and weak and his eyes were closed. She could see that each breath he took was a painful struggle to him.

Her instinct was to stand there for a long time staring at him, trying to take in his changed state, but she was afraid the bossy nurse would come back, and she slipped alongside the bed and sat on the chair, trying to shrink down and make herself as invisible as possible. She could feel the man in the bed opposite staring at her.

Close up, she could see a film of perspiration on Joel's face and hear the rasp of his lungs. His face wore a frown, as if of pain and concentration. Watching him she felt as if the years since she had last seen him were very short, like a dream which takes only moments yet in which you can experience half a lifetime. She felt as if her heart would melt with sorrow and tenderness. She sat torn between fear of disturbing him and the unbearable thought that she might be ordered to leave before he knew she was there. Slowly, trembling, she reached out her hand and laid it over his.

'Joel?'

For a moment she thought he had not heard, but then his head moved a fraction and she saw him struggle to open his eyes, as if even the effort to prise his lids apart was enormous. He looked round, eyes unfocused for a moment, then slowly rolled his head, sensing someone next to him. She felt his eyes on her.

'Joel,' she whispered, leaning towards him, finding there were tears streaming down her face. 'It's me – Maryann. I saw Darius and he told me you was here and how poorly you are.'

There was a moment while he took her in, staring at her as if he couldn't make sense of her presence and she watched his reaction fearfully. He swallowed, frowned slightly. His hand lifted, then laid over hers.

'You came . . . My little . . . nipper . . .'

This made her all the more emotional. 'Oh Joel,' she sobbed. 'It's so lovely to see you. I'm so sorry, Joel – I've wanted to say to you for ever so long that I'm sorry for running off the way I did when yer'd been so good to me. I was in a state. So many terrible things'd happened and I daint know what I was doing and I know you daint mean anything bad. You were the one person I could always go to and I can't stand to see yer looking so poorly like this.' She took his hand and kissed it again and again. She could hear his breathing becoming more agitated and she looked anxiously into his face. There were tears running down into his hair and she wiped them gently away with her fingers, knowing how unmanly it must seem to him to weep. He was trying to speak and she leaned close, barely able to hear his whisper.

'I did wrong—' He had to rest between the words to gather enough breath. 'You was . . . only a young 'un . . .' He closed his eyes as if condemning himself. 'My fault.' The final words cost him a huge effort. 'You seemed older . . . I felt for you. It weren't . . . just lust . . . Truly . . .'

'You were lovely, Joel – you were. I know that now and I'm sorry. Only I *was* young and I was in a mess . . . I've grown up a bit since then. I've thought about you – when I let myself. And I missed you ever such a lot.'

He gave a nod which seemed to encompass and elaborate everything she'd said, and he clutched her hand.

'I'll be here now – till you get better.'

Joel laid his spare hand over his chest, gasping for breath. 'I knew they'd get . . . me . . . in the end . . .'

She knew he meant his damaged lungs and a chill went through her.

'Don't say that, Joel! You're in your thirties – that's not old! You just feel it because yer sick at the moment. You can get better – you can! I'm going to come and see yer every day. Please don't give up – say you won't give up, you'll try for me, won't you!'

Slowly he brought his other hand across and cradled her hand in both of his.

'Oh Joel—' She leaned forward and kissed his cheek, barely knowing what she was saying. 'I love you *so* much.' She was laughing and crying together, but quietened herself to hear the words he whispered, still clasping her hand.

'My little . . . love, you . . . came back.'

Thirty-Three

When the tram reached Ladywood, Maryann stepped down a couple of stops early so that she could walk along Monument Road and try to get used to being back. Glancing down Waterworks Road she looked for Perrott's Folly, the old brick tower which loomed over the houses, and she passed some of the old familiar shops, St John's Church, the Dispensary, all looking the same as when she left and it gave her a strange feeling. She prepared herself for the fact that while buildings change little in six years, people do, and that she might even walk past one of her own brothers without recognizing him.

Turning down Anderson Street she was filled with a dread so strong it forced her to stop and stand nervously near the corner, trying to find the courage to go on. Again, the place looked much the same. School was out and there were kids playing on the pavement, skimming marbles along the blue bricks as they always had. She might have run along the road with Norman Griffin's keys in her hand only weeks ago. For a moment she could smell the choking smoke from the fire in her nostrils. She was going to have to see *him* again. However much she knew she was now a grown woman, that she could leave at any time, that he had no power to do anything to her, she could only feel herself as a child in relation to him. A powerless child who he

303

could use for his own cruel, disgusting appetites as he had used her sister and then destroyed her. The old anger in her rose up again until she was trembling with it.

Oh I can't, she thought. I can't go back there. I ain't got the strength. She put her case down and stood facing the wall of a house, composing herself, clenching her teeth, trying to get her shaking under control. I will not, she told herself, let him do this to me. I *won't*. Furiously she snatched up the case and marched along the road. But she still couldn't go straight to the house and walk in. She had to know how things stood.

The Martins' huckster's shop still looked just the same, the windows plastered in labels: Oxo, Cadbury's, Woodbines, the same little 'ting' of the bell as she pushed the door open. The smells hit her: soap, camphor, rubber, cough candy. For a second she saw Tony in her mind's eye as she remembered him, standing on tiptoe to peer over the counter.

'Penn'orth of rocks yer got there, bab?' Mrs Martin would say.

Maryann imagined Tony's wide-eyed nod.

Mrs Martin, her hair now white instead of metal grey, came through from the back, wiping her hands on her apron.

'Can I 'elp yer?'

''Er – Mrs Martin, it's me – Maryann Nelson.'

The woman stared at her, bewildered. 'Who?'

'Maryann – Flo Griffin's daughter. Tony and Billy's sister.'

Mrs Martin's mouth sagged open. '*No!*' she exclaimed eventually. 'Little Maryann? Ooh – I can see now, them blue eyes. Ooh my word!'

'I've been working down south and I've come back

for a visit, only I just wondered – you know, 'ow things are . . .' She jerked her head over in the direction of the house.

'Oh no – you won't find 'em over there. Daint yer know?' Her brow furrowed at Maryann's extraordinary ignorance of her own family. 'Your mother went to live back over in Sheepcote Lane when 'e left 'er. Couldn't pay the rent no more, could 'er? In a right state 'er was. But that were a good while back – five year or more. We don't see 'er round 'ere no more. Daint you know, bab?'

Maryann shook her head, her pulse racing. 'You mean Mr Griffin ain't living with them no more?'

'Ooh no – 'e took off after 'is premises went up. There was a fire, like. Gutted the 'ole damn place. You must remember that, daint yer? They've only just got it put back up now and Steven's the drapers're setting up. But your mother, Flo – well 'er version of events was 'e was never the same again after it and 'e took off and left 'er. Oh, Flo was in a right state I can tell yer.'

Maryann could tell from the way Mrs Martin was squinting at her with her head a bit to one side that any moment she was going to start interrogating her. She backed away towards the door, almost falling over a pile of galvanized buckets.

'So you say Mom's gone to Sheepcote Lane?'

'Sheepcote. Ar, that's it, bab.'

Maryann pulled the door open again. *Ting!*

'You're a right grown-up wench now, ain't yer?'

Maryann smiled. 'Ta very much, Mrs Martin.'

She passed the old house, peering closely at it. There were pale lilac curtains inside the lower window, and a black dog was lying asleep beside the step. She could sense it had all changed, would look very different inside from how she remembered, yet the thought of walking in through the front door made her flesh creep. Too many memories. Too many ghosts of the tormented little girls she and Sal had been in that house. She held on to the thought of Joel, to the love she had seen in his eyes which made her strong. Knowing she had Joel again she could face anything. Much better to keep walking and see what the present held than to linger here dwelling on the past.

The only way she could think of finding her mom in Sheepcote Lane was to ask, yard by yard, even house by house down the poor end. Poverty would have driven her to a smaller house – what fierce resentment that must've bred in her! But maybe, when Norman left her, she had been able to see him as he really was: a conman who had married her for his own vile motives: for the fact that she had two young daughters and would look after him in comfort in exchange for his money. God knows, she thought, he wasn't *rich* – not really. It was just that Mom was desperate. Maybe at last she'd be able to face the truth.

She did not need to look far. In the second back court she went into she was confronted by the sight of a woman, her back to Maryann. Her legs were thin and stringy, and her hair which had once been thick and blonde was now faded to grey, twisted and pinned up savagely behind her head. She was reaching up to unpeg a sheet from a crowded line of washing which billowed in the damp air. Maryann knew her immediately. She felt a surge of pity. Flo's bitterness and exhaustion was clear in every movement she made. Even during the war she had been quite a voluptuous woman, but now she was very thin. She kept reaching up to the line, unpegging and yanking sheets, bloomers, an apron down from it, shaking them angrily when the breeze tried to force them the wrong way. Maryann hadn't the courage to go to her in the yard. She hovered in the entry until Flo had picked up her enormous basket of washing and struggled into the end house.

It was about five o'clock. Her mom'd be cooking soon. Best go over there and get it over with. She was just stepping out across the narrow yard when two boys ran out laughing from another house. They were both about ten years old, one dark, one blond. Seeing the fairer of the two, Maryann stopped. Something about him, the way he moved, his colouring told her immediately that this was Billy. He and the other boy were tearing up and down the yard chasing one another and laughing. They saw her looking and took no notice. Both of them were in shorts cut down from longer trousers and grubby shirts hanging loose at the back. As they came closer, Maryann called, 'Billy?'

He slowed, peering at her, and came closer. His face was grubby and red from running and she saw he had a trail of freckles across his nose. From the big blue eyes, the way he held his head, she knew that he was her brother.

'Billy – it's me, Maryann. I'm your big sister.' Tears came as she said it. All those years of his life she'd missed. A little, soft thing he'd been when she left, who'd sit on her lap for a love and let her bath him. Now he was a long, skinny lad, almost grown up!

'Are yer?' She could see him searching his memory. Surely he'd been old enough when she left for him to remember her? But then she'd changed too. A sad look came over his face for a second, and she thought he was going to say something else. But then he seemed to remember the other boy with him and he wasn't going to go all soft in front of him. 'Our mom's indoors,' he said with a toss of his head. 'See yer.' And the two of them careered off again.

Gripping the handle of her case, Maryann walked along the yard. If it had been a house she'd ever lived in herself, she'd have just walked in but here she felt she must knock. She saw one of the front panes was broken and covered with cardboard, and the green paint on the door was flaking and dirty. She rapped it with her knuckles.

'Oo is it?' Even her mother's voice sounded different, thinner, somehow cracked.

Maryann pushed the door open. It was gloomy inside and it took a few seconds for her eyes to adjust. She immediately recognized the table and chairs which stood to one side of the little room as the ones they had had in the last house, bought by Norman Griffin after they left Garrett Street. Her mother was standing between the table and the range, gutting herrings which were stinking the place out. She had looked up without stopping what she was doing until she saw Maryann. Flo straightened up, holding out blood-smeared hands in front of her.

''Ello, Mom.'

The expression on Flo's face, already harsh and unsmiling, grew more taut. Maryann was shocked by just how much she had changed, as if in six years she had fallen into old age. Her face was pallid, almost yellow, the skin had lost its elasticity so that it sagged over her cheekbones. She looked hard and shrewish.

'Is that you, Maryann?'

Maryann nodded. 'I've been in service. Not in Brum.' Even now she couldn't bring herself to give away where she'd been.

Flo became suddenly aware of the mess her hands were in and picked up a damp rag from the table to wipe them. There was an ominous silence as she did it and Maryann could tell she was gathering her thoughts.

'Where's Mr Griffin?'

Flo slapped the rag back down on the table before walking round and advancing on Maryann, staring at her with her eyes full of loathing.

'Where's Mr Griffin?' she mimicked. For a few seconds she couldn't seem to find any more words. Maryann shrank back as her mother came right up close.

'Mom! What're yer doing!'

'You did it, daint yer? You set that fire at Griffin's before yer buggered off. Norman knew it was you, you evil little bitch. You destroyed my life, d'yer know that? D'you even care what yer did? You ought to be banged up in Winson Green, that's where. You ruined everything we 'ad. He walked out and left and I 'ad nowt and two boys to bring up. I've been slaving in factories ever since, thanks to you. And d'you know why 'e left? 'Cause 'e said 'e weren't staying in a family of bloody lunatics who'd taken away his livelihood. And it was all your fault, Maryann.' The words rained down, sharp and hateful. 'You ruined your own family – so 'ow d'you feel about that, eh?'

Maryann thought Flo was going to go for her throat with her fishy hands and she twisted away from her and backed across the room. She had such strong emotion rising in her she felt she might burst. The injustice of everything her mother thought and felt, the way she'd never listen or see the truth – never had. She'd never taken their side, hers and Sal's. She was beyond tears: her feelings were too raw and harsh.

309

'You're a sad, blind woman, ain't yer, Mother?' She stood clutching the back of one of the chairs as if to contain the violence that raged inside her. Her voice was low and trembling with emotion. 'Yes – I set fire to Norman Griffin's offices and I 'oped they'd burn to the ground so there was nothing left for him. But that ain't why he left you and you know it. 'E left because *we*'d gone, me and Sal, and there was nothing left for him that he wanted. 'Cause 'e didn't like grown-up women, did he? He liked little girls he could bully and do his dirty business with and turn them into ... rag dolls, with no feelings or life left of their own.' She in turn advanced on her mother. 'D'yer know what it was he did to our Sal so she lost 'er mind and he'd've done to me too if 'e'd 'ad the chance? D'yer want to know what I found in the cellar of those offices the night I went down there? Do yer?' She was shouting at the top of her voice, distraught.

'No, *no*, shut up, you lying, wicked girl ...' Flo laid her arm across her face as if to protect herself.

'No – you don't want to hear that anything might be *your* fault, *your* greed, putting money and dresses and your comfort over and above your children.' Now she'd begun to open the floodgates she couldn't stop. She was growing hysterical. 'You don't want to hear about Norman, the oh-so respectable Mr Griffin chaining our Sal to a chair and doing God knows what to 'er and most likely promising to leave her down there with a corpse for company all night. Because that's something that wouldn't be my fault or Sal's, would it? You'd have to face that you didn't see and you wouldn't see because all you could think of was saving your own skin. You daint see her stabbing at her own arms with a knife because she couldn't live with

310

herself. And it weren't you that found her with her wrists slit open, was it? You never even went to look at her after ... Was the mess too much for you, Mother? Too real for you that, was it?'

She couldn't go on. She bent over the chair with her hands over her face as sobs choked her, the long-buried grief welling up from deep inside her. After a few moments she glanced up to see her mother looking at her with a terrible, twisted expression on her face.

'Get out of my 'ouse.' Her voice lashed across the room. 'You've done enough damage to us. We've lived without yer all these years. We don't need you back 'ere now. Tek yerself and yer poison away from 'ere. I don't want yer coming 'ere again.'

Maryann wiped her eyes, chilled by the hateful finality of her mother's words. 'I want to see my brothers.'

'You ain't seeing no one. Get out!' Flo shouted. 'Get out now and don't ever come back. Never!'

311

Thirty-Four

Maryann walked back out of the yard in Sheepcote Lane so blinded by tears that she could barely see where she was going. Her mother's rejection of her was so total, so final it had cut her to the bone. They had never been close as mother and daughter but she had hoped that somehow, after all that had happened and with Norman Griffin gone, there could have been a reconcilation. Now she had lost that hope for ever.

If only Nanny Firkin was still 'ere, Maryann thought. I could've gone to her – she was proper family. She'd've been glad to see me and it would've felt like home. The thought of this made her cry even more.

As it was, the only person she could hope to turn to now was Nance. She found her feet turning almost automatically to the familiar territory of Garrett Street. Somehow she didn't doubt that the Blacks would be living in the same place. Before she went into the yard she tried to compose herself and dried her eyes. She was pleased at the thought of seeing them and even smiled slightly as a familiar sight met her eyes in the old yard: Blackie Black's 'fuckin' barrer' leaning as drunkenly as she had frequently seen its owner do, against the wall of the brewhouse.

The Blacks' door was open and Maryann peeped her head round. The family was at the table having tea.

Cathleen's squiffy eyes, Blackie's bloodshot ones and those of the six children round the table all peered at her.

'Oo're yer looking for, wench?' Cathleen said. – 'Eh, 'ang on a minute, I know you, don't I? It's . . . It can't be Maryann?' She pushed back her chair and stood up.

'It is,' Maryann said shyly.

''Eh, Blackie, it's little Maryann, our Nance's pal!' Blackie squinted at her but there was a vacant look in his eyes. He made a sound between a grunt and a whine.

'Come on in, bab!' Cathleen came and stood gazing at her. 'Don't mind Blackie – 'e ain't none too well these days. Well – look at you! Our Nance'll be ever so pleased to see yer. You ain't been round to see 'er, 'ave you?'

'No – I've only just got 'ere.' Maryann put her case down gratefully, trying to keep the tears from welling up yet again. It meant so much to be greeted kindly by people who were pleased to see her.

''Ere – 'ave a cuppa tea – it's just brewed. You seen yer mom?'

Maryann nodded.

'Well – what'd 'er say?' Cathleen was stirring the teapot vigorously.

'She daint offer me a cuppa tea, I'll tell yer that much.'

'Ooh dear – like that, was it?'

Maryann nodded, conscious that the family were all staring at her. Good heavens, – that oldest one was Perce – he was eighteen now! And young Horace who'd still been sucking his thumb and peeing his pants was a lad of nine now! There was Lizzie who'd only been a babby. And who was that? There was another little girl sitting at the table between William and George, who were now also a good deal more grown up.

'You 'ad another daughter then?' Maryann smiled at the child.

'Ar – that's our Mary,' Cathleen said. 'She were the last. Four year ago that were. I 'ad to 'ave all my – you know – taken away after. It were a blessing really, God forgive me, but I've 'ad my ten and that were enough for anyone.' She watched anxiously as Blackie pulled himself up from the table and lurched over to his old chair with the fag burns and settled into it with a loud groan. She leaned forward shaking her head and whispered, ''E ain't 'imself.'

'What's up?' Maryann whispered back.

'Oh, they don't really know. They think 'e might 'ave 'ad a bit of a turn. 'E can 'ardly speak. Not that 'e was a great talker before. I dunno.' She sighed, looking across at him worriedly. Maryann felt sorry for her, poor, worn-out woman. Cathleen and Blackie had both aged considerably.

'Any'ow, enough of our problems – where've yer been, Maryann?'

She told them a bit about Charnwood, then asked after the rest of the family.

'Where's Nance – and Charlie?'

'Oh, our Charlie's been wed a good while now – three kiddies they've got. All girls, would yer believe it! Alf and Jimmy've got one apiece. Alf was wed two year ago and Jimmy last year. They're all good wenches they've found themselves, all Catholics 'cept Jimmy's wife Lena, but she ain't no trouble.

'And our Nance married Mick just a few months

back – in the spring. She 'ad 'er nuptial mass in April. It were lovely, weren't it?'

'Me and Mary was bridesmaids,' Lizzie chipped in.

She reminded Maryann a little bit of Nancy when she was younger, with her head of black curls, although she had a softer, more feminine look about her.

'Nance'd've asked yer to the wedding only she daint know where yer were,' Cathleen said. ''Er missed yer, yer know, after yer went.'

'I know,' Maryann said. 'I missed 'er too. But I 'ad to get away.'

Cathleen nodded sympathetically.

'Where's Nance living? And what's 'er name now she's married?'

'Oh, Mrs Mallone. Mick Mallone's 'er 'usband. They only live over the back in Alexander Street. Yer can pop round and see 'er when yer've 'ad yer tea.'

'Any babbies on the way yet?' Maryann said smiling.

Cathleen shook her head. 'No – but they've only been wed a few month. It'll give 'er time to settle.' But Maryann thought she seemed rather lacking in warmth on the subject of Nance's marriage, however nice the wedding had been. She glanced at Blackie and saw that he appeared to have fallen asleep, his head lolling down on his chest.

''Ere – if you're going round to see our Nance, take the girls with yer and get 'em out of my hair for a bit, will yer? They like going round there.'

Nance was living in a front house which opened on to the street. The door was open and the two girls ran straight in.

'We've got Maryann!' she heard Lizzie shouting excitedly.

Immediately, as Maryann reached the house, Nance's face appeared at the open door, looking out with a combination of wariness and disbelief. For a second Maryann was shocked by Nance's thinness and the dull sullenness of her expression under her mop of black curls, until she registered that it really was Maryann and burst into delighted laughter.

'Oh my God – well I never! It really is – Maryann!'

Laughing and tearful at the same time, the two of them flung their arms round each other.

'Why didn't yer tell me where you was living?' Nance reproached her. 'I wouldn't've let on to anyone and I couldn't drop yer a line back or invite yer to the wedding or nothing! 'Ere – come in. It ain't much but we've got it to ourselves.' She drew Maryann inside and shut the door. 'Let me get that kettle on – or d'yer want a nip of summat stronger, eh?'

'No – tea'd be nice, Nance.'

The two little girls seemed to have disappeared upstairs. 'I've got a couple of old dollies and a few bit of clothes up there for when they come round,' Nance said. She rested the kettle on the hob, then stood back to look at Maryann.

'You ain't changed – not really. You look ever so well.'

Maryann smiled. Hadn't changed? How could Nance say that? She felt like a different person. And Nance looked different, too, in a middle-aged woman's dress and her apron. She was beginning to look just like her mom!

'I'm awright,' she said. 'Got lots to tell yer. But what about you, Nance. Look at you – a married woman!

What's your 'usband like?' She had noticed uneasily the cut healing on Nance's left cheekbone, a yellowed bruise round it. Nance seemed to feel her looking and put her hand to her cheek.

'I could tell yer everything's perfect, Maryann. Wedded bliss and that. But I've never lied to yer. 'E's a boozer like me dad only not so soft-hearted. 'E's down the pub now. 'E ain't too bad when 'e's sober but with a skinful inside 'im 'e gets all maudlin and sorry for 'isself.'

'Why's 'e sorry for 'imself?' Maryann asked.

'Oh Christ alone knows,' Nance said impatiently. ''E's one of them 'as a few and 'e 'as to wallow. 'E ain't got me expecting yet – 'e 'as a wallow about that.'

'But yer've only been wed, what a few months?'

'Three months – nearly four.'

'Well then.'

Nance shrugged. 'To tell yer the truth I'm bloody glad of it. I only married 'im to get out of 'ome. There's kids and mess and noise everywhere and now our dad's bad 'e's sat there like a dummy even when 'e ain't been on the bottle. I thought, I've got to get out of 'ere or I'm going straight round the bend. And Mick came along and 'e was willing and a Catholic so I married 'im and we kept our mom 'appy doing it proper like. And I got me own 'ouse. That's worth 'aving to put up with Mick, I can tell yer. If 'e stays down the boozer, good riddance.'

It sounded to Maryann as if there was a fair bit of bravado in what Nance was saying, making the most of a bad situation, but at least her spirit was far from being broken.

'If I don't get a bun in the oven for a year or two it'd suit me, I tell yer,' she said rattling cups. 'It's not

317

all on one side, yer know – I give 'im one back sometimes, the mardy bugger.'

While Nance finished making the tea Maryann sat down at the table in the sparsely furnished little room. There was nothing but the range, a couple of shelves for keeping their few crocks on and the table and three chairs. On the table in a jam jar was a bunch of buttercups. Maryann smiled at the sight of Nance's homemaking. She thought of the luxuriant vases of flowers at Charnwood.

'Right then—' Nance sat down with a grunt. 'You tell me all about it. For a start, where the 'ell've yer been all this time?'

With the luxury of knowing that there was little of her past Nance was ignorant of, Maryann told her: Joel, the *Esther Jane*, Charnwood, Evan and Roland Musson. And finally meeting Darius and Joel again, and what had happened when she went to see her mom – only Nance kept chipping in.

'You were never on the cut all that time, were yer? They're a rough lot, them canal workers – they're like gypos!'

She oohed and aahed when Maryann told her about Joel and Roland Musson and listened spellbound when she got to the bit about seeing Flo again. Maryann poured out everything, how she felt about Joel and how sick he was and how Darius was going to be forced to sell the *Esther Jane*.

When there was a gap in the flow, Nance put her head on one side and said, 'You're in love with 'im – really in love, ain't yer?'

Maryann smiled bashfully. 'Am I?' she said in wonder. 'Yes – I do love 'im. I *do*. I'm going to spend every minute I can with 'im and try and 'elp 'im get better.

I've missed spending so much time with him – all those years, and 'e could've married someone else but 'e daint.'

'In love . . .' Nance said wistfully. 'Well, yer one up on me there, Maryann.'

'Nance – I know this is a cheek with me coming breezing back in after all this time – but could I stop 'ere with you a while? Only I ain't got nowhere else to go and I've got to be near Joel. I've got money saved – I can pay my way and that.'

Nance looked hesitant for a moment. Then her face cleared. ''Course yer can. I'd love to 'ave the company with ole misery guts coming 'ome kalied every night. Don't take no notice of Mick if 'e says anything. You can stay and that's that.'

'Ta, Nance – oh, it is good to see you!'

Nance grinned. 'Seems like yer never left.'

Maryann couldn't help feeling it didn't seem quite like that to her. 'Did you 'ear anything about where 'e went – Mr Griffin?'

Nance shook her head. 'No, but by all accounts 'e left only a week or two after the fire. Our mom went to see yours but she wouldn't even open the door to 'er. It weren't long before she 'ad to move back over Sheepcote Lane but she still 'ad a smell under 'er nose – sorry to say it, Maryann, but Flo always thought she was above us. We ain't 'ardly seen 'er: she don't want nothing to do with my family.'

'I know,' Maryann said apologetically. She was frowning. 'Norman Griffin can't've gone that far, yer know. I wonder if 'is mom's still alive – he was all over 'er.'

Nance shrugged. 'Good riddance to 'im I'd've said. Any'ow, you don't want to go asking questions about

319

where 'e is, do yer? What about what you did to 'is business?'

'No, I s'pose ... But, Nance – what about Tony? I've got to see 'im. I've written to 'im and Billy ever since I left. How is 'e? D'you ever see 'im?'

'Oh – Tony's awright. 'E's got a job carrying hods for Paddy Murphy. Going to be a brickie. 'E's a strong lad and 'e's doing awright. I've seen him about now and then.'

'Does 'e ever say anything about me?'

'Said 'e'd heard from yer – nowt else.'

Maryann sighed, holding out her cup as Nance offered more tea. 'I saw Billy. 'E barely knew who I was.'

'Well, yer been gone a good while. You can't expect them to be all over yer from the word go.'

'No, I s'pose not . . .' Maryann was saying, when the door burst open, kicked by a heavy workman's boot which set the latch rattling.

'Oh, 'ere we go,' Nance said. 'Oh my God, Maryann!' She gasped, panic-stricken. 'I've forgotten all about making tea! Oh Jesus, I'll be for it now!'

She stood up as a stocky, dark-haired man stumped into the room. He had ruddy skin and a weatherbeaten complexion with lines under his eyes that were almost creases. Maryann's first thought was, but he's so *old*! She realized then that he was no older than Joel, but she had expected Nance's husband to be much closer to her own age. Mick Mallone must have been nearer to forty than thirty and looked rough with it. He was swaying from the drink and stood looking at the pair of them. Maryann stood up as well.

''Oo the 'ell's this?' Mick demanded.

'No, Mick – don't start,' Nance said. 'This is my pal

Maryann – I told you about 'er. I've said 'er can stop 'ere with us for a bit, 'cause 'er ain't got nowhere else to go.'

He gave Maryann a mere glance. 'Where's my dinner?'

'I'm going out to get us fish and chips,' Maryann said quickly. 'And I'll take Lizzie and Mary home. Give us a few minutes and I'll be back.'

As she went to the door, Nance shot her a powerful look of gratitude.

Thirty-Five

Carrying the fish and chips back down the road, warm and delicious smelling in their newspaper, Maryann realized how hungry she was. What a long, long day it had been! But she felt relieved after pouring her heart out to Nance. She tried to keep the thought of her mother out of her mind and instead recalled the look in Joel's eyes when she had told him she loved him. This made her so happy that she grinned at a group of children out playing, remembering how she used to play out just round the corner, waiting for her dad to come home.

Back at Nance's she found Mick slumped asleep over the table. She could hear Nance moving about upstairs and, leaving the bundles beside Mick's head, she crept up the creaky stairs to find her.

'That you, Maryann?'

'Yes – I've got the fish and chips. Mick's asleep I think.'

Nance rolled her eyes. 'Best thing. We'll wake 'im up for 'is tea. I was just making up the bed for yer.'

Once again Maryann was struck by how middle-aged Nance seemed. 'Ta, Nance – I dunno what I'd do without yer.'

'Well – pals, eh?' Nance said quite bashfully. Suddenly for a moment they were little girls again. 'Never found another pal quite like you.'

Maryann grinned. 'No – nor me.'

They woke Mick up and he sat blearily with them as they all ate out of the newspaper. The fish and chips tasted to Maryann like some of the best food she'd ever had.

'D'you get work from Marron again?' Nance asked Mick cautiously. He nodded, mouth full of chips. 'What about tomorrer?'

'Maybe.'

Maryann watched him out of the corner of her eye. Nance had told her he could only find work as a casual labourer, bits here, bits there, hanging about early morning with groups of men all looking to be taken on. Long, gruelling days in builder's yards or toiling on roads, and no security. She thought of Evan with his soft cheeks and his soft job at Charnwood, his certainty of 'getting on', and she pitied Mick Mallone. He took no notice of her at all and behaved as if she wasn't there, but she didn't really mind.

Later, when they'd all gone up to bed, Mick and Nance were arguing next door. Every word of it floated through to her as she lay on the lumpy mattress in the back bedroom.

'Yer've never got a word to say to me when yer get in – they get more out of yer down the pub than I ever do. You just expect me to be 'ere like a skivvy – tea on the table the minute you set foot in the door . . .'

'Yes – I do!' Mick yelled, his Kerry accent thickened by drink. 'And I don't think that's too much to expect you to manage when you're here all day. You've got no one else but yourself to think about, now have you?'

'Well, if I ain't got a babby coming whose fault's that then, eh?'

'Shut your blathering mouth, woman!' There was a sound of struggling.

'Stop it, Mick! Yer cowing filthy navvy, don't yer touch me!' Then a cry of pain. ' 'Ow – you bastard!'

'Fuckin' barren bitch!'

On and on they went, the shouting getting louder. Maryann sat up, all tensed up. Was this what always happened at night? Or did Nance need her help? There was another sharp yell of pain from Nancy and Maryann pushed back the bedclothes, her heart pounding, ready to rush in next door. Maybe her visit had provoked Mick beyond what was normal.

Suddenly all went quiet. She sat on the edge of the bed listening. Gradually another sound rose from the next-door room. Listening in disbelief she realized it was weeping she could hear. Mick Mallone's weeping.

Drunken bastard! she thought. He's knocked Nance about and now 'e's gone all maudlin and sorry for 'imself!

But she heard Nance's voice, soft now but with an edge of impatience, saying 'there there' and 'it's awright' until Maryann heard them climbing into bed, and at last there was quiet until Mick started snoring.

'I'm sorry about the row last night,' Nance said next morning. She was downstairs before Maryann. Mick had already gone. Her lip was cut and very swollen. She handed Maryann a cup of tea.

'Oh Nance – you shouldn't 'ave to put up with that! Have you bathed your lip? That looks ever so sore.'

'I'm awright.'

'Does that happen often?'

Nance gave a bitter laugh. 'Not every night, if that's

what yer mean. Look—' She turned, holding her teacup cradled next to her chest. 'You 'ave to understand – about me and Mick. I married 'im to get out of 'ome. 'E married me 'cause 'e wanted someone – *anyone*. 'E 'ad a wife before me – Theresa O'Sullivan she was before she married 'im. Mick doted on 'er. She was nice so far as I remember – sweet natured, gentle like. Died three year ago. They never 'ad any kids. Broke Mick's heart. 'E thought they never caught for a babby 'cause of 'er. Thought she weren't the type. Too weak and frail. But it ain't 'appening with me neither and 'e's starting to think it's 'im – probably is 'im I reckon and that ain't easy for a man to come to terms with. 'E don't love me – not really and I don't love 'im. But I feel for 'im. 'E used to be a fine man.'

'But 'e knocks you about, Nance!'

'I can stand up for myself,' she said with a sigh. 'You don't really know what the last few years've been like shut away out in the country, do yer? There've been that many out of work and the Means Test. It's been bitter 'ard for the men.' She put her cup down. 'I took what I could, Maryann. Couldn't see much else on offer . . .' Her hands went over her face suddenly.

'Oh Nance—' Maryann went to comfort her as her shoulders began to shake.

'And now I don't think 'e'll even give me a babby either. I try not to mind, but I don't know 'ow I'm going to face being married to Mick if it's just 'im and me and no one else for the rest of our lives!'

Maryann spent the morning with Nance, helping her out round the house and listening to her pour her heart out. Whatever brave face Nance was putting on about her marriage, however much she tried to laugh it off, Maryann could see how unhappy she was. She was thinking about Nance as she travelled to the hospital that afternoon to see Joel.

I'll slip Nance a bit of extra money to treat herself, Maryann thought. She had her savings and she wasn't going to go scrounging off Nance and Mick – she'd pay her board. But she could try and cheer Nance up a bit too.

She stepped off the tram and walked along Oak Tree Lane, hurrying anxiously to get to Joel. How would she find him today? She hoped he'd be just a bit better – better for seeing her perhaps?

But when she said, 'I've come to see Mr Joel Bartholomew,' to the plump, red-headed sister, the woman's expression turned very grave.

Maryann's blood seemed to freeze with dread. 'What's the matter?'

'I'm afraid Mr Bartholomew took a turn for the worse in the night.'

'Oh no ... Is 'e—? 'E's still ...'ere?' She looked wildly down the long Nightingale ward to see if she could see him.

'He's here,' the woman said stiffly. 'But perhaps not for much longer without a miracle. Are you the girl who came to see him yesterday?'

Maryann nodded, her eyes full of tears. Oh this couldn't be true, Joel couldn't die, not when they'd found each other again and they had so much between them! How could she face the future again without Joel? She wanted to give so much love to him, to make up for all their lost, lonely years.

'I really don't think ...' the woman began, but seeing Maryann begin to weep in front of her she hesitated.

'Please,' Maryann sobbed. 'I told the nurse yesterday – 'e ain't got no one else.'

The sister relented. 'You better calm down before you go to him.'

Maryann nodded, unable to speak. She wiped her face, pulled her shoulders back and walked along the ward, feeling the eyes of the other male patients on her.

Joel looked very bad. For a moment as she approached the bed she thought he wasn't breathing and his face was sunken and pale, head turned to one side like someone trying to catch the sunlight. Her tears started to fall again in spite of herself as she looked at him. He seemed so weak and defeated.

Kneeling in the narrow gap by the bed, she took his hand and brought it to her cheek.

'Oh Joel,' she whispered. 'Stay with me. Please don't go – don't die. Can you 'ear me? Joel, please open your eyes – please still be 'ere.'

Watching his face, she saw, rather than heard, his shallow breathing and waited, staring intensely at him, for a flicker of movement, some sign that he was not leaving her. For a second his lashes flickered and she thought he was going to open his eyes.

'Joel?'

But the movement stopped and left her feeling more desolate than before. He couldn't hear her. He was slipping away. She talked to him frantically in a low voice, begging him, talking about all the things they'd do when he was better, saying over and over again how she loved him, clinging to his hot hand. But there was nothing. Eventually the sister came and approached the bed.

'I think it's time to leave him now, dear.' Her

kindness terrified Maryann more than brusqueness would have done. It seemed to indicate that she was sure Joel was going to die.

'If only I could stay with 'im—' She found it unbearable to tear herself away from his hand. 'D'yer think – will 'e last the night?'

Her gaze not meeting Maryann's, the sister said, 'I'm afraid I couldn't tell you that.'

She stepped out of the ward as if into another world. It was late afternoon and sultry, the air full of acidic smells from the battery factory near by. She turned away from the city and walked numbly towards Lodge Hill Cemetery, stepping in through its gates to the tranquillity of flowerbeds and trees and gravestones. She made her way to the two graves which belonged to her, not side by side but not far apart, each with a modest headstone.

'HAROLD NELSON – 1892–1926' she read, and then, 'SALLY ANNE GRIFFIN – 1913–1928'.

The sight of Sal's gravestone brought all her rage and hurt to boiling point. Griffin! Her mom had buried Sal under that bastard's name – the one who'd all but killed her himself.

'How could she have done it?' She found herself kicking at the stone, screaming out her pain and fury. 'How could she, how *could* she?'

Not even looking to see if anyone was about, past caring, she sank to her knees and rested her head on Sal's grave, sobbing. 'Oh Sal ... oh God ... sis ... sis ...' The memory of that night she had found Sal filled her mind, of the day her dad died, and then Joel, lying there, hardly seeming to be alive even now.

Would she be visting him here too, having no one to talk to but the graves of all the people she loved? She curled up tight by Sal's grave, smelling the earth close to her face, and cried until she could cry no more.

Thirty-Six

Nance only had to look at Maryann's face when she got back.

'Oh Maryann – 'e's not . . .?'

She came to greet her, anxiously wringing a cloth in her hands. The bruising had spread round Nance's lip but the sight of her friend pulled her mind right away from her own troubles. Maryann sank down at the table.

'No. But I don't think—' She looked up at Nance, her eyes filling again even though she thought she'd cried all the tears she was capable of. 'They don't think 'e'll last the week – maybe not even the night. 'E hardly seems to be breathing. I can't bear it, Nance . . .'

'Oh Maryann, no!'

Nance pulled the other chair round and perched on it beside her, clasping Maryann's hands in her rough ones as her friend poured out her feelings.

'I was hoping 'e'd be better today, but he couldn't even open his eyes and look at me. It almost seemed he was dead already. Oh and 'e's got no one with 'im – I wish they'd've let me stay with 'im!'

'What about 'is family? Ain't there anyone round about for 'im?'

'No – there's only Darius, his brother and 'e's—' She got abruptly to her feet. 'Darius! I must let 'im know 'ow bad things are. I don't know if 'e can make it but I'll 'ave to give 'im the chance to try. Have you got a bit of paper I could write 'im a note on?'

Nancy managed to find a scrap of paper and left Maryann with it at the table while she went out to see if she could beg an envelope off one of the neighbours. She soon came back with one and Maryann addressed it to Tooley's Yard in Banbury and ran out to post it. Someone would have to read it to Darius – if he was still there. She told him in the note that she'd leave her address for him at the toll office at Farmer's Bridge. She slipped it into the box, praying Joel would hang on. The thought made her cry all over again.

She went to the hospital the next day, sick with dread. But she found Joel in much the same state as he had been in the day before. She sat beside him, willing him with all her strength and love to hold on to life.

'I'll be here, Joel, waiting for you, praying for you. Just don't leave me – I love you.'

She could hardly bear to let go of his hand and go away, she was so afraid that she might not see him alive again. She was living from moment to moment. Thinking about the future was impossible. She couldn't face it now without Joel.

That evening she went to find Tony, waiting at the end of Sheepcote Lane, hoping she could intercept him before he reached home. She stood watching both ends of the street, afraid she would not be able to recognize him and full of misgiving that if she did see him he would reject her just as angrily as her mother had.

At last when he appeared she knew immediately who he was. He turned into the road, walking briskly, whistling, a small canvas bag slung over one shoulder, his jacket slung back over the other. His boots and clothes were pale with dust and smears of cement, his cap was pushed far back on his head, showing a dark-eyed face which was also covered in muck. He was much bigger, just about her own height, quite grown up into a wiry, muscular lad. When he drew nearer and caught sight of her, he stopped in mid-whistle.

''Ello, Tony.'

He came nearer. She couldn't read his expression, except that it didn't hold surprise. Her mom must have told him she'd been back. 'Maryann?'

She was full of emotion, remembering the little boy she had left sleeping the night she ran away. 'I s'pose you thought I was never coming back.'

'Well – I dunno. I mean it's been—' He shrugged, looking down at the ground, awkward, and embarrassed by her emotion. 'Mom said you'd been to see 'er.'

'It's a wonder she could bring 'erself to mention my name,' Maryann said bitterly. 'What did 'er say?'

'Not much. Said yer wouldn't be coming again.'

Maryann wiped her eyes and looked into his face. 'What about you, Tony? You angry with me too?'

She saw a flicker of hostility, then sorrow in his dark eyes. She could sense his confused loyalties. 'Dunno. No. Not really.'

'And he left then? Norman?'

Tony nodded, raising his head. 'Mom said it were your fault.' He sounded angry, despite his denial. 'We had to come back down 'ere—' He jerked his head to indicate the lane. 'Why did yer do it, Maryann? I know 'e weren't our dad but 'e weren't all that bad. What did yer 'ave to go and ruin everyfing for?'

It was Maryann's turn to look away, shame rising in

her, the blood rushing to her cheeks. Her tears started to fall. How could she tell Tony what Norman Griffin had done to her and Sal – above all to Sal? How could she speak like that to her little brother? Little Tony who spoke in a gruff man-boy voice, who still couldn't say his 'th's properly?

'I'm sorry, Tony . . .' She couldn't help crying however hard she tried, and she stood in front of him weeping there in the street. 'I'm sorry – I had to go. *I had to do it* . . . I can't explain it to yer.'

'Why not? Don't yer think I'm grown up enough to be told what's going on, eh? I feel like a right bloody mug I do. I'm old enough to keep food on the table but I ain't old enough to be told anyfing. 'Ow about letting me in on a few fings, eh?'

'Ssh – oh Tony, please be quiet!' Maryann seized his arm. 'Don't – not in the street. I don't want people staring and gossiping. Look – come for a walk with me, away from 'ere.'

'I'll come,' Tony said, on his dignity. 'But you'd better be straight with me, Maryann. So far as Mom's concerned you were the ruin of the family. It ain't how I remember yer or think of you, but you'd better 'ave summat to say to me.' Suddenly he seemed near tears himself. She wanted to put her arms round him as she had done when he was little, but knew she mustn't.

'Oh Tony – I will tell you. Only you have to promise me you'll believe what I say. Mom never would – that's why I had to go in the end. I couldn't stand telling you if you start saying I'm a liar.'

She led him, as if automatically, to the place where they could squeeze through down to the cut, and they walked side by side away from town, breathing in the murky smell of the canal, reflections shifting on the water's surface. She found it very difficult to talk. What had happened in the past had been buried in her for so long that at first she skirted round and round what she needed to say and at last she blurted it out clumsily, knowing she owed Tony the truth.

'You daint know – you were too little. I know Mr Griffin took us to the pictures and we always had enough and didn't go short, but there was another side to him, Tony. A filthy, wicked side. And it was Sal had the worst of it. He was . . . he was . . .' Oh God, how could she say it?

She forced herself to glance round at her brother. He was watching his feet, a slight frown on his face. Maryann took in a huge, ragged breath and forced herself to go on, telling him, explaining, indirectly at first, then, uncertain if he knew what she meant, in more detail. The memories came back, raw and sickening. She stopped walking and sobbed out to him how she'd found Sal that day.

'He destroyed her. Week by week. He killed her from inside, Tony. That's what happened to your sister. She took her own life because she couldn't stand living no more after him and what it did to her. She thought she was expecting a babby as well, Tony – you won't've known that. And I . . . d'you know, that night I went down there I daint 'ave a plan. I knew I was going to do summat, I was so full of grief and anger for Sal but I daint know what. And then when I saw what I saw down there – I went mad. I was ready to do him in – destroy him and everything that was his. That was when I started the fire, and then I had to go—' Tears on her cheeks, she begged her brother, 'Don't say you don't believe me, Tony. Please don't. It's the truth – I swear to you on my life!'

She could see just how much she'd got through to him. Tony's thin face looked stunned. Eventually he said, 'Did Mom know?'

'I told 'er. I kept trying to say, but she daint want to 'ear it. All she wanted to see was the respectable side of him. I s'pose she shut it out of her mind. She was scared to frighten him off. In the end I did it for 'er.'

They stood in the dusk on the canal bank. Maryann found she could not look into his eyes. She felt dreadful after what she had had to tell him. Tony was silent for a time and she ached to know what he was thinking. At least he hadn't rejected her story straight away and told her she was a filthy liar. She sensed he was thinking hard.

'I fink I remember,' he said eventually. 'Yes – I do.'

'What?'

'Him – Griffin – coming in – of a night. When you and Sal was in the bed. It feels like a dream – but I know 'e was in there sometimes – on your bed. I remember the creaking and his voice in there.'

'Oh Tony! D'you really – you remember that?'

'I remember the bed squeaking – and 'im breathing and saying fings to yer.'

'Oh thank God!' Maryann cried. It was then, at last, she went and put her arms round him. 'Someone who knows I'm not making it up – oh Tony … I'm so happy to see you again. I've missed you so much – you and Billy, but especially you. I've been so lonely without you.'

He was awkward in her embrace at first. But then he dropped his jacket and bag on to the dry ground and his arms came round her as she cried.

'Did you get my letters?'

'Yes.'

'And the little cat I left on yer pillow?'

'Yes—' He sounded embarrassed. He was crying too.

''Ve you still got it somewhere?'

She pulled back and looked at him. Tony nodded, quickly wiping his eyes on the back of his hands.

'See – I was always thinking of you. Tony?'

'What?'

'What d'you call yourself – Nelson or Griffin?'

'Griffin.' He looked at her, ashamed, then said quietly, 'But not any more, Maryann. Never. Not after what you've told me.'

They walked on through the half-light, talking much more easily now. Maryann told Tony about Charnwood House, about the *Esther Jane* and Darius, and that he was so desperate he might have to sell her, and about Joel and how worried she was. And Tony told her something of how it had been after she left.

'When 'e saw what'd happened – with the fire, he came 'ome and knocked our mom across the kitchen. I copped 'old of Billy and took 'im outside, out the way of mean old man Griffin – 'e was like someone else that day. Frightened us.'

'He *is* someone else,' Maryann said grimly. 'That's who is really is underneath. Cruel and scheming. I wonder where 'e went to after.'

'Oh – we know where 'e is,' Tony told her, almost casually.

'*Do* you? What – somewhere near by? In Birmingham?'

'Oh yes – course. Near 'is mom.'

'Oh my God – she ain't still alive?'

'I dunno – she was a while back. 'Er must've been nearly ninety then. 'E's set 'imself up again, over on the Soho Road. The other place was insured, yer know – 'e ain't no fool.'

'No,' Maryann agreed. 'So our mom knows where 'e is?'

'Oh ar – I mean when it first happened 'e went and lived with old Mrs Griffin. Mom went over to 'ers a number of times begging 'im to come back but 'e weren't 'aving it. Said 'e'd had enough and that was that.'

Nothing there for him, Maryann thought grimly. Not without me and Sal. 'What, so Mom just gave up?'

'Had to. She wanted money off of 'im but 'e said the family'd already caused him quite enough trouble and she weren't 'aving a farthing. She come back ever so upset every time but there was nothing 'er could do. She 'ad to come to terms with it – 'e'd gone and that was that. She 'ad to make the best of it and fend for 'erself. So we moved up the old end and got on with it.'

'But she ain't going to forgive me, is she?'

'Not in a hurry, no.'

By now they'd reached the part of the bank in Ladywood where they had to scramble up and climb through the broken fence.

'It's him should be paying for all the grief he's caused – not Mom. Not us either,' Maryann said, once they were up on the road again. 'If I could just see 'im, I'd . . .' But her voice trailed off, hopelessly. What could she do? What did it matter now? The only things that mattered were that Joel was lying in hospital fighting to stay alive, and that she had seen her brother and he forgave her.

'Meet me again, will yer?' she said to him. 'And bring Billy with yer.'

Tony nodded, his eyes very dark in his pale face.

'You'd best get 'ome. You must be hungry.'

'I could go and 'ave a look – over round 'is place,' Tony said suddenly.

'Well – if you can stand the sight of 'im.' Maryann touched his arm, smiling. 'T'ra, Tony. See yer soon.'

When she got back to Nance and Mick's, Nance started up from the table as she walked in, trying to pretend she hadn't been sitting crying, and quickly wiped her eyes.

'Oh Nance – what's wrong?' Maryann wasn't fooled for a moment. 'I do wish you was happier, that I do.'

'I'm awright—' Nance hurried over to put the kettle on. 'It's just I wish Mick'd stay in a night or two sometimes. 'E never seems to be 'ere lately. But never mind, eh? How's Joel?'

'No better.' Maryann sank down at the table. ''E just seemed the same as yesterday. Oh Nance – I wish there was something I could do.'

Thirty-Seven

Maryann spent the following days in an agony of waiting. Though she was pleased to have had such a good meeting with Tony, and enjoyed Nance's company, her mind was never far from Joel. She was sick with worry. Her appetite had disappeared almost completely and she had trouble sleeping, thinking of him lying there as she saw him every day, hanging between life and death, not quite belonging to either. She often cried out her desperation in bed at night, trying to keep quiet so Nance and Mick wouldn't hear her next door.

On the other hand, they often weren't quiet themselves and Maryann realized her own presence was making things worse.

'How much longer've we got *her* hanging about for?' she heard Mick demanding one night.

Another time he made some comment about her living off them.

'She ain't 'ad a penny off of us,' Nance snapped back at him. 'So yer needn't start on like that. Maryann's got money of 'er own and she ain't mean with it neither.'

But this only seemed to increase Mick's resentment, and the added conflict she was causing between Nance and her husband made Maryann feel even more desperate. If only she could leave them in peace, but where else did she have to go?

On the third day after she had seen Tony she woke

after a broken, wretched night and lay in bed, unable to sleep but too limp and tired to get out of bed. She heard the door bang as Mick went off to work, and closed her eyes. She always felt relieved knowing he was out of the house.

She was still dozing when there came more banging. Nance was downstairs and Maryann heard voices, then Nance calling up the stairs, 'Maryann – someone to see yer!'

Bewildered, she hastily pulled her dress on and ran down without combing her hair, her mind full of irrational questions. Was it news about Joel? Had he passed away in the night? But no, of course not – no one came out to tell you. And it still felt very early.

Downstairs, she found a man with dark curly hair, looking enormous in the little room, his head almost touching the ceiling. He looked exhausted and was twisting his cap between his hands, obviously most uneasy to be in this strange place. It took her a moment to realize who he was.

'Darius – you got my letter then!' She felt so pleased to see him, as if he was a member of her own family. 'How did you get 'ere?'

'I come almost non-stop,' he said. 'After I 'eard from you. Bessie's all in. Pulled into Birnigum as it was getting light. So—' He stepped closer, urgently. 'What about Joel – have I got 'ere in time?'

'Oh Darius ...' Tears came so readily to her eyes at the moment. 'You have if 'e's the same as yesterday. I've been waiting and watching every day and 'e's been lain there, not knowing what's going on around him and his breathing's that bad. Every day when I go I don't know ...'

'Well 'ow about us go now – where is it? Is it far?'

Maryann managed a wan smile through her tears. 'We 'ave to go in the afternoon – they won't let us in now.'

''Ere—' Nance gestured shyly at the table. ''Ave a seat, Mr Bartholomew, and I'll make us some breakfast. I've even got some eggs today, thanks to Maryann.' Maryann noticed that Nance seemed quite overwhelmed by his presence.

Darius sat down rather reluctantly, as he had been all primed to spring into action straight away. Maryann sat with him and they drank tea as Nancy cooked, quietly listening and turning often from the range to look curiously at Maryann and this great, rugged visitor.

'So you came in the *Esther Jane*?' Maryann quizzed him.

''Course. What else? You got to me just in time. They'd just finished 'er up at Tooley's Yard and I was off to load up when your letter came.'

'So, you ain't sold 'er yet – to Mr Barlow?'

Darius shook his head slowly, swallowing a mouthful of tea. Maryann saw the muscles move in his thick neck. She waited for him to speak. The Bartholomews never hurried anything they wanted to say.

'Not yet. I couldn't sell 'er out from under the nose of my father without 'im being there. Nor Joel. Mr Barlow said 'e could wait.'

'So ... you didn't come the whole way single-handed?'

'No. There's a nipper come up with me this time. The Higgins family loaned me young Ernie. I left 'im asleep—' For the first time something like a smile came

341

to Darius's weathered face. Maryann saw Nance watching him, intrigued. 'That's a trip 'e won't forget in a hurry!'

'How's old Mr Bartholomew?' Maryann asked.

Darius shook his head. 'Mending – slow though. Oh, ta – very good of you.' He nodded appreciatively at Nance as she set before him a plate piled with bread and butter and *three* fried eggs. Maryann's plate held one and Nance appeared to be having only bread. Maryann raised an eyebrow at her.

''E's 'ad a long night,' Nance said, blushing. ''E deserves a good feed.'

They ate in silence for a time. Darius seemed ravenous and emptied his plate quickly, wiping up every last drop of yolk with the bread. Nance's knife and fork looked like toys in his big hands. She nibbled at her bread, seeming fascinated by Darius. Maryann also found her eyes drawn to his face as she ate. Having him here was wonderful to her, like having part of Joel. Though they looked different, there was something about the way they both moved and in the tone of their voices that was similar. She felt proud that he had appeared. But she was longing to ask him, keep on at him – you can't really sell the *Esther Jane*? You're not really going to? And her heart ached. She knew how much this would mean to Joel, how much he would struggle with every ounce of strength he had to stop it happening if he were able. But now perhaps Darius would be left alone for ever. Perhaps Joel would never . . .

Feeling tears welling in her eyes again she tore her thoughts away and looked up at Darius. He'd drunk his tea and his eyes were drooping, his whole body sagging with weariness.

'You need a sleep,' she told him. 'Would it be awright if 'e went up on my bed for a bit, Nance?'

For a second Nance looked put out, and Maryann knew she was calculating what Mick would have to say about this. But Darius would be gone long before Mick appeared.

''Course 'e can.' She smiled warmly. 'You show 'im up there, Maryann.'

Darius was dead to the world all morning. Maryann helped Nance around the house, glad to have plenty to do to while away the morning. She scrubbed the front step and helped with a load of washing, mangling it and pegging it out in the hazy sunshine, a shaft of which penetrated into the yard round the back where they were working.

'On the cut they hang the washing out along the boats,' she told Nance, shaking out a dress of her own before she pegged it on the line. It smelled rather harshly of soap.

Nance looked up, bent over the mangle. 'Do they? Fancy—' She frowned. 'I always thought them people on the cut were just a bunch of gypos. But that Darius seems a nice man.'

'They ain't gypos,' Maryann said hotly. 'And they ain't *all* rough. They just live a bit different, that's all.'

Nance looked doubtful. '*Very* different, going by what I've 'eard. Still – some of 'em are awright I s'pose.'

'Yes.' Maryann still sounded cross. ''Course they are. You want to see for yerself before you start canting on about things you don't know.'

''Eh – there's no need to bite my 'ead off—' Nance

began mangling again furiously. 'Bet you'd've said the same if yer didn't know.'

Maryann took Mick's spare trousers as they rolled through the mangle. 'S'pose so,' she conceded. 'Sorry, Nance.'

'That's awright. I know you're on edge.'

After a few moments, without looking up from the mangle, Nance said, "'E's got a wife, I s'pose?'

'No.' Maryann was stretching up to the line.

Nance looked over at her. "'E ain't married? Your Joel ain't married. I mean they're getting on, the pair of 'em. What's the matter with 'em?'

'There's nothing the matter with them!' Maryann snapped again, irritated by the way Nance said it. 'Joel 'ad a sweetheart when 'e was young and she married someone else by the end of the War. I don't know about Darius – they're working almost every hour of the day and it ain't that easy to meet up with anyone on the cut. You just don't know what it's like, Nance.'

'No. So yer keep saying. I'm just surprised a man with 'is looks ain't wed by now, that's all. 'E looks a bit of awright to me.'

'Does 'e now?' Maryann teased. 'Well – you'd better watch yerself then. Old married woman like you.'

She didn't fail to notice the blush that rushed through Nance's cheeks.

They had to wake Darius after midday. He emerged from sleep utterly bewildered as he looked round, then seeing Maryann, he sat up in a panic.

'Is it time – are we too late?'

'No – yer awright. Nance's done us a bit of dinner, and then we'll go.' She gave her hair a hasty going over

344

with her treasured brush she had had that Christmas at Charnwood. 'Don't worry – we'll be in good time.'

Don't worry! she thought later as she sat beside Darius on the tram along the Bristol Road. Well, there was a daft thing to say. The whole of her life was consumed with worry. She looked round at Darius. He didn't look any too happy on the tram. It was quite full and she could sense how uneasy and out of place he felt.

Inside the hospital was even worse. He walked along the corridor beside her, tense and silent, looking about him. Maryann felt the usual sense of panic and dread engulf her as they approached the ward but she fought against it, determined not to show Darius how bad she was feeling.

At the door she forced herself to look along, her gaze racing to the spot where Joel had been lying all that week. For a moment she couldn't take it in, could not make sense of anything, and then she saw properly as the room came into focus.

'Oh—' she gulped. 'Oh, it's awright, Darius – 'e's still there! Come on.' She found herself taking his arm, leading him down to Joel's bed.

She had grown used to the sight of how Joel had become through illness and that his beard had gone, and she had not thought to warn Darius. The shock registered in his face. Plainly Joel looked a lot worse than when Darius had last seen him.

They went to the side of the bed and Maryann searched hungrily for any sign of change. Joel still lay with his eyes closed, his breathing shallow and laboured. Each time she saw him his body seemed more slight and the sight of him filled her with pain. He was disappearing. Slowly, inexorably, day by day, the man she loved was slipping away. Darius sat on the chair, cap in hand, staring at his brother in appalled silence.

Maryann kneeled down and took Joel's hand, kissing it as she always did.

'Joel? It's me again – Maryann. And Darius – your brother – he's here with me. He's come all the way up from Banbury to see you – brought the *Esther Jane* out of Tooley's Yard and she's 'ere—' On her own she often broke down talking to him, receiving as much reply as she would from a stone, but today she wanted to be strong for Darius's sake. She looked round at him. 'D'yer want to say anything to him?'

Darius leaned forward. 'Joel. It's Darius—' He looked round the room distractedly, as if searching for the right words. 'I 'ope you're going to get better, Joel – on your feet soon, eh?' He sat back, clearly at a loss, but his gaze never left Joel's face.

'D'you 'ear that, Joel? What Darius says? Please get better and come back to us. We all need yer – Darius and me and your dad and the *Esther Jane* . . . .' More softly, she added, 'And I love you, Joel – I do love you so much.'

It was then she felt it. Just for a second. She turned with a gasp to Darius. 'He moved his hand! I felt it. 'E sort of squeezed mine – there, 'e did it again!'

'Don't 'e do that normally?'

'No – no! I've not had anything out of him. Oh Joel – can you hear us?'

Again, a pressure round her hand. Then a faint fluttering of his eyelashes. She and Darius stood waiting, absolutely still. There was nothing more, though they waited on and on.

'Nurse!' Maryann was too emotional to be frightened of the nurse. The woman came over to her, her face grave, obviously steeling herself.

'What is it?' Her voice was sharp.

''E just squeezed my hand – a few times. He squeezed my hand!'

The woman's face relaxed, looking relieved, then pleased. 'Did he, now?'

Maryann left the hospital with Darius feeling like a different person. It had been a small thing, that tiny movement that told her Joel knew he was still with them, but it changed everything. They had hope, hope which lit the day brighter than the brightest summer sun.

'I'm so glad it happened with you 'ere,' she told Darius, who seemed to be grasping just how much this meant. 'Oh – I feel so happy!' She felt like shouting and singing. 'Are you coming back to Nance's?'

'No – reckon I'll get back to the boat.'

'I tell you what, let's take Nance to see 'er. We've got to go back that way any'ow and it's not far. How about that?'

'Awright. If that's what you want.' He smiled. 'Reckon young Ernie'll just be awake by now and starving 'ungry!'

Nance was all of a tizz when they got back and asked her to come out with them. 'But I can't – I mean I've got to do the dinner, and . . .'

'Oh come on, Nance!' Maryann chivvied her, untying her apron. 'No arguments – you're coming.'

'Maryann!' Nance laughed. She could see the change in Maryann immediately.

'We'll get some liver or summat on the way back – that's nice and quick. It's a lovely day today – you don't want to spend it stuck in 'ere, do you?'

'Well – if Mr – if Darius don't mind?'

Darius shrugged. 'I can stay 'ere a bit longer. If you want to come that's all right with me.'

They walked out into the bright, hot afternoon. Darius told them he had tied up not far from Farmer's Bridge and Maryann led the way through the streets of buses and trams and hurrying people, which seemed to be as foreign as a jungle to Darius.

'Did you bring her up empty?' Maryann asked him.

'Oh no – I got a load on grain into 'er – unloaded that this morning.'

'There she is!' Maryann cried as they reached the spot. The boat sat high in the water. 'Ooh, she's looking nice, Darius – much better than when I saw 'er before.'

'She's 'ad a good going over,' he agreed. 'And a lick of paint. She was in a bad state before. Only we 'ad to keep getting ahead – there was never time.'

Young Ernie Higgins was sitting out on the bank beside the boat chewing on an apple. Darius helped Nance on board and Maryann followed.

'Oh my – it's tiny in 'ere!' Nance said, peering into the cabin. Astonished, she turned to Darius and Maryann. 'D'you live in 'ere – all year round?'

'Got nowhere else,' Darius said. 'That's it – home to us.' He smiled, obviously enjoying her amazement.

'And you lived on 'ere an' all?' she said to Maryann. 'Where on earth did yer sleep?'

Maryann took great pride in showing her the cabin, where they slept and cooked and old Mrs Bartholomew's crochet work, almost as if she'd been born to

348

the life and wasn't a newcomer 'off the bank' herself.
Nance sat at the tiny table.

'It's like playing doll's 'ouses!' She laughed. She was
more light-hearted than Maryann had yet seen her. 'I've
never seen anything so tiny. And it's ever so clean –
not like them dirty old joey boats. Ooh – ain't it nice?'

'There's nothing like it,' Maryann said, taking a seat
beside her. She looked round contentedly. Darius had
had time to polish the brasses while he was at Tooley's
Yard, and the cabin was fairly clean too. Her eye still
picked out a lot of things that needed doing. It felt like
her home.

'Oh Nance—' She squeezed her friend's hand. 'Joel's
going to get better. I know 'e is! This feels like the
happiest day of my life!'

'I'm glad for yer,' Nance said sincerely.

Darius poked his head through the door of the cabin
and smiled. 'I'll brew up a cuppa tea, shall I?'

He seemed to enjoy their company and was far more
relaxed now he was back on the cut, having come
through the ordeal of going to the hospital. They sat
drinking tea – Darius and Nance perched at the stern,
Maryann sat half twisted round on the cabin step. Darius
told Nance about the life and how they worked. Maryann could see she admired Darius and he was at ease
with her, seemed to like her. She made him laugh. And
Nance basked in the sun, her pale, thin body seeming
to relax and become more youthful away from home.
Maryann saw Darius looking at her often. If only things
were different, she thought, I do believe these two
might've had something. But it was no good thinking
of that. She thought bitterly about Mick. Shame you
could never see what was just round the corner.

'Now I've seen Joel,' Darius was saying, 'I'll go looking for a load tonight – get off in the morning. I'd thought I might 'ave to be here longer, if . . . but I'll get ahead for a bit. Keep 'er going. There's nothing I can do 'ere for now.'

'Oh – I wish I was coming with you,' Maryann said.

'I almost wish I was from what you've told me.' Nance laughed. Maryann hadn't heard her laugh like that in ages.

'Ah well.' Darius smiled. 'God knows, you'd both be welcome. I could do with more hands on board. I s'pose we'll manage though.' He nodded his head towards Ernie. 'For now.'

Thirty-Eight

'Don't tell 'im where we've been, for God's sake,' Nance implored later as they got the tea ready fast and furiously. They'd stayed too long down on the cut and had had to run back, via the butcher's. The prospect of Mick's fury if everything wasn't ready when he got home set the pair of them off and the cooking became a joke. Maryann was chopping onions frantically at the table. Nance was so dithery she dropped the liver on the floor so it had to be washed and then she got the giggles.

'Oh, look at that! What'd Mick say if 'e saw me throwing 'is tea on the floor!' Her laughter almost got the better of her as she mimicked her husband's indignation, swaggering and waving a piece of liver around in her hand like a weapon. '"Sure I don't see my dinner ready. What sort of a wife is it who can't even put a meal on the table when a man walks through the door!" Oh my Lord!' she spluttered. 'I don't know what's got into me!'

Maryann was laughing just as much, her eyes also streaming from the onions. She was bubbly with relief and hope over Joel, and really happy to see what difference a little break had made to Nance, who looked younger again suddenly, face pink from the sun and full of mirth under her mop of black curls. They were both laughing so much that for a few minutes they

351

were incapable of cooking anything at all and the liver and onions lay untouched on the table.

A rattle at the door sobered them instantly.

Nance gasped, horrified. ''E can't be back already!'

But the door didn't open.

'Must be someone else,' Nance hissed and crept over to open it. 'Oh – 'ello, Tony love.' She started giggling again with relief. ''Ow're you? Come on in. Don't mind me.'

'S'Maryann there?'

Maryann experienced a flutter of pleasure that he had come to find her. *My brother.* He had clearly just got off work again and was as grubby as the last time she saw him.

'Awright, Tony – ain't yer coming in?'

He looked awkward and anxious at the same time. 'Can yer come out – just for a bit?'

Maryann looked doubtful. 'Can you manage, Nance?'

'Yes, go on – I'll get on quicker without you setting me off.'

She walked with Tony down to the end of the street, passing men on their way home from work, a few kids playing out. Smells of cooking drifted from the houses as they walked along.

'I thought you were going to bring Billy to see me,' she reproached him.

'Not this time.' Tony seemed tense.

'What's up?'

'I know where 'e's living.'

Maryann didn't need to ask who. 'You went to see him?'

'*No.* Course not. I followed 'im home. 'E does just what 'e did when 'e was with Mom. Leaves and locks

352

up just the same time, quick pint and 'ome. 'E lives up behind the park in Handsworth.'

'And has a shop on the Soho Road? An under-taker's?'

'It's an undertaker's, but it ain't under the name of Griffin. 'E set 'imself up under a new name: Arthur Lambert. 'E's made 'isself a new life awright.'

'The slimy . . .' Maryann began, but Tony inter-rupted.

'T'ain't the main fing though. After I followed 'im home I waited for a bit to see if I could see anyfing. I daint see much, but when it was getting dark this woman come and shut the curtains at the front.'

'Woman – what, you mean . . .? Could be a landlady, couldn't it?'

'Could be. I dunno. But then, when I was getting fed up, nuffing to see – I s'pose they'd been 'aving some tea – the door come open and two girls came out and went off down the road.'

'Girls?' Maryann stopped, full of foreboding. 'How old?'

'Couldn't see for sure. Younger'un me.'

Maryann felt herself swell inside with suspicion and fury. 'Oh no – oh Tony, d'yer think . . .?'

Tony shrugged. 'Dunno – couldn't make out anyfing else.'

'No. Course yer couldn't.' She felt sorry he was involved. He was still only a kid, even if he was tall and muscular and doing a man's work. He shouldn't even have to know any of this. 'Look – thanks, Tony. For doing that.'

'What're yer going to do, sis?'

It warmed her heart to hear him call her that – already, when she'd been away so long. Made her feel she belonged. This search for Norman Griffin was bringing them together. Once again she thanked God that Tony believed her, was on her side. She couldn't have faced this alone.

'I don't know, Tony. I really don't. What *can* I do? It makes me feel bad just thinking about it.' She wouldn't say more to him, didn't want to fill his head with disturbing details.

''E wants a good 'iding, 'e does,' Tony said fiercely.

Maryann almost smiled. A 'good hiding' sounded so innocent, like something a child might be threatened with. It was the least of what she had in mind. ''E does that, Tony. And I'm going to think about how he's going to get it an' all.'

When she got back, Mick was home, eating in silence. Nance winked at her over his head but Maryann could tell the atmosphere between them was very sour. Nance was back to the cowed, weary-looking woman she had been before and Maryann felt Mick's resentment of her as soon as she walked in. She ate up her own tea quickly and said she was going to bed.

Soon after she'd gone up she heard them start downstairs, arguing, voices getting louder, savage in tone. She undressed, full of tension. It was horrible to hear.

'Don't you start carrying on like that!' she heard Nance shout. 'I 'ate it when you show yer face through the door these days, yer miserable sod. I don't know why yer bother coming 'ome the way yer keep on when you're 'ere!'

'This is my house and you'll not talk to me like that.

If I'd known what sort of a wife you'd make I'd never've married you, so I wouldn't . . .'

'Not like the blessed Saint Theresa yer mean!' Nance shrieked harshly. 'Well, 'er was never so bloody perfect as yer make out – and you never managed to get 'er a bun in the oven neither, did yer?'

It always came back to that. Maryann screwed up her eyes, hearing Nance's howl of pain and then a crash as something fell and smashed on the floor. There was more shouting, followed by a roar which almost made Maryann's heart stop.

'You bitch! You evil fecking bitch – look what you've done!'

She ran down and stopped at the bottom of the stairs, appalled. Suddenly everything was quiet. Mick was standing clutching his left forearm, blood oozing out round his fingers. Nance, mouth open in horror, was still holding the knife she'd used to slice up the pig's liver.

'Oh . . . Mick!' Nance gasped. 'What've I done?' She seized a cloth and went to him to staunch the wound but he snatched it and backed away from her.

'Don't you come near me, you mad bitch!' he snarled. 'Look what you've done to me! You're not right up top – you're not fit to be a wife to anyone.' Clutching the cloth to his arm he backed out of the door, kicked it shut so the house shook and then they heard his feet going down the path.

Nance looked stunned. Maryann went and took the bloodstained knife from her quivering hand and laid it on the table.

'He punched me.' Nance's mouth was trembling, the tears starting to come. 'It 'urt so much . . . I daint know what I was doing.' She laid her hand over her right breast. 'Punched me just 'ere.' She sat down and started to cry. Maryann poured her a nip of whiskey and put it down beside her. ''E should've never punched me there – it 'urt too much. Oh Maryann – what've I done?'

''E'll be awright. It's only a cut.'

But she knew Nance didn't just mean Mick's arm. She meant everything.

Maryann scarcely slept that night. She lay awake, awaiting the sound of Mick coming home again. Her thoughts swirled round. She was so upset for Nance, and in the night's darkness she felt full of doubt about everything and very afraid. She had felt Joel squeeze her hand and had been so hopeful, but he was still so ill. It didn't mean he was going to get better, did it? Perhaps even now he was slipping away and she'd never see him again ... She pushed this thought away but it was replaced by all the things Tony had told her about Norman Griffin.

I'm free of him, she thought. I need never have anything else to do with him. I should just give all my strength to Joel and go away and never think about any of it again. He probably has a landlady with children – or they were just visiting ... She tried as hard as she could to persuade herself that this was what was right. It was nothing to do with her. But she could not stop thinking about Sal and herself when Norman was living with them, of the trap of fear and disgust he had built round them. What if he was doing it all again and those two girls were having to live through the same hell that he had put Sal through?

She twisted back and forth in the bed, then lay on her back, hands behind her head looking at the window. There was a full moon and its light was shining through the gap between Nance's thin curtains.

'Tell me what to do,' she whispered. 'I don't want anything to do with this. Let it all just go away.' She ached for the morning to come.

She had left the hospital full of happiness yesterday, but going back today she approached it with terrible misgiving. She was weighed down by the grim thoughts brought on by lack of sleep and what had happened the night before. Mick had not come home all night.

'Oh – 'e'll've gone to 'is mom's to get fussed over,' Nance said. She was trying to take it lightly but she was pale and drawn and Maryann could tell she had not slept either.

This didn't feel like a day for anything good to happen. Her head aching, eyes watering in the sunlight from sleeplessness, she walked to the hospital.

She arrived to find Joel with his eyes open. All her dread drained away, seeing his gaze follow her hungrily towards his bed as if she was the one thing he had been waiting for. There was a little cup on the chair so she sank down on her knees by the bed and for a moment they just gazed at one another in silence. Joel tried to squeeze her hand and she could tell how weak he was.

'You're back,' she said. And burst into tears.

Joel tried to speak but the attempt produced instead a fit of coughing. He reached out for the cup and she passed it to him. He coughed painfully into it, then covered it with his hand. A nurse came and whisked it away and returned it empty a few moments later. Maryann wiped her eyes and got up to perch on the edge of the seat. Joel lay back, panting from the exertion.

'You poor thing,' she said.

Joel patted his chest. Maryann leaned over to hear him whisper, 'I think I've got half the cut in there from what's coming out.'

'But you're going to get better. I know you are. Oh Joel – I've been that worried about you. You've no idea.'

He looked very tenderly at her and she smiled tearfully and buried her head for a moment in the bedding beside him, still holding his hand and drinking in the feeling of being close to him. Then she sat up and examined him again.

'D'you feel better in yourself?'

He nodded. 'Seeing you.'

'I've been in here every day. Did you know? Did you know Darius came?'

Joel looked confused. 'Darius – in here?'

'No – I don't s'pose you remember. He stopped off to see you and then 'e went back to chase another load...' She remembered with a pang that perhaps Darius had seen Samuel Barlow again – perhaps had sold the *Esther Jane* already. She didn't know if Joel knew anything about it and she didn't want to have to tell him – not now especially. 'Anyway – your dad's on the mend. 'E's still down at your auntie's in Oxford but Darius said 'e should be back aboard soon. Darius had a young lad with 'im – Ernie Higgins I think 'is name was.'

She saw Joel nod faintly, and she could tell he was drinking in everything she was telling him. The boat was his life and she could see the hunger for it in his eyes. She leaned forward to catch his words.

'Want to get back aboard . . . soon.'

'Oh Joel – I don't think you'll be ready for a while yet.'

'Soon as I can . . .'

'All right—' She appeased him. How long would it be before he could even walk, let alone work the cut! But she didn't want to upset him.

'Maryann—' He pulled her closer.

'What, love?'

He gazed, very seriously, into her eyes. 'When I get back to 'er – will you be there this time – with me?'

He was coughing again and once more she had to wait for the seizure to pass. It exhausted him, but still he pulled her to him, full of urgency.

'Please . . . will you and me get wed?'

'Oh Joel, love—' She laid her hand against his cheek, stroking it, gently cradling his head. 'You're everything to me. Of course we will.'

He closed his eyes for a moment, quite spent, but with a smile of great joy on his face.

Thirty-Nine

The summer was slipping past. The schools closed and the streets, back yards and parks were full of the sounds of children playing.

Maryann had settled into being Nance and Mick's lodger and for the time being things were better. Mick had stayed away for three days and nights and came home with his arm bandaged and the look of a man who has been severely lectured by his mother. Mrs Mallone the elder, a staunch Catholic, wouldn't countenance the shame of a broken marriage in her family and had told him so in no uncertain terms. He arrived home at the end of a day's work and Maryann got out of the way to let him and Nance sort things out. They arrived at a truce.

'We've decided to stop arguing about us 'aving a babby,' Nance said bravely. 'We'll just 'ave to see what 'appens. And 'e said 'e should never've hit me the way 'e did and 'e don't really mind you being 'ere.'

Maryann thought that remained to be seen, but she was relieved as well. She just hoped Mick could put up with her until Joel was better.

Each day Maryann saw an improvement in Joel. He became a little stronger, bit by bit. Although he was still terribly thin his skin started to lose its deathly yellow colour, and he was able to talk more without being crippled by the agonizing cough. They talked a great deal on every visit, catching up with some of the time they had missed over the intervening years.

Sometimes Joel looked longingly at her. 'I wish we weren't sat here on full view of everyone – then I could give you a proper kiss.'

Just for a moment Maryann experienced her old surge of dread at the thought of any man touching her, and she had to reason with herself. Not every man was Norman Griffin. And this was Joel – her beloved Joel. She laughed happily. 'You *are* getting better, ain't yer?'

'Every day. I'll soon be strong enough to pick you up and carry you out of 'ere.'

She knew he'd give anything to be away from the alien place which the hospital was to him. 'Not long now,' she told him. 'Your chest'll be clear as a bell soon.'

'Oh – I don't think it'll ever be that!'

But she thought with misgiving about Joel going back to the cut. Was he going to find that his home of a lifetime no longer belonged to him? It didn't matter so much to her. It would still be the same boat, even if it did have Samuel Barlow's name painted on the side. And Darius had said there were a lot of advantages to working for someone else. They chased the loads and you got regular pay and insurance. But she still knew Joel would want to fight it.

She hadn't seen Darius since he'd visited Joel in hospital, although she left messages for him regularly. She wondered what was going on. She was almost as impatient as Joel for this time of waiting to be over so she could get away from Nancy and Mick's house and she and Joel could be together and plan their wedding.

Wedding! She was overcome with excitement and disbelief every time she thought about it. It felt so right, as if from the first time she had met Joel they had been picked out for each other and he had been just waiting for her to grow up. The two of them could go away. She imagined herself gliding off along the golden water of the cut at sunset, into a new life.

It was early one morning when she went to Handsworth and walked past Norman Griffin's new premises, reading the sign, 'Arthur Lambert'. She saw her own reflection, her tight-lipped expression, in the shop's dark window. The place wasn't open yet. She knew Norman Griffin horribly well and recalled the time of his methodical comings and goings. Oh, he was always organized, all right. You had to give him that. She waited in a shade-filled doorway on the other side of the road from his house so that he would not have to pass her. It wasn't that she didn't believe or trust Tony, only that she had to see him for herself.

He came, as she knew he would, a few minutes before nine o'clock: a black, square-shouldered figure, topped by a Homburg hat and moving at a stately pace along the street towards her. She could barely make out his face and didn't dare move closer. She clenched her fingers, digging in with her nails. He looked like any other respectable, middle-aged man who was running to fat a little. How could he look so ordinary, so harmless?

He took the keys from his pocket and unlocked the shop, then stepped inside out of sight. Maryann found she was sweating, her pulse racing. Six years had passed. She was a woman now, but the effect he had on her was just the same. She wanted to run away and never set eyes on him again.

But those little girls ... She had to know, somehow, whether they were suffering as she and Sal had suffered. If they weren't, then she could feel free to leave, never to go anywhere near Norman Griffin ever again. With slow, reluctant steps she set off towards the address Tony had given her, feeling very nervous and foolish. What on earth did she think she was going to do? A strange woman turning up, trying to talk to two girls who'd never seen her before, who'd be bound to tell their mom and then she'd tell Norman ... They wouldn't know who she was, but he almost certainly would.

I've got to find a way, she thought grimly. I just have to. When she reached the street of small terraced houses, she discovered with relief that almost opposite the address Tony had given her, number twenty-two Beechwood Road, was a side road leading into the next street and it was deep in shadow this morning, while the sun was shining brightly on the opposite side. At least she could walk less conspicuously up and down.

A half-hour passed. Some people moved up and down the pavement. A couple of women looked curiously at her as they passed. Another half-hour. A clock struck ten in the distance. Maryann was beginning to feel very bored and worried that people were watching her.

I'll come back tomorrow, she was thinking, when she saw the door open and someone coming out! She stood in the shade and watched. First she saw one girl appear with long auburn hair and carrying a shopping basket. Maryann guessed her age to be about twelve. She was followed by another, smaller girl, very similar looking though her hair was curlier and not as long as her older sister's. They were dressed in buttery yellow frocks, like a pair of pretty dolls. They obviously weren't living in the depths of poverty. But then they wouldn't be, would they? Maryann thought bitterly.

Then she saw their mother appear on the step, her own auburn hair coiled up at the back and a pleasant, though tense-looking face. She was leaning forwards, supporting herself on two sticks, and it was clear she had great difficulty in negotiating her way down. She handed one stick to the younger child and was helped down the front step by her older daughter. Taking up with both sticks again she waited while the older girl shut the front door, and then they began to make their way along the road. Maryann realized that there was going to be no danger of losing them. In fact, it was going to be hard to follow and not be seen because she was having to walk so slowly. The woman was apparently able-bodied in every other respect than in her right leg, which left her body at the hip at such an awkward angle that her walking on it was greatly hampered and twisted her from side to side as she did so.

She followed the grindingly slow progress of this family as they made their way round the shops fetching their groceries. Maryann saw that the girls were quite used to this routine and helped carry everything, or sometimes went into shops for their mother who called instructions to them if the entrance was particularly awkward for her. They seemed close and amiable together. She learned that the older girl was called Amy.

When they finally reached home, Maryann waited, and at last saw the two of them emerge from the house alone and set off towards Handsworth Park. Amy was carrying a hoop and they were skipping along quite fast. With a pang she saw herself and Sal, before, when their real dad was alive and they'd gone off to play like that with Tony in tow, scurrying off to the rezzer on hot summer afternoons. Maryann had to hurry now to keep up with them.

Once they reached the park they started throwing the hoop. There were other children playing in the park and Maryann relaxed, feeling she could stroll round them, keeping an eye on them. They kept busy with their hoop amid the yells and laughter of the other children. Maryann watched them carefully and in a very short time noticed something that made them stand out from the other children around them. They played with great intensity and never once did she see them laugh or even smile. They seemed only to notice each other, as if they were sealed in, away from everyone outside. Maryann knew that feeling. She saw the younger one surreptitiously touch herself, just for a second, between her legs, wincing. It was a gesture that probably no one else would have noticed. But Maryann began to know then, really know. She had to be absolutely sure though.

Moving round, she positioned herself in the path of the hoop that the older one was holding behind her head ready to lob overarm. It bounced and skittered across the grass. The younger girl ran but Maryann got there first, catching it as it spun past her.

'Oh – caught it for yer!' She smiled as the girl ran urgently towards her. 'Here you are, love.' She held it out but when the girl took it, Maryann held on so she couldn't just run off.

The girl tugged at it, frowning furiously when Maryann didn't immediately let go.

'It's awright – I'm not taking it away. It was just coming at me so fast I caught it.' Out of the corner of her eye she saw the older girl running towards them. 'It's a nice one, ain't it? Who bought you that then?'

There was no reply.

The older sister arrived, looking very wary.

'I just caught your hoop – you threw it so hard,' Maryann said.

'Sorry,' she said, dully.

'No – it's awright.' Maryann gently released the hoop, asking as she did so, 'You must have a mom who's good at sewing – did she make your lovely dresses?'

Amy nodded. She seemed to see that Maryann was being friendly. While she still looked solemn, the hostility drained out of her expression. She stood holding the hoop against her legs, with her weight on one foot, the other leg bent back, the toe of her black rubber pump resting on the ground.

'Well, she's better at sewing than I am.' She fought desperately for a reason to keep them with her and fumbled in her pocket. 'Look – I've got some toffees. D'yer fancy one?'

The girls looked at each other, then nodded in unison.

'Here y'are.' Maryann sat down hoping they would do the same, but they stood above her, the toffees bulging in their cheeks. They each had freckles, the older one just across the bridge of her nose, while the younger one had them scattered, golden, all over her face.

Maryann wanted to be gentle with them, befriend them, but she was also worried they'd run off before she could ask them anything, so she came straight to her questions. 'So – your mom or dad not out with you?'

Amy shook her head.

'Your dad's at work I expect?'

The two girls seemed to draw physically close, together as their eyes lost contact with hers and looked down at the ground. The fierce tone of the older girl's voice as she half spoke, half whispered, brought Maryann's flesh up in goose pimples.

'E ain't our dad.'

The emotions were there for anyone who knew how to read them the fear, the disgust and loathing. And for Maryann it was like listening to herself speak, as if her own soul had addressed her from out of the young girl's mouth.

She kept them with her for as long as she could. They accepted another toffee but still wouldn't sit down.

'What's your name?' she asked the older one. Of the two she had the longer face, was rather pretty with her autumn looks. But her gaze slid distractedly away when Maryann spoke to her. She might meet her eyes for a fraction of a second, then she would stare away across the park towards the trees or look down at her feet.

'I'm Amy. This is Margaret.'

Margaret's gaze didn't leave the ground. She was standing with her weight on the outside of her feet, concentratedly chewing her toffee. Hers was the rounder face, hair more carroty, expression closed tight as a trap.

'How old're you then, Margaret?'

'She's nine,' Amy said. 'I'm twelve.'

Maryann longed to ply them with questions but she did not want to frighten them. Margaret had still not said a word to her. 'You'd better get back to your game then,' she said. 'D'you come to the park every day?'

Amy nodded in her vague way, eyes sweeping the park. Margaret put her head on one side and looked sulky.

'Might see you again then.' Maryann got up. 'T'ra for now. Have a nice game.'

They returned immediately to their hoop as if she had never existed.

She found them the next day sitting on the grass not far from the park entrance, the hoop lying on the ground beside them, each wearing turquoise dresses and a white bow in their hair. They were turned slightly towards each other, their heads bowed, and Maryann thought that from the way they were sitting they must be busy playing or making daisy chains. As she came closer, though, she saw they were not doing anything.

'Amy? Margaret? Hello there – thought I might see you again.'

Margaret, as ever, kept her head down, but Amy glanced up and her mouth almost twitched into a smile. Maryann sat down on the grass beside them. What she said next had taken some careful thought.

'I never said what my name was when I saw yer yesterday. I'm Esther. Esther Bartholomew.' She didn't want to tell them fibs. But nor did she want to ask them to keep her meeting them a secret from their mother. If she told them her real name though, and they mentioned it in front of Norman ... She went cold at the very thought. ''Ere – I brought some bull's-eyes today – d'yer fancy one? I never go anywhere without a bag of rocks.'

When the girls were both sucking their sweets, she

took the plunge. 'So you live with your mom and stepdad, do you?'

She got no reaction from little Margaret, but Amy nodded, tugging furiously with her thumb and fore-finger at the short, dry grass.

'What happened to your real father?'

'He went away.' Amy spoke so quietly Maryann could barely hear.

'Oh dear, did he? How old were you when he went away?'

'Nine.'

'And has your stepdad been with you a long time?'

Amy nodded. A long time could mean anything, Maryann realized. Most likely it seemed like an eternity to them.

'I had a stepdad when I was your age,' she told them. 'My own father died in an accident and our mom got married again.' She took a deep breath. 'I daint like 'im. In fact I hated 'im.'

Amy looked at her, her expression betraying nothing more than mild curiosity. She was tapping her foot up and down on the grass.

'Is your stepfather nice to yer?'

''E's awright. Takes us to the pictures, and that, sometimes.'

'D'you like going to the pictures, Margaret?'

The girl's head seemed to sink further down, her hair hanging over her face. There was a long silence.

'You're a quiet one,' Maryann said gently.

'She don't speak,' Amy said.

'Not to anyone?'

'Only me. Sometimes.'

'I s'pose you'll be back at school soon.'

369

Amy nodded. 'Next week.'

'D'yer like school?'

'S'awright.'

She could think of nothing to say which might lift their apparent dull acceptance of life. It was as if there was a wall round the two of them. How could she, a stranger, break through it? She didn't want to frighten the girls. Mostly she wanted to put her arms round them and comfort them.

She left them that day, feeling desperate, as if she had let both them and herself down.

That afternoon when she went to see Joel again, she didn't mention Amy and Margaret. She hadn't told Nancy either. She couldn't bring herself to speak of it. And if it was hard for her, she knew that it was well nigh impossible for those little girls to put into words what was happening to them. She couldn't go barging into their family and confront Norman. After all, who would believe her? Her own mother hadn't. It seemed hopeless, the seal of privacy around respectable family life behind which a man's tormenting habits could hide and grow monstrous. Whatever could she really do to help them and stop Norman Griffin's vileness – for good?

Forty

'What're yer wearing that long face for?' Nance asked the next morning. She was clearing away the remains of Mick's breakfast – a bloater and bread and butter – screwing up her nose at the fishy smell. Maryann leaned over to wipe the table, glad that her hair swung forward to hide her face.

'*Have* I got a long face on?'

'Yes, you 'ave. I thought everything was awright – you said Joel was looking much better yesterday.'

'Oh – 'e is – I was just thinking, that's all.' Maryann quickly rearranged her expression along less perplexed lines and stood straight, shaking back her hair. The strain of the past weeks showed in her face, even though she tried to look calm.

She couldn't tell Nance just how much those two little girls were possessing her. She lay awake at night thinking of them. One minute she was telling herself she was imagining it all. They were well dressed and cared for, they played in the park like any other children. She should stop thinking she had any place in their lives. But it was the tiny signs which she understood so intimately that gave them away. Margaret's silence, the shame that made Amy's eyes slide away from anyone's gaze, the very way they held their bodies, never quite at ease. They were suffering and only she could imagine how. What could she do? She felt furious at her helplessness. That night she had resolved before she went to sleep that she would go and see the girls' mother and speak to her. At least tell her what she suspected, alert her to what might be going on in her home. Now, this morning, this seemed preposterous. Maryann ran the cloth over the table, mopping up rings of tea and crumbs. She must talk to Amy and Margaret again first, see if she could get them to trust her, open up to her.

'How long d'yer think it's going to be before Joel can go out of the hospital?' Nance was saying, scraping off Mick's plate into a piece of newspaper.

'Wish I knew, Nance. 'E's so weak it's hard to watch 'im sometimes. 'E can barely stand out of bed. Sometimes I want to just pick him up and carry him he looks that thin.' She went and rinsed out the cloth in the pail of water Nance kept out the back. 'I just want 'im out, Nance. All this time I've been away and now 'e's stuck in there. It feels as if we'll never be able to be together.'

'Oh – you will.' Nance turned and looked through the door at her, wistfully. 'You're ever so lucky. You know – starting out right with someone.'

Maryann came back in from the scullery. 'But you and Mick're getting on better. I mean you ain't been fighting and carrying on like you did before . . .'

'No – I know.' Nance pushed her hands down behind the belt of her apron. She looked miserable. 'But there's no *feeling* between us. Never was really – we both sort of went along with it. I'd never 'ad those feelings, see. So I daint know I was missing anything. But I know there's summat more and you've got it – you and Joel. It's made me see . . . And now I'm stuck with 'im for ever . . .' She stopped, looking down miserably. 'I've always tried to be good, you know, Maryann. Listened to what the priests said and done what I was told. But I don't 'alf 'ave some bad thoughts lately. I don't even dare go to confession and say what's been going through my mind.'

'Oh Nance . . .' Maryann, who'd never had to go to confession in her life, struggled to find the right words, but failed and just stood looking at her, full of pity.

Nance put her hands over her face for a moment, then drew them away and turned round. 'Well – this won't get nowt done. I'd better get cleared away and off up the shops.'

'I'll finish clearing up,' Maryann said. 'You go on out. It'll make you feel better.'

When Nance had gone she washed and dried the breakfast things as usual, swept the room and got ready to go out, feeling nervous and unsettled. Should she talk more to the girls today? Tell them the truth: that their stepfather had also been hers? Would that be the best thing? But her heart was heavy. What did she think she was trying to do – break up a family? Thrust them out of one kind of suffering into another – the insecurity and poverty into which she had condemned her own mother?

It was raining gently outside, through a heavy, late summer warmth. She took her coat and started off down the road. But before she had got very far she saw a tall figure turn in at the end of the street, walking towards her through the drizzle with an unmistakable gait. Her pulse quickened.

'Darius!' Overjoyed, cheeks flushing a healthier pink, she ran down the road to meet him. He smiled, seeing her dashing along the street, impatiently pushing strands of her black hair out of her face. 'When did yer get in? I daint know when we'd see yer again!'

'I'm glad to see *you*,' he said. 'I wasn't sure I'd find the right place again.'

'You just caught me – I was off out. Come on down to the 'ouse. Nance is out shopping but she'll be back soon. Oh Darius, you should see Joel – 'e's looking so much better than last time you was 'ere.'

'Oh—' Darius seemed to sag with relief. 'Thank 'eavens for that. I've been thinking, round and round, what we're gunna do. My father's still not right and I've 'ad to keep Ernie on. I couldn't think 'ow I could manage – even selling out. Joel looked that bad – I thought 'e might not come through after all. Is 'e going to be in there much longer?'

'I don't know – he's ever so keen to get going. You know Joel. He'd be out of there by now if he had the strength to move hisself.'

Darius chuckled. Once more he seemed very tired, but more relaxed now he had heard the good news. He sat at the table in Nance's house and Maryann stoked the fire and put the kettle on again.

'You'd like some breakfast, wouldn't yer?'

'Wouldn't mind – if you've enough. Been going most of the night again.'

'We ain't got much in till Nance gets back, but 'er won't be long.'

'Oh – a cuppa'd do me.'

'You can 'ave that for a start – our Nance'll feed you up like a turkey cock.'

She made tea for them both, scraping out the last of the condensed milk, and sat down, beaming at him. 'I've got summat to tell you.' She couldn't wait any longer. It already felt as if he was her brother. 'Me and Joel, we . . . well, 'e asked me if we'd get wed.'

Darius stared at her, swallowing a mouthful of tea.

A smile spread slowly across his face. 'What – and yer'd come and . . .?'

'Live on the *Esther Jane* – course we would. Where else d'yer think Joel'd ever live?' She was full of excitement. 'I'm so glad you've come now because I was afraid you'd already've sold her and you don't need to – we can all work her together and stay as Number Ones . . .'

Darius held up one of his huge, callused hands. 'Now – 'old your 'orses a minute. You don't know the life, Maryann – not 'ow things've got now. For a start, we could all keep the *Esther Jane* going, but you and Joel ain't gunna want me about for long if you're wed, with a family coming along. That's one thing. Now I'd go back and work a Fellows' boat down London like I done before and leave you to it once Joel's got 'is strength back if that were just it. But it's all changing. We just ain't keeping ahead and getting the loads we need. Now – I've thought long and hard about this, and tomorrow Essy Barlow's gunna be 'ere and 'e's taking on the *Esther Jane* – and what's more—' He held his hand up again to prevent Maryann from interrupting. 'There're going to be changes. 'E's promised to put a motor in 'er and we'll work a pair again. When you and Joel are ready to work 'er together you can 'ave 'er for your home with my blessing, but that's 'ow it'll 'ave to be. I don't like it neither, but we're going to 'ave to 'just to it. That's the only way we're gunna keep up.'

'A motor? You mean – no more Bessie?'

'No more Bessie, and a lot of noise and stink besides. But it's the only way forward. There's more and more moty boats now and they shift the loads. We ent keeping up – simple as that.'

Maryann was digesting this when the door opened and Nancy appeared, panting with two heavy bags of shopping, her coat shiny with rain.

'Oh—' She had expected the house to be empty and was really taken aback. 'Ello ... Darius.' She seemed very flustered and turned away to put the bags down, but not before Maryann saw how much she was blushing.

'Can I get Darius a bit of breakfast? 'E's been on the go a long while again.'

'No – let me get it,' Nance said at once.

'Very good of you, Nancy,' Darius said gruffly.

'No – it's – I'm glad to. I wish I'd've known you was coming – I'd've got a bit of bacon in ...'

While Nance fussed about cooking eggs and sawing doorsteps off a loaf of bread, Maryann reported to her what Darius had said. Nance presented him with a moutainous breakfast of eggs and fried bread and bread and butter, then sat down with some satisfaction to watch him eat it.

'You come to visit yer brother again then, 'ave yer?' she asked.

Darius nodded, his strong jaws working away. 'Thought I'd see Joel. And deal with Mr Barlow tomorrow ...' He paused, then added, 'I just wondered. Today's the last day she'll be our boat, proper. D'you want to come out on 'er for a bit – see 'ow she really goes before they stick a moty on 'er?'

Maryann was just about to answer when she realized his question had been addressed to Nance. After all, she was no stranger to the *Esther Jane*!

'Ooh, well ... today? What, now like?' Nance seemed to swell with excitement.

'The day'll be over, else. See, a bloke at Gas Street

said if we go down the Worcester and Birnigum Cut it
goes past the back of the chocolate fact'ry and we can
turn down by Selly Oak Wharf – and you said that's
near Joel's 'ospital.'

'Yes, it is,' Maryann said. 'We could go and see him
from there. We'll 'ave to stop 'im breaking out of the
'ospital to come and see 'er! Oh go on, Nance – it'll be
lovely, look – the rain's going off already.'

Nance was all smiles. 'Oh – go on then. I'd like that,
Darius – I really would.'

Maryann could tell from her expression that this was
something of an understatement.

'Poor old Bessie – she's tired,' Maryann said as they
slid out away from Gas Street amid a busy to-ing and
fro-ing of joeys, some empty and riding high, others
laden and low in the water. The sky was hazy with
cloud and smoke, but the rain had gone off and it was
clearing up.

'Well – we'll go gently. Tomorrow she can 'ave a
long rest,' Darius said.

Young Ernie, who'd worked his way up with
Darius, was quite happy to spend a day away on the
bank. Nance had stepped aboard saying, 'Just think,
Maryann – this'll be your home soon. How on earth
are you going to manage?'

Maryann laughed, patting Jep, who had greeted them
wagging not just his tail but the whole of his body.
She felt she could manage anything so long as Joel
was going to get better and be beside her. 'I'll 'ave to
get good strong arms, that's all! It's a killer on yer
shoulders working on 'ere.'

'Bet I could manage,' Nance said, prodding her

muscles. Nancy had always had a robust frame and now she was thinner she looked wiry and strong, like a greyhound.

Maryann saw Darius watching Nance appraisingly. 'Reckon you could,' he said.

They wound along between the smoking factories, the wharves and warehouses, down the Worcester Canal, moving south. As they glided out through the Edgbaston tunnel to Bournbrook then Selly Oak, the route became greener. Trains chugged past to their right and occasionally the sun broke through the cloud and transformed the dull, scummy ripples to silver. After a short time Maryann had taken up her favourite position on the cabin roof, her hand stroking Jep who sat panting beside her. Coots and moorhens scooted away from the bow of the boat. Butterflies shimmered round flowers in the grass. She took deep, contented breaths. However hard this life, whatever the struggle, this was what she wanted: this was her place and these were her people. Somehow it seemed to have chosen her.

Nance stayed with Darius at the stern and Maryann could hear him instructing her how to work the tiller. Often she heard Nancy's laughter and smiled. It was so good to hear Nancy enjoying herself. She felt herself swelling with happiness, everything else forgotten except that she was here and Joel was getting better. She throbbed with love and longing for him. If only he could be here today, it would be perfect!

They tied up at Selly Oak. Jep pottered off to explore the towpath while they ate bread and cheese that Nancy had brought. Darius had some plums on board, the skins a beautiful reddish orange that seemed to contain the very sunshine that had ripened them. They were sweet and delicious, and they spat the stones overboard.

'So're we gunna turn round 'ere then?' Nance asked.

Darius laughed. 'You can't just turn 'er anywhere. The cut's narrower than the boat – look.'

'Oh yes—' Nance chuckled. 'So it is. I never thought about that before!'

'You 'ave to find a winding 'ole where you can turn – it's just keep going otherwise.'

All morning he had been explaining things to her. Maryann had never heard him speak anything like as much before. She watched them as they perched together at the stern, eating their lunch. It was only then it truly dawned on her. It was so clear in their eyes, the way Darius looked at Nance, her radiance in his presence. However much they tried to hide it, to behave normally, she could see the two of them were falling deeply in love, and she was filled with dread and sorrow.

Maryann turned away from them. What Nance had said this morning, *But now I know there's summat more . . .* Had she just been talking about what Maryann and Joel had? She hadn't, had she? She had been saying so much more. She could hear their voices behind her, and it only increased her sense of disquiet. She thought of Mick and pitied him. But she pitied Nance just as much, and Darius for his lonely, hard-working existence.

There came another peal of laughter from Nance; a youthful, carefree sound.

God, Nance, Maryann thought, just keep yourself under control.

Whatever happened, if they gave rein to their feelings, someone was going to end up broken-hearted.

*

'Look who I've brought!'

Joel was just waking as they arrived and Maryann leaned down and kissed him tenderly. He returned the kiss, clasping her hand, then caught sight of his brother.

'Darius!' He made a couple of attempts and finally managed to haul himself up. 'Damn it – I keep forgetting I'm weak as a kitten!'

'This is my friend Nance – she's putting me up for the time being.'

'Putting up with 'er more like.' Nance laughed. 'Nice to meet yer at last.'

'We'll go out for now,' Maryann said, taking Nance's arm firmly. She had words to say to her. 'Let you two 'ave a chat.' She knew Darius was going to have to tell Joel about Mr Barlow.

'What's going on, Nance?' she demanded in a fierce whisper, once they were out in the corridor. There was a constant flow of people up and down, nurses and visitors, so no one took much notice of them.

'What're you on about?'

'You – making up to Darius, that's what.' Maryann found she was furious and boiling over with frustration. Of course Darius and Nance were right together! It stood out a mile. When she was with him, Nance was the happy, laughing person she had been before her marriage. She should be able to be with him and spend her life with him. But it couldn't be like that because Nance was Mrs Mallone and Mrs Mallone she would have to stay.

Nance looked crestfallen. 'Oh Lor', Maryann – does it show that much? I never meant it – I know 'ow wrong it is. Only whenever I'm near 'im I just can't help myself. I know 'e likes me – you can tell, can't yer? I just feel so *right* when 'e's here. Oh, I'd give anything. . . .' She looked appealingly at Maryann. 'Look – I know why yer going on at me. But Darius'll be gone soon and once you're away I'll never see 'im again. I'll just 'ave to swallow the fact. Let me enjoy today, that's all.' With tears in her voice she finished, 'Then I'll 'ave to get back to my proper life.'

They pulled back into the Gas Street wharves in the cool late afternoon.

Maryann had been leading Bessie for the last part of the journey, patting her and talking to her to encourage her. Despite the horse's obvious weariness she seemed happy enough to plod along. There were few flies to bother her and it wasn't too hot.

'I'm going to miss you, Bessie,' she murmured, kissing her hot, smooth neck. 'What's going to become of you, eh?'

When she had gone back in to see Joel, Maryann looked anxiously to see how he was taking the news about the *Esther Jane*, but he looked calm enough.

'You've told 'im then?' she asked Darius.

'We'll still have our home.' Joel looked at her and she swelled inside with happiness. 'After all this I'm happy knowing I'm going to be alive. Everything else comes after that.'

As the afternoon wore on, she felt increasingly that she should leave Darius and Nance alone together and give them a chance to say anything that needed to be said.

She was walking ahead of the *Esther Jane* with Bessie, but once when she looked back she saw that Darius had an arm round Nance's shoulders, their faces were close as they talked with obvious intensity. The shortage of time together had speeded up events. Maryann looked away, full of sorrow.

When they had tied up and stabled Bessie and it was time to say goodbye, Nance could contain herself no longer. Maryann had come back from the stables, tearful at parting with Bessie, to find her and Darius in each other's arms. Seeing it was time to go home, Nance also burst into tears.

'Oh, I can't leave yer, Darius. I can't – it ain't right. Today's been the best day of my life – I just want to stay with you!'

'I know,' he said, gently trying to loose her from him, though Maryann could see how little he really wanted to. 'But you can't just come with me, Nancy. You're married – it'd be wrong.'

'Why's it wrong when I don't love 'im? I love *you*. Oh, I've said it now—' She stood sobbing, distraught, beside the *Esther Jane*. 'But that's how it is. I've never loved 'im and now I'm stuck with 'im and it ain't right!'

'Oh Nancy . . .' Darius put his hand on her shoulder, casting a desperate look at Maryann. 'You don't know what I'd give for things to be different . . . I'd like you as my wife, and that's the truth of it . . .'

Still weeping, Nance thrashed her hands back and forth through the air in furious frustration. 'It ain't fair. Why do things 'ave to be as they are – eh? Why did I go and say I'd marry Mick? It was so stupid – *stupid* . . . as if 'e was the only man who was ever going to come along!'

'Come on, Nance—' Maryann said gently. 'We're going to 'ave to get home . . .'

'Go on—' Darius said, his voice cracking. 'Please – go now.'

They held each other one last time before Darius pulled away and stepped down into the *Esther Jane*. He ducked into the cabin as if he could not bear to watch them both walk away.

Forty-One

On Monday morning Maryann set off to find Amy and Margaret again. It was a cool, overcast morning with a definite nip of autumn and she was worried that the girls might not come to the park. If they didn't come out she would be forced to go to the house. She knew she had to see them.

It had been a difficult weekend. Nance was as low as Maryann had ever seen her and she had spent as much time with her as possible, trying to console her and keep her mind away from Darius. Maryann had gone to Mass with her and Mick, and Nance kept filling up with tears all the way through.

'What the hell's the matter with you?' Mick demanded when they stepped outside the church.

'Nothing *you*'d ever understand,' Nance snarled at him which sent Mick swearing off into the distance in a temper.

'I feel as if my life's over,' Nance sobbed to Maryann.

All weekend she had been casting hateful looks at Mick. Maryann felt terrible for her, but they both knew Nance was going to have to settle down and forget Darius.

On Sunday when Maryann went to see Joel he was sitting up waiting for her.

'They've said another week or so and I can be off

out of here!' He beamed. 'Oh – I've almost forgotten what it's like to breathe in fresh air. Just the idea of being able to go out and walk round outside seems – well, I can hardly take it in!'

'Oh Joel – I can't wait until we can be together,' Maryann said. She was desperate to leave Nance's house with all its unhappiness. Although she felt guilty about leaving Nance there was nothing she could do about her situation. She longed to get on with her life with Joel after all the waiting.

'We'll 'ave to start fixing up a wedding day.' Joel looked into her eyes with a sense of wonder. 'Little Maryann – and you're going to be my wife.'

She smiled back, face alight with happiness. 'Soon as we can manage,' she said.

He stroked a finger gently down her cheek. 'We can share everything that comes – best mates, eh?'

She thought about this as she walked to Handsworth. Joel had said they could get married in Oxford, near to where his auntie lived and where old Darius Bartholomew was recuperating.

'But if you want to get wed here – so your family can come,' he said. 'We could think of that instead?'

'No,' she said firmly. 'My mom won't come wherever my wedding is. I might be able to get our Tony down for it, but your family's my family now, Joel. Oxford's lovely and it'll suit me fine.'

She felt strong and joyful inside, as if nothing could ever harm her again, Joel's love warming and strengthening her. Her only anxiety was his leaving hospital so soon. Where were they going to go if Darius didn't get back? But even this didn't seem insurmountable. She still had some money left. If necessary they'd have to rent somewhere until the *Esther Jane* was ready. She wouldn't stay with Nance any longer than she had to. She felt she'd already brought enough trouble into her life.

Turning into the park she looked round for the girls. It was much quieter today, an end of summer quiet. School was due to begin the next day. With a sinking feeling of dread she thought for a moment that they weren't there. It was almost midday – this was when she had found them before.

After a moment strolling round she spotted them over by the pond, both kneeling, peering down into the water. Her heart went out to them.

'Hello, girls,' she said softly.

Still kneeling side by side, they swivelled round together so that the tops of their heads were almost touching. Their eyes held the usual closed blankness, though she thought she saw a flicker of welcome in the older girl's expression. Amy stood up slowly.

'Hello.'

Margaret turned away.

'I thought I'd come and see you – school tomorrow, ain't it?'

Amy nodded.

'I've er . . . I've got some nice peanut toffee – d'yer want some?' She felt like a wicked witch in a fairy story, luring them with sweets, but she had to get them to come and sit with her somehow. Margaret just shook her head and carried on facing the other way.

'I'll 'ave a bit,' Amy said. 'Please,' she added.

''Ere – I'll sit down next to yer,' Maryann said, tucking the skirt under her on the grass, sitting quite close to Margaret. Even if she couldn't get her to come and sit with them she wanted to be sure she heard what she was going to say. Amy sat on her left, chewing the toffee, her legs bent, leaning sideways on one arm.

There was no point in dilly-dallying. She had to say something.

'Look, Amy – you must've thought it was a bit strange me coming and seeing yer in the park. I mean it's been nice for me getting to know you a bit – but there's another reason why I've been coming.'

Amy's hair was hanging half across her face and she didn't look up but Maryann could tell she was listening.

'I've seen your stepfather – going to his shop and that. I know he calls himself Arthur Lambert, but the truth is, that ain't his name. Or at least that ain't always been his name.' Her heart was beating terribly hard. Was she wrong to do this, was she? She forced herself on. 'The thing is – I used to know 'im under another name. He was called Norman Griffin and he was my stepfather an' all – when my sister and me were not much older than you are now. And . . .'

She swallowed, almost unable to go on. Amy cast her a quick glance, then looked down again. Margaret was sitting by the water, absolutely still.

'The thing is – when 'e was living with us, he daint treat us like . . . like a dad ought've done. He was . . . bad. 'E . . .' She took a deep, shuddering breath. 'Oh God help me for saying this to yer!' She spoke with her gaze fixed on Amy's face, watching for her reaction to her words. She didn't want to leave them in any doubt as to what she was admitting to them, but she was trembling as she spoke.

'He was wicked, the way he was with us. At night he came to our rooms and . . . and made us do things –

things children ain't s'posed to do – and he made us feel dirty and different to everyone else . . .'

She couldn't go on. Her voice was choked with tears. Looking at Amy she saw that the girl had turned her head and it was tilted so that her hair completely hid her face. She had brought her hand up and pressed it tightly over her lips. The gesture spoke more loudly than any words.

Maryann wiped her eyes, trying to control herself. Very slowly and gently she reached out her hand and pushed the girl's hair aside.

'Amy? I was so frightened of speaking out of turn and getting it wrong. Is it . . . is he still the same?'

She released Amy's hair and watched her. There was a long pause during which Maryann almost despaired of an answer. But then the coppery hair began to quiver and she saw the girl was nodding. A quick, frightened nod.

'Oh God,' Maryann gasped. 'You're saying yes, ain't you, Amy?'

This time the nod was more definite.

'You poor things . . .' She wanted to reach out and take the child in her arms, but she restrained herself. Half whispering she said, 'What about . . . Margaret?'

Again the nod, more vigorously this time.

'Your mom – does she know anything about it?'

This time a shake of the head.

They all sat in silence for a minute. Margaret had still not turned round.

Maryann sat thinking furiously. Her own mother had not believed her. Why should theirs be any different? She had her life to protect, her security. And Norman was so smooth and respectable. Why would the woman listen to a complete stranger?

'There's one more thing I want to tell you, Amy. My name's not Esther Bartholomew like I told you. I daint want to tell you my real name in case you mentioned it at home in front of him. I'm Maryann Nelson – you can call me Maryann. Look, I can't promise you anything, Amy. I don't know if I can make it stop – if I was to see your mom. She won't want to hear it. But d'you want me to try?'

Amy's head swung round and for the first time she looked into Maryann's eyes. Her own were full of tears. Never had Maryann seen a more desperate, yearning face.

'Please,' she whispered. 'Make it stop.'

'Come on then.' Maryann stood up and Amy did the same. 'It's now or never, Amy.'

She looked warily at the younger girl. Amy went to her.

'Margaret – come on. We're going 'ome. This lady's coming with us.'

Margaret slowly, almost mechanically it seemed, got to her feet and turned to come with them. As she did so the blank expression in her young eyes chilled Maryann to the bone.

Maryann brought her hand up to knock at the door. Amy had been about to open it but she said, 'No – wait. I can't just go walking into your mom's house. I'll knock first.'

She was terrified, her knees like jelly, yet somewhere in her she was also triumphant. No longer did she have to feel wicked, to be told she was imagining things. She was not alone. She and these girls could stand together.

389

'She'll be cross,' Amy said uncomfortably as Mary-ann knocked. 'Takes 'er a while to get to the door.'

They heard her moving painfully along the hall. When the door opened Maryann suddenly found herself looking into the face of the auburn-haired woman. There were lines across her forehead and at the corners of her mouth which indicated that she suffered pain. She had pale skin, lightly freckled, wide eyes of a deep blue and a gentle, patient expression. Maryann was reassured. Her face was not the tight, bitter mask her mother had taken on through her hardships.

'Oh—' the woman said, eyeing her daughters. 'Is summat the matter? I hope they haven't done anything wrong?'

'No—' Maryann smiled nervously. 'Nothing like that. Only – I've met your daughters over in the park a few times recently and we've got a bit friendly like. There's a reason why I was looking out for them ... D'you think I could come in and talk to you for a minute or two? There's summat I'd like to say to you.' She glanced at Amy and Margaret but their faces were blank once more.

'Well – awright then,' the woman said doubtfully. 'I 'ope it won't take long though. I've got the dinner on.'

She led them into the nearest room, which was the front parlour. Maryann was not in a state to take in much detail except that the room was very clean and neatly arrayed, with polished brasses by the grate and moss green curtains.

'Sit down, won't you?' the woman said, easing herself into a chair. They were positioned either side of the fire and there was a rag rug between them in bright colours. Maryann could smell lavender. Nervously she took off her straw hat and sat holding it on her lap.

'Why don't you run along, girls?' Janet Richards said.

'Oh – no, please,' Maryann said quickly. 'They need to stay.'

'But I thought you said – I mean they're not in trouble . . .?' She frowned anxiously.

'No – at least, not the way you mean. Oh dear, this is so . . .' She clasped her hands under her hat to try and stop them shaking. 'I don't know where to start.'

Janet was beginning to look as if she doubted her own wisdom in letting this stranger into the house, so Maryann plunged in and began talking quickly, explaining, trying not to put things too harshly nor to skirt round the truth. The girls stood close by.

'See – as soon as I saw him again I knew it was him,' she explained. ''E weren't called Arthur Lambert when 'e lived with our mom – Norman Griffin was his name. But it was him, and when I saw your daughters, the way they were, I just knew. It's hard to explain unless you've suffered it yourself. No one'd believe me when I was their age. My mother turned against me – she still won't see me. And today I asked Amy whether 'e was . . . well, doing the same to her and Margaret and when she said 'e was I just couldn't let it rest. I know this'll be a shock to you and you must think I'm terrible to interfere, but I had to come and say something rather than let them go through the same . . .' She ran out of steam at last.

The woman's expression was frozen. Shock, fear, disbelief all competed and for a time she couldn't speak.

'Amy—' she gasped eventually. 'Amy? What's she saying – who is she? And what've you been telling her?'

'Oh, don't be angry with them!' Maryann implored

her. She all but got down on her knees in front of the woman to plead with her. The girls stood listening, hanging their heads. She wanted them to speak up and plead with their mother, but she knew they couldn't do it. 'They shouldn't get in any trouble for telling me. They've been through enough – it's him you want to ask questions of. He's the one who takes over people's families, wrecks their lives. I know 'e looks like a gentleman and 'e's polite and well dressed and everything but underneath 'e's summat else – there's a side to 'im only a few of us have seen.'

The woman's eyes narrowed into slits, the look of sweetness quite gone from her face. She struggled to her feet, raising her walking stick as if she was going to hit Maryann, who hastily stood up as well.

'Who *are* you?' she hissed. 'What d'you think you're about, coming into my house and coming out with this *filth* in front of my two young girls? What've you been saying to them – poisoning their minds and filling them with these dirty lies. What do you want? You must be wrong in the head. Why didn't you say this woman'd been hanging around yer, Amy? What's she been saying to yer? Did she tell yer to come and make up stories about your father?'

Maryann's hand went to her throat as she watched Amy. For a second, which seemed eternal, the girl stood motionless. Then she raised her head a little and her face was burning red. Eyes still looking at the floor, she said, 'She daint make me, Mom. It's true. It's what 'e does – to Margaret and me. 'E does . . .' Her mother was shaking her head in horror. ''E *does*, Mom – upstairs, at bedtime.'

They all froze then, because there came the sound of the front door opening and a man's heavy tread entering the house. The front door was closed, loudly, and his footsteps moved through to the back.

'Janet!' They heard a moment later, 'Janet?'

She looked round at her daughters and at Maryann with utter contempt. Maryann, feeling her legs give way, sank down on to the chair.

'He's come home for his dinner.' Janet's mouth twisted bitterly. 'Now we'll see, won't we? Arthur!' she called. 'We're in the front.'

The door opened and Maryann found herself face to face with Norman Griffin.

Forty-Two

He looked so wide, filling the doorframe, standing
there in his black coat. There was a long silence. In a
corner of her mind, Maryann could hear the clock
ticking and a horse's hooves passing in the street. His
glance swept round the room, rested on her for a
fleeting moment during which her pulse seemed to stop,
then passed over to his family.

He had shown not a flicker of recognition. Have I
changed that much? Maryann thought. Looking at him
she was stunned once more by his familiarity, as if even
now when he was fatter and his hair thinned she could
remember every pore of the skin on his face, every
quiver of expression. Her body, seeming in his presence
to remember even more, his loathsome touch, felt
turned to water. If she had not already been sitting
down she would have collapsed.

'My dear? What's going on?'

Janet Lambert was standing, leaning on her stick, the
girls near to her. 'Oh Arthur,' she said and then burst
into tears. He was beside her immediately.

'Whatever's the matter, love? What's been going on?
Who's your visitor?' His words dripped concern like
syrup.

'She came in with the girls – she's been saying the
most terrible things, Arthur . . . And now Amy's saying

them too – the same lies ... I can't even bring myself to tell you ...'

He turned, looked at Amy and Margaret, then Maryann felt his eyes boring into her.

'What's going on in my 'ouse? Who're you?'

She thought her anger might choke her. She managed to stand up, clutching folds of her skirt in her hands to steady herself. 'You know perfectly well who I am, Mr Griffin,' she spat at him. 'I'm Maryann Nelson. Remember – your stepdaughter? And under the law you're still married to my mother, Mrs Florence Griffin.'

She heard Janet Lambert gasp. 'Arthur no! She must have the wrong person. What's she saying?'

Norman Griffin gave a bewildered shrug that could have won him a part in a troop of actors. 'I've no idea, my dear – where on earth did you pick 'er up from? Has she got loose from the asylum or summat?' He even managed a chuckle. 'Never heard anything like it. Why did you let her in?'

'You know who I am!' Maryann shouted at him. She could feel herself becoming hysterical. There was such a pressure rising inside her that she felt as if she might explode.

'D'you think I'd ever forget the man who did things to me that shouldn't be done to an animal, you vile, filthy pig?' She faced Janet Lambert. 'He's the one who came to our room night after night and interfered with us so's we prayed every day that night would never come. D'you think anyone'd ever forget that? And now' – she turned on Janet Lambert – 'you've got two daughters praying the same thing. Because from the day you let that *animal* into the house they lost their childhood. They were never safe again. Tell her Amy—' She stepped over to the girl and held her shoulder.

Speaking softly she said, 'You know what you told me – say it to your mom. Tell her the truth or he'll just go on and on and you'll never get away from it.'

Amy's shoulders were shaking. She put her hands over her face. Her mother watched, appalled, her eyes stretched wide. Maryann squeezed her shoulder.

'Come on then, Amy.' Norman's voice was soft, mocking. 'Let's hear it then. All the terrible things I do to yer – buying you nice frocks and taking you both to the pictures. Tell us all about that. Oh – and we're going to the zoo next weekend, aren't we – better get that off yer chest as well.'

'Amy?' her mom said quietly. 'Have you got anything to say or was it just this woman talked you into it – got you to make up a story?'

As Amy sobbed, Margaret remained in stony silence. Her gaze never left the floor.

Norman turned to the girls' mother. 'I don't know who this woman is or what she wants, but the last thing I'd ever want is for you to think badly of me or have any suspicions about me. Is there anything else you want to ask her before I put her out of our house?'

Janet looked round desperately at all four of them: her daughters, silent except for Amy's weeping, at Norman who was looking at her in wide-eyed appeal, and at Maryann who was staring pleadingly at Amy, her own face wet with tears. She stepped towards Maryann, a hateful expression in her eyes.

'How could you come and say such terrible things to us. What's wrong with you?'

'But they're true – every one of them! Look at your daughters! They're too frightened of him to speak. When did Margaret last speak at all? And that's what he's done to them – you've got to believe me. Why else would I come to you – you're strangers to me. But I saw your daughters and I saw myself in them . . .' Her weeping took her over then. 'Oh why doesn't anyone ever believe us?'

'That's quite enough of that.' Norman suddenly laid both his hands on Maryann's shoulders and began to propel her fowards. 'Get out of my house, away from my wife and daughters with your filthy lies . . .'

'If she's your wife then you're a bigamist!' Maryann shrieked helplessly. She twisted round. 'Amy – Amy, I wanted to 'elp you. I did – I wanted to be there with you.'

Amy looked across at her, her face blotchy with tears. Suddenly they heard her voice raised in a howl. 'But you *won't* be here, will you?'

That was Maryann's last sight of her as Norman propelled her to the front door. In the few seconds before Janet managed to limp out into the hall he spun Maryann round and forced her up against the front door, one hand against her throat. This time there was no doubt as to whether he recognized her. His eyes were malicious slits.

'Don't you *ever* come near me again, or you'll regret it. You know I mean what I say, don't you, Maryann?' He pulled her back and opening the door, handed her out into the street.

'I know you!' she yelled, spinning round. 'I know who you are even if they don't!'

The door slammed, sealing the family in behind its solid green exterior.

For a moment she stared at it, stunned, then took off along the road.

*

She slid down into a deep black hole that afternoon, wandering the streets with no thought as to where she was going. Seeing Norman Griffin again at such close quarters, his physical presence, his denial of her had stripped her in just a few moments of the calmness and sense of identity she had painfully erected for herself over the years. She had come crashing back down into her childhood emotions. The child who had lain in her bed looking up into the empty darkness, helpless against the progress of Norman's feet up the stairs. Never again, she had said, never again will I let him have power over me – yet just a few minutes with him and she felt close to disintegration. She walked and walked, in such a state she saw nothing of the people, houses, factories, parks around her.

At some point in the afternoon she found herself walking along the boundary of a cemetery and when she reached the gate she went in and sat down in a quiet spot on the damp grass, looking out across the graves, scattered and tilted like old men's teeth. The sky was hazy and it was still warm. She gave no thought to whether she was warm or cold, hungry or tired. She tried to think clearly but only terrible, negative things came to her.

I can't stand up to this. Sal couldn't and I can't. Sal's dead and I'd be better off dead, peaceful like these people in here. I can't face anyone again. I can't marry Joel. Can't do anything . . . There's nothing left . . . And she had let those girls down so badly. She had utterly betrayed them. She kept hearing Amy's last despairing cry, 'But you *won't* be there . . .' What would Norman do to them now?

She lay on her side on the grass, wishing there was something that could cover her: a blanket, a mantle of leaves or a thick fall of snow, or that she could burrow into the earth like an animal, anything so that she could hide her grief and self-disgust away. Curled up tightly, she could smell the grass, the earth. Birds chirruped in the trees. Eventually, overwrought and exhausted, she fell asleep.

It was dusk by the time she turned into Nance's road, the light going and the air full of smoke, trapped in the breezeless space between the houses. She was trembling with weariness and lack of food and couldn't put on a brave face to hide her leaden despair.

Nance was sitting at the table darning a sock with sharp, angry movements but she got to her feet immediately. 'What's 'appened? You look terrible!'

Maryann sank down at the table and began to weep wretchedly. 'Oh Nance . . .'

'What is it? It's not Joel, is it?'

Maryann shook her head. 'I ain't seen Joel today. It's *him* . . . I've seen him, his family. . . .' Nance sat back down again as it all came pouring out. Norman Griffin, Amy and Margaret, everything.

'I wanted to save Amy and Margaret and all I've done is let them down and make everything much worse for them and I can't do a thing now. I can't marry Joel – I can't even face seeing him. I feel like I did that time I ran away from him before – I thought it was all better, but it ain't. I ain't normal, Nance. I'd be better off finishing myself off, that I would.'

'What *are* you going on about?' Nance blazed at her. 'You love Joel and 'e loves you! What the 'ell's got into yer? You can't let that bastard wreck yer life for you the way 'e did Sal's! You and Joel are made for each other. How can yer even think about saying that? If I had even a tiny bit of a chance to marry Darius I'd be off like a shot and there's nothing standing in your way, Maryann. You're lucky – just you remember that!'

Maryann put her face in her hands, shaking her head. Through her fingers she said, 'I don't feel lucky. I feel dirty and disgusting. You can't be happy, Nance – so why do I deserve to be?' Face wet with tears, she looked up at her friend.

'Oh Maryann,' Nance said sadly, her anger gone. 'I know I don't know 'ow it feels to 've 'ad all that going on with him and Sal and that. Only – there must be a way of making things right. If you let 'im wreck yer chances with Joel he'll've spoiled all yer life ... Look – you ain't in a state to think about anything. Let me get you a bite to eat and a cuppa tea and then you can 'ave a sleep. You'll see everything straighter in the morning. I saved yer a helping of stew – soon get it heated up. And there's apple and custard.'

'Ta, Nance,' Maryann said dully, wiping her eyes on her sleeves, grateful for Nance's mothering. 'Don't know what I'd do without you.'

Nance gave a crooked smile. 'You don't 'alf look a sight, you do.'

Maryann looked down at herself. She knew her hair was all hanging down. Her hands were grubby and there was mud on her grey skirt and shoes. She got up to wash her hands in the scullery.

'Where's Mick?'

She saw Nance's expression tighten. 'Not been 'ome yet.'

'What – not for 'is tea? That ain't like him.'

'Nope.' Nance stirred the stew fiercely.

Maryann went to her. 'You don't think summat's happened to him – an accident?'

Nance shrugged. 'If it 'as, no one's been to tell me about it.'

Maryann sat to eat her tea and did feel a little less wretched after it. She and Nance sat drinking tea together and still there was no sign of Mick. The hands of the clock moved past ten o'clock and Maryann found she could no longer keep awake.

'I'll have to go up,' she said. 'I'll doze off down 'ere else.'

'I was just thinking,' Nance said. 'Them little girls – you could at least tell them where you live – you know, just in case like.'

Maryann got to her feet. 'But this is your address.'

'Well – if it'd make yer feel any better, I don't mind them knowing that. For the time being.'

'Awright, thanks, Nance.' Maryann was grateful but felt suddenly hopeless again. How could she even get it to them?

'You go on up,' Nance said. 'A good sleep'll sort you out.'

But a good sleep was not what she was destined to have that night.

Forty-Three

Before Nance had come up to bed the front door
opened with a bang that shook the house. Within
moments the shouting and screaming had begun and
Maryann was jerked out of a deep sleep. She soon
realized that Mick and Nancy were fighting with a
ferocity beyond anything that had gone before, and she
climbed out of bed, disorientated from being woken so
suddenly. She hated interfering between them, but it
sounded as if someone would have to. As she put on
her shoes and slipped a cardigan over her nightdress,
she heard crashing and the splintering sound of china
breaking and she ran downstairs.

Mick was so drunk he couldn't stand without swaying perilously. He still had his work jacket on, covered
in muck, his face was puffy and florid and he was
standing by the humble little shelf they had in the living
room to keep their few crocks on, picking them up one
by one and hurling them across towards the far end of
the room.

'Stop it!' Nance shouted, pushing at him. 'You'll
break the whole lot, yer kalied bastard!' He swung
round and smacked her in the mouth and Nance
groaned, reeling back away from him, too stunned
to have a go at him. He reached round for another
cup, lurched to one side and seized hold of the shelf
to save himself. It came off the wall with a crunch

and everything crashed down, plates, cups, saucers, Mick falling with it, ending up in a pile of broken china. He hit his head on the wall and there was a split second's quiet.

'Look what yer've done, yer drunken Irish navvy!' Nance had recovered enough to run at him, so beside herself with fury that she kneeled down, oblivious to the shards of white china all over the place, and began raining blows down on her insensible husband. There was blood trickling from the left side of her mouth and another shiny mark on her cheek.

'I hate you!' she yelled, hitting and slapping. 'Hate you, hate you, yer fucking useless bastard. Yer not even a proper man, are yer? Yer useless to anyone ... I bloody hate yer ...' She was sobbing hysterically.

'Nance!' Maryann could barely get near her. 'Nance – stop hitting 'im – I think 'e's knocked himself out – look!'

'Good! I 'ope 'e bloody kills hisself!'

'*Nance!*' She succeeded in grabbing both of Nance's arms at once and held on, gritting her teeth while Nance fought like a rabbit in a sack before suddenly going limp. Maryann let go of her and gingerly went over to Mick, afraid for a moment that the bang on the head had really done him in.

'Is 'e awright?' Nance suddenly sounded frightened.

Maryann prodded Mick and he stirred, groaning.

'Oh, 'e's awright,' Nancy said, disgusted. 'Can't even knock 'isself out properly, the silly bugger.'

'What the hell was all that about?'

Nance's face crumpled. 'His brother Paddy – 'e's gone and got Marie in the family way *again*. That'll be their fifth, popping them out like peas every year and God can't spare us even one – just one little babby—'

403

Her voice cracked and she let out a howl of distress. 'Oh Maryann – if we could at least 'ave a babby I could think of staying with 'im without wanting to cut my own throat.'

'Oh Nance...' Maryann kneeled down with her amid the wreckage and held her tight. 'Poor old Nance...'

'What 'm I going to do, Maryann? I'm going to go round the bend living like this.'

Maryann rocked her, feeling desperately sorry. There was nothing she felt she could say.

'I feel as if there must be summat I did when I was younger to deserve punishing like this.'

'Oh, yer didn't do anything. Course yer didn't.'

'I'd better go and see Father Maguire and make a clean breast of everything that's been going through me 'ead,' she said. 'I might be able to stand it better then.'

There came another moan from beside them and suddenly Mick sat slowly up, rubbing his head. 'Christ Almighty.'

'Don't blaspheme, yer bleedin' navvy,' Nance snarled at him.

He stared blearily at the chaos of breakage round him, saw Nance and Maryann staring at him in disgust and groaned, 'Oh God save us.' Slowly, like a great ox, he lumbered to his feet and disappeared up the stairs.

'Well,' Nance said dully. 'Now yer can go back to sleep.'

'Not before we've cleared up.'

'Maryann—' Nance took hold of her wrist as she squatted, about to get up.

'What?'

'Go and see Joel tomorrow.'

Maryann hung her head, not meeting Nance's eyes.

She barely slept at all after that, hearing Nancy crying next door, Mick snoring, and all their troubles churning round in her head. She couldn't stop thinking about Amy and Margaret as well, full of frustration, anger and pity. In the morning she woke early from an uneasy doze, her head aching. But she got up, dressed silently and slipped out of the house. There was at least one small thing she could do.

There was a mist and the streets looked ghostly but she was glad of its grey obscurity in which to hide herself. When she got to Handsworth she waited in the side street where she had stood before. As time passed the streets took on a purposeful atmosphere. Children started coming out of the houses in their school clothes and scurrying down the road. Soon, the door of the Lamberts' house opened and she saw Amy and Margaret come out. Maryann shrank back. Janet stood for a few moments with her arms folded, her hair a bright flame in the pale morning, face turned to watch her girls. Then at last she stepped back and the door closed. Maryann slipped round quickly after them.

They were almost at the school gates when she caught up with them. She watched them tenderly from behind. They stood out amid the rag-taggle bunch of children as among the best dressed and neatest. Amy's hair had been plaited immaculately and each plait tied with a blue ribbon and Margaret's was put up in bunches, big bows tied with the same ribbon. As ever she was walking with her head jutting forwards, eyes fixed on the ground.

'Amy—' Maryann spoke softly, but her urgency was clear. Amy turned and gasped, seeing her. They stopped for a moment, letting the other children stream past them.

'What d'*you* want? Mom'll kill us if she sees yer!'

'Don't worry – I won't get you into trouble. You awright?'

Amy's gaze slid away. She swallowed. Nodded.

'I'm sorry, Amy. I'm so sorry,' Maryann said helplessly. She felt a huge lump rise in her throat. 'I was hoping yer mom'd listen – but then she daint know me from Adam, does she? I don't know what else to – 'cept I brought you this—' She slipped a scrap of paper into Amy's hand with Nancy's address on. 'That's where I live just now. It's my friend's house. I won't always be there but if you need help, go to her. She's kind, and she can get in touch with me . . .'

'Where'll you be then?' Amy asked.

'I don't know where I'll be—' It was her turn to look away. 'Look – yer'd better go now. I can't do any more for yer, not the way things are. But remember – if you want to get away, go to Nancy. I know she'll 'elp yer. Don't let yer mom see that though.'

She saw Amy look down at the piece of paper and nod.

'Tara then—'

And they were gone, two little figures amid the tide of other children.

*

Nance looked terrible. Her face was all in a mess, she was exhausted and in a foul temper. Mick had woken with a splitting head, said he wasn't effing well going to work and rolled over back to sleep. When he woke later in the morning he was contrite and gave Nance the money to buy some more crockery as they scarcely had enough left for a cup of tea between them. Maryann had wondered about buying some on the way home but resisted the thought. It wouldn't do Mick's pride any good having her chipping in again. Nance went out and came back with a few cheap willow-pattern crocks and an even more raging temper.

'If 'e ain't pouring 'is wages down 'is throat 'e's up to these sort of tricks,' she said, slamming the parcel down on the table so hard Maryann wondered if anything inside was left intact. 'Moan, moan, moan about not 'aving enough and now we 'ave to go and spend it on summat we 'ad already. 'E can 'ave bread and lard for 'is dinner and like it 'cause we ain't got enough for anything else.'

'Well, Nance – I could give yer . . .' Maryann began.

'No! Yer bloody couldn't! You've done quite enough. Let 'im put up with it. That'll teach 'im where 'is boozing and carrying on gets us!'

Whatever Maryann did to try and help, she got her head snapped off. She'd have to leave this house soon, she knew, however much Nance kept begging her to stay. She was only making everything worse.

After they'd had their bit of dinner and Mick had slouched off out somewhere, Nance turned on her. 'Now – you get yerself down to that 'ospital.'

Maryann was washing up the new plates. She didn't answer.

407

'Maryann?'

She hung her head over the sink. 'I can't, Nance. Not today. I'm not myself today. I just can't tell yer 'ow bad I feel . . . I can't face 'im.'

'Well, what're yer going to do?'

'I'm going to bed. 'Ave a sleep. I can't do it, Nance – not today . . .' She felt her voice crack with tears.

'Right—' Nance pulled her apron off and flicked it so hard down on a chair that the cloth made a snapping noise in the air. 'I've 'ad enough. If you're too bloody stubborn to go, I'll go meself.'

'Nance!'

But she was already out of the front door and off down the road.

'Nance – what the 'ell're yer playing at?' She was already a good way down the street, striding furiously along. She turned for a second, gave Maryann a look of complete exasperation, then carried on at the same breakneck pace.

'Oh Nance . . .' Maryann stood biting her nails, helplessly watching her friend disappear. She wasn't sure which she felt most, anxiety or gratitude.

'Maryann . . .'

There was a persistent tapping on her arm. Nance was standing over her and the light in the room had changed. She must have slept for hours.

'Nance – what time is it?' She sat up at once. 'Did yer see him? What did you say to him?'

'Plenty,' Nance said non-committally. The bruising on her face looked worse in the shadowy light. 'Come down – I've got the kettle on.'

Maryann scrambled guiltily off the bed. 'I never thought I'd sleep that long . . .'

'Come on,' Nance said grimly. 'Get yerself downstairs.'

Maryann frowned at her tone. Whatever had happened? Full of misgiving she followed Nance down the stairs, clothes all rumpled. Nance reached the bottom and stood back to watch her. Maryann got halfway down, then gasped.

'Oh my . . . what're *you* doing here? How did . . .?' She looked back and forth between them.

'Couldn't stop 'im,' Nance said, beginning to smile. 'Any'ow – I'm popping round to spend a penny – back in a few minutes.'

He was sitting in the chair by the fire. His cropped hair had grown a little, he had not been shaved for a few days and he was just beginning to look more like the old Joel. He looked across at her, a gentle, loving smile of anticipation on his face and started trying to get up.

'No—' She was across to him immediately. 'You mustn't . . . You must be worn out! How did you get here?'

'Trams.' He reached out and took her hand, holding it between his two enormous ones. 'She said you was in trouble . . . family troubles like and you was upset. So I came – wasn't staying in there a moment longer than I 'ad to. You awright, little 'un?'

She was overcome by tears at the sight of him, at his loving tone. 'Yes . . . no. Oh Joel, I don't know – I'm sorry . . .'

He pulled her closer. ''Cause I know you when you get all in a state – running off like a rabbit. Couldn't 'ave that, could I? Come 'ere, my lovely – come and sit with me.'

Her resistance broke like a dam as he pulled her on to his lap and she sat crying, her head tucked close to his neck as his hand smoothed her hair. Her worry poured out of her, her shame that she could have doubted her feelings for him.

''Eh now – there's no need for all this, is there?'

'Oh Joel,' she sobbed. 'I'm sorry.'

'Sorry – what for? There's nothing to be sorry about – you got me out of there, dint you?'

'Are you all right? Aren't you too weak?' She wiped her eyes and sat back to look at him.

'It was hard going – still wheezing like anything, but it's getting better. Bit by bit, every day.' He smiled at her joyfully, and reached up to wipe a tear off her cheek. She tried to smile back.

'Now what's up?'

'I'll tell you,' she said wearily. 'But not now. I saw my stepfather . . .'

His face darkened. 'Oh. I see.'

'It'll keep. Now I've seen you.'

He pulled her closer again. 'Your Nance'll be back in a minute. You got a kiss for me before she does?'

'Oh Joel, course I 'ave.'

They held each other close and she kissed him, full of love and gratitude, and felt the strength of his passion for her in the kiss he gave her back.

'We'll start again away from 'ere,' he told her. 'You need never see 'im again.'

Maryann looked into his face. 'I do love you such a lot.'

Nance came in to find her still sitting on Joel's knee

with a watery smile on her face and steam gushing in great clouds out of the kettle.

'God in heaven,' Nance said, rushing to lift it off the heat. 'Don't crush the life out of 'im, will yer?'

Forty-Four

They had waited in dread that night for Mick to come home. But he was back in good time, sober and contrite.

'This is Joel Bartholomew, Mick,' Nancy said nervously as he walked in. 'Maryann's intended.' Joel stood up with an effort which made him cough and held out his hand.

'How do, Mick. Your wife said I could stop 'ere for a few days until our boat's ready.' Seeing Mick frown, he explained, 'I'm a boatman – on the cut.'

'Oh – right then.' Mick nodded.

'If you don't like it, we'll move on somewhere else. It's your home . . .'

'Joel's just come out of the 'ospital,' Nance explained.

Mick nodded again. 'Ah – right. Well – sit down.' Nance immediately laid Mick's plate of tea in front of him and winked at Maryann as if to say, 'So far so good.'

They ate in silence but the atmosphere was not hostile, and when Maryann got up to clear the dishes away she heard Joel say, 'D'you fancy a pint then, Mick?'

'Joel!' Maryann said. 'You've 'ardly got the strength to stand up let alone get to the pub!'

'It ain't far!' Joel grinned. 'Anyway – 'ow'm I going

to get my strength back without a few pints inside me? I can tell you, Mick, it's been a good long while since I've 'ad anything but tea and slops.'

Mick looked warily at Nancy.

'Just don't let 'im overdo it,' she said to Joel. 'And you look after 'im, Mick. The poor feller's only out of 'is sickbed.'

'I'll do that,' Mick said. He looked relieved. 'You don't look too well,' he said to Joel. 'We'll take it easy now.'

Nance raised her eyebrows at Maryann. When the men had gone the two of them looked at each other and laughed.

'Jesus,' Nance said. 'They'd be dragging themselves off their deathbeds if it meant getting a drink inside them.'

But she looked pleased too. It was the most harmonious evening they'd had in ages.

The week passed quite peacefully, though it was a time of mixed feelings for Maryann. She was so happy Joel was out of hospital and they spent hours talking. She unburdened herself to him about Amy and Margaret and he agreed there was not much else she could do. But it was unsettling being here. They both wanted now to be off, to start their new life. Every day one of them – usually Maryann – went to see if there was any message from Darius, but so far they'd heard nothing. The weekend came and went. Tony and Billy came to see them. Billy was a young bruiser of a lad, and though they got on all right, Maryann knew it was going to be hard to see much of her brothers once she and Joel were working the cut, and this was a cause of sadness. All she could do was do her best to keep in touch.

Nancy had gone to confession on Saturday night and came back looking stern after a lecture from Father Maguire.

''E said I've got to put anything else out of my mind and sort out my marriage. And 'e told me God sometimes doesn't give people children for a reason.' She looked bleakly at Maryann. 'I mean I know 'e's right really, about my marriage and that. And Mick's really trying hard at the moment. But if God's got 'is reasons for not giving me a babby I wish 'e'd bloody well let me know what they are! – Ooh, Lord forgive me . . .'

She went to Mass with Mick on the Sunday, leaving Maryann and Joel a blissful couple of hours alone. Joel was asleep at first. Maryann had insisted he have her bed upstairs and wouldn't listen to any argument.

'You're the one that needs to get better and the sooner you do, the sooner we can go.'

He slept a huge amount. 'This is the first time I've had any peace at night,' he said. 'In there there was always someone coughing or summat going on. I haven't slept so well in months.'

He slept late that Sunday. At last, before Nance and Mick came back, Maryann took a cup of tea up for him and for a few moments watched him sleeping. His hair was longer, he was gradually letting his beard grow back and, slowly, her Joel was reappearing. He looked so pale and thin, though, and his coughing was still terrible at times. She sat by him thinking what a fool she'd been. He was so steadfast in his love for her. Through all the bad things that had gone on – were still going on – he had always been there, strong and gentle. He had been the one really good thing in her life.

She leaned over and tenderly kissed his face, pressing little kisses on his eyelids, cheeks, forehead until he stirred and woke to look at her. A smile spread across his face. 'Well – that's a nice way to wake up.'

'I brought you some tea. Nance and Mick've gone to Mass. I should've let you sleep but I wanted to see you before they get back.'

Joel pushed himself up. 'You should've woke me earlier.'

'No – I want you better.' She handed him the tea and he downed it in several big gulps, then put the cup down. He shuffled over in the bed, patting the space beside him.

'Come on in and sit with me. You'll 'ave to get used to a narrow bed on the *Esther Jane*.'

Maryann hesitated, blushing.

'It's all right, little bird – I just mean sit with me.' He held his arm out to embrace her. 'Come on – I won't bite. Promise.'

She slipped her shoes off and climbed in beside him, resting back against his warm arm. Blushing even more, without looking round at him, she said, 'I do ... I mean ... Oh dear, I don't know how to say this.' How could she tell him she wanted him, that she wanted to be held and touched, that when they were married she wanted to be his the way married people were supposed to – only she was afraid of herself, of finding she couldn't bear to do it when her only experiences of it had meant pain and fear?

'I do want – you know – to be properly married, Joel.'

415

He squeezed her gently. 'I know, love. And I'm not him, you know. I'm not your stepfather. I wouldn't want to hurt you, ever – you know that now, don't you?'

She rested her head against him. 'Yes,' she whispered. 'Course I do.' She leaned round and her lips reached for his, wanting to show him, to give all her love to him and he kissed her back, his arms pulling her close.

They stayed there snuggled close together, looking round at the bare room with its whitewashed walls and the little window behind them.

'I've scarcely ever been in a house before,' Joel said. 'I mean it's all right – a lot more space, of course. But I couldn't live like this. Not in one place all the time. Don't think I could breathe proper. D'you think you can live on the move all the time?'

'Think so. That feels the right way to live to me. So long as you're there.'

'It's a tough life, Maryann.'

She nodded. 'It's what I want though. That life – with you. I wish Darius'd get here, don't you?'

'Well – we've waited this long – a few more days don't make a lot of difference.'

'Poor Darius.' Maryann sighed. She'd told Joel about Nance and his brother. 'There's so much unhappiness we're leaving behind and nothing I can do. I just wish we could go now.'

'I know—' Longingly, he pulled her closer into his arms. 'I don't 'alf feel like the lucky one.'

'Joel! He's coming! There's a message from Darius – he should be up 'ere some time on Thursday!' Maryann came panting into the house two days later to find Joel sitting talking to Nancy as she worked.

Even in her excitement she noticed Nancy taking special care to control her expression. Maryann bit her lip. It seemed awful even to mention Darius's name if it upset her, but he was Joel's brother – what else could she do?

''E's got the moty in then,' Joel said. 'I wonder how 'e's managing?'

''E said it'd be easier,' Nancy said, attempting to join in the conversation brightly.

'Should be in the long run,' Joel said. 'But it'll all take getting used to.'

From then on, while they were waiting for Darius, everything changed. Joel and Maryann were full of expectation. Nancy, though, however hard she tried, became more and more glum as the time passed. By Wednesday afternoon, she was finding it impossible to remain cheerful at all. Maryann felt terribly awkward. It had been a peaceful week with Joel and Mick hitting it off well enough and Nance having company, and Maryann knew the parting was going to be hard.

On the Wednesday night Joel and Mick went out for a farewell drink while Maryann and Nance stayed in. Maryann tried to keep her talking, but Nance stared desolately into the fire. For a time they sat in silence. The clock struck ten with its mellow chime and roused Maryann from her thoughts.

'It'll be better when we've gone.' She sat forward in her chair, leaning closer to her friend. 'It's only making everything worse, us being here and talking about Darius – it's rubbing salt in the wound.'

Nance's face in the firelight looked hard in her

unhappiness. Maryann thought about her prettiness when she was with Darius on the cut.

'You and Mick,' Maryann persisted gently. 'I mean – things seem a bit better . . .'

Nance's lips began to tremble as she spoke. 'I s'pose they are. I think it's 'aving Joel 'ere – just knowing 'e can come 'ome and . . .' She lost control of her voice and the tears broke through. '. . . and not just find me 'ere . . . Oh God, Maryann, I know I married 'im in the sight of God and I know what the right thing to do is, but it's breaking my heart, it's so hard! I want to see Darius again more than anything else in the world, but I don't know as I can manage to see him. I don't think I could bear it.' She kept wiping her eyes furiously as if it was disloyal even to weep.

Maryann was just about to suggest that she try and keep Darius away from the house when she met him the next day, when they heard a knocking sound.

Nance frowned. 'Was that ours?' She looked round at the door.

The noise came again, and another sound of someone crying outside. Both of them got up and went cautiously to the door.

'Anyone in there?'

Nance opened the door, and in the dim light they saw a young, rather startled-looking policeman, and beside him a mane of red hair and a terrified, tear-stained face looking up at them. At the sight of Maryann she began sobbing uncontrollably.

'Amy?' Maryann went to her immediately and put her arm round her. She took in that the child was wearing a coat over her nightdress, her bare legs pushed into her boots. 'Are you awright? What's happened?'

The policeman was parking his bike up against the

wall. 'I found 'er, wandering about – over Winson Green way. In a right state she was – all she'd say was she 'ad to get over 'ere. You know 'er then?'

'Yes—' Maryann guided Amy into the room as she gulped and trembled. 'This is one of them,' she said to Nance over her shoulder. 'I wonder what in God's name's happened?'

'Oh my word,' Nance said, full of pity.

'Wouldn't say nowt to me,' the constable complained from the doorway. 'Thought the best thing to do was bring 'er here on my bike.'

Maryann put her hands firmly on the young girl's shoulders, trying to calm her. 'Amy – it's awright. You're safe here, love. You can talk to us – no one can hurt you here . . .' Seeing the distraught state of the girl brought Maryann close to tears herself. What had he done? What terrible harm had that cruel, self-obsessed man inflicted now?

Amy could scarcely get the words out. 'Sh-sh-sh . . .'

'It's awright—' Maryann caressed her shoulders. 'Slowly now.'

Amy took a great gulp of air and burst out, 'It's Margaret – I think sh-she's killed him.'

Forty-Five

That evening had, outwardly, begun like any other. Amy and Margaret came home from school, spent their few blissful hours alone at home with their mother before their stepfather arrived home. Janet had cooked mince for tea with potatoes and gravy and they had all sat to eat together. Margaret said nothing, as usual. Their stepfather asked polite, jovial questions about how school had been and about their mother's day. The conversation was strained. Afterwards, as it grew dark, they had put on the gas lamps in the front room, and Norman lit the wick in his brass oil lamp and placed it with its glowing light on the little table in the corner. He'd sat down to read the *Mail*, for the duration of that dreadful pause between tea and his stretching in the chair and saying, 'It's time you wenches were up in bed.'

To anyone watching it would have seemed a normal evening.

Yet the girls were living in constant fear and dread. Since Maryann's visit, nothing had been the same. Before, he had used them, abused them, convinced them of their subservience. But now it had become something much worse.

The night after Maryann had been, he had come up for the usual 'bedtime story'. Amy and Margaret got ready for bed, as ever, with feverish haste because if he was upstairs when they were still changing his hands were everywhere, pinching, poking. He stood in the doorway for a moment, smoking a cigarette, leaning on the frame with a nonchalant air, taking his time.

'So,' he said softly. 'You thought you could get away with squealing on me, did yer?' He gave a low laugh, then took a drag on the cigarette. Its tip flared orange for a second. 'Did you really?' Smoke curled from his nostrils. 'Poor little things – that was silly. Wasn't it? Very silly. I don't like that. I think I need to show you how much I don't like it.'

He yanked the thin pillow out from under Margaret's head and with both hands pushed it down over her face. Amy heard herself whimper and saw Margaret's hand clawing at him, her young body fighting against suffocation. He forced it down over her for what seemed an age, his expression a cruel grimace. Amy felt she was going to burst. She could bear it no longer.

'Get off her!'

She sprang off her bed and flung herself at him. He was perched at an angle on the edge and her weight threw him aside. Amy dragged the pillow away from Margaret's face and Margaret sat up, panting, frantic.

'You could've killed her!'

He was half sprawled across Margaret's bed and the look he gave her chilled her to her very core. Inside him, where most people had a heart and soul, was a place of hard, emotionless cruelty. She backed away from him.

'So – you're getting uppity now an' all, are yer?'

He advanced on her slowly.

'No!' Amy moaned. She curled herself at the top of her bed, her knees brought up to her chest. 'No – don't touch me ... don't, please ... I'll do anything, but don't ...'

But it was no use. It made no difference. Whatever she said or did would never make any difference, she could see that now.

This evening he had come up, his plume of loathsome blue smoke trailing after him. Once again he stood, as he liked to do, in the doorway, like a man looking down a menu, choosing, relishing. He strolled over to Margaret and sat down. With the cigarette jutting at the corner of his mouth he whipped back her bedclothes. Amy jumped violently. She saw him yank Margaret over on to her back and pull up her nightdress. Then, clamping his left hand over her mouth, he took the cigarette out of his mouth and stubbed it hard into her stomach. Amy's hands went over her own mouth. Margaret's body lifted off the bed, writhing. A thin, terrible noise was coming from her. He held his hand there until Margaret quietened, then removed it.

'Now—' He wagged his finger at her. 'Don't do it again.'

Do what? Amy thought wildly, biting on her fist to stop herself shouting out. What had she done?

'I've put my mark on you, wench. You show anyone and there'll be worse. I can do much worse than that.'

Margaret was gasping, crying in agony. Amy slid down the bed and blocked her ears. She knew he wouldn't have finished, that cruelty always led to something else, it excited him. She closed her eyes, pressed her hands over her ears while he raped her sister. Then he buttoned himself up tidily and went downstairs. Margaret lay, absolutely silent.

Amy went over to her. 'D'you want me to put summat on it for you?'

She stroked her sister's shoulder but Margaret was quite still, eyes closed, like a dead person. She must've have been in great pain but she made not a sound. Not knowing what else to do, Amy waited for a long time until she thought Margaret must really be asleep. At last, she crept back to bed.

It was almost an hour later when she heard Margaret moving about. She got up and just stood for a moment as if she was in a trance.

Amy turned over. 'Margaret?'

She waited a moment longer, like a little ghost in her bare feet, then went out of the room. Amy sat up, wondering if Margaret was sleepwalking. She heard her going down the stairs and through the open door, the faint sound of her mother clinking cups in the kitchen. Uneasily, Amy got out of bed and stood shivering at the top of the stairs, waiting to hear her mother's voice ordering Margaret back to bed. Was she going to show her the burn? It must hurt so badly. Amy trembled at the thought. He'd said she mustn't! What if she did – what would he do then?

She heard nothing and crept further downstairs. Her mother was still in the kitchen. Where had Margaret gone? Amy stood on the bottom step. And it was then she heard the crash, the sound of glass breaking from the front room, a shout from her stepfather, 'What've yer done, yer little vixen?' then high, agonized screaming which grew louder and more panic-stricken. Amy knew it was not Margaret who was screaming.

'Arthur?' Janet hobbled from the kitchen. 'Amy, whatever's going on?'

423

Amy reached the front room first. For a split second she thought the room was on fire but saw an instant later that the blaze was confined to her stepfather. Flames were leaping all over the top half of him, shooting out from his hair, his clothing, and he was leaping a wild jig around the room, shrieking in agony as the fire took hold of his hair and clothes. As she came to the room he flung himself down on the floor, rolling back and forth trying to douse the flames but they refused to be put out and leaped back into life in the places where his body left the floor and met the air again. Not far away, Margaret stood with her arms folded, her expression blank. Near him on the floor lay his brass lamp, its glass shattered. His head must have been doused with paraffin.

'Oh—' Janet Lambert gasped. 'Margaret – oh Margaret, what've you done? Help him, one of you – get the rug round him!' She pulled herself frantically across the room on her sticks. 'Help him I said!' she cried. 'Don't just stand there.'

But her daughters offered no help at all. Margaret stood quite still as if she hadn't heard. Amy slipped upstairs, running as if possessed, and fetched her boots. Throwing her coat over her nightdress she slid past the front parlour, past the sobbing screams, past her mother beating helplessly at the flames and out into the night, running, running to the one person who she knew would help and understand.

The story she managed, in her distress, to sob out to Maryann and the policeman was a brief, disjointed summary of this.

'What'll happen to her? She must've smashed the lamp right over 'is head. What if Margaret's killed him? Will she go to prison? They mustn't put her in prison, it ain't right – it was him, he drove her to it! He burned her with his cigarette.'

The young policeman appeared rather out of his depth. 'Look – I don't s'pose it's as bad as you think,' he said.

'Of course it's as bad as she thinks,' Maryann stormed at him. 'Ain't you heard what she just said? The man's an evil bloody maniac!'

'I see,' the policeman said uneasily. 'Look – you keep 'er here for tonight and look after her. I'll get over there now and see what's happening and tell her mother where she is. The address is . . .?'

'Blimey – that's a good distance away, that is . . .' He was just writing it down laboriously in his notebook when Joel and Mick rolled in from the pub.

'What's all this then?' Mick started aggressively. Joel looked at Maryann, her arm round Amy's shoulders and guessed who the girl was.

'Now, Mick—' Nance stepped in. 'Don't you go getting on yer 'igh 'orse. The wench is in trouble and 'er'll be stopping 'ere tonight. You just keep quiet.'

Amy looked fearfully at Mick's red, rough-looking face.

'It's awright,' Maryann whispered to her. 'He won't hurt you. This is Joel – the man I'm going to marry—'

''Ow do.' Joel smiled kindly at her. 'You'll be all right here. We'll look after you.'

They saw the policeman out.

'You can sleep down here with me,' Maryann reassured Amy.

425

'Oh no you don't,' Joel said. 'You're having the bed, you two, and no arguments.'

It took Amy a long time to calm down enough to fall asleep. Even after she had gone off, her body twitched in a disturbed way. Maryann lay with her arm wrapped round the child, making soothing noises, trying to comfort her. But her own mind was spinning round. She would have to take her back the next day to her mother. What sort of reaction was she going to get? And what would happen to Margaret? Was Norman really dead as Amy feared? It was a long time before she got any sleep herself.

The next morning Maryann, Nance and Amy went straight to Handsworth.

'I'm glad you're with me,' Maryann said to Nance on the tram. She felt horribly nervous at the thought of facing Amy's mother.

The house had a very quiet feel about it when they got there and Maryann wondered if anyone was in. But after she knocked on the door, they heard Janet Lambert pulling herself along the hall to open it. Maryann gripped Amy's hand as the door swung open.

All her remorse and worry was evident in Janet Lambert's sleepless, tear-stained face. 'Oh – Amy!' she cried and Amy, also crying, ran into her arms. 'Oh love – are you awright?' Janet sobbed. 'I'm sorry – I'm so, so sorry, Amy ... Oh my God, as long as you're awright...'

Maryann and Nance watched as the two of them cried in each other's arms.

'Oh my girls – how could he've done it – all this time?'

Maryann felt her own overwrought emotions surfacing and it was all she could do to stop herself crying as well. To see Amy was at last believed by her mother and accepted back tore at her heart.

Janet looked over Amy's head at her, her eyes full of shame. 'Come in,' she said.

Once more they sat in the little parlour room, Amy on the arm of her mother's chair, leaning close to her.

'This is Nancy – my friend,' Maryann said. 'I'm living with her at the moment so it's her house Amy stayed at last night.'

'Good of yer,' Janet said absent-mindedly. Nance nodded, sympathetically.

'Where's Margaret?' Amy asked.

'They took her away.' The woman was distraught, tears running down her face as she spoke. 'The ambulance came for him. He was burnt terrible. They took her as well. I don't know what I'm going to do . . .'

'Did she show you?' Amy whispered.

They all knew she meant the burn that Norman Griffin had inflicted on her, the bruises.

Janet lowered her head, nodding. 'They want to make that better – only they think there's other things the matter with 'er – her mind. Oh . . . my little girl. What've I done? Why couldn't I see it? He was always so kind, such a gentleman with me! I just couldn't believe he could ever . . . I mean he was never even demanding that way, you know, with me . . .'

'He was just the same with us,' Maryann told her. Now she saw how sorry the woman was, how she wanted to do right by her daughters, she felt great sympathy for her. 'My sister took her own life because of him.'

Janet's head jerked up. She looked deeply shocked. 'Did she? You never said . . .'

427

'You wouldn't've believed me.'

'No.' She shook her head. 'I wouldn't. It's like having two whole different lives, different *worlds* going on in your house at the same time. You look at him, the way he is, and you can't believe ... I mean you can't believe *anyone* could do things like that, can you? I still can't ...' She shook her head as if to reassemble her thoughts. 'Still can't ...'

'I know,' Maryann said gently. 'He's the one with summat wrong in his mind. He's like a devil. He's going to live then?'

'They think so.'

There was silence for a moment. Janet pulled Amy on to her lap and held her.

'Whatever happens, we'll be together now – we'll manage somehow. I'll never let him near you.'

Forty-Six

Maryann cried all the way home, as if releasing years of pent-up sadness and however much Nance tried to comfort her she was unable to stop. And Nance was feeling so miserable that she was tearful herself.

'If only my mom'd been like that.' Maryann sobbed. She knew people were having a good look at her but she was past caring. 'I mean I know Janet daint believe them to begin with – but seeing 'em like that, her cuddling Amy ... She wants the best for her girls at heart. But that poor Margaret – what ever's going to happen to her?'

'I s'pect 'er'll be awright,' Nance said doubtfully, adding, 'the poor little mites.'

Maryann was even less hopeful. Nance hadn't seen what Margaret was like. 'I feel terrible leaving with all this going on. But we'll come and see them – and you, as often as we can.'

Nance nodded, staring bleakly ahead of her.

When they got back home, Joel saw what state she was in and came and took her in his arms. Nance began bustling about to hide her own emotion. There was no one to embrace her.

'She believes them now,' Maryann said into Joel's chest. 'Whatever else happens, she's on their side.'

'Thank 'eavens,' Joel said. 'That poor little nipper. What about him?'

'Oh – he'll live, they say.' Her voice was savage. 'I'm glad for Margaret's sake anyway.'

When they'd told him what had happened Maryann whispered to Joel, 'No sign of Darius yet then?' They were almost certain he was due in that day.

'Thought 'e might've got 'ere by now,' Joel said, shaking his head. 'Still . . .'

'We could go down there and wait for him,' Maryann suggested.

'What's all the whispering about?' Nance demanded sharply.

Maryann looked into the dregs of her teacup. 'We was just saying – maybe it'd be better – for you, like – if we was to go and wait down by the cut for when Darius gets in.'

Nance came and stood by the table, hands on hips. 'No need for that – I think me and Darius both know how to behave,' she said tartly. 'And Joel don't look as if he could walk another step at the moment. He wants to save 'is strength for later, that 'e does. I don't know how 'e's going to manage on that boat.'

'Darius'll be there – and me. We can make sure he takes it easy.'

Maryann was tensed with anticipation. After the events of last night and now this waiting she felt very churned up and unsettled. And she was dreading having to say goodbye to Nance. If only they could just go, be there on the *Esther Jane* without all this to-do!

The afternoon crawled by. Nance declared she wasn't going to lift a finger that day to do anything in the house. There'd be plenty of time for that when they'd all gone. Maryann thought of Nance's days stretching ahead, full of work, just her and Mick, and she pitied her terribly. Nance had a home and a husband all right, but her life seemed so empty.

They sat reminiscing that afternoon, each trying to take each other's mind off the coming departure, laughing about their antics and Blackie Black with his barrow.

'Poor old Dad,' Nance said. 'Never managed much with 'is life neither, did 'e? 'E was always on about how 'e was going to get us out of Ladywood to somewhere better – soon as 'e had a shilling on him 'e was off down the pub.' She shook her head. 'The old sod. I can 'ardly stand to go and see 'im. 'E ain't going anywhere now.' Blackie's health was failing week by week. 'It's a good job our mom's got all the boys to bring in some money.' She looked across at Maryann. 'You not going to go and see yer mom again before yer go?'

Maryann bit her lip. 'I can't, Nance. Mom's made it clear what her attitude is to me. Tony said she's never said a word about seeing me and I ain't crawling to her again if she don't want me.'

'But what about Amy and Margaret – if you told 'er what's happened to Mr Griffin?'

'It makes no difference now. It's too late, Nance. She daint believe anything I said when it really mattered. Joel's my family now – 'e was always the one who was good to me in any case. Me and Mom were never close.'

Nance stared at her, smiling gently, her old friend with her wayward black hair and face that was still rather impish even now, in her twenties.

'You – a bargee – I can't believe it.'

'We ain't bargees.' Maryann sat up straighter. 'We're

Number Ones. Well – we were. I'll miss yer, Nance – but I'll be back. We always were best pals, eh?'

Late in the afternoon, when the waiting was becoming almost unbearable, at last there came a tap at the door. Maryann saw Nance's face tense up as Joel opened the door and they all saw Darius's stern features lifted into a rather flustered smile.

'At last!' Joel cried. 'I thought them moty boats was s'posed to be quicker.'

Darius stepped in, acknowledging everyone with a nod. 'The trouble I've 'ad with the bloody thing – there's been many a time today I'd've said we'd be better off going back to 'aving a horse any day. Once she got going though, she did put on a bit of speed. Takes getting used to I can tell you – she vibrates fit to shake your teeth out! Anyway – I've got a load on so we're all set. You ready then, are you?'

'Can I get you a cup of tea, Darius?' Nance asked softly.

'Nancy.' He nodded again, not meeting her eyes. 'Er – no ta. I think we'll be getting on.'

Nance nodded. Maryann could tell how much it hurt her that Darius was being so distant with her, but what choice did he have?

'Come on—' she said briskly. The less drawn-out the farewells the better, she thought. 'Let's get moving. You got everything, Joel?'

She had her case with her things in and Joel had a small bundle. They had few possessions and even if they had had more, there was little space for anything on the *Esther Jane*.

When they had gathered themselves together, Nance

suddenly untied her apron and said, 'Look – I don't want to say goodbye 'ere. I'll come down with yer—'

'You sure that's a good idea?' Maryann asked anxiously. It just seemed like prolonging the agony.

'It's awright,' Nance said staunchly. 'I just want to see yer off properly.'

Darius said he'd brought the boat through to Gas Street as it was nearer, and he'd already picked up a load of brass fittings to take south the next day. There was only about half a mile to walk. They took it slowly for Joel's sake. Maryann was concerned about how very easily he tired. She walked ahead with him, and Nancy and Darius followed at a distance which increased gradually as they went along. Maryann could just hear their voices, lowered, talking urgently. By the time they reached the cut, Nance was in tears. Maryann saw that while Darius was talking earnestly to her, trying to comfort her, he refrained from putting his arm round her shoulders.

The sun was beginning to set, glinting on windows, casting gold on the dark water and turning the chimney stacks and warehouses round them into black silhouettes. They had to step across a couple of other boats to reach the *Esther Jane*, turning their faces away, as was the custom, from the private living quarters of their occupants. When Joel stepped down into the *Esther Jane* his legs almost gave way. Maryann caught him.

'No work for you,' she said. 'You've got a lot of resting to do.'

But he sat beside the tiller, panting a little, and looked round in sheer delight. The boat was sitting quite low in the water, filled with sacks of brassware.

'Home – at last. It's felt like an eternity – 'specially in that 'ospital.'

'Saved your life though,' Darius said.

Joel nodded. 'They did. But I reckon it was someone else 'ere coming back to me really did it.' He laid his arm round Maryann's shoulder. She nestled into his embrace, though painfully aware of Nance's presence. They were all squeezed in at the back together. 'You'll 'ave to show me what they done to 'er.' Joel eyed the new chimney of the Bolinder motor jutting out of the *Esther Jane*'s cabin roof. 'When I've got my breath back.'

There was an awkward silence. A sliver of cloud crossed the setting sun and for a moment a chill darkness passed over everything, the gold leeching out of the ripples.

'Well,' Nance said, with a huge effort at cheerfulness. 'I'd best be getting back then. Get Mick's tea or there'll be trouble.'

'You've been very good to us,' Joel said. 'I'm ever so grateful to you, Nance.'

'Oh – that's awright,' she said, struggling not to cry.

She and Maryann flung their arms round one another.

'Thanks, Nance – for everything. We'll be back to see yer – often as we can.'

'You'd better—' Her voice was choked. 'Hark at me – I must go.' Hastily she held out her hand. 'Goodbye – Darius.'

'Tara.' He spoke very quietly, painfully reluctant to let go of her hand.

She turned and climbed back over on to the bank. 'Don't go falling in, any of yer!' she called, and Maryann could hear her tearfulness. She watched Darius as Nance gave a final wave and slipped away into the dusk

434

which lay in thick folds along the wharves. His eyes didn't leave her until she was out of sight.

Though they spent the evening busily, somehow Nance was still with them. Darius and Joel spent some time peering into the engine as Darius explained how it worked and how they had to maintain it, while Maryann fried up their evening meal and then they sat in the tiny cabin together: Darius on the step, his plate held in his enormous hands; Maryann and Joel at the table under the little lamp bracket. It was as cosy as she remembered and she felt herself glowing with happiness. Here she was, on the *Esther Jane* with her two favourite people in all the world.

'Soon as Joel's up to scratch,' Darius announced, 'I'll go back and work for Fellows, Morton and Clayton. That way we'll 'ave another wage coming in. I don't think our dad's going to be up to coming back on the cut. You two can make this your 'ome. Essy Barlow'll give us another butty to tow so you can get a decent load.' Putting the motor in had taken up some of the space previously occupied by cargo.

Joel nodded. He knew how sore Darius was about Nance, but they would not put this into words. And on the cut necessity meant getting work and keeping moving at all costs. 'Thanks,' he said. 'You've held everything together, Darius. I 'ope it won't be long now – this blessed chest of mine.'

'Keep her in the family any'ow,' Darius went on. 'You'll 'ave another family growing up on 'ere.'

As soon as they'd eaten, Joel said he had to lie down and Darius pulled down the cross bench for him. Blushing, Maryann wondered where she was going to sleep. She'd have the bench, she decided – until she was married. The two brothers could sleep together.

As soon as Joel was settled, Darius said, 'I'll be off out for a couple of pints,' and out he went.

Maryann finished the washing-up. Joel was quiet, sleeping, she thought. She tried to put the plates away quietly, not clatter them and wake him. She eyed the cabin. She'd get the place spick and span again. She wasn't having any of the other boatwomen saying she couldn't keep it nice. The crochet work was looking worn and grey. She was going to learn how to do it and make her own, all fresh! When they were tied up somewhere she'd get one of the women to teach her.

Turning, she saw Joel was watching her.

'Ooh – you made me jump!' She laughed. 'I thought you was asleep!'

'Come and get in 'ere with me.'

'Joel! We ain't married!'

'We will be soon enough. Go on. Just a cuddle.'

She went and sat beside him. 'I thought you were tired?'

'Not that tired.'

'What if Darius comes back?'

'He won't. Why d'you think 'e went out?'

She unfastened her frock and lay down beside him in her slip. They lay very close together on the narrow bed, looking at one another in the rosy light of the cabin. She saw the speckled colour of his lashes and his loving expression.

'Back home.' He smiled. 'Maryann – my lovely Maryann.'

She stroked his face. After a week at Nance's his cheeks were covered by a down of gingery hair. 'Your beard's coming back. You're starting to look right again.'

He laughed. 'That's nice to know.' His arm pulled

her even closer and they kissed. Their bodies were pressed together and in panic she realized how aroused he was. 'That's not the only thing that's coming back,' he murmured.

She stiffened and he sensed it immediately.

'It's all right.' He kissed her flushed cheek, drawing back a little, and stroked her hair. 'It's awright, little 'un. I ent going to force myself on you without your say so. It just shows how much I love you, that's all.' He kissed her face in between talking to her. 'You're my little bird and I don't want you flying away. Just let me love you a bit tonight – bit by bit. I want you to love me too – not to find me horrible.'

She felt herself relax at his assurances. This was Joel – she had always been able to trust him.

'Oh Joel – I could never find you horrible. And I know how long you've waited. It's just – we ain't married and I'm – I'm a bit frightened of it . . .'

'I know . . . I know. But don't be frightened, lovely one . . . You're meant to like it.'

Gently, slowly, he began to love her body into life. She was moved by his desire for her as he stroked her.

'Your hands are softer these days,' she said.

'Oh – that won't last long on 'ere!'

She began to relax as he ran his hands under her slip and touched her breasts. Gradually he pulled the slip down and kissed her and the sensation made her gasp. Excitement rose in her, sudden and strange. For a moment her mind rebelled – no, no, it was wrong to feel this, it was horrible! And she tensed, but when he continued to touch her and she saw the pent-up pleasure and need in his face she tried to relax. No, it wasn't wrong. It had to be right. She and Joel could make it right.

She clung to him, stroking him. 'Oh Joel . . . oh . . .'

'It's all right—' He moved his hand between her legs and she flinched, then forced herself to relax. All the vile poking and prodding that Norman Griffin had done flashed back to her for those moments and she moaned, forcing her eyes open.

'It's all right, my love,' he kept saying. 'I don't want to hurt you – just to love you . . . love you, little bird . . .'

After a time he leaned close, his breathing very quick. 'Can I – please?'

She knew she couldn't refuse him. She loved him too much to refuse him anything and she gave a tiny nod. She must do it for him.

That first moment, feeling the weight of him and his moving inside her she almost screamed, but she watched him, seeing the love in his face, the way he didn't abandon her for his own pleasure but stayed with her, looking into her eyes. 'My love . . . my love,' he gasped. 'Oh my little love . . .' When he had reached his climax he kissed her again and again, and they lay holding one another tenderly.

Maryann was full of wonder, of relief. They'd done it! She knew it was something every married woman had to get over with. And it was going to be all right. With Joel it could be. She could be married in every sense, and not have to dread any part of it.

She woke next morning before dawn, cramped and stiff, and lay looking round, for a few moments, beside Joel's warm back. There was very little to see, but she could just make out the dark shape of the range and hear Darius breathing loudly on the other bench. She was here, on the *Esther Jane*! It was really going to be her home. How long would it be before she could stop pinching herself and really believe it?

And last night – Oh Lor', she thought. Did I really . . .? The thought that they'd fallen asleep and Darius must have come back and found them both side by side and dead to the world was mortifying. But this was outweighed by her happiness. She smiled, sleepily. It'll be all right, I can love him – I can be a normal woman! It was really too late to worry about Darius now. The next night she'd suggest sleeping on the other bed. But she found herself hoping Darius would refuse to let her.

She kissed Joel's warm back, then eased herself off the bed, pulled her clothes on in the dark and crept out, taking the bowl to relieve herself, thankful that there was little sound from anywhere around. Then she went back in and lit the lamp and got the range going to put a kettle on and by the time she'd done that, Darius was up and she heard others around them beginning to stir.

'We need to be on our way,' Darius said. 'I'm going to get her going.'

Maryann got a huge shock when Darius started the engine. It felt all wrong without old Bessie hauling away on the bank. He had said the boat vibrated, but when all the china in the cabin started rattling and she felt as if she was being shaken up inside a salt cellar, she realized life was going to be very different from when the *Esther Jane* had Bessie pulling them serenely through the water. Soon she could also smell the acrid fumes from the funnel as well as the constant phut-phutting sound of the engine. It woke Joel.

'It's *horrible*,' she said, dismayed. 'How on earth're we s'posed to get used to this?'

Joel didn't look too happy either. 'Darius says you

do get used to it after a bit. Thing is, Maryann – it's this or selling her altogether. At least we've got our home, eh?'

'I s'pose so,' she conceded, handing him a cup of tea. She smiled shyly, kissing him. 'Our home. That sounds nice, don't it?'

Darius swung in through the door. 'We'll untie and be off now—'

The boat seemed to make a lot of noise starting off, but when they were moving, she settled down to a more regular sound. They eased away from the other moored boats. Joel stood at the stern, watching in amazement in the pale dawn light.

They were just straightening up to move off when they all heard a cry from on the bank, a voice shouting with all its strength, '*Maryann! Darius!*'

'My God—' Maryann peered through the door out into the dim light. 'That sounds like Nancy!'

'*Wait! Don't go – wait, wait!*'

Darius instantly steered the *Esther Jane* towards the bank where Nancy was frantically shouting and running to keep up with them. He brought her in rather awkwardly and they bumped the side, almost causing Maryann to fall over.

Nance was panting so hard she could scarcely speak. Darius held out his hand and she jumped in.

'Nance – what the hell're yer playing at?' Maryann was quite annoyed. She'd said her goodbyes – that was that. Why spin it out even longer? She saw, though, that Nance had a fresh shiner on her left eye, which was only half open.

In any case, it was not Maryann Nance wanted to speak to. All her attention was fixed on Darius. 'I 'aven't slept a wink!' she panted. 'It's no good – I'm coming with yer! 'E gave me this as a present last night—' She pointed at her eye. 'I ain't never going back, Darius – it's you I want to be with – for ever!'

Darius's face took on a look of wonder and disbelief. 'But . . .' he stuttered. 'Nance – you, I mean . . .'

'Nance – what're you saying?' Maryann asked her. 'What about Mick – I mean, you said you'd never . . .?'

'I know what I said. I married 'im, I took vows in church and I can't divorce 'im and I'm most likely damned into the bargain. But it's you I love, Darius. I've never felt the way I feel when I'm with you – *ever* before. I've only got one life and I can't spend it with 'im when I can hardly stand the sight of 'im and 'e knocks me about and there'll be no babbies neither. It ain't a marriage, it's a prison sentence. If you'd not come along, Darius, I might never've known I could fall in love. I know we can't make it legal and regular but out 'ere it don't seem to matter. It's you I want to spend my life with – if you'll 'ave me.'

'If I'll have *you*?' Darius said. He could scarcely believe what he was hearing. He handed the tiller to Joel and pulled Nance into his arms. 'How can you even ask, girl?' He was laughing with sheer joy.

'Flamin 'ell, Nance!' Maryann was only just beginning to take in what had happened. 'Joel – this family's getting bigger every minute.'

Nance, laughing and crying at once, hugged each of them in turn. 'I can't believe I'm doing this! I'm going to wake up any moment!'

'Well,' Darius took command of the *Esther Jane* once more, 'let's get going before you do.'

With the water churning behind them, they weaved their way through the shadowy Birmingham Cut and out towards the fresher country air.

Forty-Seven

December 1934

The day of their wedding, Maryann woke in the little house where she and Joel were staying with old Darius's sister in Oxford. Joel's father was still in poor health and was staying on the bank for the forseeable future.

Maryann had been given a bed upstairs and Joel was sleeping on an old sofa down in the tiny back room. She could see that the sun was shining brightly behind the curtains and she climbed out of bed, shivering as she pulled her woolly on and then going to draw back the curtain. The sight that met her eyes made her laugh with pleasure. It was a diamond-hard, cold day, creaking with ice and from the roof hung huge icicles glinting in the bright sunlight. The rooftops were white and the tree she could see a little way along the street looked as if it had been dipped in icing sugar. She couldn't have asked for better than this sparkling white perfection.

Old Mrs Simons, Joel's aunt, had married away from the cut and spent her wedded life in Oxford, where her late husband had a grocer's shop. She was a diminutive lady with scrubbed pink cheeks, little spectacles and she wore black, old-fashioned bombazine dresses with white lace collars. She was delighted that Joel and Maryann had decided to be married at St Barnabas Church, just a couple of streets away, and where she attended regularly.

'Now, moy dear,' she said to Maryann later in the morning when they were ensconced together upstairs away from the men and she was helping Maryann dress. 'Just you stand still so's I don't nick you with this.' She bent over with a needle and thread in one hand, finishing a seam in the woollen dress Maryann had chosen. It was second-hand but in good condition and a lovely violet-blue colour. 'Looks very nice with your pretty hair.' Maryann's hair was fastened back in a shiny, raven twist behind her head, and with her rosy cheeks and bright, happy eyes she looked very beautiful.

Mrs Simons stood back and clasped her hands in front of her breast, her china thimble still on one finger, beaming with excitement. 'We haven't had a wedding in this family for such a time – what with all poor Esther's boys . . . the War, you know. I began to think Joel and Darius'd never settle. . . .' She drifted off sadly, then regained her state of glee. 'But it always makes me feel young again, a wedding! Now just you remember, moy dear – they're good men in this family, good sound men. But sometimes you do have to take a firm hand with them.'

'Do you?' Maryann asked, surprised.

'Oh yes.' Mrs Simons neatly packed away her needles and thread. 'Give 'em half the chance and they treat you like a man – like a *packhorse*, moy dear, to tell the truth – have you toiling day and night. Just remember to get Joel to treat you proper, however much strovin' there is to be done. You 'ave to pull your weight of course, on the cut, but don't let 'im forget you're a woman for a moment, that's my advice – specially when you're carrying a child. Nothing worse for child-bearing than toiling like an animal day in day out. Saw my mother's life come to an end through it, so I should know.'

'I'll try.' Maryann smiled.

She had a smart, royal blue hat with a white feather in it to top off her outfit, and blue shoes with an elegant heel.

'I suppose this is the last time I'll feel this smart in many a year.' She laughed.

'Well, you're realistic, I'll give you that,' Mrs Simons said. She squeezed Maryann's hand and stood on tiptoe to kiss her. 'Joel's a good boy – always has been. I hope you'll be very happy, moy dear, and have a big, healthy family.'

It was unconventional, she knew, but as she had no one there in the way of family, Maryann asked old Mr Bartholomew to walk up the aisle with her and present her to his son. She did feel rather wistful that morning. Even Tony wasn't going to travel all the way down from Birmingham, although he had written her a letter. She knew there was no question of her mother coming. But Nancy and Darius were there, Nancy acting as her 'assistant'.

'I don't know whether I'm a bridesmaid or a matron of honour!' Nance joked.

She and Darius were working another of Samuel Barlow's boats and had managed to reach Oxford that morning by the skin of their teeth in time for the wedding.

And old Darius Bartholomew seemed delighted that Maryann was marrying Joel. 'I'd 'ardly've known you,' he said, looking her up and down when he first saw her. 'You was only a child when last I saw you.'

She would have known him anywhere. He was certainly shrunken and more stooped in stature compared with how she had first seen him, but his beard and bushy white eyebrows and his tanned, leathery features were unmistakable. He was rather splendidly dressed in an ancient suit which shone with wear, a red cravat in the neck of his shirt. She remembered how intimidating she had found him in the past. Now she felt only respect and fondness. It felt absolutely right when he took her arm and led her along the aisle while the organ was playing the wedding march, and she saw Joel dressed up – for the first time ever probably – in a black suit, his beard trimmed, waiting for her before the altar. Mr Bartholomew gallantly handed her to his waiting son with an expression of great solemnity. Maryann was surprised to find that her legs were trembling so much she could barely stand.

When they came out, their few well-wishers sprinkled them with rice and Joel kissed her in the doorway of the church as the others watched and cheered. A man took their photograph.

Nance kissed her enthusiastically, almost knocking both their hats off in the process. Nance's was perched precariously on her curls.

'I'm ever so 'appy for yer, Maryann! You look really lovely.'

'Ta, Nance – you do an' all.' Maryann linked arms with Joel on one side and Nancy on the other as they all walked along to the pub where they went afterwards to celebrate. It was lovely outside but so cold that they were anxious to get into the warmth and they walked briskly, watched by a few curious passers-by in the little Oxford back street with its rows of neat terraces.

Nance looked a picture of health. In the three

445

months since she'd been with Darius she seemed to have filled out and her eyes were alive with happiness.

'I've got muscles on me like bed-knobs!' She laughed. 'Eh Darius – bring the bride a drink, will yer!'

They were a small wedding party, but they settled down very happily together. Old Mrs Simons became quite merry drinking glasses of ginger wine. Maryann sat between Nancy and Joel.

'Well – there's not many of us, but we wish you well,' Mrs Simons said, raising her glass. 'You're a lovely girl and I know you'll make our Joel very happy.'

They all drank to Joel and Maryann's health. Nance nudged Maryann.

'My wedding to Mick was quite a big do and look where that got me,' she said quietly. 'You be happy, my girl.'

'I'll do my best,' Maryann said. She thought to herself that if she'd had the finest wedding in the land she couldn't be happier. She laid her hand over Joel's under the table and he smiled and leaned close to kiss her.

Maryann and Nance had a good old chinwag about adjusting to life on the cut, catching up on the past couple of months. After a month apart, when Darius had gone off to earn some money with Fellows, Morton and Clayton and Nance had stayed on the *Esther Jane*, the two of them had got their own Barlow boat and Joel had said he felt strong enough to cope – especially now the boat had an engine.

'I tell yer, Maryann,' Nance said. 'Some nights I'm so tired I'm near falling asleep standing up and I'm dreaming the engine's still going at night even when it ain't.' Maryann nodded her agreement. 'I never knew what work was till I went off with Darius. 'E's 'ad a right go at me a few times when I get things wrong. Still, I learned a lot off Joel when I was still with you so it could be worse. And I tell yer summat, I wouldn't swap it for the world – when yer get up in the morning and look out on the fields all white with frost and the sun coming up – never seen anything like that in my life before.'

'You don't miss the old life then?' Maryann asked.

'Sometimes, when I'm trying to do a wash and get it hung out and moving about in that cabin I curse it and wish I 'ad a house to live in. But then when I think back – when I did 'ave, I've never felt so miserable in all my life.' She looked sober for a moment. 'No. I couldn't go back. I mean I'll 'ave to go back *some time* soon – I've writ me mom, trying to explain. I know I've done Mick wrong and sometimes it weighs heavy on me. But we love each other, me and Darius. I 'ope Mick finds some way of getting on without me – but I wanted a life, Maryann . . .'

Her brown eyes earnestly sought Maryann's, needing reassurance. Maryann patted her hand. ''Course you did.'

'You been back to Brum?'

'I was there only last week. Went to see if Tony and Billy could come down for the wedding but Tony daint seem to think 'e could. And I went to see Amy and her mom.'

'Oh – how are they? What's 'appened to *him*?'

'*He*,' Maryann said, 'is still in hospital. Janet said his face and the top of him's burnt so bad you can scarcely recognize him. She was sort of shuddering as she told me. Said 'e's a terrible sight – it all got infected and it's taking time to heal.'

'Serves the bastard right.'

'She said she daint think he'll find any more young widows with families to charm his way into. Said they'd run away at the sight of him.'

'What about those poor girls of 'ers?'

'She and Amy are just living quietly together. She's taking in some sewing – it's very hard for 'er to get by but they're managing. She says she don't care what she has to do just so long as she can keep Amy safe. Amy seems awright – much more cheerful, though heaven knows – the scars run deep, Nance . . .'

'Poor child. What about Margaret though?'

'Well—' Maryann's face clouded. 'They've still got 'er in the asylum. She ain't right. God alone knows what he did to her. Her mom's worried to death and she visits, but she's that busy trying to make ends meet. She says they can still barely get the kid to say a word.'

Nance made a hissing sound through her teeth and was interrupted before she could say anything by Joel leaning over.

'My dad wants to say summat.'

They all looked at old Darius Bartholomew. Slowly he got to his feet and his stooped figure loomed above them.

'It's a very happy day for us all today,' he began ponderously, then stopped and cleared his throat. 'Turns out I've known the lass what's marrying our Joel since she were a nipper, and a fine young woman she's turned out to be.' He paused and Maryann smiled, blushing with surprise. 'It's a pity today couldn't be the wedding of both my living sons. My Esther Jane, God rest 'er, would've taken both daughters-in-law to 'er heart, even if they was off the bank.' It was Nancy's turn to go red. Darius said no more about her situation. It was a difficult one, but they could all see how she and Darius were together and Nancy, who was sturdy and a good worker on the boat, had been accepted.

'I don't have no finery to give you both on your wedding day, 'cept my blessing. But there is things I'd like to give to you. My working days on the cut're over now and it's no use in thinking they ain't. So . . .' He indicated to his sister to pass up a cloth bag from beside the chair and dipped his hand into it. 'This 'un's for you, Joel.' It was his second windlass, the one he'd had to use all the time after Maryann so shamefully lost the first.

Joel soberly nodded his thanks. Both of them knew what it meant: old Darius was handing over the *Esther Jane* after a lifetime's work.

'And there's summat for you too, missy.' From the bag he drew something black and crumpled, and as he opened it out with his twisted hands, Maryann gasped, seeing the honour that was being conferred on her. It was Esther Jane's black bonnet.

'Oh—' She hesitated then, seeing Joel smiling, took it gingerly from the old man's outstretched hand. 'I – I don't think I deserve this . . .'

'Well—' Darius sank into his seat and picked up his glass. 'Time'll tell. But you're a boatwoman now. A Bartholomew. My Esther was my best mate on the cut through good days and bad. Now it's your turn and Joel's. You look after each other, eh – and you two an' all—' He nodded at Darius and Nance who had tears in her eyes.

They all raised their glasses and Joel turned to Maryann, his face full of love.

'Best mates.'

She clinked her glass against his and kissed him. 'Best mates.'

Joel and Maryann had said their farewells for the moment to the family. Darius and Nance were going straight back to pick up a load and get ahead. Darius said they'd be likely to work the Grand Union next.

'Might not see yer for a bit,' Nance said as she and Maryann hugged each other goodbye. 'We'll get back on the Oxford soon as we can.'

'Try and get to Napton for Christmas!' Joel said.

That evening they moved the *Esther Jane* out away from the town and tied up in a beautiful, isolated spot where fields stretched out all around them and the only thing filling the middle distance were the sharp outlines of winter trees against a white half-moon. They left old Jep snoozing in the cabin and stepped out on to the bank in the moonlight. The cold was so intense it seemed to come down on them like a weight, but the sky was full of stars and they wanted to enjoy the sight of it. Joel put his arm round Maryann and they stood close together in silence for a few moments, looking across the silver fields, hearing the gentle slap of the water against the bank. A bird screeched somewhere in the distance, a high, lonely sound. Maryann shivered and snuggled closer to Joel.

'It's so beautiful,' she said. 'Feels as if there's no one around for miles.'

'Probably ain't.'

She looked up at him, the pale sheen of moonlight on his face. He was filling out gradually and beginning to look like his strong, burly self. She could hear, though, the loud wheezing of his lungs, an utterly comforting sound because it had always been one which accompanied him, but also a worrying sign of his vulnerability. She knew how close to death he had been, the risk that any illnesses meant to him in the damp atmosphere of the cut. She stood on tiptoe and kissed his face, overflowing with love and gratitude. She would treasure every day with him.

He took her in his arms. 'So – what happened to the girl who said she would always be called Maryann Nelson?'

She laughed. 'Fancy you remembering that!'

'You were very strong on it at the time. Funny, scrawny little thing you were.'

'I know – well, thanks for changing my mind. Maryann Bartholomew'll do me well. 'S a funny thing – being married does feel different. Even though we've been living on here – I just feel properly married now, 'stead of "living in sin"!'

'Can't 'ave you living in sin, can we?'

'Even if Nance is.'

'Ah well – what else can they do, eh?'

'And they're happy,' she said.

'And you?'

She hesitated. 'Happier than you know . . . Joel?'

'Umm?'

'I think, in fact I'm sure – I'm expecting.'

'A baby – a little 'un?'

She could hear his excitement and she nodded solemnly.

'Oh,' he said, awed. 'My Maryann. That's lovely, that is.' Suddenly, laughing, he lifted her off the ground. 'Oh love – a little 'un!'

They held each other close.

'Come the summer,' Joel said, kissing her nose, 'we could lie out in the fields of a night ... no one about.'

'By summer,' she laughed, 'I'll have a belly on me like a barrel!'

'Well – tonight ...'

'Not tonight, no,' Maryann said firmly, pulling on his hand. 'I'm turning rigid with cold already. Come on – let's go in.'

They took one last look at the star-flecked sky, the friendly land spreading out around them, then, still holding hands, they stepped back into the cosy little cabin.

Epilogue

August 1936

'If it's a girl,' Maryann was saying, 'let's call her Ada.'

'Or Sally,' Joel said. 'After your sister.'

'We'd better have two girls then.' Maryann laughed.

She and Joel were walking out along the road away from Banbury towards Charnwood House, on a boiling August afternoon, ripe wheat stretching away on either side of them, swaying and rustling in the languorous breeze. On Joel's shoulders, his legs jutting forward each side of his father's face was their little son Joel, who had had his first birthday the month before. Maryann, who was four months into another pregnancy, was still looking trim.

'Margaret's a nice name,' she mused. 'Only it feels unlucky – poor little Margaret.'

'And Margaret's – well, she's not dead like our Ada and your Sally, is she?' Joel said carefully.

'Might just as well be, where she is.' Her voice was so hard and bitter, Joel reached out and touched her shoulder and little Joel gave a squeak of panic as his father loosed one of his legs.

Margaret, like Sal, was someone Maryann tried hard never to think about. Such thoughts had great power to make her feel sick with rage and sorrow and as there was nothing she could do, she pushed them away.

There had been plenty else to think about over the past couple of years. Most of her first year on the cut had been spent pregnant and she found it completely exhausting, with the added worry that if she was able to do less Joel would be forced to work even harder and could fall sick again, so however tired or heavy she was feeling she pushed herself on. Little Joel was born slightly early, on the *Esther Jane* with a nurse present, and Maryann had then been faced with the challenge of bringing up a child in the confined space of the boat. It was all right when he was a tiny baby, but as he grew and began to move about she worried constantly for his safety. More and more she heard stories about infants losing their lives on the cut through accidents or sickness and she became acutely protective of him. But he was a steady, sensible little fellow, even as a young toddler, and he had come well through his first year. She longed now for a daughter who would be a companion for him as he grew up.

Every so often they saw Nancy and Darius. Blackie Black had died of a seizure back in the winter of 1935 and Nance had gone home to visit. While she was there she was afraid she'd have to face Mick. Cathleen told her that a few months after Nancy went, Mick had left too, taken off and no one knew where. Cathleen, in her usual placid way, had not made an issue of her daughter's actions and was more concerned that they remain on good terms.

Nance and Darius had had a baby son, who in the family tradition they had called Darius and who must, Maryann calculated, have been conceived on about the first night the two of them were together, a fact which gave Nance enormous satisfaction after the agonies of living with Mick.

Every time they passed through Banbury, Maryann had thought fondly of Charnwood and she said to Joel she'd like to go back and visit. She often remembered them all, especially Mrs Letcombe, and she wondered whether Roland Musson had found the courage to leave and make a life for himself, and whether Miss Pamela was married now. She even wondered about Evan. Up until now though, they'd always been passing through or too busy or tired to make the effort. Today, however, it was the *Esther Jane*'s turn to revisit Tooley's Yard, and the beautiful, sultry day seemed to be calling them out across the fields.

When they turned in at the gate of Charnwood she said, 'Oh – this does feel peculiar. It all looks just the same as it did – only the trees've come on a bit more.'

As they neared the house Joel said, 'My goodness – this is a smart place. Can't think why you ever wanted to leave!'

'I daint, for a long time. But I met Darius, remember? And he told me that *someone* was very poorly in hospital . . .'

'Ah yes.' Joel laughed.

'We'll have to go in the servants' entrance,' Maryann said. They went round the back of the house, with the wistaria sprawling across the back. As she glanced across the garden, Maryann's eye was caught by a figure sitting in a sunny spot near the wall of the rose garden. There was a new bench that had not been there before, and on it sat a figure dressed completely in black.

'That looks like Mrs Musson,' Maryann whispered, frowning. 'The lady of the house. She looks to be in mourning, wouldn't you say? That hat's got net on and everything. I wonder – it could be the anniversary of John's death. That was her oldest son, killed in the war. Or I wonder if Mr Musson . . .'

Someone must have opened the front door as she

spoke because there was a sudden frenzied barking and Freddie the fox terrier tore round towards them, followed at a waddling pace by Lily Langtree, the spaniel who had been quite fat when Maryann was working there and had now expanded into a dog of truly corpulent proportions. Little Joel laughed and pointed at them, but other than sniffing at the visitors' legs and barking loudly the dogs did nothing else except run back round the end of the house.

'Well, they ain't changed.'

Inside, they found that not a huge amount had changed among the servants either. She found Mrs Letcombe, looking exactly the same, seated in her little room, dozing over her knitting in the warm afternoon.

'My dear, it's very nice to see you,' she said, kissing Maryann and greeting both Joels warmly. She loved small children, and took little Joel on to her lap immediately. 'Oh – and this little fellow must have a piece of Cook's best seed cake. Come on now – we'll all have a nice cup of tea. Oh, I am glad things have turned out well for you, Maryann. You left in such a hurry, I was rather afraid that Evan drove you away – he was always more forward than he ought to be.'

They filled in the news of the past two years. Evan and Alice had got married, but were still living and working at Charnwood. Sid the gardener had died unexpectedly – 'His heart, they think,' Mrs Letcombe said as they all sat at the kitchen table with the tea and cake and little Joel tottering around practising his new walking skills. 'Otherwise down here, things are really much the same. It's a settled sort of house. But upstairs—' She rolled her eyes. 'Oh dear me.'

'What's happened?' Maryann said. 'I saw Mrs Musson – all in black.'

'Terrible. Only last month. It was Master Roland. Went off to that war in Spain. Upped and went. Said war was the only thing he knew and if he couldn't make a life here he might as well go back to that. So he went and fought for Franco. He lasted just three weeks.' She shook her head sorrowfully. 'That poor, poor boy.'

'No!' Maryann let the news sink in. She wanted to weep. The image of him roaring through the quiet countryside on his motorcycle came to her, as if nothing of stillness or quietness could satisfy his troubled mind. 'How terrible,' she said. 'Poor Mrs Musson.'

'Nothing'll console her. Two sons gone – there's only Master Hugh left and somehow she doesn't seem to have the same affinity with him. Miss Pamela's married now of course. To a farmer chappie, over near Thame and she seems happy enough.' She turned to Joel. 'And what is it you do for a living?'

When he told her, Mrs Letcombe seemed quite taken aback at first, then she laughed. 'I thought you were looking very brown and sturdy,' she said to Maryann. 'Well – I'd never've put you down as doing that but you look as if it's suiting you.'

'Oh – it is.' She laughed. 'Most days, any'ow!'

They spent a very friendly hour in the kitchen and she kissed Maryann again when they left. 'Come and see us again, won't you? With all your lovely children as they arrive.' She chucked little Joel's cheek as Maryann held him. 'Sorry you didn't see anyone else.'

But Maryann was glad. She hadn't wanted to see Evan or the others especially. As they left she looked down the garden and saw that the bench where Mrs Musson had been sitting was empty, and she was filled with a great sense of poignancy. Handing Joel their son

457

to lift back on to his shoulders she slipped her arm through his. Among so many sad things, so much pain and unhappiness, her own joy seemed miraculous: a hard-won, precariously existing miracle.

'I'm glad I came to see them,' she said as they set off along the road. 'But I don't think I'll want to come again.' She felt oddly lost now, out in the country, without that sinuous line of water to guide her, to show her where she belonged.

'Today is today,' she said to Joel suddenly. He looked down at her, not quite sure what she meant. 'No one can take today away, whatever else happens.'

He did understand. 'No. Let's try and make a good tomorrow too.'

'Come on.' She squeezed his arm affectionately. 'Let's get back to the cut. Let's go home.'